# PRAISE FOR AMY CLIPSTON

"Amy Clipston has once again penned a sweet romance that will have her readers rooting for a heroine who deserves her own happily-ever-after. Crystal Glick is a selfless, nurturing woman who has spent her life caring for others—to the detriment of her dream of a family of her own. Duane Bontrager is a much older widow with three nearly grown sons. Readers are in for a treat as these two overcome one obstacle after another to be together. The real stars of the show, however, are Crystal's nieces and nephews. They're enchanting. Grab a cup of coffee, a piece of pie, *Foundation of Love*, and settle in for a lovely Clipston story."

—KELLY IRVIN, AUTHOR OF *THE BEEKEEPER'S SON* AND *UPON A SPRING BREEZE*

"A heartwarming story that works as both a standalone romance and a satisfying series installment."

—PUBLISHERS WEEKLY ON *THE COFFEE CORNER*

"Clipston always writes unique and compelling stories and this is a good collection of light reading for evenings."

—PARKERSBURG NEWS AND SENTINEL ON *AN AMISH SINGING*

"Amy Clipston's characters are always so endearing and well-developed, and Salina and Will in *The Farm Stand* are some of my favorites. I enjoyed how their business relationship melded into a close friendship, and then eventually turned into so much more. *The Farm Stand* honors the Amish community in the very best of ways. I loved it."

—SHELLEY SHEPARD GRAY, *NEW YORK TIMES* AND *USA TODAY* BESTSELLING AUTHOR

"This series is an enjoyable treat to those who enjoy the genre and will keep readers wanting more to see what happens next at the Marketplace."

—PARKERSBURG NEWS AND SENTINEL ON *THE FARM STAND*

"Clipston begins her Amish Marketplace series with this pleasing story of love and competition . . . This sweet tale will please fans of Clipston's wholesome Amish romances."

—PUBLISHERS WEEKLY ON *THE BAKE SHOP*

"Fans of Amish fiction will love Amy Clipston's latest, *The Bake Shop*. It's filled with warm and cozy moments as Jeff and Christiana find their way from strangers to friendship to love."

—ROBIN LEE HATCHER, BESTSELLING AUTHOR OF
*WHO I AM WITH YOU* AND *CROSS MY HEART*

"Clipston closes out this heartrending series with a thoughtful consideration of how Amish rules can tear families apart, as well as a reminder that God's path is not always what one might expect. Readers old and new will find the novel's issues intriguing and its hard-won resolution reassuring."

—*HOPE BY THE BOOK*, BOOKMARKED REVIEW,
ON *A WELCOME AT OUR DOOR*

"A sweet romance with an endearing heroine, this is a good wrap-up of the series."

—*PARKERSBURG NEWS AND SENTINEL* ON *A WELCOME AT OUR DOOR*

"*Seasons of an Amish Garden* follows the year through short stories as friends create a memorial garden to celebrate a life. Revealing the underbelly of main characters, a trademark talent of Amy Clipston, makes them relatable and endearing. One story slides into the next, woven together effortlessly with the author's knowledge of the Amish life. Once started, you can't put this book down."

—SUZANNE WOODS FISHER, BESTSELLING AUTHOR OF *THE DEVOTED*

"With endearing characters that readers will want to get a happily ever after, this is a story of romance and family to savor."

—*PARKERSBURG NEWS AND SENTINEL* ON *A SEAT BY THE HEARTH*

"[*A Seat by the Hearth*] is a moving portrait of a disgraced woman attempting to reenter her childhood community . . . This will please Clipston's fans and also win over newcomers to Lancaster County."

—*PUBLISHERS WEEKLY*

"This story shares the power of forgiveness and hope and, above all, faith in God's Word and His promises."

—*HOPE BY THE BOOK*, BOOKMARKED
REVIEW, ON *A SEAT BY THE HEARTH*

"This story of profound loss and deep friendship will leave readers with the certain knowledge that hope exists and love grows through faith in our God of second chances."

—KELLY IRVIN, AUTHOR OF *THE BEEKEEPER'S SON* AND
*UPON A SPRING BREEZE*, ON *ROOM ON THE PORCH SWING*

"This heartbreaking series continues to take a fearlessly honest look at grief, as hopelessness threatens to steal what happiness Allen has treasured within his marriage and recent fatherhood. Clipston takes these feelings seriously without sugarcoating any aspect of the mourning process, allowing her characters to make their painful but ultimately joyous journey back to love and faith. Readers who have made this tough and ongoing pilgrimage themselves will appreciate the author's realistic portrayal of coming to terms with loss in order to continue living with hope and happiness."

—*RT BOOK REVIEWS*, 4 STARS, ON *ROOM ON THE PORCH SWING*

"A story of grief as well as new beginnings, this is a lovely Amish tale and the start of a great new series."

—*PARKERSBURG NEWS AND SENTINEL* ON *A PLACE AT OUR TABLE*

"Themes of family, forgiveness, love, and strength are woven throughout the story . . . a great choice for all readers of Amish fiction."

—*CBA MARKET MAGAZINE* ON *A PLACE AT OUR TABLE*

"This debut title in a new series offers an emotionally charged and engaging read headed by sympathetically drawn and believable protagonists. The meaty issues of trust and faith make this a solid book group choice."

—*LIBRARY JOURNAL* ON *A PLACE AT OUR TABLE*

# FOUNDATION
# OF LOVE

# OTHER BOOKS BY AMY CLIPSTON

**CONTEMPORARY ROMANCE**
*The Heart of Splendid Lake*
*The View from Coral Cove*
(Available May 2022)

**THE AMISH MARKETPLACE SERIES**
*The Bake Shop*
*The Farm Stand*
*The Coffee Corner*
*The Jam and Jelly Nook*

**THE AMISH HOMESTEAD SERIES**
*A Place at Our Table*
*Room on the Porch Swing*
*A Seat by the Hearth*
*A Welcome at Our Door*

**THE AMISH HEIRLOOM SERIES**
*The Forgotten Recipe*
*The Courtship Basket*
*The Cherished Quilt*
*The Beloved Hope Chest*

**THE HEARTS OF THE LANCASTER GRAND HOTEL SERIES**
*A Hopeful Heart*
*A Mother's Secret*
*A Dream of Home*
*A Simple Prayer*

**THE KAUFFMAN AMISH BAKERY SERIES**
*A Gift of Grace*
*A Promise of Hope*
*A Place of Peace*
*A Life of Joy*
*A Season of Love*

**YOUNG ADULT**
*Roadside Assistance*
*Reckless Heart*
*Destination Unknown*
*Miles from Nowhere*

**STORY COLLECTIONS**
*Amish Sweethearts*
*Seasons of an Amish Garden*
*An Amish Singing*

**STORIES**
*A Plain and Simple Christmas*
*Naomi's Gift* included in *An Amish Christmas Gift*
*A Spoonful of Love* included in *An Amish Kitchen*
*Love Birds* included in *An Amish Market*
*Love and Buggy Rides* included in *An Amish Harvest*
*Summer Storms* included in *An Amish Summer*
*The Christmas Cat* included in *An Amish Christmas Love*
*Home Sweet Home* included in *An Amish Winter*
*A Son for Always* included in *An Amish Spring*
*A Legacy of Love* included in *An Amish Heirloom*
*No Place Like Home* included in *An Amish Homecoming*
*Their True Home* included in *An Amish Reunion*
*Cookies and Cheer* included in *An Amish Christmas Bakery*
*Baskets of Sunshine* included in *An Amish Picnic*
*Evergreen Love* included in *An Amish Christmas Wedding*
*Bundles of Blessings* included in *Amish Midwives*
*Building a Dream* included in *An Amish Barn Raising*
*A Class for Laurel* included in *An Amish Schoolroom*
*Patchwork Promises* included in *An Amish Quilting Bee*

**NONFICTION**
*The Gift of Love*

# FOUNDATION OF LOVE

An Amish Legacy Novel

AMY CLIPSTON

ZONDERVAN®

ZONDERVAN

*Foundation of Love*

Copyright © 2022 by Amy Clipston

Requests for information should be addressed to:

Zondervan, 3900 Sparks Dr. SE, Grand Rapids, Michigan 49546

ISBN 978-0-310-36433-7

*Printed in the United States of America*

*For Zac Weikal with appreciation.*
*Thank you for sharing your talent,*
*knowledge, and expertise with me.*
*You are a blessing!*

# GLOSSARY

*ach:* oh
*aenti:* aunt
*appeditlich:* delicious
*Ausbund:* Amish hymnal
*bedauerlich:* sad
*boppli:* baby
*bopplin:* babies
*brot:* bread
*bruder:* brother
*bruderskind:* niece/nephew
*bruderskinner:* nieces/nephews
*bu:* boy
*buwe:* boys
*daadihaus:* small house provided for retired parents
*daed:* father
*danki:* thank you
*dat:* dad
*Dietsch:* Pennsylvania Dutch, the Amish language (a German dialect)
*dochder:* daughter
*dochdern:* daughters

*Englisher:* a non-Amish person

*fraa:* wife

*freind:* friend

*freinden:* friends

*froh:* happy

*gegisch:* silly

*gern gschehne:* you're welcome

*Gude mariye:* Good morning

*gut:* good

*Gut nacht:* Good night

*haus:* house

*Ich liebe dich:* I love you

*kaffi:* coffee

*kapp:* prayer covering or cap

*kichli:* cookie

*kichlin:* cookies

*kinner:* children

*krank:* sick

*kuche:* cake

*kumm:* come

*liewe:* love, a term of endearment

*maed:* young women, girls

*maedel:* young woman

*mamm:* mom

*mei:* my

*naerfich:* nervous

*narrisch:* crazy

*Ordnung:* The oral tradition of practices required and forbidden in the Amish faith.

*schee:* pretty

*schtupp:* family room
*schweschder:* sister
*schweschdere:* sisters
*sohn:* son
*Was iss letz?:* What's wrong?
*Wie geht's:* How do you do? or Good day!
*wunderbaar:* wonderful
*ya:* yes
*zwillingbopplin:* twins

# AN AMISH LEGACY SERIES FAMILY TREES

**Connie (deceased) m.**
**Duane Bontrager**
|
Tyler

Korey

Jayden

**Arlene (deceased) m.**
**Perry (deceased) Glick**
|
Kane m. Leona

Crystal

**Wanda m. Hershel Stoltzfus**
|
Monroe

Clemons

Jared m. Jeannie

Owen

**Tricia m. Harley**
**(deceased) Mast**
|
Kathleen

Ella May

Dora

**Leona m. Kane Glick**
|
Alisha

Nate

Jevon

Hope

Evelyn "Evie" (Morgan's twin)

Morgan (Evelyn's twin)

# A NOTE TO THE READER

WHILE THIS NOVEL IS SET AGAINST THE REAL BACKDROP OF Lancaster County, Pennsylvania, the characters are fictional. There is no intended resemblance between the characters in this book and any real members of the Amish and Mennonite communities. As with any work of fiction, I've taken license in some areas of research as a means of creating the necessary circumstances for my characters. My research was thorough; however, it would be impossible to be completely accurate in details and description since each and every community differs. Therefore, any inaccuracies in the Amish and Mennonite lifestyles portrayed in this book are completely due to fictional license.

# CHAPTER 1

THE EARLY APRIL SUN WARMED THE BACK OF DUANE Bontrager's neck as he climbed the porch steps of the large, white farmhouse. He looked up and smiled at the cloudless, azure sky while birds sang in nearby trees. It was another perfect spring day.

"Kane has four barns and a *daadihaus*," Jayden, his youngest son, said, pointing behind them. "Does he want the roofs replaced on all of the buildings?"

"He mentioned the barns and the main house in the message, but he didn't say anything about a *daadihaus*," Duane explained. "He said all of his roofs were damaged in that storm we had last fall. He's been waiting to fix them."

Duane took in the large pasture dotted with cows and the row of four red barns, each looking as if they hadn't been painted in a decade or more. The red paint had long faded and the doors hung at odd angles. Even the pasture fence needed a new coat of paint and many slats repaired or replaced. Perhaps the farmer had decided it was time to finally do some much-needed maintenance on his property, starting with the roofs.

Jayden rubbed his chin. "This is a big job, *Dat*."

Duane adjusted his straw hat on his head and, squaring his

shoulders, pointed toward the back door. "*Ya*, which is why I wanted to get out here and give him an estimate before we missed our chance at it."

He walked to the back door, knocked, and waited. Beyond the door, he heard children crying and yelling. He glanced over at Jayden, who grimaced before Duane rapped on the door again, harder this time.

After a moment, the racket became louder and then a back door opened, revealing an Amish woman balancing a red-faced, screaming toddler on her hip while an identical toddler held on to the skirt of her dark-green dress and black apron and howled. Both toddlers wore light-pink dresses and had heads of thick red curls.

The woman looked up at Duane and sighed, her pretty face seeming resigned as the toddlers continued to wail. She had striking features—an ivory complexion with bright, intelligent green eyes that reminded him of the lush green pastures behind him. And the hair peeking out from under her prayer covering was a deeper shade of red than the toddlers'. He surmised she was in her early thirties.

"*Wie geht's?*" she asked, her voice barely audible over the sobbing children.

"Hi." Duane raised his hand. "I'm here to speak with Kane Glick. He left me a message asking for an estimate to replace your roofs."

She held her free hand up to her ear. "Could you repeat that?" she said over the cries.

"I said—" Duane began, raising his voice.

"Excuse me." The woman turned and hollered, "Alisha!" She peered over her shoulder at Duane and gave him a sheepish expression.

A moment later, a girl with long blond braids and blue eyes, who looked to be approximately ten years old, appeared behind her.

"I need you to take your *schweschdere*," the redhead yelled over the fussing as she attempted to peel the wailing toddler from her waist.

Alisha looked behind her and called, "Hope! *Kumm!*"

A smaller girl, whom Duane guessed was around four, scrambled over, her long, light-brown hair in braids and her bright-hazel eyes shining.

Alisha gently untangled the toddler holding on to the redhead's skirts and guided her toward Hope, who took the crying toddler by the hand and steered her through the mudroom where they stood and out toward a doorway. Then Alisha lifted the second screaming child from the redhead's arms, and the woman thanked the girl before she also disappeared through the doorway, the cries fading in the distance.

The redhead smoothed her hands down her dress and apron as her lips turned up in a pretty smile. "I'm so sorry. They're teething. Molars, you know. Now I can hear you as well as my thoughts." She laughed. "How may I help you two?" She divided a look between Duane and Jayden.

"I'm Duane Bontrager, and this is *mei sohn* Jayden. We're here to give Kane an estimate on the roofing job."

She snapped her fingers. "Oh, right. It's Saturday. I forgot you were coming today. Kane is out in the barns somewhere. Hang on one minute. I'll get one of the *buwe* to take you out there. I believe Jevon came back inside a few minutes ago." She disappeared into the house.

"One of the *buwe*?" Jayden muttered beside him. "How many *kinner* do they have?"

Duane grinned. "It sounds like quite a few."

The redhead appeared a few moments later beside a small blond boy. "This is Jevon." She bent down beside him. "This is Duane and Jayden. Would you please take them out to see your *dat*?"

The boy nodded, and Duane assumed he was around five years old. Then Jevon rushed out the door and down the steps.

"It's this way." Jevon pointed toward the row of barns.

The redhead gave him a thumbs-up. "You're in *gut* hands."

Jayden followed the boy, and they started toward the barns.

"It was nice meeting you," the woman told Duane.

"What was your name?" he asked.

"Oh, I'm sorry. In all the chaos, I never introduced myself. I'm Crystal Glick."

"Nice to meet you, Crystal." He nodded and then jogged down the steps and caught up with Jayden. "That Crystal has her hands full. I remember those days with *kinner* running all around the *haus*. Although, your *mamm* never had that much craziness, except when your *bruders* were both in diapers. Your *mamm* wanted a houseful, but you and your *bruders* were blessings enough."

Duane's heart twisted. He would never overcome the grief of losing his *fraa*. Sometimes it felt as if they'd lost her just yesterday instead of eighteen months ago.

As they moved toward the first barn, Duane took a closer look at faded paint flecking off the side of the barn and the doors, which looked as if they might fall off their hinges. He turned toward the other two large barns, which were in the same state of disrepair.

Beyond them, he took in the fence, noticing more missing slats than he'd observed from the porch. It looked as if the poor old fence hadn't been painted or repaired in several years. The *daadihaus* also looked as if it could use a coat of paint and a good scrubbing of the windows.

The aroma of animals and wet hay overwhelmed Duane as he approached the barn. He and Jayden stopped at the barn door as Jevon rushed inside.

*"Dat!"* Jevon shouted. *"Dat!"*

A few moments later, a tall man with reddish-brown hair, a matching beard, and a long nose stepped out of the barn, wiping his hands on a red rag. Jevon and another boy, who looked to be about twice Jevon's age, sidled up to him as he smiled.

The man shoved the rag into his pocket and then held out his hand. "I'm Kane. I assume you're Duane Bontrager."

Duane shook his hand. "*Ya*, that's right. And this is *mei sohn* Jayden."

"Nice to meet you both." Kane jammed his thumb toward Jevon and the other boy who stood behind him. "These are *mei sohns*. This is Nate, and you've already met Jevon."

The boys waved at Duane and Jayden and then raced back toward the house.

"So, how long have you been in business?" Kane asked.

"I've had my own roofing business for about twenty years," Duane said. "I renamed it Bontrager and Sons when my former helpers moved on to other jobs and my *buwe* were old enough to help me with the work."

Kane rubbed his long reddish beard. "*Gut, gut*. You come highly recommended. Do you live here in Gordonville?"

"No, but we're not far from here in Bird-in-Hand."

"Great. You can see that my farm needs some attention. I've put it off for years since there's always so much work to do around here, but *mei fraa* insisted we start cleaning it up this spring. The roofs are my first priority. I need them replaced on my main *haus* and barns. We're not using the *daadihaus*, so I'm not going to worry about it just now. Next I'll hire someone to paint the barns as well as paint and repair the fencing." He rubbed his hands together. "So, I suppose you need to measure my roofs before you can give me a price."

Duane nodded toward the pickup truck waiting patiently in the driveway. "My driver has all of our equipment, including our ladders. We'll measure and then give the breakdown of our pricing."

"All right then," Kane said.

Duane and Jayden collected the measuring wheel, clipboard, and tallest ladder, and soon they were measuring the barn roofs before moving to the house.

While Duane stood on the roof of the house, he looked down to the ground toward an elaborate wooden swing, where four of the children played. Crystal stood nearby wearing a sweater with one of the redheaded toddlers perched on her hip and the other grasping her apron.

Duane shook his head, amazed at her patience as she spoke to Alisha and then to Jevon. She looked down, addressing the toddler on her hip before kissing the little one's head. Crystal seemed completely at ease, as if she were born to be a mother. She absently rocked back and forth, looking content with the toddler glued to her hip while resting her cheek on her shoulder.

As if reading his thoughts, Crystal tented her eyes with her free hand and looked up at the roof. Duane nodded at her and then returned to his task.

After they were done, Duane and Jayden descended the ladder, and Duane calculated their figures while Jayden stowed their supplies. Duane wrote up an estimate and delivered it to Kane, who was working in the dairy barn.

"This is around what I had expected," Kane said as he read the estimate. "When are you available to start?"

"We're finishing up a job today and then we have two more next week, but they'll each take only a day. We can start here on Wednesday."

Kane held out his hand. "That works for me. I'll expect to see you then."

"Perfect," Duane said, shaking on the deal. Then Kane spun on his heel and headed back to his chores.

As Duane approached the truck, he looked toward where Crystal stood with the children just as the back door opened and another woman walked down the porch steps. With blond hair under her prayer covering, she appeared to be in her midthirties, and by the way her stomach was distended and by how she rested her hands on her lower back, it was obvious she was expecting a child. He recalled how his late wife, Connie, would knead her sore back with her fingers while she was pregnant with each of their three sons.

He tried not to stare, but questions swirled through his mind as the blonde walked over to Crystal and then sat down on a nearby bench. He wondered if the blond woman was a relative visiting Crystal and Kane, but it was none of Duane's business.

He strolled over to the four-door pickup truck and climbed into the front passenger seat beside his driver, Drew Cooper. "*Danki* for waiting for us," he told Drew.

Drew, a friendly man with graying dark-brown hair and kind eyes, smiled. "You're always welcome."

"How did it go, *Dat*?" Jayden asked from the seat behind him.

Duane settled on the seat and buckled in. "We got the job."

"Yes!" Jayden clapped.

"Congratulations," Drew said as he put the truck into gear.

"Thank you, Drew." Duane breathed a sigh of relief.

Business had been slow during the winter months, and he'd prayed that the Lord would see fit to send them work in the spring. He was grateful his prayers had finally been answered when Kane Glick had left a message regarding the work he needed done on his barns and farmhouse.

Duane released another long breath of gratitude, quietly thanking God for this answered prayer.

Duane climbed out of the truck at the worksite where his two older sons, Tyler and Korey, stood on the roof of a two-story home owned by an *Englisher* who had seen Duane's advertisement in the local paper.

Tyler, his oldest son, descended the ladder and met him at the top of the driveway. At twenty-four, Tyler was tall like his father and brothers and had dark-brown hair, resembling Duane's and Korey's, but he had inherited hazel eyes from his mother, as Jayden had. He swiped the back of his hand over his brow. "What happened?"

"We got the job." Duane patted one of Tyler's broad shoulders.

Tyler's grin was bright. "Praise God. Kore and I are almost done here, and then we have those two jobs in Strasburg, but we can knock them out on Monday and Tuesday. We can start it on Wednesday."

"That's exactly what I told Kane."

"How'd it go?" Korey yelled from the roof. His mirrored sunglasses blocked his deep-brown eyes, and his dark-brown hair was covered by a straw hat.

Although he was sixteen months younger than Tyler, Connie had often referred to Korey and Tyler as "the twins," since they were so close in age. But Duane often thought of them as night and day.

Tyler glowered at his middle brother. "Come down here and ask, Kore! Don't stand up there and bellow!"

"You're not *mei daed*," Korey bit back. "So quit acting like it."

"He needs to grow up," Tyler muttered while walking over to their large cooler filled with water.

Duane sighed and turned toward Jayden, who shook his head as he picked up a hammer and then started up the ladder.

Despite his oldest sons' near constant bickering, he was grateful to have his three sons working for him. He wouldn't have it any other way.

"All right," Duane announced. "Let's finish this job up so we can enjoy the rest of the weekend." Then he grabbed a hammer and box of nails and ambled toward the ladder, feeling satisfied from another day of hard work with his sons.

# CHAPTER 2

"Now you're all clean, okay, Evie?" Crystal whispered to her little niece, who was balanced on her hip while she held her twin sister's hand and guided her down the steep stairs toward the kitchen later that afternoon. "And you're clean too now, Morgan," she told Evie's twin.

Alisha, Crystal's faithful helper, appeared at the bottom of the stairs. "*Mamm* said she still isn't feeling well, and she asked me to ask you to start supper. Do you need me, *Aenti*?"

Oh, how Crystal appreciated her eldest niece! Without her, she'd never be able to finish her chores and care for the twins, which seemed to be her full-time job since Leona, her sister-in-law, was expecting her seventh and eighth babies in July and hadn't felt well throughout this entire pregnancy.

Crystal touched Alisha's cheek. "Oh, *mei liewe*. What would I do without you? Would you please play with your *schweschdere* so that I can cook?"

"*Ya!*" Alisha's pretty face lit up in a smile.

"You're an angel."

Alisha took Morgan's hand and nudged her away from Crystal's skirt. "Let's go play with Hope, okay, Morgan?"

"Okay!" Morgan smiled and allowed Alisha to guide her toward the family room, where toys were spread out, and Hope played with a doll.

Hope held the doll up toward Morgan, who waddled over to her, laughing.

Alisha reached for Evie next. "May I hold you, Evie?"

"No! I want *Aenti* Kisstal!" Evie turned away from her sister, pressing her face into Crystal's neck.

Crystal swallowed a sigh. Evie seemed to have been attached to Crystal since the day she'd been born, but it had gotten worse when she'd started teething and had trouble sleeping. While Crystal cherished her nieces and nephews, she found it a bit suffocating when they preferred her instead of their parents or siblings.

"Evie," Crystal began, careful to keep her voice calm, "I need you to play with your *schweschdere* so that I can make supper, okay?"

"No!" Evie's voice was muffled by Crystal's neck.

Alisha's pretty blue eyes widened.

Crystal's patience began to wear thin. "Evie, I need you to listen to Alisha or our family will go hungry tonight. Do you want everyone to be hungry?"

Evie met Crystal's gaze and shook her head, her strawberry-blond curls bobbing with the motion.

"That's what I thought. Would you please be a *gut* girl for me?"

Evie nodded.

*"Wunderbaar."* Crystal set Evie on the floor, and while Alisha led Evie into the family room, she made a beeline into the kitchen.

She glanced at the clock on the wall, and she felt a rush of panic. It was nearly four o'clock! She had to get food in the oven quickly.

If only Leona would have asked her earlier in the afternoon to take on the cooking. Her sister-in-law had seemed to be feeling better when she'd joined Crystal and the children outside by the swing set, and when Leona had gone to lie down, she'd told Crystal she had a headache and planned to take a short nap. She'd expected Leona to get back up before long, but now Crystal would have to scrape something together.

She opened the propane-powered refrigerator, and her spirit lifted when she found the two packages of chicken breasts she'd picked up at the grocery store yesterday. Thank goodness she hadn't stored them in the freezer!

"Baked chicken it is," she mumbled. She flipped on the oven and searched the pantry for some Shake 'N Bake. *There it is!* Then her mind wandered as she pulled out a pan and opened the box of her favorite time-saving seasoning.

Sounds of her nieces playing in the family room filtered into the kitchen as Crystal set the pieces of seasoned chicken onto a baking sheet. How she loved listening to her nieces and nephews enjoying each other's company!

Crystal slipped the baking sheet into the oven and then opened the pantry door, searching for a couple of cans of mixed vegetables.

Soon vegetables were cooking in a pot while the delicious aroma of chicken permeated the kitchen. Crystal located a bag of rolls, and after dividing them up in two baskets, she put one on each end of the table.

She smiled as she placed plates, utensils, and cups by each place. Though tasks like cooking a meal might feel mundane to some, she was grateful the Lord had given her a purpose after she had lost her father. Although God hadn't seen fit to make her a mother, at least she was able to help care for her nieces and nephews instead of living alone in the big house where she'd been raised.

"It smells *appeditlich*."

Crystal looked over her shoulder and saw Leona standing in the doorway, yawning and massaging her lower back with her fingers. "Are you feeling better, Leona?"

Leona shrugged and yawned again. "My feet and my back never stop aching. I can't imagine how I'll survive the summer feeling this way."

"Well, it's a *gut* thing you're due in July and won't have to suffer through August and September." Crystal began filling the cups with a pitcher of water she kept in the refrigerator.

"Is there anything I can do to help?"

"Please tell Alisha to call her *dat* and *bruders* in. Then we can get the *zwillingbopplin* in their highchairs."

Leona moved to the doorway leading to the family room. "Alisha, please tell your *dat* and *bruders* to come in for supper."

While Alisha jogged outside to fetch her father and brothers, Crystal helped Leona get the twins settled in their highchairs and Hope in her booster seat before they brought the food to the table.

Soon, all nine members of the Glick family were seated around the long oak table, and after a silent prayer, they began filling their plates with chicken and veggies.

Crystal buttered two rolls and then handed them to the twins before buttering rolls for Jevon and Hope.

"The roofers are going to start on Wednesday," Kane announced from his seat at the end of the table.

Leona nodded from the other end of the table. "So, their price was *gut*?"

"*Ya*, it was competitive and close to what I had hoped for." Kane nodded and wiped his reddish-brown beard with a paper napkin.

Crystal's thoughts drifted to her brief encounter with Duane Bontrager while she cut up a piece of chicken for the twins. Duane looked to be in his midforties with the flecks of gray threaded through his dark-brown hair and matching beard, and he was also tall like her brother.

Although she'd only spoken to him for a few moments, she'd been struck by his easy demeanor and his warm smile. He seemed like a kind man. She had been impressed by his patience with her wailing nieces. Some men would have been irritated or rude while she had worked to silence the children, but he seemed more amused than anything.

"Did they say how long the job will take?" Leona asked.

"No, but I didn't ask," Kane said. "I imagine it will take a few days. Most roofers hope to finish their jobs quickly so they can move on to the next."

After serving chicken and vegetables to Hope, Jevon, and the twins, Crystal finally prepared a plate for herself. She hadn't realized how hungry she was until she tasted the flavorful chicken. Lunch had been more than five hours earlier, and she'd been too busy to make herself a snack.

"We have to get up early tomorrow for church," Kane said.

Leona nodded. "*Ya*, that's right."

"*Brot!*" Evie hollered when her roll was gone.

Crystal smiled over at her niece. "There's no need to yell." Then she buttered another roll for her.

"May I have one too, *Aenti*?" Hope asked.

"Of course you may since you have such *gut* manners." Crystal touched her nose.

"Me too, *Aenti*," Jevon said.

Crystal nodded at him. "Of course."

After Crystal finished buttering rolls for the kids, she returned to her chicken, which was now cold, but she continued eating it while Kane and Leona discussed church tomorrow and their plans for next week.

Soon their plates were clean, and Crystal served a container of cookies she had baked a few days ago, along with coffee for the adults. After dessert, Crystal began gathering up the plates and utensils.

Leona groaned as she stood and began kneading her lower back. "Alisha, would you please get the *zwillingbopplin* and Hope into the bathtub?"

"*Ya, Mamm.*" Alisha grabbed a wet rag and mopped Evie's face. "You need a bath, Evie."

Evie groaned and turned her head.

Hope smiled. "I like getting a bath."

"Bath! Bath!" Morgan hollered.

Alisha wiped Morgan's face next. "*Ya*, that's right. It's time for your bath." Then she helped the twins down from their highchairs and led them and Hope toward the downstairs bathroom.

Shaking her head and smiling, Crystal placed the dishes in the sink and turned on the faucet. She glanced behind her as Kane gave Leona a quick kiss before he headed back out through the mudroom with his two sons in tow.

Crystal felt a familiar tug at her heart. The love between her brother and sister-in-law had been obvious since they had met when Kane was twenty-one and Leona was nineteen. From the beginning of their relationship, Crystal had witnessed them holding hands, stealing kisses, and whispering to each other when they thought no one was paying attention.

If only Crystal could have found that kind of love too. She'd never expected to be unmarried at the age of thirty-three. In fact, she'd thought she was going to marry her ex-boyfriend five years ago, but he had chosen a job opportunity in Ohio over a future with her.

She quickly reminded herself to be grateful that Kane and Leona had generously welcomed her into their home when her father had died and left her alone. Being a part of this wonderful family was enough to sustain her for a lifetime. At least, she kept praying to the Lord that it would be.

Leona set an armful of cups on the counter and then rubbed her back again.

"Why don't you go sit?" Crystal said. "I can handle this."

"Are you sure?"

"Of course."

"I don't know what we'd do without you, Crystal." Leona gave Crystal's shoulder a gentle squeeze and then disappeared into the family room.

Crystal sighed and collected the rest of the dishes, utensils, cups, and serving platters from the table. As she began scrubbing the dishes, she wondered what it would have been like to have a family of her own.

She'd never know how it felt to be a wife or a mother, but she was grateful God had blessed her with the family she had.

"I cooked, so you three can decide who does the dishes," Korey announced as he carried a stack of dishes to the counter. "I'll go take care of the animals."

Jayden lifted a sand-colored eyebrow as he retrieved their empty glasses. "You cooked? You made sub sandwiches, Kore, not a pot roast."

"Oh, pot roast," Tyler said, his voice sounding wistful. "That sounds amazing. Remember Mom's pot roasts?"

Jayden nodded. "They were the best."

Duane felt a tug at his heart. Everything Connie cooked had been wonderful. He pressed his lips together. How he missed her. He'd never get over losing her.

Tyler set a handful of utensils in the sink and then opened the freezer. "Do we have a roast?"

"I'll add it to the list." Duane blew out a sigh and located the shopping list he'd started earlier in the week.

Jayden set the glasses on the counter and then turned on the water in the sink and added dish detergent.

Duane shooed him away. "I'll do the dishes. Why don't you help your *bruder* in the barn?"

"But you did the dishes last night, *Dat*."

"It's fine. Go."

"*Danki*." Jayden headed toward the mudroom.

Duane crossed to the table, where Tyler had scooped up the utensils.

"What are you going to make for tomorrow?" Tyler asked.

Duane shook his head. "Well, I guess I could throw a casserole together tonight and heat it up tomorrow since we can't cook on Sundays. I'll see what we have in the fridge."

"Or we could do sandwiches again."

"Since we had sandwiches tonight and we'll have sandwiches for church lunch, I really won't want to eat a sandwich again for supper tomorrow night while you all are at youth group. If I put together an easy casserole and bake it tomorrow night, then we'll have the leftovers on Monday. I'll be killing two birds with one stone." Duane moved to the counter and opened Connie's favorite cookbook and began perusing the casserole recipes.

If only he'd made it to the market yesterday. At times, he was overwhelmed by everything he had to remember in order to keep his business and the house running.

He took a deep breath. He just did the best he could. It had only been eighteen months since Connie had passed, and he felt as if he was taking life one day at a time without her, figuring it out as he went along.

He was grateful he had his sons and his business. The rest would fall into place with constant prayer and God's help—but they were all still adjusting to their difficult new normal.

Duane found the recipe for cheeseburger pie and he felt his shoulders relax. Not only was it an easy recipe, but it was one of his sons' favorites. Plus, he most likely had all the ingredients on hand.

Tyler sidled up to him. "Do you need help?"

"*Ya. Danki.* See if there's some defrosted ground beef in the refrigerator, and I'll get out a pan." Duane set the pan out on the counter and then gathered up the rest of the ingredients—an onion, salt, shredded cheese, eggs, milk, and Bisquick. For once, he already had everything he needed!

Duane and Tyler worked in silence for a few moments as they put the recipe together.

"Do we have any other jobs coming up?" Tyler asked as he mixed the ingredients in a large bowl.

"I checked my cell phone earlier, and I had two messages. I need to check the messages in the barn too. I'll call all of the customers back on Monday."

"*Gut.*" Tyler gave him a sideways glance. "I can call them back if you'd like. I really want to take a bigger role in the company. I think I'm ready."

Duane smiled. "All right."

"I can even go with you when you give the estimates. Maybe you can even let me write them up. I have an idea that will help with your bookkeeping too. And I was thinking we should run more ads in the newspaper and maybe on the internet."

"Sounds *gut.*" Duane studied his eldest son. "You seem so focused on work, but you haven't mentioned any *maed* lately. Is there a *maedel* you like from youth group?"

"What?" Tyler laughed. "No."

"Why not? You're almost twenty-five. I was married at twenty-two, and you made me a *daed* when I was twenty-three."

Tyler held his hands up. "Whoa. There's no special *maedel* in my life. Right now I just want to help you grow our company." He paused, then turned back to mixing. "You don't say it out loud, but I can tell you worry about a steady income. Let me help you shoulder some of that worry. That's more important than dating."

Duane shook his head as he covered the baking pan with aluminum foil. "The business is fine. In fact, it's better than fine. This big job next week will sustain us for a while, even if we only have small jobs for the next month or so until the weather warms up. You need to consider your future and not worry about work so much. Think about dating, Tyler."

"When I find the *maedel* that the Lord has chosen for me, I'll start dating. Right now, my focus is helping you and the business."

Duane's heart squeezed, and he gave Tyler's shoulder a pat. "Your *mamm* would be so proud of you."

"*Danki.*" Tyler's voice was hoarse. "I miss her so much, *Dat.* I don't know what to do with the grief sometimes." He swallowed and blinked, his hazel eyes glistening in the light of the propane lamp above them.

Duane sniffed and looked away. He had to be strong for his sons. "I know, *sohn*. I do too."

"I'm going to shower." Tyler headed up the stairs, his footfalls echoing.

Duane set the casserole in the refrigerator and then leaned back against the counter. He glanced across the kitchen, memories of Connie filling his mind.

It felt as if it was just yesterday that she had stood at the counter, washing dishes, while he snuck up behind her and kissed her cheek. He could still hear her giggle and see her gorgeous smile, her hazel eyes shining in the bright sunlight that spilled in from the window above the sink. She was beautiful, so very beautiful, and she was still beautiful even after cancer had ravaged her body and spirit.

Oh, how his heart ached for her. He missed their late-night talks on the porch when they would sit together on the swing, hold hands, and discuss everything from their sons to the business to their plans for the future.

The plans they never were able to see come to fruition.

Duane closed his eyes and rubbed his temples. Connie had been his first love, the love of his life. He'd never understand why the Lord saw fit to take her when she was only forty-five years old and had so much more life to live.

But it wasn't Duane's place to question God's will. Instead, he would always cherish the twenty-four years he had enjoyed as her husband. He and Connie had been blessed with children early in their marriage, and he admired the mother she became.

He could still hear her singing to the boys at night while rocking them to sleep. She rarely raised her voice, even when Tyler and Korey would wrestle in mud puddles and then run through the house, leaving a trail of mess behind them.

Connie had been loving, supportive, and patient, even when Duane lost his temper. She'd been his everything, and then she was gone, leaving him to struggle to be the best parent he could for their sons. Most of the time, he felt inept.

But he would push on, doing his best with the Lord's help.

Standing up straight, Duane began to pray.

"*Danki* for the time I had with Connie, Lord," he whispered. "Please heal my and *mei sohns'* broken hearts."

Then he walked toward his first-floor bedroom, which still felt cold and lonely without his loving wife by his side.

# CHAPTER 3

CRYSTAL SAT IN THE UNMARRIED WOMEN'S SECTION OF THE Blank family's barn during the service the following morning. Evie balanced on Crystal's lap, Morgan was perched on the bench to her left, and Hope was at her right as the bishop talked on about the book of John.

As she adjusted Evie on her lap, Crystal looked across the barn to the married women's section, where she spotted Leona sitting between two of her friends, absently rubbing her abdomen. Alisha sat beside her mother with her back straight and her eyes trained on the bishop.

Crystal turned her attention to Jeannie Stoltzfus, her best friend since first grade, sitting a few rows behind them, flanked by their mutual friends, Lorraine Fisher and Jolene Esch. Jeannie, like Leona, rubbed her abdomen while listening to the sermon, and Crystal smiled.

Her best friend had married Jared Stoltzfus three years ago. She had married one of Crystal's ex-boyfriend's older brothers, and she was delighted for her. She would never have any ill feelings toward Jared, even though his younger brother Owen had broken her heart. After all, Jeannie and Jared were in love, and he treated her well. And after hoping and praying for some time, they were finally expecting their first child.

Crystal couldn't have been more delighted for Jeannie. She only wanted the best for her friend, and in the back of her mind, she held on to a thread of hope that someday she would sit over in the married women's section with her friends.

When Crystal scanned the married men's section, she found Jevon and Nate sitting with their father. Jevon stared down at his lap while Nate and Kane kept their attention on the preacher.

When Evie moaned and then squirmed, Crystal retrieved a small, plastic container filled with Cheerios and handed it to her.

"Have a snack," she whispered in her niece's ear. "We need to be quiet and listen to the bishop."

Evie squirmed some more.

Hope leaned over and shushed her.

"No," Evie whimpered, nuzzling her face in Crystal's shoulder.

Crystal tried to calm her, but Evie only groaned louder. When a woman sitting in front of her turned and glared at Crystal, her cheeks warmed. It was time for her to remove Evie from the church service.

Balancing Evie on her hip, she hoisted her diaper bag onto her shoulder and stood, grateful she had chosen a spot at the end of the bench to allow for an easy exit in case Evie or Morgan acted up. She took Morgan's hand and nodded for Hope to follow while Evie continued to fuss. Now she had to figure out how to get Morgan and Hope over to Leona without making an even bigger spectacle of herself.

As if reading her mind, Alisha met her at the end of the aisle and took Morgan's and Hope's hands. Crystal nodded a thank-you to her and then hurried out into the cool April air. Despite the bright sun, she shivered and pulled her heavy black sweater over her and Evie while breathing in the aroma of animals mixed with moist earth.

Evie's wails grew louder, and Crystal sighed.

"It's okay, *mei liewe*. I know your teeth hurt. We'll get you changed, and you'll feel better, okay?"

Crystal walked up the Blank family's porch steps and entered the large kitchen, which was empty since everyone was attending the church service. She crossed to the family room and set Evie down on the sofa. Then she pulled out a small mat and changed Evie's diaper. Crystal tickled her niece's belly and toes until she laughed, grateful the crying spell ceased.

After dressing Evie, Crystal took her outside and walked her around Ruth Blank's garden, pointing out the colorful flowers, a few bees, and a lovely butterfly. Evie sighed and rested her chin on Crystal's shoulder.

"You're tired, *mei liewe*. You need a nap."

Evie yawned, and her eyelids drooped.

Crystal rubbed her back and walked around the garden until the congregation began filing out of the barn. She spotted her sister-in-law walking out with Alisha, Hope, and Morgan, and she rushed over to meet them.

"I'm sorry Evie is so cranky today." Leona reached her arms out. "Evie, come to me."

Evie snuggled in deeper, burying her face in Crystal's neck. "I want *Aenti*." Her voice was muffled.

"I'm so sorry." Leona shook her head.

"It's all right. I'll take the *zwillingbopplin* to the kitchen and feed them lunch."

Alisha held Morgan's hand. "I'll help you."

"*Danki*, Alisha," Crystal said as they headed toward the kitchen. Once there, Crystal fed the twins and Hope while the men ate lunch in the barn. When it was time for the women to eat, Kane took over caring for the children. Then Crystal made her way to the barn, found her friends, and slipped onto the bench beside Jeannie and across from Jolene and Lorraine.

Jolene smiled over at her as she dropped a small pile of pretzels on her plate. "Evie was antsy today, huh?" With her dark-brown hair and deep-brown eyes, Jolene was attractive and had started dating her husband soon after they were baptized when they were eighteen. They'd married when Jolene was twenty-three, and now had five children.

"*Ya*, she was." Crystal chuckled as she sipped her cup of coffee. "She's been cranky since I got her up this morning. Teething is rough on the *kinner*."

Lorraine nodded. "Oh, I understand. Mattie woke up in a bad mood this morning too," she said, motioning to the youngest of her three children.

"I look forward to those days, even the cranky ones." Jeannie smiled down at her protruding belly.

Crystal had always thought Jeannie was one of the prettiest young women in their youth group, with her hair that reminded her of sunshine and her eyes resembling the clear azure sky.

"Your *boppli* will be here before you know it," Crystal told her. "Your due date is only two months away. June is coming so fast."

Jolene snickered, her dark eyes sparkling as she smothered a piece of bread with peanut butter. "*Ya*, get your sleep now."

"I won't mind losing sleep. I just want to meet this little angel." Jeannie placed two pieces of lunch meat on her bread. "How is Leona doing?"

Crystal picked up a pretzel. "She's managing as best she can. She has a lot of lower back pain and foot pain."

"So, you're taking care of the *kinner* and doing all of her chores, right?" Jolene frowned.

Crystal shrugged. "I don't mind."

Lorraine and Jolene shared a knowing look.

Crystal held her hand up. "I know what you're going to say, and she's not taking advantage of me. I love *mei bruderskinner* and would do anything for them. I'm just grateful Kane and Leona welcomed me into their home after *mei dat* died. If not, then I'd be alone."

Lorraine looked left and right and then leaned forward and lowered her voice. "I think Evie is so attached to you because you've been her *mamm* since she was born."

"*Ya*, it's true," Jolene said.

Frustration boiled beneath Crystal's skin. She glanced behind her and spotted Leona eating lunch and chatting with friends at the next table. Then she bent toward Lorraine. "I enjoy caring for Evie and her siblings. She's close to her *mamm* too."

"So then why is she always hanging on you when I see her?" Jolene asked.

Crystal turned her attention to her food and popped another pretzel in her mouth. She needed to change the subject.

Lorraine held up her cup of coffee. "She'll be even more clingy when the *zwillingbopplin* are born."

"That's perfectly normal. Hope was the same way when Evie and Morgan came along." Crystal looked over at Jeannie, who continued to eat her piece of bread. "How are your parents?"

Jeannie's smile was warm. "Just fine. *Mei mamm* has been doing a lot of quilting."

While her best friend talked on about her mother, Crystal worked to tamp down her feelings. She couldn't understand why her friends didn't see how appreciative she was to have her brother and his family. Perhaps someday they would understand her point of view.

Since the Lord hadn't given her a family of her own, she would always count her blessings and enjoy her nieces and nephews. If only she could convince her heart to stop yearning for children of her own.

Duane nodded to friends in his congregation as he walked toward his buggy after lunch that afternoon. He had enjoyed the service as well as eating lunch with his friends. Now he was ready to go home to his quiet house while his sons spent the afternoon playing volleyball and singing hymns with the members of their youth group.

He glanced toward the line of horses and buggies sitting nearby awaiting their owners to guide them home. He smiled when he spotted Korey leaning against his buggy and grinning while Michelle Lantz, one of the young women from his youth group, talked to him.

Warmth surged in Duane's chest as he recalled his youth group days and how he had courted Connie. Perhaps one of his sons would begin dating soon and then decide to marry. How he looked forward to seeing his sons settle down and start families of their own.

But then, whenever his sons moved on, he'd be left alone in his house. His chest constricted as loneliness crept in.

"Duane!"

He turned at the sound of his name and spotted the bishop, Wilmer Flaud, hurrying toward him. With his long white beard and matching hair, horn-rimmed glasses, and bulbous nose, Wilmer was a short, portly, elderly man who rarely smiled and commanded respect when he spoke.

Duane pasted a smile on his face. "Wilmer. You're looking well. I enjoyed your sermon today. It was very thought provoking."

"*Ya, ya.*" Wilmer's wave seemed dismissive. "I wanted to speak with you about something." Then he beckoned Duane to follow him over to a nearby tree, away from the crowd heading toward their buggies.

Duane followed him. "What is it?"

"You and your sons run that roofing company."

"That's right."

"I need you to help out Tricia Mast." Then he gestured toward a group of women talking nearby. "As you know, her husband passed away almost a year ago, leaving her and her three *kinner* alone without any male relatives to support her financially."

"Yes, I know."

"The men in the congregation have been helping her out with the milkings and maintenance on her farm. Rufus Swarey mentioned that she has a leaky roof. In fact, she has some buckets scattered throughout the upstairs. Could you make some time to help her soon?"

"Of course. I'll check my schedule right away."

"*Gut, gut.* I can cross that off my list. *Danki*, and have a *gut* week, Duane." With that, the bishop spun on his heel and started toward another group of men. "Elmer. I need to speak with you!"

Duane rubbed his beard as he gazed over toward where Tricia

Mast stood talking with the group of women. Her three daughters were close by—all under the age of twelve.

Tricia was in her late thirties and attractive with her light-brown hair and lovely gray eyes. She was friendly, and he recalled Tricia talking to Connie on many occasions at church. He'd been sorry to hear that her husband, Harley, had passed away unexpectedly nearly a year ago. Like Tricia, Harley had been outgoing and pleasant, and Duane recalled the love in his eyes for his wife and children.

"What did the bishop want?"

Duane turned to Tyler, who sidled up to him. "He wants us to help Tricia Mast. The men in the congregation have been tending to her farm since her husband died, and she has a leaky roof."

"Do you want me to come home with you, and we can look at our schedule together and figure out where we can fit her in?"

"No rush, Ty." Duane bit back a grin. "Go have fun with your youth group. We'll figure that out later. I'll see you tonight." Duane clapped his eldest son on the shoulder and then headed toward his buggy.

He would go home to his quiet house and spend the rest of the afternoon alone. Oh, how he missed having a companion at his side. Connie had left a permanent hole in his heart.

# CHAPTER 4

"It's a *schee* night." Leona pulled one of Kane's heavy sweaters over her middle while she sat on a rocking chair on the back porch beside Crystal later that evening.

Crystal shivered and hugged her own sweater against her body. "It's cold, but it will warm up soon. Before you know it, May will be here."

She peered up at the clear evening sky, taking in the stars sparkling down. Frogs croaked in the distance as the smell of a nearby woodburning fireplace filled her senses. She loved this time of night—when the children were asleep and she could relax. She shifted on her rocking chair and turned toward Leona, who smiled as she cradled her abdomen.

"Are they kicking?" Crystal asked.

Leona nodded and then reached out, grasped Crystal's hand, and placed it on her belly. When Crystal felt the little *bump bump*, her eyes filled with tears.

"Oh my goodness." The miracle of life overwhelmed Crystal, and she felt a sudden crush of yearning.

Once again, she wondered if God would ever give her the opportunity to be a wife and a mother. Perhaps the chance had passed her by while her friends had all been blessed beyond measure. Somehow it didn't seem fair, but everything happened for a reason. God had a plan for everyone, she knew.

Crystal cleared her throat and sniffed while working to keep her emotions in check.

Leona released Crystal's hand and gave her a concerned look. "You okay?"

"*Ya.*" Crystal forced her lips into a smile. "I'm just happy that soon my *bruderskinner* will arrive. We have a lot of work to do first."

Leona sighed. "I know. I have to talk to Kane about getting another crib. We'll have the *bopplin* in with us at first and then we'll have to put the *bopplin* in with Evie and Morgan. I told Kane we really need to add on to this *haus*. We're running out of bedrooms." She laughed.

Worry wrapped around Crystal and squeezed. Would they run out of room for her? She nodded toward the *daadihaus* that had been empty since Leona's parents moved to her sister's farm. "Kane could clean up the *daadihaus* for me, and then you'd have my bedroom for the *zwillingbopplin*."

"Oh, no, no, no. We don't want you in a separate *haus*. You'd be too far away from the *kinner*. Evie would not do well if you were in a different *haus*. I didn't mean to make it sound like you're in the way."

Although Crystal nodded, insecurity rolled over her. Then her friends' conversation from lunch about how Leona depended on her too much echoed in her mind. Her friends were wrong. This was her family, and she belonged here.

The back door creaked open, and Kane stepped outside before it clicked shut. "What a *schee* night."

"I know." Leona smiled up at him and patted the rocker beside her. "Join us."

Kane lowered himself into the chair beside his wife.

"Oh! The *bopplin* are kicking again." Leona grabbed his hand and directed it to the right spot.

Kane grinned. "Oh my. Those *buwe* are strong."

"Or girls," Leona teased.

An intimate expression passed between the couple, and Crystal felt out of place. She cleared her throat and stood. "I'm going to take a shower and head to bed."

"*Gut nacht*," Kane said as she walked past him.

Leona smiled. "Sleep well."

Crystal nodded and then hurried into the house. As she started upstairs toward her room, she felt uneasy once again. She hoped she wouldn't eventually wear out her welcome with her brother's family. If she did, then she wouldn't know where to go.

Later that evening, voices sounded from the mudroom before the back door banged shut. Duane folded up the copy of the Amish newspaper, *The Budget*, that he'd been reading in the family room. Relief tumbled through him. He was grateful his sons were home. The house had been too quiet all afternoon.

Duane walked out into the kitchen and leaned against the counter. "How was youth group?"

"*Gut.*" Jayden retrieved a glass from the drainboard and filled it with water before taking a long drink.

"It was the usual." Tyler headed for the stairs. "I get the shower first. *Gut nacht, Dat,*" he called over his shoulder.

Duane met Korey's gaze. "I saw you talking to Michelle Lantz after the service."

Korey shrugged. "*Ya,* I was."

"Do you like her?" Duane prodded.

"She's nice and *schee.*" Korey moved to the counter, filled his own glass with water, and took a sip.

Jayden smirked. "He does like her. He's just not admitting it. I saw them talking while we were playing volleyball. They seemed to be getting along really well."

"That's fantastic." Duane pointed at Jayden. "What about you? Do you have a special *maedel*?"

Jayden shook his head. "No." He set his empty glass in the sink.

Now it was Korey's turn to smirk. "Jay is too shy to talk to *maed.* He wouldn't even know what to say."

"So? I'm only nineteen and I'm not in a rush." Jayden headed for the stairs. "I get the shower next. *Gut nacht, Dat.*" His heavy footfalls echoed in the stairwell.

"*Gut nacht,*" Duane called after him and then he turned toward Korey. "So, tell me more about Michelle. Are you going to ask her out?"

"Maybe." Korey turned his back on his father and began washing the glasses.

"You can talk to me. I won't tell your *bruders.*"

Korey tilted his head. "I like her, but I just don't want to rush into anything. I'm not in a hurry to settle down and get married." He looked down at the toes of his socks. "I know you were a *dat* at my age, but I'm not ready for that kind of commitment."

"No one is telling you to marry Michelle, but if you like her, you might want to try dating her and see how it goes. That's one step toward a future."

Korey looked up, frowning. "Please don't pressure me."

"No one is pressuring you. I just want my *sohns* to be *froh* like I was with your *mamm*."

Korey swallowed. "I miss her so much." His voice was soft and thick. "I think about her all the time. When I come downstairs in the morning, I still think she'll be here making us a huge breakfast with bacon, eggs, toast, and fruit. Sometimes I'm sure I can smell it." He gestured toward the stove. "And then when we come home after youth group, I expect to see her sitting in her favorite chair next to yours, reading a book while you read the paper. But when I walk in, she's not here." He cleared his throat roughly.

Duane's eyes burned as he looked down at the worn linoleum floor. *Keep it together! Don't let your son see you cry! You have to be stronger than this.*

"Sometimes I even think I can hear her voice." Korey sniffed. "But other times, I forget what her voice sounded like when she sang to us."

Duane sucked in a breath. "I understand."

Korey bit his lip and looked down at the floor. "You need to talk about her, so we don't forget her completely."

"I'll try. It's just difficult for me to talk about her sometimes." Duane's heart twisted.

Korey met his gaze. His eyes narrowed for a moment and then recovered. "*Ya*, so I'll let you know about Michelle. Right now, we're just talking."

"*Gut.* Take your time, *sohn.*" Duane patted his shoulder. "The Lord will lead you down the right path."

"I know. *Gut nacht, Dat.*"

"See you in the morning," Duane called after him as Korey headed up the stairs.

Duane sagged back against the counter once again and rubbed his temples where a headache brewed. He'd spent all afternoon alone in his house, and the loneliness was deafening.

And when he'd seen Korey talking to Michelle, the truth had hit him: Soon all three of his sons would date, become engaged, and then leave him all alone. He might see them at jobs if they continued to work for him, but he'd spend his evenings by himself. An image of Connie's beautiful face filled his mind's eye, and the notion filled him with more grief and sadness than he could bear.

How would he learn to live with the constant loneliness when his once busy home became as silent as a tomb?

Duane knocked on the Glick family's back door Wednesday morning. Birds sang in nearby trees, and two squirrels chased each other toward the pasture fence while the aroma of animals washed over him.

He pivoted toward the large barn, where his sons unloaded his driver's truck and set up their day. Beyond the back door, he heard sounds of children talking and screeching, and he smiled, recalling how Crystal had appeared at the door with the crying toddler.

The back door opened with a creak, and the blond woman he had seen standing out by the swing set with the children and Crystal on Saturday stood in the doorway.

She rested her hands on her protruding belly and smiled at him. *"Gude mariye."*

"*Gude mariye*," he said. "I'm Duane Bontrager, and I just wanted to let you know *mei sohns* and I are going to get started roofing the barns."

"Oh, right. Kane said you were coming today. He's out in the barn. Feel free to go find him if you have any questions."

"*Danki.*"

The woman smiled before closing the door and disappearing into the house.

Duane ambled down the porch steps toward the barn and thought of Crystal, wondering where she was this morning.

As he approached the barn, he turned his thoughts toward work, and he rubbed his hands together.

"All right," Duane called to his sons. "It's time to earn our living. Jayden, get our tallest ladder."

Crystal climbed out of the passenger seat of her brother's driver's van later that morning. She cupped her hand to mouth to stifle a yawn and walked to the back of the van as the driver opened the tailgate, revealing a mountain of grocery bags. Then she yawned again.

Evie had kept her up last night, but she had to run to the grocery store. Now she needed to muster the energy to carry in the groceries and stow them.

When loud voices sounded, Crystal tented her hand over her eyes as she peered out toward the largest barn. She spotted Duane and three young men working on the roof. She watched them for a moment and felt a twinge of curiosity. She guessed that the three younger men were in their twenties, but she couldn't be certain from her view.

She studied them, wondering if they were Duane's sons. After all, Duane had a beard, indicating he was married, and he looked old enough to have children that were in their twenties.

"*Aenti!*" Jevon scrambled down the porch steps with Hope in tow.

Crystal smiled at her niece and nephew. "Are you here to help?"

Hope nodded and her long, light-brown braids bounced over her shoulders. Then she bent her little arm and raised her chin. "I'm strong! I can carry something heavy."

"What a good helper." Crystal bit back a chuckle as she handed the four-year-old a bag with two loaves of bread in it. "Is this too heavy for you?"

Hope shook her head and then scampered up the back steps.

Jevon picked up two bags while Crystal struggled with four and followed him into the kitchen, where Leona sat at the kitchen table. Crystal directed her niece and nephew to set their bags on the table, and they complied before hurrying outside for more.

Leona pushed herself up from the table and rubbed her lower back with her fingers. "I'll start putting everything away."

After several trips, the kitchen table was covered with grocery bags. Crystal's posture sagged. Now she faced the tedious task of putting everything away.

Leona set two boxes of cereal and four cans of soup in the pantry, and then she sank down onto a nearby chair. "My feet and back are just killing me, and I can't shake this headache."

"I'm sorry to hear that." Crystal picked up two jars of tomato sauce and carried them to the pantry just as Evie and Morgan began to cry out. She turned toward Leona. "Where are the *zwillingbopplin*?"

Leona pointed toward the doorway. "In the *schtupp* in their play yard."

Crystal stared at the sea of grocery bags as anxiety gripped her. Then she did a mental headshake and looked at Jevon and Hope who were busy stacking cans of soup in the pantry. She could get all her chores done. After all, she did it every day.

"Hope, would you please go play with the *zwillingbopplin* until I'm done in here?" Crystal asked.

Hope raced out of the kitchen. *"Ya, Aenti."*

*"Danki,"* Crystal called after her.

Soon the crying stopped, and giggles sounded from the family room. Crystal felt her shoulders relax as she and Jevon finished putting away the groceries.

When she walked into the family room, she found Hope sitting on the floor, making faces at the twins while they giggled. How she enjoyed the sweet sound of their laughter!

Hope turned to her. "They think I'm *gegisch*."

*"Danki*, Hope. You're a big help." Crystal touched Hope's cheek. "Would you help me get the *zwillingbopplin* to their room? We can change their diapers."

Crystal and Hope led the twins upstairs, and after Crystal changed their diapers, she set them in their cribs for a nap.

*"Aenti*, could we make lemonade for the men working on the barn?" Hope asked as they descended the stairs.

"That's a nice idea, but let's ask your *mamm* first."

Hope scuttled down the last few steps and then dashed into the kitchen, where Leona sat nursing a glass of water. *"Mamm!* Can me and *Aenti* make lemonade for the men outside?"

Crystal walked into the kitchen and stood by the counter while Leona beamed down at Hope.

"That would be sweet, Hope." Leona angled her body toward Crystal. "Did the *zwillingbopplin* go in for their nap?"

"*Ya*, they did."

"*Danki*." Leona leaned on the table as she stood. "My headache is only getting worse. I'm going to take a nap. Call me if you need me."

"We'll be fine. You get some rest and feel better." Crystal opened the pantry and found the lemonade mix. Then she retrieved a plastic pitcher from the nearby cabinet.

"I want to help." Hope joined her at the counter.

Crystal pulled a chair over and helped Hope stand on it. She poured the powder into the pitcher and added water.

"Here you go." Crystal handed her a wooden spoon. "You can stir."

Hope's forehead wrinkled, and she stuck her tongue out while stirring with all her might.

Crystal smiled. How she loved spending time with her sweet niece! She couldn't wait to see Hope's happy face when she carried the pitcher out to Duane Bontrager and the other three men. Surely they would appreciate lemonade and a break.

# CHAPTER 5

"I WANT TO CARRY THE PITCHER," HOPE ANNOUNCED AS Crystal dropped a tray of ice cubes into the pitcher of lemonade.

Crystal grimaced as she envisioned Hope tripping and dumping the pitcher all over herself and the ground. What a sticky mess that would be! "It's awfully heavy."

"I'm very strong like *mei bruders*. See?" Hope squeezed her bicep.

Crystal couldn't stop her laugh. "I know you are, but why don't you carry the cups instead?"

Hope shook her head. "I'll be careful. I promise, *Aenti* Kisstal."

"How about I carry it, but you help me pour it for the men?"

Hope beamed at this option. "Okay!"

"Perfect." Crystal gathered up a stack of Styrofoam cups and handed them to Hope. "When we get out there, why don't you ask the men if they want some of our special lemonade?"

Hope dashed out the door, down the porch steps, and through the grass. "Yay!"

"Slow down, *mei liewe*," Crystal called, rushing after her.

When they reached the barn, they found Duane standing by the ladder while the three young men worked on the roof. Duane looked over and gave them a warm smile.

Hope rushed toward him. "Are you firsty?"

"As a matter of fact, I am thirsty." His lips twitched.

"Would you like some lemonade?"

He glanced over at Crystal and then crouched down beside Hope. "Did *you* make the lemonade?"

"Uh-huh!" Hope nodded with vigor and held up a cup. "I'll pour it for you." Then she pointed toward the roof. "Would those men like some too?"

Duane smirked. "I'll find out, but I have a question for you first. What's your name?"

She pointed to her chest. "I'm Hope."

"It's nice to meet you, Hope. I'm Duane." He pointed toward the roof. "Those are my three *sohns*—Tyler, Korey, and Jayden."

Hope squinted up at them. "They're all tall like you and *mei dat.*"

"*Ya*, they are." Duane grinned over at Crystal. "It's nice to see you again."

"You too." Crystal gestured toward Hope. "This was her idea. She wanted to make lemonade for you and your *sohns.*"

"We appreciate it." Duane pointed toward a large beverage cooler with a spigot. "All we brought with us is water."

One of the young men stood at the edge of the roof. "What do you have down there?"

"Get your *bruders* and come down and meet our new *freinden*," Duane told him.

"We made you lemonade!" Hope hollered up to him, yelling a little too loud and making Crystal snicker.

The young man grinned, and his smile reminded Crystal of Duane's.

"Lemonade?" the young man asked. "How did you know that was my favorite?"

Hope gasped and turned to Crystal. "It's his favorite!"

Crystal's heart swelled at Hope's excitement. "You had a *gut* idea, Hope."

She looked over and found Duane watching her. When he smiled, she noticed how handsome he was with his dark eyes, graying brown hair and beard, his broad shoulders, and his trim waist. There was something about him that drew her in, but then a wave of embarrassment swept through her. How could she allow herself to feel this way? Duane was a married man!

Duane moved to the ladder and held on to the bottom as the three young men climbed down. While they were all tall men, two had dark hair while the one she had met last week had sandy-brown hair.

The one who had called down to Hope crouched beside her just as Duane had. "I'm Tyler. What's your name?"

"I'm Hope." She pointed to Crystal. "Me and *mei aenti* Kisstal made you lemonade. *Aenti* Kisstal said I can help her pour, but she didn't want me to carry the pitcher. She says it's too heavy, but I'm strong like *mei bruders*." To prove her point, she flexed her arm. "See?"

Tyler grinned. "Wow. You sure are."

Duane and his other two sons chuckled.

"*Danki* for making us lemonade." Tyler stood up straight and pointed to the man with dark hair behind him. "This is *mei bruder* Korey."

"Hi, Hope." Korey nodded, his eyes hidden by mirrored sunglasses.

Then he pointed to the man with sandy-brown hair. "And this is *mei bruder* Jayden."

The other man waved at her.

Crystal held up the pitcher. "Why don't we pour that lemonade?"

"Let me help." Hope reached for the pitcher.

Duane sidled up to Crystal. "I'll hold the cups for you."

"*Danki,*" she told him.

While Duane held up each cup, Crystal guided the pitcher for Hope. Duane handed out the full cups to his sons and then took a cup for himself.

Korey took a sip and then held up his cup. "Hope, this is the best lemonade I've ever had."

"I have to agree," Duane said.

"Yay!" Hope clapped and then pointed to the pitcher. "I'd like a cup, peease, *Aenti.*"

"Of course." Crystal poured a cup for her, and Hope took a long drink.

"*Ya,* it's *gut.*" Hope pointed at Crystal. "You drink a cup too."

"Allow me." Duane set his cup on a nearby picnic table. Then he took the pitcher from Crystal, poured her a cup of lemonade, and handed it to her before setting the pitcher on the table.

"*Danki.*" She took a sip and nodded. "It will do."

Duane raised his cup as if toasting her.

Hope walked over to the three *bruders* and pointed at Tyler. "How old are you?"

"I'm twenty-four." Tyler pointed at Korey. "He's twenty-three, and Jayden is the *boppli.* He's nineteen."

"Hey," Jayden protested.

Hope cackled. "He isn't a *boppli!*"

"Exactly." Jayden gave her a high-five.

Crystal grinned. "I think Hope just made some new *freinden.*"

"I was thinking the same thing." Duane turned toward her. "She called you *aenti.* She's your *bruderskind?*"

"*Ya.* Did you think she was mine?"

"I just assumed since you said your last name was Glick, that this was your farm."

"Oh, no." Crystal waved off the comment. "And all of the *kinner* are Kane and Leona's—even the *zwillingbopplin*."

"Ah. I see." Duane sipped more lemonade.

"People often think the *zwillingbopplin* are mine since they have red hair. I live here, and I help take care of them."

"Interesting." He seemed to study her. "I'm sure your *bruder* and his *fraa* appreciate your help with all of the *kinner*."

"*Ya*. There will be eight soon."

"Eight." Duane seemed to get a faraway look his in eyes as if remembering something. "*Mei fraa* wanted a big family, but we were grateful that the Lord saw fit to give us three."

"They seem like nice young men." Crystal pointed to where his sons continued to talk and laugh with Hope. "You're blessed."

Duane set his empty cup on the table. "*Ya*, I am, and I have a feeling your *bruderskinner* are blessed to have you."

Crystal took in his kind expression and once again felt drawn to him, despite herself.

She pointed toward the pitcher. "Would you like us to leave the lemonade out here for you?"

"That would be nice. *Danki*."

"*Gern gschehne*." She turned her attention to her niece. "Hope, we need to let Duane and his *sohns* get back to work."

Hope waved at them and then dropped her empty cup into a bag of trash. "See you later."

Tyler smiled at Crystal. "*Danki* for the lemonade."

"It was a nice break," Korey said.

"I'm so *froh* you liked it." Crystal turned toward Duane. "Have a *gut* day."

Hope threaded her fingers with Crystal's as they started toward the house.

"Let's make them some *kichlin*," Hope said.

"We'll ask your *mamm* first." Crystal glanced over her shoulder and found Duane watching her, and once again, she felt a stirring in her heart.

She did her best to redirect her thoughts. "If your *mamm* says it's okay, we could make chocolate chip *kichlin*."

"*Ya!*" Hope released Crystal's hand and trotted ahead of her toward the back porch.

Later that afternoon, Duane looked down from the roof just as Crystal, Hope, and Jevon walked toward the barn, each of them carrying a plate.

He smiled. How he had enjoyed talking with Crystal earlier! He guessed she was in her thirties, and he'd spent most of the day thinking about her and wondering why such a sweet, friendly, and attractive young woman was helping to raise her brother's children instead of children of her own.

"Looks like our little *freind* is back with another snack," Tyler announced.

Jayden smacked Tyler's arm. "I think she has a crush on you."

"Hold on now. I thought she liked me," Korey teased.

Duane snickered as he crossed the roof to the ladder. "Let's go see what they brought us this time." He climbed down just as Crystal and the children approached. "Hi there."

Hope walked over to him with Jevon at her side. "This is *mei bruder* Jevon. We made you *kichlin*!" She held up a plate of chocolate chip cookies.

"Oh my goodness!" Duane exclaimed as he breathed in the scrumptious aroma. "How nice of you." He met Crystal's gaze, and she gave him a warm smile. She had some of the loveliest green eyes he'd ever seen. "You're spoiling *mei sohns* and me."

She nodded toward her niece. "This was Hope's idea again."

The ladder creaked as Duane's three sons came down to the ground.

*"Kichlin!"* Korey announced. "Yum!"

Tyler rubbed his flat abdomen. "Chocolate chip. My favorite."

Duane picked up the nearby bottle of hand sanitizer. "Clean your hands, boys." He pumped some into his hands and then held the bottle out to Jayden.

While his sons cleaned their hands and then swiped cookies from Hope's and Jevon's plates, Duane moved over to where Crystal stood and chose the largest cookie on her plate. "What a nice afternoon snack."

"I had to do something since it looked like you and your *sohns* hadn't eaten yet today."

He raised an eyebrow, surprised by her sense of humor. When she laughed, he enjoyed the sweet lilt.

"I'm kidding." She peered up at the roof. "How's it going?"

"There was a lot of damage, so we're replacing the entire roof. We stripped off the old one this morning."

"How long have you—" she began.

"When did you—" he started.

They both laughed, and her cheeks flushed as she looked down.

"You first," he said.

"No, you."

He shook his head. "I insist. You go first." He took another cookie from the plate.

"Fine. How long have you been in business?"

"Twenty years now," Duane said. "It was originally called Bontrager's Roofing, but I renamed it Bontrager and Sons when they were old enough to help me run the business. I used to have a couple of helpers, but they moved on to other jobs. It was perfect timing when *mei buwe* were ready to work for me." He glanced toward where his sons talked and laughed with Jevon and Hope.

"Tyler favors you."

Duane cocked his head. "You think so?"

"He has your smile." She looked sheepish. "Anyway, what were you going to ask *me*?"

"How long have you lived here?"

"Almost four years. I had been living with *mei dat* a few miles from here." She pointed toward the house. "Kane took over Leona's *dat*'s farm, and her parents moved in with her *schweschder* in the *daadihaus* on their farm. When *mei dat* passed, Kane decided to sell *mei dat*'s property and asked me to move in and help them. I moved in three years ago when I was thirty. Our *mamm* had already passed, back when I was sixteen."

Duane's heart twisted. "I'm sorry for the loss of your parents."

"*Danki.*"

"So, you're thirty-three."

"That's right."

He studied her, once again contemplating why a woman who was so lovely would be single.

She held up the plate. "Take more *kichlin*. We have plenty more saved in the kitchen for the *kinner*."

"*Danki.*" He retrieved another cookie from the plate.

"Who taught you how to roof?"

"*Mei dat*. He had a company."

"Oh."

He looked past her toward the house, where Leona led the twins out to the play area. "The *zwillingbopplin* do resemble you."

She laughed as she pivoted toward the house. "*Ya*, I'm told that when I take them shopping." She shook her head. "I can't believe *mei bruder* will have eight *kinner* soon. It will be a blessing. They will keep me busy for sure."

Crystal faced him once again. "Well, we should let you get back to work so you can get home at a decent time." She tilted her head. "Do you live close by?"

"Not far from here. We're in Bird-in-Hand."

"I hope you enjoy the rest of the afternoon. I might see you again if Hope decides you and your *sohns* need more snacks."

"We won't complain. We enjoy them. In fact, we finished the lemonade."

"*Gut.*" She set the plate of cookies on the table and picked up the empty pitcher. Then she looked over at her niece and nephew, who were still talking to Duane's sons. "Hope. Jevon. Let's get back to the *haus* and let Duane and his *sohns* finish their work."

Hope and Jevon said good-bye to Duane's sons, who thanked them for the cookies.

"Have a *gut* afternoon," Crystal told Duane and his sons.

"You too."

"That's enough of a break," Tyler announced. "We have a roof to finish. Let's go."

"You never let up," Korey mumbled.

Jayden shook his head and started up the ladder.

While his sons climbed back up toward the barn roof, Duane

picked up another cookie and then turned toward the house. Crystal followed her niece and nephew toward the swing set. The four children played on the swings, and Crystal took a seat on a bench beside Leona.

"Hey, *Dat!*" Jayden called down to him.

Duane tented his hand over his eyes and looked up toward his youngest son. *"Ya?"*

"Would you please finish the *kichli* and bring up another box of nails?"

Duane grinned. "I'll be right there."

He followed Jayden's directions before climbing the ladder to where his sons were busy hammering shingles.

"What are you making for supper tonight, Korey?" Duane asked as he handed the box to Jayden and then retrieved his hammer.

Korey faced him, scowling. "It's not my night. It's Tyler's." He pointed his hammer toward his older brother.

"Oh no. I cooked on Monday." Tyler shook his head.

"No, you didn't!" Korey snipped. "We had leftover casserole on Monday."

Tyler nodded. "Right, and I warmed it up."

"I get so tired of their tiffs." Jayden sighed.

Duane exhaled, also exasperated by the bickering. "All right. I suppose I'll go to the market on the way home and pick something up."

"Why does Kore always get away with not cooking?" Tyler demanded.

Korey stood up straight. "Get away with it? I made sub sandwiches last week. Doesn't that count?"

"Okay, okay. We're at a jobsite. We need to be professional."

Duane pinched the bridge of his nose. "I said I'll go to the market tonight. Korey can cook tomorrow night. Now drop it before I get angry."

Tyler frowned as he returned to hammering while Korey did the same.

Duane looked over toward the swing set and spotted Crystal pushing Jevon on a swing. As if she could feel his stare, she turned toward the barn and waved. He smiled and waved back.

For some strange reason, he couldn't wait to talk to her again.

# CHAPTER 6

Duane thanked the man at the deli and then set the roasted chicken in his shopping cart later that afternoon.

He shook his head and tried to imagine what Connie would say if she knew he was buying a meal that had already been prepared. Oh, how disappointed she'd be! She'd also tell him that he was spoiling their sons by not insisting that they take their turn cooking.

But if she were here, then he wouldn't have to struggle to not only keep food on the table but also to work full-time running a business to earn the money to buy the food for the table. That familiar grief swirled in his chest. If only the cancer hadn't taken his beloved wife . . .

"Duane!"

He spun as Tricia Mast walked over to him. He raised a hand. "Oh, hi, Tricia."

"Picking up supper?" She pointed to his shopping cart.

He leaned forward on the cart handle. "*Ya*. We're working on a big job over in Gordonville. Tyler and I stopped at the market while Jayden and Korey had our driver take them home so they could take care of our animals."

"Oh." She pointed down at her full cart. "I was able to get out without the *kinner*. It's always a treat, even if it's grocery shopping."

He laughed. "I remember those days."

"What is the big job you have in Gordonville?"

"It's a farm with four barns and also a *haus*, of course. The owner asked me to replace all the roofs. It's a blessing for my family."

"That's *gut*."

"Wilmer mentioned that you need some roofing done at your *haus*. I plan to come by soon to take a look. We've been busy working on this big project, but I haven't forgotten."

"*Danki*. I appreciate that you're going to work me in."

He studied her pretty face and considered their similar circumstances. "How are you doing?"

"I'm fine." Her smile seemed forced.

Duane leaned toward her. "How are you *really* doing?"

She examined her short, clean fingernails.

"Tricia, you don't have to tell me everything, but remember I know how difficult it is to suddenly be alone."

She met his gaze, and her gray eyes seemed to shimmer in the light of the fluorescents buzzing above them. "My grief comes in waves. Some days are more difficult than others."

Duane moved his shopping cart closer to the deli counter as an *English* couple walked past them. Then he turned toward Tricia once again. "I understand. Some days I'm doing great, and then I'll see something that reminds me of Connie and I'll feel lost again. Last week it was her cookbook. I was looking for a casserole recipe, and it brought back some memories of being with her in the kitchen."

"Exactly." Tricia's voice sounded gruff, and she cleared her throat.

Tyler walked over carrying two bags of potato chips. "I see you're done shopping, Tyler."

"I like chips." His eldest son shrugged and then smiled at Tricia. "Hi, Tricia."

"Hello." Tricia pointed in the direction of the cashier. "I need to head on home. Have a *gut nacht*."

"You too. And I'll be in touch about your roof," Duane told her before she steered her cart toward the front of the store. "You ready?" he asked his eldest son, angling his cart toward the next aisle.

"I thought after the doctor's appointment, Kane and I could go to lunch and then run a few errands. Do you mind, Crystal?" Leona asked the following morning.

Crystal scrubbed the last breakfast dish and then rinsed it before setting it in the drainboard. "No, of course not."

"Oh *gut*. Kane and I never get to spend time alone. It will almost be like a date." Leona grabbed a dishcloth, dunked it in the soapy water, and then walked over to the table.

When she heard the rumble of an engine, Crystal looked over her shoulder toward the windows that faced the line of barns and the pasture. Duane's driver's work truck rumbled down the rock driveway toward the large barn. She smiled to herself as she recalled their conversations yesterday.

Just then Alisha and Nate rushed into the kitchen.

"We're leaving for school," Alisha said, pulling on her sweater.

Leona kissed each of them on the head before they started toward the door. "Have a *gut* day."

"Wait!" Crystal grabbed their lunch boxes and then rushed after them. "Your lunches!"

Alisha spun and grabbed both of them from her. *"Danki."*

*"Gern gschehne."* Crystal touched their heads. "See you later."

Her niece and nephew waved before rushing through the mudroom toward the back door. Then the storm door creaked open before banging shut.

Leona clucked her tongue as she returned to wiping down the kitchen table. "What would we do without you, Crystal?"

Crystal shrugged off the comment as she finished washing the dishes and setting them in the drainboard. Then she turned her attention to the twins sitting in the highchairs, singing non-sense songs to each other with their faces covered with pieces of scrambled eggs, cinnamon rolls, and globs of butter.

"I'll get the *zwillingbopplin* cleaned up."

Leona dropped the dishcloth into the sink and then started toward the doorway. *"Danki.* I'm going to get ready for my appoint-ment. I'll check on Hope and Jevon in the *schtupp* on the way to my bedroom."

Crystal cleaned up the twins and then carried them to the family room, where she changed their diapers on the sofa before setting them in their play yard with two board books. Hope and Jevon sat at the coffee table coloring.

Then she went back to the kitchen to finish tidying up. After grabbing the dustpan and broom, Crystal began sweeping up the crumbs from breakfast. She stopped to peek out the back windows and spotted Duane talking to his sons while they stood by the tall ladder.

Leaning on the broom, she recalled their conversation yes-terday and what he had said about his wife yearning for a larger family. Crystal had appreciated how kind and patient Duane had been with Hope and Jevon. Duane seemed like such a warm, friendly, and good man. She could tell he adored his sons, and she was certain he was a warm and loving husband as well.

Crystal returned to sweeping while pondering what Duane's wife looked like. Surely she was a beautiful woman, who took good care of her husband and sons.

"Our ride is here." Leona appeared in the doorway in a fresh blue dress and black apron, with a black sweater hanging over her arm. She turned toward the family room. "Be *gut* for your *aenti, kinner*," she told the children.

Kane took Leona's hand. "We'll see you later, Crystal."

Crystal waved as her brother and sister-in-law disappeared through the mudroom doorway.

She finished sweeping and then peeked in on the kids in the family room. Thankfully, the twins still sat in the play yard looking at books while Jevon and Hope continued to entertain themselves.

Crystal took the quiet opportunity to plan supper. She found her favorite casserole cookbook in the cabinet and flipped through it. Then she leaned down to retrieve a casserole dish. When she yanked on the cabinet knob, the door flew off in her hand, sending her backward. She landed on the floor on her bottom with the cabinet door in her hand.

"Oof!" she exclaimed with a start.

She stood up and placed the cabinet door on the counter before rubbing her sore bottom.

*"Aenti?"* Jevon appeared in the doorway and then walked over to her. "Are you all right?"

Hope hurried in behind him. "What happened?"

"Oh nothing, just a mishap with the cabinet door." Crystal examined the hinges.

If only she had a screwdriver. She looked inside the exposed cabinet and imagined the twins crawling into it, pulling out all the pots and pans, throwing them around, hitting each other with them, and getting injured. She cringed.

She turned to Jevon. "Would you please go outside and ask Duane if he has any tools? Tell him I need a screwdriver, okay?"

"*Ya.*" Jevon scooted toward the back door.

"May I go with him?" Hope asked.

"I need you to stay in the *schtupp* and keep an eye on the *zwillingbopplin* for me so I can get supper ready. That would be a great help."

"Okay."

"*Danki, mei liewe.*"

While Hope darted back into the family room, Crystal leaned back against the counter and hoped Duane wouldn't mind helping her fix the cabinet door.

Tyler pointed toward the Glicks' house while he stood on the barn roof. "We have some company."

"Who is it?" Duane set his hammer down, swiped his sleeve over his forehead, and then stood. He peered out to see Jevon scuttling toward the barn.

Duane walked over to the edge of the roof. "Hi, Jevon. What's up?"

Jevon rested his hands on his hips and took a deep breath. "*Mei aenti* needs your help. She wants to know if you have any tools. She needs a screwdriver. It's an emergency!"

Well, this was unexpected.

"I'll be right down." Duane turned toward his sons, who watched him with curious expressions. "Crystal needs help. I have to grab my toolbox. Apparently, it's an emergency."

Jayden's forehead crinkled. "Doesn't Kane have tools?"

"That's what I was thinking," Korey chimed in.

Tyler pointed toward the house. "I saw Kane and his *fraa* leave in a car earlier."

"Oh. Now it makes sense," Jayden said.

Tyler set his hammer on the roof. "Do you want my help, *Dat*?"

"Sure."

Duane and Tyler rushed down the ladder, gathered up their two toolboxes, and hurried with Jevon toward the house.

# CHAPTER 7

When they reached the back porch, Duane followed Jevon and Tyler into the house, where Crystal stood at the counter.

"What's happened?" Duane asked her.

"I'm sorry to bother you, but Kane went with Leona to her doctor's appointment and to run some errands. I don't feel comfortable leaving the *kinner* in the *haus* alone while I go search for a screwdriver in the barn." She held up a cabinet door. "This came off in my hand."

Duane grinned. "Oh. I was worried. Jevon said it was an emergency."

"He did?" She grimaced and blushed. "I'm so sorry."

Jevon tapped Tyler's leg. Then he took Tyler's hand in his and yanked him toward a nearby doorway. "Want to see what I drew? It's in the *schtupp*."

"Um. Okay." Tyler lifted a shoulder in a shrug and handed his toolbox to Duane. "Here you go."

Duane took the toolbox and then looked at Crystal before they both started laughing. He loved the sound of her laughter and the way her whole face lit up.

"I'm so sorry, Duane. I told him to ask you if you had a

screwdriver. I've reminded Kane over and over that the hinges were loose, but I suppose it kept slipping his mind."

"It's no problem at all." Duane walked over to the counter and set the two toolboxes down. "I always keep toolboxes at the jobsite since we never know when we'll need them." He pointed toward the cabinet. "I'll take a look."

"*Danki.*"

Duane examined the screws and then retrieved a screwdriver from the toolbox.

"I'm going to go check on the *kinner,*" Crystal said as she headed toward the doorway.

Duane tried screwing the hinges back in place, but the holes were stripped. He sighed.

He crossed the room to the doorway of the large family room, which included three sofas, two recliners, three wing chairs, a coffee table, and a play yard. Tyler knelt on the floor between Hope and Jevon while they colored, the twins bounced in the play yard, and Crystal stood over Tyler, nodding as Jevon showed them a drawing.

Crystal turned and smiled as she closed the distance between them. "Did you fix it already?"

"No, actually. The holes are stripped."

"Oh well. *Danki* for looking at it. I can ask Kane to fix it when he gets home."

"Actually, I can do a fix if you have wood glue and a toothpick."

She pointed toward the kitchen behind him. "I'm sure I have toothpicks, and I think there's some wood glue in the utility room."

They stepped into the kitchen together, and Crystal gathered up the supplies and then walked over to the counter.

AMY CLIPSTON

"*Danki.* I just have to make sure the glue is dry before I put the screws back in," he explained.

"I appreciate it." She pointed toward the family room. "I'm going to try to get the *zwillingbopplin* down for a nap."

"Okay." Duane sat down on the floor and began applying wood glue to the toothpick before pushing it into the hole.

Whines and cries of protests sounded from the family room, and he imagined Crystal trying to convince the twins to go to their room for their nap. Duane smiled, recalling his own sons behaving the same way when they were cranky toddlers.

"You got this under control?"

Duane looked up at Tyler standing over him. "I do."

"Then I'll head back outside. We have to stay on schedule."

"I'll be done here soon."

"No problem," Tyler said. "I'll make sure we're on track." He disappeared through the mudroom.

After Duane finished gluing the toothpick in the hole, he stood and washed his hands at the sink. He spotted the cookbook on the counter and skimmed the recipes listed on the page. Slipping a napkin in to save the page, he flipped through the cookbook, checking out other casserole recipes.

He peeked up at the ceiling when he heard a toddler howl above him, and he shook his head. Poor Crystal must have been struggling to get the twins to settle down for their morning nap.

While he continued perusing the cookbook, he heard more commotion upstairs and then running water and the sounds of toddlers whining, along with the muffled sound of Crystal's voice. He glanced over at the stove where the percolator sat. When he opened it, he found it had some coffee in it.

He considered how forward it would be to warm up the coffee

for himself and Crystal. On one hand, she might think he was making himself too much at home, but on the other, she might appreciate a cup of coffee and some conversation after wrestling the twins for their nap.

Against his better judgment, he turned the burner on under the percolator and searched for two mugs, a bowl of sugar, spoons, and creamer. Then he carried the cookbook to the table and continued reading it while he waited for Crystal to return.

The delicious aroma of coffee filled the large kitchen as the sound of water draining out of the tub and footsteps sounded above him, along with more whining and protesting. Then footsteps echoed in a nearby stairwell and then stopped in the family room.

"Do you two need anything?" Crystal asked in the next room.

"No, *Aenti*," Jevon said.

"We're still coloring," Hope responded.

"*Gut*. I'm going to check on Duane." Crystal entered the kitchen and gave him a sheepish expression. "I'm so sorry." She held up two toddler-size matching blue dresses. "When I changed Evie and Morgan, I found that Morgan had, well . . . ah." She shook her head. "I wound up giving them each a quick bath."

Duane held his hand up. "Understood. I've been there."

"Anyway, I'm sorry that I—" Her pretty green eyes focused on the table and she smiled. "How did you know I needed a cup of *kaffi*?"

He gave her a palms-up. "Just a *gut* guess, I suppose." He pointed toward the cabinet. "I need to wait until the glue dries before I can put the door back on, so I thought we might share a cup before I go back out to work."

"Oh, I hate taking so much of your time."

"*Mei sohns* need to learn how to run the jobsite without me. I do hope to retire someday." He chuckled.

"Give me one moment." She disappeared through a nearby doorway and then returned without the damp clothing. "I'd love to only do laundry once a week, but it's not that simple when you have six *kinner* . . ." Her voice trailed off as she moved to the sink and washed her hands.

Duane glanced around the kitchen, suddenly getting the impression that Crystal did more than her fair share of chores around the house. "Have a seat."

"I was just thinking about those cinnamon buns I made this morning. Would you like one?"

"Of course I would."

She retrieved a container and plates and then brought them to the table while he filled their mugs with coffee. Then they sat down across from each other.

Crystal set a cinnamon bun on a plate and then handed it to him. "I'm so sorry for asking for help this morning. I've mentioned to Kane at least a dozen times that the cabinet door was loose, but he's been a little busy lately."

"Stop apologizing. I'm glad I could help." Duane stirred cream and sugar into his mug.

"*Danki.*" She placed a cinnamon bun on a plate for herself. Then she added cream and sugar to her mug of coffee before taking a sip. "This hits the spot."

Duane took a bite of the bun, and his taste buds danced with delight at the sweet flavor. "Spectacular."

She laughed. "*Danki,* but I can't take credit for making them from scratch. It's just an easy mix I picked up at the grocery store."

"But you did mix them up and bake them." He lifted his mug to toast her and then took a sip. The coffee hit the spot as well.

"The *zwillingbopplin* had me up early this morning, well before everyone else."

He set his mug on the table and tilted his head as her words sank in. "You get up with the *zwillingbopplin*?"

Crystal shrugged as she broke off a piece of cinnamon bun. "Their room is beside mine upstairs, so I hear them. And Evie is pretty attached to me."

Silence stretched between them as they both ate more of their buns and sipped their coffee.

She set her mug down and pointed to the cookbook beside him. "Were you looking for new recipes?" she asked, sounding as if she were teasing him.

"I was actually. I'm always looking for easy casseroles."

"Oh *ya*?" Her expression filled with a wide smile. "You like to cook?"

"I don't necessarily like it, but I was forced to learn how to do it."

She studied him as if he were an intricate puzzle. "Does your *fraa* have a job outside the home? Or does she not like to cook?"

He wiped his beard with a paper napkin and then took a deep breath. "I'm a widower." He would never get used to saying that word.

"I'm . . . I'm so sorry. I-I had no idea," Crystal sputtered, frowning.

"*Danki*, but you had no way of knowing." He sipped more coffee while she stared at him.

"I can't even begin to imagine the depth of your grief." She hesitated. "May I ask when you lost her?"

Duane dipped his chin and peered down at the oak table, running his fingers over the wood-grain pattern to avoid the sympathy and shock in her expression. "Eighteen months ago. Cancer. She was only forty-five. She fought hard, and we prayed and prayed for her recovery, but the Lord decided it was her time."

"It must be so difficult for you and your *sohns*." Crystal's voice was soft and warm.

"It is. I rely a lot on prayer and keep my eyes on Jesus."

"That's the best plan." She paused. "But according to my experience, the grief hits you when you least expect it, like having the wind knocked out of you."

He looked up, and when his gaze locked with hers, he found sympathy and understanding in her pretty face. And for the first time, he noticed tiny freckles marching across her petite nose. "I'd have to agree with you there."

"Losing parents isn't the same as losing a spouse, but I'm still grieving them. *Mei mamm* was my best friend, and I'll never recover from her death. *Mei dat* and I were close too, but it was different." She suddenly smiled and pushed the container of cinnamon buns over to him. "Would you like another one?"

"No, *danki*. I'm full." He rubbed his middle. Then he pointed to the cookbook. "I marked the page where you had the cookbook open. Which recipe are you going to make tonight?" He moved the book closer to her.

She opened the book and examined the page. "I was going to make this tuna casserole. The *kinner* love it." She turned the book to face him and pointed to the recipe.

He read it. "It's an easy one."

"Have you made one like it?"

He shook his head. "I use Connie's favorite cookbook, and there aren't many casseroles in there that the *buwe* like."

She smiled. "Connie is a *schee* name."

He sipped more coffee.

Crystal's face seemed to fill with questions, but she remained silent as she drank more coffee.

"You look anxious to ask me something."

She hesitated and then her expression relaxed. "What was Connie like?"

Surprised by the question, Duane sat back in his chair as memories filled him.

Crystal grimaced. "I'm sorry. That was a strange thing for me to ask. You don't need to answer."

"No, actually, it's refreshing. Most people are afraid to discuss Connie. They act as if I might break if I talk about her." He drank the last sip of coffee as he considered where to start.

"Connie was *schee*. She had dark-brown hair and hazel eyes. She was quiet and thoughtful, but when she spoke, people listened because she usually had something profound to say. She was insightful. She would have a perspective on things that most people wouldn't see. Jayden reminds me of her, but I think Tyler looks most like her."

He thought back to his youth and chuckled. "I actually had a crush on her for as long as I can remember. We grew up together and started dating after we were baptized. We were married when we were twenty-two. And then we had Tyler the following year."

Crystal hesitated as if contemplating something. "So, you're forty-seven," she finally said.

"That's right." He felt his smile waver. "I never thought I'd become a widower this young. It's not something that you think will happen to you until it does."

"I'm sorry." She paused for a moment. "She sounds like she was lovely."

"She was. The *buwe* and I will always miss her."

She smiled. "I know you will, but you're a great *dat*. Don't ever doubt that you're doing a *gut* job. I'm so impressed by how patient and kind your *sohns* are with *mei bruderskinner*."

"I appreciate that very much."

They smiled at each other, and for a split-second, he felt a tug at his heart as he took in her pretty face.

He shifted in his seat and cleared his throat before craning his neck over his shoulder to glance at the clock. "The glue should be dry now."

He pushed back his seat and stood. Then he started gathering up their mugs.

"Oh no." She covered his hand with hers and then pulled away as if his skin was on fire. "I'll take care of that."

*"Danki."* He retrieved his screwdriver, the screws, and the cabinet door before kneeling on the floor and reattaching the cabinet door.

While he worked, Crystal cleared the table and washed their mugs, spoons, and plates in the sink.

"I can write down some of my favorite casserole recipes for you," she suddenly said as she set the mugs in the drainboard.

He looked up at her. "Really? I would appreciate it."

"I picked up that casserole cookbook at a used bookstore I like to visit when I go to the grocery store. The next time I go, I'll see if there's another copy and get it for you."

*"Danki.* Just let me know how much it costs." Warmth surged in his chest at her generosity.

When he was done installing the cabinet door, he stood and stowed his screwdriver in the toolbox. Then he leaned down and tested the hinges.

"*Gut* as new," he said opening and closing the door a few times. "*Danki* so much."

He picked up the two toolboxes. "*Gern gschehne*. And thank you for the wonderful snack. I'm sure I'll see you later."

"You will." She smiled.

Duane headed out the back door and down the porch steps toward the barn. As his work boots crunched up the path, he contemplated Crystal's sweet demeanor. Conversation between them had flowed with ease, and he'd enjoyed talking with her. In fact, he was disappointed when it was time to finish fixing the cabinet and return to work.

But at the same time, he felt so old in her presence. He was aware that their fourteen-year age difference would be a hindrance to getting to know her better. Clearly, Crystal would be a wonderful mother and wife to someone God had in mind for her—some man in his thirties who was ready to start a family.

Her future husband would be a blessed man. A very blessed man indeed.

# CHAPTER 8

LATER THAT AFTERNOON, CRYSTAL SAT AT THE KITCHEN TABLE copying down recipes from her cookbook for Duane. She flipped through the book, hoping to find simple meals that he and his sons might enjoy.

Her heart clenched as she recalled the grief she'd witnessed in his warm brown eyes as he spoke about his late wife. She'd never expected him to share that he was a widower. She had been so surprised and honored at how he'd opened up to her, and she'd been disappointed when he left the kitchen and returned to work. He'd been so easy to talk to. Conversation had flowed between them, and it reminded her of how she and Owen, her ex-boyfriend, used to talk to each other.

She finished copying down a recipe for broccoli chicken divan just as tires crunching on the driveway sounded from outside.

Crystal grabbed her sweater before hurrying out the back door.

"How'd it go?" Crystal asked Leona when she met Crystal at the back of the van.

Leona frowned and rubbed her distended abdomen. Worry filtered through Crystal at the sight. "The doctor is very concerned with my blood pressure," Leona said. "She said it's too high, which is why I'm having headaches."

"*Ach* no!" Crystal gasped and touched Leona's hand. "Are the *bopplin* okay?"

"*Ya*, they are for now, but rest is the best thing for them and me. She said that I need to keep my feet up. The goal is to get these babies to mid-July."

"You need to go sit, then," Crystal said.

"But we stopped for a few groceries at the store, and I should help—"

"Kane and I will handle them." Crystal opened the tailgate and began gathering up bags in her arms.

"How are the *kinner*?"

"*Gut*. The *zwillingbopplin* and Hope are napping, and Jevon is resting with a book in his bed."

"*Danki*. I appreciate all you do." Leona patted Crystal's back.

Kane came around to the rear of the van and nodded at Crystal before taking two bags and then starting toward the house. "Leona, you need to go rest. That's what the doctor ordered."

"I know." Leona picked up one bag and followed him.

Crystal peered out toward the barn and spotted Duane up on the roof, on his knees while hammering. The roof of the large barn looked as if it was almost done, and she felt a strange disappointment filter through her.

She didn't want Duane to finish the project, which was ridiculous. Not only did he have four more roofs to fix, but it would be silly to not want him to leave. After all, they weren't even friends. They'd only shared a few conversations.

"Crystal? You okay?"

"Huh?" Crystal jumped and spun toward the steps, where

Leona stood watching her. "Sorry. I was lost in thought." She hurried up the porch steps and trailed Leona through the mudroom and into the kitchen, where they deposited the bags on the kitchen table.

"I'll go pay our driver," Kane said before heading back outside.

Crystal began storing the supplies while Leona emptied a bag and lined the contents up on the counter.

"Sit, Leona," Crystal said. "High blood pressure is dangerous. You need to take care of yourself."

Leona gingerly lowered herself onto a kitchen chair, and Crystal brought her a glass of cold water poured from the pitcher in the refrigerator. Then she returned to unpacking groceries.

A few minutes later, Kane returned.

"*Mamm! Dat!*" Jevon hurried into the kitchen, his little face full of excitement. "There was an emergency while you were gone!"

"What happened?" Kane asked.

"It wasn't an emergency." Crystal pivoted toward her brother and sister-in-law's concerned expressions. "I was putting together a casserole for tonight, and when I went to get a pan out of this cabinet, the door came off in my hand." She pointed to the pesky cabinet.

Jevon grabbed a box of crackers and struggled to open it. "I had to run out to get Duane to help."

"Give me that before you destroy the box, Jevon." Leona took the box and started to open it.

Kane shook his head. "I'm so sorry, Crystal. You've been after me to fix that for a month, and I completely forgot."

"It's okay. Duane was able to fix it. The holes were stripped, but he fixed it with wood glue and toothpicks."

Kane grinned. "That's brilliant."

"I don't get it." Leona scrunched her nose as she handed Jevon a few crackers.

Crystal explained how Duane had glued the toothpicks in the hole, let them dry, and then run the screws in. "The toothpicks give the screws something to grab on to."

"Oh." Leona nodded slowly, but still looked confused.

"I need to get out to the barn." Kane kissed Leona on the cheek. "I'll be in later." Then he started toward the back door.

Jevon rushed after him. "*Dat!* I want to help you."

"All right." Kane mussed his son's blond hair. "Come on, kiddo."

Kane and Jevon disappeared through the mudroom, and Crystal carried two loaves of bread over to the breadbox and slid them inside.

"Why are you writing down recipes?"

Crystal turned toward where Leona sat at the table, pointing at her notepad.

"They're for Duane."

"Why?" Leona smirked. "Can't his *fraa* cook?"

"It's not that." Crystal returned to the table and picked up two variety packs of lunch meat. "He lost his *fraa* eighteen months ago, and he said he's always looking for easy casserole recipes."

Leona frowned. "I'm sorry. I didn't mean to make light of it."

"You didn't know, and I didn't either before today. I said something similar when he asked about my cookbook. I offered to share some of my favorites."

"That's kind of you." Leona looked down at the notepad, flipping through it. "Ooh, you wrote down the tuna casserole."

"That's what I'm making tonight."

"My favorite." Leona cupped her hand to her head. "I'm wiped out after all of that running around. Would you mind if I took a nap?"

"Of course not. Your priority is to take *gut* care of yourself and those *bopplin*. I'm going to finish putting the groceries away and then write down more recipes for Duane."

"*Danki.*" Leona yawned as she headed out of the kitchen toward her bedroom.

Crystal set the lunch meat in the refrigerator and walked over to the windows that faced the back of the house. She peered out to where Kane stood talking to Duane by the barn. Then the men shared a laugh, which made Crystal smile.

Warmth swirled in her chest as she imagined bringing the recipes out to him. She couldn't wait to talk to him again.

Duane disconnected the call on his cell phone and dropped it into his pocket later that afternoon. He turned toward their stack of tools just as he spotted Crystal walking toward him. His pulse kicked up as he ambled toward her and met her halfway down the path.

"We were just cleaning up for the day," he said, smiling. "My driver is on his way."

"I'm glad I didn't miss you. I wanted to give you this." She held out an envelope with his name written in pretty cursive penmanship. "I wrote down some of my favorite casserole recipes."

"I appreciate this so much."

"I just hope the recipes will take some pressure off you when you plan your meals." She jammed her thumb back toward the house. "I have a casserole in the oven, and I need to set the table. Have a *gut* evening."

"You too." Duane watched her as she padded back toward the house. Then he started toward the barn, where his three sons studied him with curious expressions.

Korey nodded in the direction of the house. "What did Crystal give you?"

"Casserole recipes." Duane held up the envelope. "We discussed cooking while I was waiting for the wood glue to dry."

Jayden grinned. "Recipes? So that means you're cooking again tonight, huh?"

"No, I'm not. You're going to make chicken salad with the leftover roast from last night."

Jayden frowned as Korey and Tyler laughed.

"That's enough joking around," Duane said. "Our ride will be here soon. Let's finish cleaning up."

While his sons returned to the task of picking up the worksite, Duane faced the house once again. Would he see Crystal again tomorrow?

The following morning Crystal swept the back porch after cleaning up the breakfast dishes and getting Alisha and Nate off to school. The beautiful early April Friday morning sky above her was bright blue and dotted with white, puffy clouds. She looked out toward the pasture and found two rabbits hopping toward one of her brother's smaller barns, where Duane and his sons were perched, stripping off the old roof.

Crystal leaned on the broom and watched them for a few moments. When Duane stood, faced the house, and waved at her, she smiled as she returned the greeting.

After she finished sweeping the porch, she looked out toward her garden, and she felt as if it was calling to her. How she loved to work in the garden! Although it was technically Leona's garden, Crystal had taken over maintaining it. Leona had quickly admitted she appreciated the help since she'd never enjoyed getting her hands dirty and preferred sewing.

Crystal walked over to her garden, which was desperately in need of attention. She stepped into the small shed Kane had built for her supplies, and she found a bucket and her gardening stool. Then she sat down and began yanking the weeds that had infested her bed and dropped them into the bucket.

It felt so good to dig in the dirt! Not only did gardening help clear her mind and give her quiet time to talk to God, but it also made her feel closer to her mother. Some of her best memories of *Mamm* were spent in their garden together weeding, planting, and talking. Oh, how she missed those times!

If only *Mamm* were here to spend time with her precious grandchildren. She'd love each one of them! And if *Mamm* had lived, would Crystal's life have turned out differently? Would she have married and started a family of her own?

The question gripped Crystal's heart as she ripped another pesky weed from the ground and dropped it into the bucket. She continued working until the flower bed was nearly free of weeds, enjoying the feel of the warm sun on her back while birds sang in nearby trees and squirrels scurried past, squeaking and chirping loudly.

When the sound of a yowling child filled the air, her gaze flew toward the porch, where Leona stood holding one of the twins.

Crystal gasped and jumped up. "Leona! You should be resting!" She dashed over and up the stairs, removing her gardening gloves.

"I know." Leona looked exhausted. "The *zwillingbopplin* were sleeping, and then Evie woke up screaming. She's inconsolable. I'm sure it's due to her teething. I gave her some painkiller and numbing medicine, but it's not working. I've tried everything else I could think of—walking the floor with her, changing her diaper, singing to her, and giving her a snack." She held the child out to Crystal. "Would you please take her? I have a splitting headache and can't hear myself think."

Crystal set her gardening gloves on the porch railing and wiped her hands down her apron. "*Ach.* Of course! You are supposed to keep your feet up. Why didn't you call for me?"

"I didn't want to bother you since you never get to work in the garden, and you love it so much."

"I'll handle Evie." Crystal took a sobbing Evie into her arms. "*Was iss letz, mei liewe?*"

Evie buried her face in Crystal's neck, and Leona sighed.

"*Danki*, Crystal. I'm going to make lunch."

"It's lunchtime already?" Crystal asked, raising her voice above Evie's sobs.

"*Ya.* It's almost twelve. Kane will be in any minute now looking for his lunch."

"Do you want me to make lunch for us?"

"No, I can set out some lunch meat, condiments, chips, and bread. You just calm down Evie. I promise I'll rest after I set out the food." Leona ambled toward the back door.

Crystal bounced Evie on her hip. "There's no need to cry, Evie. It's okay."

The toddler lifted her head and sniffed. Crystal retrieved a tissue from her apron pocket and wiped her eyes and nose before shoving the tissue back into her pocket.

"Chicks! Want chicks!" Evie announced, pointing toward the chicken coop.

"All right, *mei liewe*. Let's go see the chickens."

Crystal carried Evie toward the coop, her shoes crunching on the rock path. "It's Alisha's job to feed the chickens and collect the eggs. When you're bigger, you can help her."

She glanced over toward the barn, where Duane and his sons sat at a nearby picnic table eating their lunch. Tyler looked over and waved. She returned the greeting just as Evie shifted in her arms, but she caught the toddler just before she slipped.

"Chicks! Want chicks!" Evie whined as she bounced in Crystal's arms and struggled to get free.

"Let's walk together." Crystal set the toddler on the ground and held her hand out to her. "Hold my hand, little one."

Evie took off running.

"Slow down, Evie! You're going to fall!" Crystal dashed after her.

When they reached the coop, Evie screeched as she held on to the chicken wire while the birds pecked the ground. She grinned at Crystal and pointed toward the birds. "Chicks! Chicks!"

"*Ya*, that's right." Crystal stooped down beside her. "They're eating lunch, which is what we should be doing. Let's go back to the *haus* so I can help your *mamm*." She held out her hand. "*Kumm*."

Evie spun, screeching with delight as she sprinted toward the picnic table where Duane and his sons sat.

"*Ach* no. Evie! Slow down!"

Crystal rushed after the toddler, her cheeks heating as Evie shrieked, drawing the attention of Duane and his sons, who chuckled. Each of the men had sandwiches and chips on their plates, along with a cup of water. A sandwich bag full of carrot sticks sat in the center of the table.

When Jayden opened the bag, grabbed a handful of carrot sticks, and set them on his plate, Evie ran up to him and reached toward the carrot stick he held in his hand.

"Carrot!" the toddler exclaimed.

"Evie," Crystal scolded. "That's Jayden's lunch."

"Carrot!" Evie whined.

Crystal was certain her face might burst into flames as she reached for Evie and took her hand. "I'm so sorry." She looked down at Evie's frown. "*Kumm*. Our lunch is inside. Your *mamm* is making it now."

"No!" Evie shook her head.

Crystal looked over at Duane, who grinned at her. "Someone needs a nap," she said.

"No nap!" Evie stretched toward Jayden again. "Carrot!"

Jayden gave Crystal a sheepish smile as he held up the vegetable. "Would it be okay if I gave it to her?"

Crystal rubbed her temples as she debated what to do. If she told Jayden to give her the carrot stick, then she would be rewarding bad behavior. But if she said no, then she would have to drag Evie toward the house while she continued her tantrum, which would be even more embarrassing.

Duane sat on the end of the bench across from Jayden. He leaned forward, his expression serene. "Evie? May I speak with you?" he asked, his voice calm.

Evie stopped whining, blinked, and turned her attention to Duane. She rubbed her eyes as she studied him.

Surprise and relief gripped Crystal.

"Evie, do you know how to get the carrot stick?" Duane kept his voice soft.

The toddler shook her head and sniffed.

"*Kumm*," Duane said, and she walked over to him. He leaned down to her level. "If you asked Jayden nicely, he would be *froh* to give you a carrot stick. But let's ask your *aenti* first if you may have one." He met Crystal's gaze and winked at her.

She stilled, surprised by the familiarity of the gesture and how it sent a thrill twirling through her. No man had ever made her feel that way since her ex-boyfriend, Owen.

"*Aenti* Kisstal," Evie said, pulling Crystal back to the present. The toddler pointed to Jayden's vegetable. "I have carrot? Pease?"

Crystal bent down and brushed her fingers through Evie's red curls. "Since you asked nicely, *ya*, you may have one."

Evie clapped and stomped her feet. Then she turned her attention to Jayden. "Carrot? Peeeease?"

"Here you go." Jayden held out the vegetable, and Evie took it with her tiny hand.

Duane looked over at Crystal, and she mouthed, "*Danki*."

He nodded and then scooted over on the bench and patted the empty spot. "Have a seat."

Crystal sank down beside him, perching herself on the edge of the bench.

Across from her, Evie finished the carrot stick. "Another? Peeease?"

Duane's sons laughed as Jayden gave her another carrot stick.

"You really have a gift with *kinner*," Crystal told Duane, careful to keep her voice low.

"Not really. I remember it worked well with Korey once, and it always seems more effective to talk to them rather than yell."

Korey snorted beside him. "I remember plenty of times you yelled at me, *Dat*."

"And you probably deserved it," Tyler quipped. "After all, you were the one who always got us into trouble, Kore."

Jayden divided a look between his older brothers, looking unconvinced. "I don't think you were always innocent, Ty. *Dat* has yelled at all of us."

Duane held up the bag of carrots toward Crystal. "Would you like some?"

"Oh, no. *Danki*, though. I need to get Evie back to the *haus* for lunch and a nap."

"No nap!" Evie announced before asking for another carrot.

Duane leaned closer to her and lowered his voice. "You need to spell out those trigger words."

She glanced over at him and swallowed against her dry throat. He was so handsome that he nearly took her breath away.

"*Ya*, I am learning that." She hoped her voice didn't betray her. She nodded toward the barn. "How's the roof coming along?"

"We should have this barn done today. I saw you working in your garden earlier. Do you like gardening?" He nodded in the direction of the house.

"Very much. I always—"

"Crystal! Evie! Lunch is ready!" Leona yelled. Crystal looked toward the house, where Leona leaned out the door.

Evie scampered toward her mother with her arms in the air. "*Mamm!*"

"You better go catch her," Duane said with a laugh.

Crystal hopped up. "*Danki* for sharing your lunch with Evie."

"We enjoyed it," Duane said, his smile warm and inviting.

As Crystal jogged after her niece, she felt her stomach sink as the truth hit her: She was developing a crush on Duane.

# CHAPTER 9

DUANE SAT IN HIS PHONE SHANTY LATER THAT EVENING AND dialed the voicemail. While he carried a cell phone for business purposes, he also kept a house phone for personal calls and to use for advertising his business. He found it was easier to advertise his home number to cut down on calls while at the jobsite.

He poised his pen on his notepad. When the voicemail started, he was delighted to find two messages asking for estimates and then a message for his sons from their friend Toby, reminding them about his birthday party.

Duane jotted down notes, then ripped the sheet of paper with the messages off the notepad. He made his way into the house, where he found Korey pouring a large can of soup into a pot while Tyler set the table and Jayden stood beside him flipping two sandwiches in a pan.

Duane moved to the sink and began scrubbing his hands. "What's for supper?"

"Grilled cheese and tomato soup." Korey lifted his chin with pride.

"As long as we eat, I don't care. I'm starved," Tyler announced.

Korey's expression became wistful. "It was one of *Mamm*'s favorites. That's why I wanted to make it."

Jayden bit his lower lip and swallowed. "She did love it. I remember that."

Duane felt a tug at his heart but said nothing, even though memories of Connie swirled through his mind.

"So, were there any messages, *Dat*?" Tyler asked.

"*Ya*, there were, and there was one for all of you from Toby. He wanted to remind you about his birthday party tomorrow night. He said to be there at six."

Tyler frowned. "Would it be all right if I went?"

"Why not?" Duane dried his hands with a paper towel.

"Well, if I go, then you'll have to finish up alone at the worksite."

Duane smiled. "*Danki*, Tyler, but I'll handle it. You three should enjoy time with your *freinden*. Before you know it, you'll be married and have more responsibilities and less time for fun."

"But we have to stay on schedule with our jobs."

"Leaving early one day won't put us behind, Tyler. I promise."

Tyler nodded but seemed unconvinced. He returned to filling their drinking glasses with water.

"Were there any other messages?" Jayden asked, maneuvering a spatula under the sandwiches.

"*Ya*, two potential customers left messages about estimates. I'll call them back after supper and make appointments."

"That's great news." Jayden flipped the grilled cheese sandwiches onto a plate and handed it to Duane. "Here you go." Then he began buttering another piece of bread.

Duane set the plate on the table, and the savory aromas made his stomach gurgle. Lunch had been more than six hours ago. He felt his lips turn up in a smile as he recalled his lunchtime encounter with Crystal and Evie. He had enjoyed spending time with them both.

It seemed as if it had been a lifetime ago when his sons had been that small. Memories of his three sons toddling around had filled his mind as he'd worked to calm down little Evie. Chatting with Crystal, if only for a moment, had been an unexpected gift. He'd contemplated their conversation in the kitchen more than once, and he'd longed to talk with her again.

If only they'd had more time. He wanted to know more about her, but soon their project would be finished.

"Do we have a gift for Toby?" Korey asked as he ladled the soup into a bowl.

Tyler set the empty pitcher on the counter. "I guess we'll have to pick something up tomorrow."

"We could go by the hardware store and get him a couple of tools." Jayden dropped two more sandwiches onto the pan, which sizzled in response.

Duane smiled to himself. He had always enjoyed witnessing the friendship between his three sons, which he sometimes secretly envied. As an only child of older parents, he hadn't experienced the joy of siblings, but he was grateful the Lord had given him and Connie the chance to have a family—even if Connie had only experienced it for a short while.

*Connie.*

His chest constricted.

Tyler's hand on Duane's shoulder startled him. "You okay, *Dat*?"

"*Ya.*" Duane nodded at his eldest son.

Korey carried two bowls of soup to the table. "So, if we have to go to the hardware store and then get cleaned up, I guess we have to leave a little earlier than planned tomorrow, huh?"

"That's true. Will that be all right, *Dat*?" Tyler moved to the stove and began ladling out more soup.

"Tyler, I said I can handle the work, so stop worrying. The business is doing fine. You need to have a social life too," Duane said.

"Okay, *Dat*." Tyler looked over his shoulder at Korey. "Will Michelle be at the party?"

Korey shrugged. "I don't know."

"Why don't you call her and find out?" Duane suggested.

Korey pursed his lips. "Do you think that's a *gut* idea?"

"You like her, right?" Duane asked.

Korey rubbed the back of his neck. "I think I do."

"Sounds like you're overthinking it," Tyler told him. "Just get to know her and see what happens."

"Exactly," Duane said with a smile. His eldest son was wise.

Crystal carried a basket out toward the chicken coop late the following afternoon. The air was chilly, and the sky was clogged with gray clouds as she breathed in the familiar scents of springtime. Since Alisha had offered to scrub and mop the bathrooms earlier while Crystal hung out laundry, Crystal was happy to collect the eggs for her.

She looked out toward one of the smaller barns, where Duane stood on the roof alone. She had heard his driver's truck pull up earlier and then leave, and she'd been curious, assuming his driver had dropped off more supplies. However, it seemed his sons had left early.

Crystal gathered up the eggs and then turned toward the barn, where Duane now stood looking toward her. He waved from above and then motioned for her to join him.

Crystal's heart did a funny little dance as she walked toward him. Duane started down the ladder, and she met him at the bottom.

He swiped the sleeve of his shirt over his forehead. "I haven't seen you all day."

"Did your three employees quit?" She nodded toward the barn.

He laughed, and she enjoyed the sound. "No, but they left early for a birthday party."

"How fun." She pointed toward the roof. "You finished the two small barns today. You do great work."

"*Danki*. We just have the *haus* left to do. We'll do it on Monday."

"So soon?" Disappointment filled her. Monday would be the last day she'd see him. She had to make the most of their time together now.

"*Ya.*" He leaned back against the ladder. "We never got to finish our conversation yesterday. You were telling me about your love of gardening before Leona called you and Evie in for lunch."

"Oh." She was surprised he recalled what they'd been discussing. "It's one of my favorite hobbies."

"Did you grow up gardening?" His coffee-colored eyes seemed to assess her.

She set the basket of eggs on the picnic table. "*Mei mamm* and I loved to garden together. We would spend hours talking and working while we planted flowers and vegetables, weeded, or harvested. It was our special time."

"It had to be so difficult to lose her at such a young age. Was she *krank*?"

The compassion in his eyes sent warmth surging through

her. "She had a heart attack in her sleep. It was completely unexpected. *Mei dat* thought she was sleeping in late, but when he went to check on her, she was already gone."

He clucked his tongue. "I'm so sorry."

"*Danki.*" She cleared her throat against a swelling ball of grief. "Have you tried any of the casseroles yet?"

"No, not yet, but I plan to. Last night was Korey's night to cook."

"Oh *ya*?" She grinned. "What did he make?"

Duane smiled. "Grilled cheese and tomato soup, which was one of Connie's favorites. And he talked Jayden into helping him. He's the one who always seems to convince others to help him out. Connie used to say he could sell water to a fish."

Crystal laughed. "Your *sohns* are so nice and mannerly. You must be so proud of them."

"*Danki.* I'm grateful to have them." He stood up straight. "I'm sure you're ready to go in for supper now, and I should call my driver. I hope you have a *gut* Sunday tomorrow." He pulled his cell phone from his pocket.

"Do you have plans for supper?"

He stilled and then shook his head. "I was going to have a sandwich. Why?"

"Stay for supper. I made barbecued meatloaf, and I always make too much. We'll have leftovers for days."

He shook his head. "*Ach* no, I wouldn't want to impose."

"You're not imposing, and no one should eat alone."

Duane paused, and Crystal's nerves lit up as she waited. "Okay," he finally said. "If you insist. I'm afraid I'll be quite the mess after a day's work, though."

"I do insist, and I don't care about any mess!"

Duane laughed. "Well, I suppose I'll have to believe you. Let me finish cleaning up here, and then I'll come in."

"Perfect." She picked up the basket of eggs. "I'll see you inside."

Excitement filled her as she headed toward the house. Any time with Duane she could get, she would take.

# CHAPTER 10

AFTER PUTTING AWAY HIS TOOLS, DUANE KNOCKED ON THE back door to Kane's house. He smiled as he heard children playing together inside.

He'd been equally surprised and honored when Crystal invited him to stay for supper. The brief encounter earlier had been the highlight of his day.

Footsteps sounded and then Crystal appeared at the back door. "You don't need to knock." She graced him with a beautiful smile as she opened the door wide. "Come in."

*"Danki."* He stepped into the mudroom, and the delicious smell of meatloaf filled his senses as he hung his straw hat on a peg on the wall and kicked off his work boots.

She leaned in close to him, and the trace of her flowery shampoo sent a strange awareness zinging through him. "I have to warn you. Meals in this *haus* are loud and chaotic."

"That sounds refreshing."

"Okay, but I warned you . . ." she sang before stepping into the large kitchen, where the family was seated around the long oak table.

The toddlers were perched in matching highchairs, chattering nonsense words, while Hope and the two boys sat at the table. Alisha carried two large bowls of mashed potatoes to the table, and Leona stood by the counter, rubbing her lower back with her hands and frowning.

"Leona," Crystal admonished her. "I told you to sit. The doctor said to stay off your feet, but you've been working so much today."

Leona sighed as she moved toward the table. "I know."

Kane sat at the head of the table. "Duane! We're so glad you could join us tonight."

"*Danki* for the invitation." Duane pointed toward the sink. "I'm going to wash my hands."

"Help yourself," Kane said.

Duane crossed the room and stood at the sink.

Crystal slipped past him and grabbed two pot holders before opening the oven door. "Excuse me."

"No problem." He glanced over at her as he scrubbed his hands.

"Let me help you, *Aenti*." Alisha appeared at her side with pot holders and helped retrieve the three pans of meatloaf.

Then Alisha rushed to the table and set out three trivets before helping carry the meatloaf pans to the table.

Leona took a seat and smiled at Alisha. "*Danki* for helping your *aenti*."

Crystal hurried to the counter and grabbed a knife from the block and a butter dish from the refrigerator. Alisha brought two large bowls of green beans to the table, putting one at each end before sitting between Leona and Hope.

"May I help you at all?" Duane offered.

Crystal pointed to a large bowl of salad and a bottle of home-made dressing. "Would you please grab those?"

"I'd be glad to." Duane set them in the center of the table.

Crystal stood by the table. "I think that's everything."

Leona rubbed her belly. "It's *wunderbaar. Danki*, Crystal."

"Come sit by me, Duane," Kane announced.

Disappointment filled Duane as he sat beside Kane, and Crystal sank into a seat between the two highchairs. He'd imagined sitting nearer to Crystal, but he held on to hope that he'd have time to speak with her after the meal.

They all bowed their heads for a silent prayer and then began filling their plates with the delicious food. Voices and the sound of utensils scraping plates filled the large kitchen. Their arms reaching toward the platters and bowls reminded Duane of a picture of a giant octopus next to the letter *O* that one of his boys had once colored in an alphabet coloring book.

*"Aenti!"* one of the toddlers called. "Want!"

"Please be patient." Crystal's voice was calm.

Duane turned his attention toward the other end of the table, where Crystal placed mashed potatoes on each of the twins' highchairs. Then she began cutting up a piece of meatloaf and added it to their trays, along with a scoop of green beans.

*"Aenti,"* Hope began, "would you please cut up a piece for me?"

Crystal smiled at her. "Of course I will."

Duane couldn't take his eyes off Crystal while she served the children. It was clear that Crystal put her nieces and nephews before herself. She was such an incredible woman.

"So, Duane, I'm really impressed with your work," Kane said while scooping salad into a bowl. "You also work so quickly and efficiently. I see why you came so highly recommended."

Duane nodded as Kane handed him the bowl. *"Danki."* He scooped salad into his bowl and then added dressing. "Crystal told me that you took over this farm from Leona's parents."

"*Ya*, that's right. *Mei dat* worked at a hardware store over in Strasburg until he became *krank* and had to retire."

"I'm sorry to hear that. What happened to your *dat*?" Duane asked.

"He had uncontrolled diabetes that progressed to kidney failure. He was on dialysis for years before he passed away. Crystal took *gut* care of him."

Duane's eyes snapped to Crystal.

She met his gaze and shrugged. "That's what you do for family."

"*Aenti* Kisstal," one of the twins whined. "More potatoes peeeeeease."

"Let me take care of Hope first." Her own supper sat untouched on her plate while she cut up meatloaf for Hope and then dropped small mountains of mashed potatoes on the highchair trays for the twins.

Duane's mind churned with the information Kane had just shared—Crystal had nursed her ailing father until he passed away and then moved in with Kane and began raising his children. Crystal had never had the opportunity to have a life of her own. He studied her, wondering if she'd even had a chance to have a boyfriend.

Crystal's eyes caught his, and she gave him a hesitant smile. When he smiled in return, he took in her natural beauty. She was such a special woman—so caring, patient, and kind. She clearly gave her all to her family. She deserved a family of her own, but it seemed impossible she would ever find one when she was so entangled in her brother's.

"So, Duane," Kane continued, "did you grow up in Bird-in-Hand?"

"I did."

"What did your father do for a living?"

"He was a roofer too. My parents were married later in life, so I was an only child. Both of my parents were in their forties when I was born."

"That's *gut* that he taught you a profession. I had to learn about dairy farming on my own. It's a lot of work to care for the cows, handle the milkings, and keep up the farm. You can see I haven't done a *gut* job of that."

Leona chuckled. "I warned him when we got engaged. *Mei mamm* said she was blinded by love when she met *mei dat*. She had no idea how much work it was to be a farmer's *fraa*."

"And the work doesn't end," Kane continued. "I plan to hire someone soon to mend and paint the fence around the pasture, fix the barn doors, and paint the barns, the *daadihaus*, and the *haus*."

"And fix the chicken coop," Alisha chimed in.

Kane sighed. "*Ya*, and the chicken coop. The list is endless. I'll look into hiring some help after the roofs are done."

The men spent the remainder of supper talking about work. While Duane spoke with Kane, he snuck frequent glances toward the end of the table, where Crystal split her time between eating and taking care of the three youngest members of the Glick family.

After supper, Crystal and Alisha served chocolate pie and coffee, and Kane moved from talking to Duane about work to discussing their childhood. When their dessert was gone, Kane invited Duane to join him in the family room to continue their conversation.

And much to Duane's disappointment, Crystal remained in the kitchen with the children and Leona.

Crystal couldn't have been more frustrated. She had invited Duane to stay for supper with the expectation of having a conversation with him, but her brother had monopolized the meal and dessert before inviting Duane to join him in the family room, ruining any chance she had to talk to him.

She swallowed back her exasperation and turned her attention to carrying the dirty dishes to the counter and filling one side of the sink with hot, soapy water.

"I'm going to give the *kinner* a bath," Leona announced. "They can play in the water for a while."

Crystal looked over from the sink toward where Leona stood in the doorway with Evie on her hip and Hope and Morgan beside her. "Okay, but be sure to sit as much as you can. I'm afraid you aren't listening to your doctor."

"I will, Crystal." Leona sighed before disappearing through the doorway.

Alisha carried a handful of utensils to the sink. "I'll help with the dishes."

"*Danki,*" Crystal told her.

While Nate and Jevon joined their father and Duane in the family room, Alisha and Crystal worked in silence. Crystal could hear the murmur of conversation in the family room as her hope deflated like a balloon. By the time the dishes were done and the kitchen was clean, it would be time for Duane to go home.

What a letdown!

"I like your *freind,*" Alisha said, snapping Crystal from her thoughts.

Crystal spun to face her niece. "What?"

"Duane. He's nice." Alisha nodded her head toward the doorway leading to the family room.

Crystal smiled. "I like him too." *Very much!*

They were still putting away the dishes when Kane, his sons, and Duane walked into the kitchen. Crystal's stomach dipped.

Kane pointed toward the mudroom. "We're going to walk outside."

Duane gave Crystal an apologetic expression before he followed Kane outside, and Crystal's disappointment threatened to pull her under. Now she wouldn't be able to talk to him until Monday—the last day she would have reason to see him.

*"Aenti,"* Alisha said. "What would you like me to do with the leftover meatloaf?"

A smile spread on Crystal's lips as an idea filled her mind. "Let's put it in a container. Pack up the leftover salad, mashed potatoes, and green beans too."

Once the food was packed up in four containers, Crystal placed them all in a paper bag and started for the door.

"I'll be right back," she called to her niece over her shoulder.

Then Crystal darted out to the porch and stopped in her tracks as Duane walked up the stairs toward her.

She breathed a sigh of relief. "You're still here. I thought for sure I'd missed you."

"Did you really think I'd leave without saying good-bye to you?" He grinned, and her heart thudded against her rib cage.

She held up the bag. "I have leftovers for you and your *sohns.*"

"Oh no." He waved off the offer. "I don't expect you to feed my family."

"I insist."

He took the bag. "Fine, if you insist. The meatloaf was *appeditlich,* and I won't mind enjoying it again. *Danki* so much."

"I thought it might be a nice break from grilled cheese and tomato soup." She held her hand up. "Not that there's anything wrong with that. Don't tell Korey I criticized his choice of supper."

He laughed, and the warm sound sent a thrill through her. "I promise I won't tell him."

"Did you call your driver?"

"*Ya*, I did. He should be here shortly." He frowned as if he was just as disappointed as she was that their time together had almost come to an end.

"I was hoping we would have had more time to talk." She inwardly cringed, fearing she'd been too honest and forward.

"I was thinking the same thing, but I do appreciate the fantastic meal and the company. It was a nice change from being home alone while *mei sohns* are off with their youth group."

"Do you have church tomorrow?"

He shook his head. "No, it's our off-Sunday."

"It's our off-Sunday too."

"Have a restful day." He held his hand out, and when she shook it, heat ricocheted up her arm.

At that moment, a mixture of excitement and fear gripped her. Surely Duane Bontrager would never have feelings for a woman like her. She was ordinary and not beautiful like Jeannie, who had always stolen the attention of the young men in their community. The only man who had ever taken an interest in Crystal was Owen, and he had left her behind so easily. Crystal had sometimes wondered if something was wrong with her and if she hadn't found a husband simply because she was too plain.

But still, she couldn't deny that she felt drawn to him.

Headlights bounced off their largest barn as Duane's driver's pickup truck parked beside the house.

"That's my ride," he said. "I look forward to seeing you on Monday."

*"Gut nacht."* She leaned forward on the railing while Duane jogged down the porch steps and loped over to the pickup truck.

Duane waved at Kane walking up the path from the barn with his sons in tow. Then Duane climbed into the pickup, and the truck backed down the driveway before the rumble of the engine and the taillights faded into the distance.

Kane climbed the back steps and stopped on the porch while his sons disappeared into the house. He studied Crystal. "Isn't he a bit old for you?"

She blinked, hoping to mask the surprise at her brother's intuition. *"Freinden* are never too old."

Before he could respond, she scooted into the house.

# CHAPTER 11

CRYSTAL PADDED INTO THE KITCHEN SUNDAY EVENING AFTER all the children were settled in their beds.

She peeked out the back windows where the beautiful sunset bathed the sky in brilliant hues of yellow, orange, and red while Kane and Leona sat on the glider together. Murmurs of their conversation filtered in through the open window, and when Kane leaned over and whispered something in his wife's ear, she giggled in response.

Disappointment pressed down on Crystal's back, and she slumped against the counter. Memories of her time with Owen crashed through her mind, mixing with the familiar confusion.

If she had accepted his proposal and moved to Ohio with him five years ago, maybe she would have had a family of her own by now. Still, she couldn't bring herself to uproot her father when he depended so much on the doctors and the staff at the dialysis center he had grown to trust so deeply. At the time, Owen's insistence that her father would have adjusted to a new team of doctors in Ohio seemed like such a selfish stance to take, especially when he wasn't even sure the construction business he planned to open with his cousin would be a success.

But now as she stood in the kitchen witnessing the love between her brother and his wife, she found herself once again doubting the decision to reject Owen's plan. She tried to suppress her worry that Owen was supposed to be the love of her life, meaning she missed her only chance at creating her own family, her own happiness.

She adored her nieces and nephews, but no matter how she tried, she couldn't stop that yearning that gripped her heart and bubbled up inside of her at unexpected times.

She often wondered if life would have been different if Owen had chosen to stay in Gordonville. But when she had proposed that idea, he told her no, since he had already committed to his cousin. That was when she knew he'd chosen work over her. And that realization had hurt the worst.

Crystal pushed off the counter and poured herself a glass of water. As she drank, she hoped the cold liquid would wash away her loneliness and doubt.

While she prayed daily for the Lord to bring love into her life, she was certain life had passed her by. She would continue to count her many blessings, but deep in her heart, she couldn't stop herself from craving more.

"Have a *gut* day," Crystal called as Nate and Alisha hurried out the back door for school the following morning.

"Bye, *Aenti!*" Alisha called over her shoulder.

The sound of loud voices filled the air, and Crystal stepped out onto the porch and tented her hand above her eyes before looking up toward the roof, where Tyler and Korey worked stripping off the old shingles.

"*Gude mariye,*" she called up to them.

Korey waved, his eyes shrouded with his mirrored sunglasses. "Hi, Crystal."

"*Wie geht's?*" Tyler asked.

"*Gut.*" She leaned back on the porch railing. "How was your party Saturday night?"

"It was fun," Korey said. "Most of our youth group came. How was your Sunday?"

She shrugged. "We all just stayed here. It was quiet and relaxing."

Tyler pointed toward the clear blue sky. "It's a *schee* day, and it finally warmed up a bit."

"*Ya,* that's right." Crystal glanced behind her toward where Kane and Duane stood talking by the large dairy barn, and her heart gave a little bump. Oh, how she hoped they would have a chance to talk before the day was over.

Kane met her gaze and waved. "Crystal! You have a message."

"Oh." She looked up at Tyler and Korey. "Excuse me." She descended the porch steps just as Jayden walked over. "Hi, Jayden."

"Morning." He nodded as he continued to the ladder.

Crystal's pulse took flight as she hurried down the path toward the barn where Kane and Duane stood.

Duane looked handsome clad in a dark-green shirt, dark-colored trousers, and straw hat. He blessed her with a bright smile as she approached him, and her knees wobbled.

"*Gude mariye.* How was your Sunday?" he asked.

"Restful. Yours?" she asked.

He nodded. "It was *gut.*"

She turned to her brother. "What was the message?"

"Jeannie called," Kane said. "She wants you to call her right away."

Crystal's insides turned and dropped as worry coursed through her. *Please, God! Let her baby be okay!* She turned to Duane. "Excuse me."

"Of course," Duane said.

Crystal rushed into the barn and dialed the number for Jeannie's phone shanty. She held her breath until someone picked up the receiver.

"Hello?" her best friend said.

"Jeannie!" Crystal breathed. *"Was iss letz?"*

"Hi! Nothing is wrong."

"Oh, praise God!" Crystal sank down onto the chair by the phone. "Kane told me to call you right away, and I got so worried."

"I'm sorry for worrying you. I was wondering if you could meet me for lunch today. I have an appointment in town, and we haven't had much time to talk. I know it's last minute. I meant to call you last week, but it's been so busy. Is there any chance you can meet me?"

"*Ya!* I'd love to." Excitement filled Crystal. It was rare that she could enjoy an outing with a friend.

They discussed a time and a place and then she headed out of the barn. Her heartbeat kicked up as she stepped outside and looked around for Duane, hoping to find him outside the barn. Then her excitement dissolved when she spotted him on the roof of the house helping his sons.

She rambled down the path toward the house, and when he looked up, he smiled and waved at her. She waved in return and then continued into the house to finish up her morning's chores.

Duane pushed open the passenger door of Drew's truck at lunchtime. "Thank you for letting me run out to do this estimate. I appreciate it," he told his driver. "It was the only time I could fit it in."

"Take your time," Drew said.

Duane jogged up the porch steps of Tricia's two-story white farmhouse and knocked on her door. He had left her a message Saturday night asking if he could stop by at lunchtime today to give her the estimate. Thankfully, the schedule worked for her. He knocked and soon heard footfalls moving toward the door.

The door opened, and Tricia smiled up at him. "Hi, Duane."

"*Wie geht's?* I'm here to look at your roof."

"Oh, *danki.*" She pointed toward the roof. "It's been leaking in the girls' rooms for some time. I've been meaning to ask for help, but then I had mentioned it to the bishop, and he said he'd take care of it."

He took in the anxiety in her lovely gray eyes and felt the depth of her grief. "How are you holding up?"

"I'm trusting in the Lord."

"Tricia, you can talk to me."

She sniffed. "I'm overwhelmed." Her voice sounded raspy. "I lost Harley, and then we had the fire and lost most of our herd. Now the cows that are left aren't producing like they should. A few men in the congregation are coming over to handle the milkings, so I'm doing what I can—sewing for neighbors, cleaning for a few others, hosting dinners for *Englishers* at night, but it's just so much. I still have to do my chores—cooking, cleaning, and laundry.

"Then I got the news that the county did a tax assessment and is raising our taxes, and I'm so close to depleting my savings as it is. I don't have enough money to pay that bill, and the deadline is coming up so quickly. It just seems like no matter what I do, I'm still going to lose this place. I don't know what my girls and I will do . . ." her voice trailed off.

"The community will take care of you."

She nodded, but he could see the doubt shining in her eyes.

"I'll take a look at the roof."

Duane retrieved the ladder, climbed up on to the roof, and began inspecting its condition. The sky was crystal-blue and cloudless while a warm mid-April breeze blew the scent of moist earth, trees, and flowers over him as he worked.

When he peered down toward the back of the house, he spotted Tricia on the back porch, hanging out laundry. He saw the children's clothes, and his heart clutched. Harley had left her with three school-age daughters ranging from seven to eleven years old. He understood the uncertainty of a life alone, but the added stress of possibly losing her home was too much.

He tried to keep his mind on his work, measuring and writing on his clipboard, but Crystal had lingered around the edge of his thoughts since he had left her brother's house Saturday night. He'd gone to bed thinking of her both Saturday night and last night and then awoke in the morning still pondering her.

He wondered if he should evict her from his mind. She was a sweet and special friend, but that was all she would ever be. After all, their age difference seemed too great. Not to mention the difference in their life experiences.

The idea that today was the last day he'd see her sent disappointment threading through him. He hoped he'd have time to talk to her before he left this evening.

Duane finished up his calculations and then climbed down

and found Tricia hanging out her daughters' dresses on the line. "Well, I have what I need. I believe *mei sohns* and I can fit the roof in this week."

"How much will it cost?"

"I don't expect you to pay me." He slipped his clipboard under his arm.

"No, that's not right."

"But you already have your hands full, and you don't need more financial stress." Then an idea hit him. "Perhaps you can mend some shirts and trousers for *mei sohns* and me in exchange for the roof. I can do it, but I'm not very *gut* at it."

Her brow furrowed. "Mending clothes in exchange for a new roof hardly seems like a fair deal."

"You haven't seen how many pairs of trousers I had in mind."

Tricia gave a burst of laughter, and Duane joined in, enjoying the warmth that filled her pretty face. He was grateful he could offer her a moment of relief from her worries.

"Well, I'm *froh* to help you out as much as I can," Tricia said. "Bring me your clothes that need mending."

*"Danki."* He studied her. "I'm sorry for all you're going through. Do you have any family members helping you out at all?"

She sighed. "No. I don't have any *bruders*, and my parents are gone. Harley's *bruder* moved to Colorado years ago. Since I don't have any male relatives, I have to rely on the community, which means my problems are interfering with other people's lives." Her frown returned. "I feel so guilty every time one of the men has to come over to help with the milkings, but it does free me up to try to make some money to sustain my family for as long as I can."

He started to reach for her hand to comfort her, but then he stopped. "It's not your fault. We're called to care for each other, so the men and I are helping you because it's our way. We wouldn't think twice about helping each other."

"I know you're right. It's all out of my control, and I need to just keep praying. I never imagined I'd become a widow in my thirties or with *mei kinner* still so young." She pulled a tissue from her pocket and wiped her eyes and nose. "It was the Lord's will. He chose to take Harley, and I don't doubt his plan. It's just—well, it's just difficult."

"*Ya*, and some days are worse than others." He shifted his weight and fingered his clipboard. "How are the *kinner* doing?"

Tricia shook her head. "They have *gut* days and bad days just like you said. Some nights they sob for him. I just try to be strong." She picked up an apron from the laundry basket. "How about your *sohns*?"

"They still are emotional. They don't seem to cry as much—at least not in front of me—but they still grieve her. I don't think that will ever change."

"How do you comfort them?"

Duane shrugged. "I just tell them I miss her too. I offer my sympathy and my love. I think it's all we can do." He paused to gather his thoughts. "We'll never get over the loss. I know they say time heals all wounds, but I'll always have a hole in my heart."

"*Ya*, that's true."

"Special days are more difficult than others—holidays, birthdays, milestones. I just do my best to get through it and pray often." He paused. "And finding someone to talk to helps. Someone who understands."

She smiled. "It does help to have someone who understands. The most difficult days are the ones when I allow myself to think about how much Harley is missing with the *kinner.* He'd be so proud of them."

"*Ya.*" Duane smiled. "Korey has a *maedel* in his youth group that he seems to like. In the back of my mind, I ponder when *mei sohns* will start dating and then get married. Not only will Connie miss their courtships, their weddings, and their *kinner,* but when they're married, they'll be gone."

"And the *haus* will be quiet." Tricia finished his thought.

"Exactly." He felt himself relax. He appreciated that she understood how he felt. It was refreshing to have a friend who could relate.

"Duane!"

Turning, Duane spotted the bishop ambling toward him from the barn. "I didn't realize Wilmer was here."

"He came by to help with the animals today."

Duane greeted Wilmer as he climbed the stairs. "*Wie geht's?* It's a *schee* day."

"*Ya, ya,* it is." Wilmer pointed toward the roof. "Did you give it a look?"

Duane nodded. "I did. I was just telling Tricia that we can fit her in this week."

"*Gut.*" Wilmer turned his dark eyes to Tricia. "The community fund will pay for your roof. I'll discuss it with the deacon."

"That's not necessary. Tricia is going to do some work for me in exchange," Duane said.

Tricia shook her head. "If you insist, Duane."

"I do." He nodded.

Wilmer looked back and forth between them. "Well, at least let the community fund pay for the supplies. Then you can donate your time."

"That's perfect," Duane said. "If you'll excuse me. I need to get back to finish a job." He moved toward the stairs. "Enjoy the rest of your day."

"You too," Tricia said.

"Good-bye," Wilmer called after him.

After loading up his ladder, Duane climbed into the cab of Drew's truck. "Thank you for waiting."

"It's no problem at all," Drew said as he backed his truck out of Tricia's driveway.

Duane considered all that Tricia was facing, and his heart went out to her. He wouldn't dream of charging her for the work when other men in the community were already donating their time, and he would appreciate the help with the mending since he had managed to ruin one pair of trousers already.

As Drew motored them down the road toward Gordonville, Duane's thoughts turned to Crystal. He smiled as he imagined her pretty face and gorgeous smile. He couldn't wait to see her this afternoon. He would do his best to cherish the remainder of the last day working at her brother's house, and though he would miss Crystal's friendship, he hoped one day they might be reunited once again.

# CHAPTER 12

"HOW WAS YOUR APPOINTMENT?" CRYSTAL ASKED JEANNIE AS she sat across from her at the Bird-in-Hand Family Restaurant.

Conversations twirled around them in the packed dining room while the delicious smells of roast beef and chicken filled the air from the long buffet. Crystal and Jeannie sat in a booth by the windows facing the traffic passing by on Old Philadelphia Pike.

Jeannie seemed to glow as she smiled, her blue eyes shining. "It went great. I'm on track to deliver in early June. My due date is still June seventh." She rubbed her hand over her belly. "I'm so grateful and blessed. I thought it wouldn't happen for us."

"I'm so *froh* for you too." Crystal reached across the table and squeezed her friend's hand.

"I can't wait to meet this little person. Jared and I are discussing names."

"Oh *ya*?" Crystal leaned forward. "Can you share?"

Jeannie bit her upper lip. "I'll tell you, but it's a secret."

Crystal pretended to lock her lips and toss away the invisible key.

"Okay. We're thinking Lila for a girl and Dennis for a boy."

"What *wunderbaar* names. I love them!"

Just then their server, a pretty young Mennonite woman, came by and gave them glasses of water before taking their order. Then she hurried toward the kitchen.

"*Ya*, everyone is so excited. Our *boppli* will be the seventh grandchild."

"What a blessing," Crystal said.

Jeannie studied Crystal and something unreadable flickered across her pretty face. "Jared spoke to Owen last week. His garage construction business is failing, and he's considering moving back to Gordonville."

Crystal's eyes widened, and she gripped the edge of the table.

"Have you considered forgiving him?"

Crystal relaxed her face and tried her best to give a casual shrug. "I already forgave him. It's our way to forgive, so that wasn't ever an issue."

"You already know that he never married, and you never married. So, if you two worked things out, then there's still a possibility that we could be *schweschdere*." Jeannie grinned as she said the words Crystal had heard nearly a thousand times when Jeannie had started dating Jared six years ago.

Back then, Jeannie often talked about becoming sisters when they married the Stoltzfus brothers. But Crystal soon realized Jared was a different kind of man from his brother. Jared had kept his promises. Jared had chosen to cherish Jeannie. Owen had chosen to chase a dream in another state.

"I don't think that would happen if he came back." Crystal worked to keep her words even despite the storm brewing in her chest. "We missed our chance for a future."

Jeannie opened her mouth to respond as their server appeared with their lunch. The young woman set Jeannie's BLT and coleslaw in front of her and then handed Crystal her roasted turkey sandwich and fries.

Once the young woman was gone, Jeannie leaned toward Crystal. "Why do you think you've missed your chance? Owen told Jared that he has no ties in Ohio. You're not married, and you're not dating anyone. You're helping Kane and Leona raise their *kinner*. Don't you want a home and a family of your own?"

Crystal narrowed her eyes as she picked up a fry. "Of course I want those things."

"So, what's the problem?"

Crystal huffed out a breath. "Why would I trust him again?"

"Because he's been gone nearly five years, and he's grown up. Maybe now he'd put you first. He might realize how much he lost when he left, and when he sees you again, he'll regret what he gave up when he moved away."

Crystal stared down at her plate. What could she say that would help Jeannie understand?

Jeannie huffed out a breath. "Crystal, you're my best *freind*. We've grown up together. You're one of the most important people in my life. I want to see you *froh*. If Owen has grown up, he might be able to make all of your dreams of a family come true." She picked up her sandwich and took a bite.

Crystal bit into her own sandwich and considered Jeannie's assessment of Owen. Still, in the back of her mind his parting words echoed, "If you loved me, you'd move to Ohio with me."

At the memory, she shook her head. He had abandoned her when she'd needed him most. And after he left, her father took a turn for the worse and died six months later. It had been the most horrific time of her life—other than when she lost her precious mother.

Trusting Owen again would only lead to more heartbreak.

"What are you thinking?" Jeannie asked before sampling the coleslaw.

"Owen never put me first. He was always too selfish, and I doubt he's changed. I was doing my best to care for *mei dat*, and he couldn't understand how moving my *dat* to another state would have been devastating for both him and me." She took another bite of her sandwich.

"But what if he *has* changed? Then you could finally have some happiness in your life."

Crystal stopped chewing and stared at her friend. Then she swallowed. "*Mei bruderskinner* give me plenty of happiness."

"But you would have your own family if you married." Jeannie touched her belly again. "Don't you want this?"

Exhausted by the conversation, Crystal wiped her mouth with a napkin, then returned it to her lap. "Let's talk about something else. Has Jared put the crib together yet?"

They spent the remainder of lunch discussing Jeannie's baby, and then they turned to news about their friends.

After lunch, they walked out to the parking lot. When Crystal's gaze moved to the used bookstore across the street, an idea took shape in her mind. She spun to face her best friend. "Do you have a few minutes?"

"*Ya.* Why?"

"Could we walk into the bookstore?"

Jeannie shrugged. "Sure."

They waited until it was safe to cross the busy street before hurrying into the store. Crystal breathed in the comforting scent of books before moving through the knot of customers and finding her way to the cookbook section.

"I'm going to go look at some novels," Jeannie announced before continuing down the aisle.

Crystal perused the shelves until she found two casserole cookbooks that offered a variety of recipes. She smiled and excitement gripped her as she imagined handing the books to Duane. Then she made her way to the cashier and paid for what she had chosen.

She met Jeannie at the doorway, and they walked outside together.

Crystal turned to her friend while they waited for the busy road to clear so that they could cross once again. "You didn't find anything?"

"No. What did you buy?" Jeannie pointed to Crystal's bag.

Crystal pulled the cookbooks out. "They have easy casserole recipes."

"Oh." Jeannie's nose scrunched. "You needed cookbooks?"

"No. They're for a *freind*."

"Which *freind*?"

"His name is Duane. He and his *sohns* are the roofers working at the farm."

Jeannie's eyebrows formed a *V* as she studied Crystal, and then she laughed. "You bought cookbooks for a roofer who has *sohns*. Does his *fraa* not know how to cook?"

"He's a widower."

"Oh," Jeannie said and then her eyes widened as she gasped. "Oh! So you like him?" She grabbed Crystal's arm and towed her over to a nearby bench where they both sat. "It's no wonder you're not interested in seeing Owen again! Why didn't you mention him earlier? Tell me *everything*! What does he look like? Is he handsome?"

"Calm down. We're only *freinden*, and they're finishing the last roof today. We talked about recipes last week. He was interested in my casserole cookbook, so I thought I'd pick up one for him as sort of a parting gift." *And hopefully he'll remember me.*

"Well, maybe he'll come to visit you, and you can get to know each other better. You never know where that could lead." Jeannie tilted her head. "You mentioned his *sohns*. How old are they?"

Crystal cleared her throat as Kane's comment about Duane's age echoed in her mind. "Two are in their twenties and the youngest is nineteen."

"Wait a minute." Jeanne's brow puckered. "How old is Duane?"

"Forty-seven."

*"Forty-seven?"*

"Shh," Crystal hissed as a passerby stared at them.

Jeannie looked aghast. "Why would you be interested in a man who's almost fifty?"

"He's handsome and he's nice. And he's not *that* much older than me."

"Well, a man who's almost fifty most likely doesn't want more *kinner*."

"It doesn't matter. I'll probably never see him again after today." Disappointment rushed through Crystal as she looked out toward the line of cars moving past them on Old Philadelphia Pike.

"Listen, Crystal, Jared has a few really nice single *freinden* who are in their midthirties. They would be interested in settling down and starting a family."

Crystal stood. "I need to get home. I have more chores to do. *Danki* for inviting me to lunch."

"Hey." Jeannie pushed herself up from the bench and touched

Crystal's arm. "I didn't mean to upset you. I just want you to have a *froh* life like I do. I want the best for you."

Crystal hugged her friend. "I know, and I appreciate it. But trust me when I tell you that I am *froh*."

"Just don't give up on your dream of having a family. You're young enough to be a *mamm*. We're the same age, and I'm having my first."

"I know."

"Let's go meet our drivers." Jeannie looped her arm in Crystal's, and they started toward the crosswalk.

*"Aenti!"* Hope rushed down the porch steps toward the van when Crystal arrived home. "Will you come in and read me a story before I go in for my nap? *Mamm* said I should ask you since she's busy sewing."

"Of course." Crystal glanced up at the roof and frowned.

Nearly half of it was covered with new shingles. The day was coming to an end too quickly, which meant she was running out of time to talk to Duane.

Crystal looked toward the porch, where Leona stood, hands on hips.

Leona shook her head. "She's been sitting at the window waiting for you to get home. Would you mind taking care of her while I finish another maternity dress? This one is getting too tight."

"Of course I don't mind."

*"Danki.* And before you say it, I feel fine. Plus, I'm sitting while I'm sewing."

"I understand." Crystal smiled.

Hope grabbed Crystal's hand and began to tug. "I know which book I want you to read."

Crystal peered up at the roof once again as Duane turned toward her and waved. She held up the bag of books and hoped she would have time to give them to him before he left for the day and walked out of her life.

But more importantly, she prayed their friendship would mean something to him, and he would someday return to see her.

# CHAPTER 13

D<small>UANE STOOD WITH</small> K<small>ANE LATER THAT AFTERNOON WHILE</small> his sons cleaned up the worksite and loaded their supplies and tools in his driver's truck.

"You did a fantastic job." Kane glanced around his property. "I'll definitely recommend you to *mei freinden* and neighbors."

Duane shook his hand. "*Danki*. We should be done cleaning up shortly."

Disappointment filled Duane as he looked toward Kane's house. He'd spent all afternoon hoping and praying Crystal would visit him, but she never came out of the house. Instead, she'd exchanged brief waves with him, and that was it.

Perhaps their friendship meant more to him than it did to her. He frowned at the idea and tried to ignore his feelings as he ambled over to the pile of tools, carried them to the truck, and set them in the bed.

Once everything was loaded, Duane turned toward the house as his sons climbed into the wide back seat of the king cab truck. Discouragement whipped over him when he found the porch empty, and he was certain he'd imagined the connection he'd felt to Crystal. It had all been in his mind.

He wrenched the passenger door open and started climbing into the truck.

"Wait! Duane!"

He spun toward the house just as Crystal jogged down the path toward him, carrying a plastic bag. She looked beautiful today dressed in a dark-green dress that complemented her emerald eyes and fiery-red hair.

"Please wait." She hurried over to him and then took deep breaths and pressed her free hand to her chest. "I suppose I need to exercise."

He chuckled. "How was your day?"

"Frustrating. I've been trying to get outside to talk to you, but my chores have kept me hopping. I'm so sorry about that."

Relief came over him. She *did* care! "It's not your fault. I'm just glad I had a chance to see you before I left."

"I have something for you." She held the bag out toward him.

"What's this?"

"Just a parting gift for you to remember me by."

His mouth dried as he took in her beautiful face. He opened the bag and pulled out two cookbooks, and he was so overwhelmed by the gesture that he was speechless for a moment.

"I was in a bookstore today and thought of you. I hope you use them in *gut* health."

He couldn't even put into words how much the gift meant to him. He looked at her and his chest tightened with sadness. He didn't want to say good-bye to her and their friendship.

"What a kind gesture, Crystal. *Danki.*" His voice sounded throaty.

"*Gern gschehne.*" She looked toward the truck and waved at his sons and then started to back away from him. "I'm so glad I met you, Duane. Take care."

"You too." He stood by the truck as she darted back to the house and disappeared inside.

At that moment, he knew he cared for her.

Duane hung a pair of Korey's trousers on the clothesline late Monday afternoon, two weeks later. The early May air was warm, and the sky above him was bright blue as birds sang their familiar songs in nearby trees. He breathed in the scent of flowers and smiled. How he loved the spring!

Since he and his sons had finished a job early, they had come home and started on chores. While Korey cooked, Jayden cleaned the bathrooms, and Tyler took care of the animals, Duane had started the laundry.

As he looked down at the basket of clean clothes, he smiled. He had completed Tricia's roof last week, and he was grateful she had mended some shirts and trousers for Duane and the boys. It was a great help to them. He had enjoyed a short conversation with her when he'd stopped by to pick up their clothes. She still hadn't found a solution to her predicament with her farm, but she wasn't giving up hope yet. And he admired her faith and tenacity.

The back door creaked open and clicked shut, and then Jayden appeared beside him. "Let me help you."

"*Danki,*" Duane said as Jayden handed him another pair of trousers. Then Duane hung the trousers on to the line, which extended from the porch to the barn.

Soon they had an assembly line with Jayden handing Duane

the clothes, and Duane hanging them up before moving the clothesline out toward the barn.

"*Dat!*" Tyler suddenly hollered as he loped out of the barn toward the porch. "I just checked the messages, and someone wants us to come out for an estimate."

"Fantastic. What else did they say?"

"He's located out on Osceola Mill Road in Gordonville. Do you want me to do the estimate?'

Duane's heart came to life. The customer lived on the same road as Kane's farm! "I'll call them back and handle it after I finish hanging out the clothes."

"But I'm ready to handle this, *Dat*. You know I plan to take the business over someday."

"I know, but I can take care of it today, Tyler."

Frowning, Tyler turned and headed back toward the barn.

Duane's heart felt light as he hung another pair of trousers on the clothesline. Crystal had permeated his thoughts for the past two weeks, especially when he used the cookbooks she had given him. He missed her, even though he was certain she only wanted to be friends. He'd longed to stop by to see her but couldn't think of a valid excuse for a visit. But now, going to a prospective customer's house on the same road was plenty of reason for him. He couldn't wait!

Jayden handed Duane a shirt, and Duane hung it on the line while he considered what he might say to Crystal when he saw her. Perhaps he could tell her how much he liked the cookbooks. That might be the easiest conversation starter.

"I'll finish up the laundry. You go call the customer back." Jayden pointed toward the clothesline.

"*Danki.*" Duane hurried down the steps toward the barn, his pulse picking up speed as he imagined heading back to Osceola Mill Road and seeing Crystal again.

Later that afternoon, Crystal opened the mailbox and pulled out a stack of letters. She had meant to check the box earlier but had gotten sidetracked with her chores.

She flipped through the stack of letters as she started up the driveway.

"Crystal!"

She stopped, spun, and spotted Duane hurrying toward her. His horse was tied to the fence near the bottom of the driveway. "Duane. What a nice surprise!"

Thoughts of him had been her constant companion since she'd last seen him two weeks ago. She was certain she had imagined him, but there he was—gracing her with a bright smile as he strode up the driveway toward her.

Duane looked handsome wearing his straw hat, a tan shirt, and dark trousers. Happiness buzzed through her as he approached.

"Have you tried out your new cookbooks?"

"*Ya*, I have, and the *buwe* and I are enjoying them. *Danki* again for picking them up for me."

"I'm thrilled you like them." Oh, how she'd missed him!

He jammed his thumb toward the farm across the street. "I was just over at the Beiler farm for an estimate. Kane recommended me, and I'm so grateful."

"Oh *gut*." She hugged the mail to her chest as she imagined

Duane working across the street and coming to visit her for lunch. Oh, she couldn't wait! "When will the job start?"

"In a couple of weeks. We have some others to finish first."

"That's fantastic."

He seemed to study her. "How's your family?"

"Keeping me busy." She beckoned for him to follow her into the house. "Hope and I made brownies earlier. Would you like some to take home?"

"How could a man refuse brownies?"

They walked up to the porch together and then inside the house, where Alisha and Hope were setting the table. The delicious smells of chicken potpie permeated her senses.

"Duane!" Hope announced as she ran over to him.

"Great to see you, Hope." He grinned down at her and then tapped her nose with the tip of his finger.

Crystal's heart turned over in her chest as she took in the warmth in his eyes for her niece. He was such a gentle, kind man.

Alisha set a glass on the table and then waved to him. "Hi, Duane."

"Hi, Alisha. How's school?" he asked.

"It's going well. I've been helping the younger *kinner* with their math papers."

Duane leaned on a kitchen chair. "That's fantastic." Then he glanced around the kitchen. "Where's everyone else?"

"Leona is changing the *zwillingbopplin,* and the *buwe* are helping their *dat* in the barn." Crystal crossed to the counter and retrieved the pan of brownies she had baked earlier and set them into the container for Duane.

Duane sidled up to her. "What smells so *gut*?"

"Chicken potpie." Crystal smiled up at him.

"*Mei aenti* makes the best chicken potpie," Alisha said as she gathered up a handful of utensils from the nearby drawer. "You should stay for supper and have some."

Crystal set more brownies in the container. "That's a great idea." She grinned at Duane. "You're always welcome here."

"Can you stay, Duane?" Hope asked. "Please?"

Duane shook his head, and Crystal tried to swallow her disappointment. "Oh, *danki*, but I can't. *Mei sohns* are expecting me at home."

"You could call them and tell them that you're going to be late," Hope suggested as she reached for napkins.

Duane touched her head. "Maybe some other time."

"If you say so." Hope frowned.

Crystal closed the container of brownies and handed it to him. "Here you go."

"*Danki.*" He held up the container. "We will enjoy these."

Hope tapped his arm, and he looked down at her. "Do you know the best way to eat brownies?"

He grinned. "No, I don't. Please tell me."

"Warm them up and then put ice cream on top of them. Yum!" Hope rubbed her belly.

Duane chuckled. "You're right. That *is* the best way to eat them."

Hope nodded and then joined her sister at the table, where they set out the utensils.

Duane smiled at Crystal. "I have to go, but it was so *gut* seeing you and the *kinner*."

"You too. Tell your *sohns* we said hello," Crystal said. "And don't be a stranger."

"I won't," he told her. Then he said good-bye to the girls and headed toward the door.

Crystal stood by the counter as Duane disappeared through the mudroom. Then she heard the storm door creak open and click shut, and he was gone.

Hope turned toward Crystal. "Duane is so nice."

Crystal smiled. "He is," she said. *I like him a whole lot.*

"We have a special dessert tonight." Duane pulled the brownies from the oven, flipped off the oven, and set the pan on a trivet on the table later that evening.

Korey set four bowls on the table while Jayden pulled out a container of vanilla ice cream and set it next to the brownies.

Tyler grinned. "Brownie sundaes. Fantastic."

"*Mamm* loved them," Korey said, his expression melancholy.

Jayden nodded. "Remember how much she loved pralines and cream?"

"*Ya*, it was her favorite, along with vanilla shakes. She'd never have strawberry, but she loved vanilla." Korey glanced at Duane, who nodded and looked down.

Memories of Connie flickered in his mind, and his chest tightened with the knot of grief. He sucked in a breath, hoping to hold back his emotions.

"Where'd you get the brownies, *Dat*?" Jayden asked.

"I stopped to see Crystal after I talked to Hans Beiler about the estimate." Duane put a brownie in his bowl and then added two scoops of vanilla on top before passing the container to Korey. "She wanted us to have some brownies that she and Hope baked earlier, and she told me to tell you all hello."

"That's nice," Jayden said.

"I'm so glad we got that job. Before you know it, we'll be booked into June." Tyler dropped a large brownie into his bowl.

Duane nodded. "That's what I'm hoping."

"I think we should run more ads in the Amish and *English* newspapers," Tyler added.

Duane picked up his spoon. "*Ya*, I was thinking of that too."

"I'm putting together a business plan for us. I started on it last night. I'll show it to you when I'm done. I think we can really increase the number of jobs."

"Great," Duane said.

They spent the remainder of their dessert talking about the business. After they were done eating, Tyler and Jayden headed out to the barn to care for their animals while Duane gathered up their dirty dishes, and Korey filled the sink with soapy water.

When Duane set the bowls and spoons on the counter, Korey gave Duane a sheepish expression.

"*Dat*, I need to ask you something."

"Okay . . ." Duane leaned against the counter.

Korey seemed twitchy as he cleared his throat. "How did you know that you wanted to date *Mamm*?"

Duane smiled as memories filled his mind. "We got along well and we never ran out of things to say to each other. I thought she was the most beautiful *maedel* in youth group." He tapped his chest over his heart. "I just knew in here that I wanted to be more than just her *freind*."

As if avoiding Duane's curious stare, Korey set the stack of bowls in the sink and began scrubbing them.

"Is this about Michelle?" Duane asked.

Korey shrugged and set the clean bowls in the drainboard.

Duane began drying them. "Korey, if you like her, then ask her out."

"I might."

"Hey." Duane touched Korey's shoulder. "What are you afraid of?"

Korey set his jaw. "What if I ask her out, and we don't click?"

"That's what dating is all about. You're getting to know the *maedel*, and she's getting to know you. If you don't click, then you end the relationship and remain *freinden*."

Korey picked up the stack of their dinner dishes and placed them in the sink.

Duane studied his middle son. "Are you feeling pressured to marry her?"

"No, it's not that. I just don't want to rush into something I might regret later."

Duane rubbed his shoulder. "Just take your time and see where God leads you."

Korey nodded.

As Duane walked over to the table to gather up their drinking glasses, his thoughts turned once again to Crystal. He wondered if she had a boyfriend. If so, she had never mentioned one.

And if not, would she ever consider dating a man like him?

Crystal rolled over onto her side and stared toward the sliver of light sneaking in past the dark-green shade covering her window. She felt as if she'd been waiting for sleep to find her for hours.

Although she'd tried to relax and fall asleep, she couldn't stop her mind from replaying her encounter with Duane earlier in the day. Every time she closed her eyes, she imagined his smile, his laugh, and the way he'd interacted with her nieces. She sighed, trying to imagine what it would be like to have Duane in her life permanently—as a boyfriend or more.

She groaned as she rolled onto her back. *Stop torturing yourself!*

Just then she heard one of the twins cry out. She pushed herself up out of bed, flipped on her lantern, and then headed over to the twins' room next door, where they both stood in their cribs and sobbed.

"*Ach, mei liewes.* There's no reason to cry. *Aenti* is here." She set the lantern down on their dresser and then wiped their faces with a tissue.

Crystal climbed into the single bed beside their cribs and snuggled down on the pillow. "Let's go to sleep now."

The twins sat down in their cribs and continued to whimper.

"How about I sing?" Crystal cleared her throat. "Jesus loves me, this I know. For the Bible tells me so . . ."

While she sang, the twins continued to moan and sniff—and Crystal prepared herself for what was certain to be a long night.

# CHAPTER 14

"Would you please go to the store?" Leona asked as she stood at the kitchen counter on Wednesday a week later.

Crystal yawned as she carried a stack of dishes to the sink. She started the water before adding detergent. "I was planning to go tomorrow. I didn't get much sleep last night. The *zwillingbopplin* kept me up and then woke up early."

"I wouldn't ask you, but we're out of bread. Plus, the *zwillingbopplin* finished their favorite cereal. You know they'll scream for it tomorrow." Leona moved to the pantry. "We also need soup, and I need some ground beef and chili powder if we want chili this week."

"Of course. And you should sit. How are you feeling?"

"I'm okay. *Danki* for going."

Just then Evie arched her back and started screaming from her highchair.

Leona sighed and walked over to her. "What is it, Evie?"

Evie yelled louder, and Morgan joined in, the kitchen now echoing with their wails.

"*Aenti?*" Hope grabbed onto Crystal's apron and tugged. "Can I go with you to the store?"

Crystal hesitated. While she adored her helpful niece, she preferred her shopping trips to go as quickly and as smoothly as possible, especially after a sleepless night. She glanced over at Leona, who was busy trying to calm the twins by offering them crackers. When that didn't work, she removed the tray from Evie's highchair and pulled her into her arms.

"I think your *mamm* would appreciate your help with the *zwillingbopplin*. Right, Leona?" Crystal hoped Leona would read her tone and understand she preferred to go to the store alone.

Leona gave Crystal a weary expression. "I have my hands full here. It would be helpful if you took Hope with you."

"I'll be your helper, *Aenti*. I promise." Hope yanked Crystal's apron again.

Crystal smiled down at her niece. "I know you will."

While Leona tended to the twins, Crystal finished cleaning up the breakfast dishes, and Hope did her best to sweep the kitchen with her little broom.

As Crystal walked out to the barn to call Kane's driver, she looked up at the bright-blue sky and breathed in the fragrance of mid-May. She looked out toward her garden and felt a tug at her heart. How she longed to sit on a gardening stool and soak up the sun while working in the soil.

But the gardening would have to wait. Leona needed her help, and she would do anything to make sure Leona took care of herself and her unborn babies. She looked up at the sky again and then began to pray:

"Lord, please stop this bitterness and resentment that's consuming me today. Help me keep my eyes focused on you."

Then she continued into the barn, toward the phone.

Duane stepped out of the hardware store with his bags full of supplies and started down the sidewalk. When he saw a redheaded Amish woman pushing a little girl with light-brown braids in a stroller, he did a double take. Then his pulse jumped.

"Crystal!" he called, hurrying after her. "Crystal!"

She stopped and turned, and her pretty lips turned up in a wide smile. "Duane."

Hope leaned out of the stroller and waved both of her arms. Then she looked up at Crystal. "It's Duane, *Aenti*! We like Duane."

"*Ya*, we sure do." Crystal nodded at her niece, and Duane was almost certain she blushed as she looked over at him.

"What brings you out here today?"

Crystal pulled a piece of paper from her apron pocket. "Grocery list." She pointed to the bags in his hand. "I see you've been to the hardware store."

"*Ya*, I needed more nails, a new hammer, and a few other things." He peered across the parking lot, and an idea formed in his mind. "Are you in a hurry?"

"Not really. Why?"

"Would you like to have a snack?" He gestured toward the ice cream parlor.

Crystal followed his gaze. "Our driver had to run an errand, so we have a little bit of extra time." She leaned down toward her niece. "Hope, would you like some ice cream?"

"*Ya!* Please!" The four-year-old nodded with such vigor that her braids bounced off her shoulders.

"Let's go then."

They walked across the parking lot together and then entered the restaurant, where the sweet smell of ice cream teased Duane's senses and the buzz of conversations filled the air. The ice cream parlor was decorated in an old-time theme with a black-and-white checkerboard tile floor and red booths, while posters of ice cream cones, banana splits, and sundaes peppered the white walls.

Duane pointed to the menu above the counter where young women wearing Mennonite prayer coverings served the customers. "Do you know what you want?"

"Cookies and cream with chocolate sprinkles!" Hope announced loud enough that the elderly Amish couple at a nearby table peered over and smiled.

"Cone or cup?" Duane asked.

"Cup, please," Crystal said quickly.

"Okay," Duane said. "And what do you want, Crystal?"

Crystal's pretty pink lips twisted as she studied the menu. "I'm debating between peanut butter cup and vanilla fudge swirl."

"How about a cup with a scoop of both?" he suggested.

"Perfect." Crystal began unzipping her purse.

Duane reached over and placed his hand on top of hers, and his skin started to burn, his pulse tripling. She looked up at him, her beautiful emerald eyes wide. "Do you really think I'd invite you for ice cream and allow you to pay?"

Her lips turned up in a smile. "I suppose not."

"Why don't you find us a table while I get our treats?" He released her hand and then nodded over to an empty booth. His hand felt cold without her touch.

While Crystal and Hope went to sit, Duane stood in line. After ordering and paying for their ice cream, he balanced their treats on a tray and brought it over to the table.

Duane sat down across from Crystal and Hope and then set

Hope's kid's-size cup in front of her. "One cookies and cream with chocolate sprinkles."

"Yay!" Hope exclaimed, reaching her little arms out for the treat.

Crystal handed Hope a stack of napkins. "Try not to get it all over you like the last time you had ice cream."

Hope looked serious. "I won't, *Aenti*." Then she smiled at Duane. "*Danki*, Duane."

"You're so welcome." He pushed Crystal's over to her. "And here's your peanut butter cup and vanilla fudge swirl."

"*Danki*." Crystal picked up her spoon and dug in. "Oh, it's just *appeditlich*. Isn't ice cream heavenly?"

He grinned. "*Ya*, it is."

"What did you get?" Crystal asked before spooning more ice cream into her mouth.

He pointed his spoon at his cup. "Butter pecan."

"That's *mei dat*'s favorite," Hope said before eating more ice cream.

"Is that so?" Duane asked.

Hope nodded. "*Mei mamm* likes vanilla smothered in chocolate sauce."

"How about that?" Duane smiled at Hope, and when he looked over at Crystal, he found her watching him with a warm expression that sent a jolt through him.

Crystal ate more ice cream and then covered her mouth to stifle a yawn. "Excuse me."

Duane wiped his mouth and beard with a napkin. "You okay?"

"*Ya*. I had a tough night."

Concern gripped him. "What happened?"

"The *zwillingbopplin* kept me up, but I'm fine." It was then that he noticed the shadows under her pretty eyes.

Hope frowned. "They woke me up too, but I was able to roll over and go back to sleep. They never wake up Alisha, though. She was snoring." She leaned forward and whispered loudly. "She snores like a bear. That's what Nate says. He can hear her in his room."

Duane bit back a grin at Hope's comments as he spooned more butter pecan into his mouth. While he chewed, he pondered what Crystal had shared. "How often do the *zwillingbopplin* keep you up?"

"It's been nearly every night for the past week. I wonder if their teething is keeping them up or if it's bad dreams." She sighed. "But I'm grateful I can help Leona. The doctor told her to take it easy. She's worried about Leona's blood pressure."

Then she smiled. "It's just a phase, and the *zwillingbopplin* will get through it. I remember when Hope had trouble sleeping and now she sleeps like a champ." She bumped her shoulder against her niece, who smiled up at her with ice cream outlining her mouth.

Duane couldn't shake the feeling that Leona took advantage of Crystal, but it was none of his business.

"How's work?" Crystal asked.

"*Gut.* We're roofing a home over in Ronks. We should be finished with it this afternoon, and then we have a job over in Paradise."

"Will you be back out by us next week like you originally thought?"

"We will." He spooned the last of his ice cream into his mouth and then wiped his mouth and beard again.

"*Gut.*" She smiled as she finished her ice cream. "That was fantastic."

"It hit the spot, like *Dat* says," Hope chimed in, and both Duane and Crystal laughed.

"Oh, how sweet!" An *Englisher* woman with purple glasses and wearing a pink T-shirt with a horse and buggy on it approached the table. She glanced around the table and then her brown eyes landed on Duane. "Is this your daughter and your granddaughter?"

Duane swallowed. He peeked over at Crystal, and her cheeks reddened as she looked down at her empty cup.

Hope patted Crystal's arm. "She's *mei aenti.*"

"That's so nice. Have a blessed day," the woman sang before strolling toward the exit.

Crystal cleared her throat. "This was so fun. *Danki* again for the ice cream."

"*Gern gschehne,*" Duane said as he gathered up their empty cups. "*Danki* for having a snack with me."

"I'm so glad we ran into you."

Duane stood and dropped their cups, spoons, and napkins in the nearby trash can before retrieving the stroller and opening it for her.

"*Danki,*" Crystal said as she steered Hope to the stroller.

They exited the ice cream parlor together, and Duane tried to shake the embarrassment from the woman who had assumed he was Crystal's father and Hope's grandfather. His mind kept replaying the scene and envisioning Crystal's humiliation.

He swallowed a groan as they crossed the parking lot and headed toward the grocery store. Certainly Crystal would never want to date a man who looked as if he were old enough to be her father. After all, she would want to plan a future with a man who could have children with her, and what if he wasn't able to have more? He would never forgive himself for being a hindrance to her greatest desires.

Disappointment hit him square in the chest, almost knocking the wind out of him. If dating her was out of the question, then he would concentrate on being her friend.

When they reached the grocery store, she faced him. "I hope to see you soon."

"Me too." Duane looked down at Hope. "You be a *gut* helper for your *aenti*."

"I will." Hope held up her hand, and he gave her a high-five.

Then Duane turned his attention back to Crystal. "Take care."

"Be sure to visit when you're working across the street," Crystal said.

*"Ya!"* Hope hollered.

"I promise I will." Then he watched them make their way toward the grocery store.

"How'd it go?" Leona asked from the doorway to the family room.

Crystal looked over from the pantry where she and Hope were busy stacking cans of soup. "There was a sale on soups and vegetables," she said.

*"Gut."* Leona moved to the table and pulled out three loaves of bread and carried them to the breadbox. "You were gone an awfully long time."

"We had ice cream," Hope announced as she handed Crystal two more cans of chicken noodle.

Leona lifted an eyebrow at Crystal. "Ice cream?"

"*Ya*, with Duane. We bumped into him, and he offered to buy." Hope retrieved two cans of beef with barley from the bag and carried them over to Crystal.

The skin between Leona's eyes pinched as she studied Crystal. "Well, that's interesting . . ."

Crystal tried to look casual. While she didn't plan to keep secrets from her sister-in-law, she also wasn't ready to talk about her growing feelings for Duane.

Hope helped Crystal stack the remainder of the vegetables and soups in the large pantry while Leona put away the ground beef, chili powder, and cereal.

"*Danki* for your help, Hope," Leona told her. "Why don't you go look at books for a while?"

"Okay, *Mamm*." Hope scampered off into the family room.

When Leona turned to Crystal, she crossed her arms. "Isn't Duane a bit old for you?"

Crystal felt as if she'd been slapped. "We're just *freinden*, Leona."

"I saw you give him a gift on the last day he worked here, and Hope told me you gave him brownies when he stopped by last week."

Crystal began gathering up the empty grocery bags and jamming them all into one bag. "I didn't say I wanted to date him. We just happened to see him, and he asked us to have ice cream with him. That's it. We're not dating. I don't think he's even interested in me."

"Listen. I'm concerned. He's not—"

The back door suddenly opened, and Kane burst into the

kitchen, cutting off his wife's words. "Crystal! Jeannie's *mamm* just called. Jeannie had a *boppli*. It's a girl."

Crystal gasped, cupping her hand to her mouth. "A girl!"

"Oh, what a blessing," Leona said, her face lighting up. Then she rested her hand on her belly. "Ours will come soon, Kane."

"*Ya*, that's right." Kane and Leona shared a special look.

"I'll have to get a gift for when I go see her." Happiness curled in Crystal's chest as she imagined her best friend holding her new baby girl. She couldn't wait to meet the little angel!

As she put away the grocery bags, Crystal tried to push away the resentment that nipped at her after Leona's criticism of Duane. Not only was he a kind and thoughtful man, but he was a good father. In fact, he was just the kind of man Crystal would choose for a boyfriend, no matter what Leona thought of his age. As far as Crystal was concerned, age had nothing to do with a person's true character.

# CHAPTER 15

DUANE STEPPED OUT OF THE BARN SUNDAY AFTERNOON AFTER enjoying the church service and lunch at Bishop Wilmer Flaud's farm. It was another warm and beautiful mid-May day, and he smiled when he spotted a calico barn cat chasing a gray squirrel up a nearby tree. He waved to his sons before they climbed into buggies and headed off to the afternoon's youth gathering.

He pivoted just as Tricia walked over to him, smiling.

"Duane. Hi. *Wie geht's?*"

"Hi, Tricia. How's your roof holding up?"

"Perfectly. *Danki.*"

"And how are *you* holding up?"

"I'm okay." She shrugged. "The *kinner* had a tough week with some crying spells, but I remember what you said about just being strong for them and letting them grieve."

He looked down and kicked a rock with the toe of his black shoe. "*Ya*, it's not easy." He nodded. "I appreciate all of the sewing you did for me."

"It certainly wasn't enough. Pease feel free to bring more by if you need it."

"That's a very kind offer."

"Well, I should go. Have a *gut* week."

As Tricia walked away, Duane noticed the bishop watching him intently. Curious.

When he started toward his buggy, Duane spotted two of his oldest friends and decided to visit with them before leaving. "Ed! Ray!" he called, moving in their direction.

"How's business?" Ed Allgyer asked as Duane joined them.

Like Duane, Ed was in his late forties and had married in his twenties. But Ed had four daughters and ran a dairy farm. Ed and Duane stood with their mutual friend, Ray Lambert, who had also grown up with them. He had six children—five boys and a girl—and also ran a dairy farm.

Duane nodded at Ed. "It's been *gut*. Busy. How about you?"

"The same." Ed gestured toward Ray. "Ray and I have been splitting our time between our farms and Tricia Mast's."

"Is that right?" Duane asked and they nodded. "I fixed her roof a month ago. She had a few bad leaks."

Ray frowned and glanced around before lowering his voice. "*Ya*, her farm needs a lot of work. It's getting a bit tiresome."

"I'm sure she appreciates the help. She did some sewing for me since *mei sohns* and I donated our time. I was grateful. I can fix roofs and tinker with wooden toys, but I can't sew at all."

Ray rubbed his graying dark-brown beard. "I know that she needs the help, but it would be *wunderbaar* if she found someone to help her permanently."

"Or if she married again," Ed chimed in.

"Even better," Ray said. He looked past Duane. "Oh, there's *mei fraa*. You two have a great week."

"Take care," Ed called after him. Then he shook Duane's hand. "Always *gut* seeing you."

"You too," Duane said, then returned to his buggy.

He couldn't wait to get home. Duane looked forward to spending the afternoon reading the mystery novel he had picked up at the library last week. Then he planned to warm up the casserole recipe he had decided to try from one of the cookbooks Crystal had given him.

He had just begun climbing into the buggy when he heard someone call his name. He turned, and he felt the happiness drain out of him as the bishop waddled over. The older man's dark, beady eyes were narrowed, and his expression stoic.

"Duane! I've been looking for you," Wilmer exclaimed.

"Hi, Wilmer. *Wie geht's?*" Duane smiled.

"Fine, fine." Wilmer waved off the pleasantries. "Do you have plans for this afternoon?" the older man asked.

Duane hesitated. He couldn't lie to the bishop, but his only plans were with his newest novel and a casserole. "Not really."

Wilmer beckoned Duane to follow him toward the house. "*Gut, gut.* It's settled then. Stay and visit."

"Okay." Duane felt his brow furrow. What did the bishop have up his sleeve?

Later that afternoon, Duane sat beside Tricia on a rocking chair on Wilmer's back porch. He lifted his glass of iced tea and looked out over Wilmer's rolling, lush green patchwork of fields.

He had spent more than an hour visiting with Wilmer, his son, and his adult grandsons in the family room, discussing their work, while Tricia talked with the bishop's wife, Marlena, and the other ladies in the kitchen. Then the bishop had abruptly suggested Duane and Tricia go out to the porch to talk.

Now they sat beside each other sipping their iced tea while birds sang in the nearby trees, the colorful flowers in Marlena's garden seemed to smile over at them, and Tricia's three daughters played nearby on the elaborate wooden swing set.

Duane quickly figured out what the bishop had planned: to encourage Duane and Tricia to date. Duane would play along for the afternoon and then go back to his home and his life. While he appreciated Tricia's friendship, he wasn't interested in dating her. Still, having someone to talk to on Sunday on a lovely afternoon instead of sitting alone in his house was a welcome change.

"How's work for you?" Tricia suddenly asked.

"*Gut.* Busy." Duane set his glass on the small table between them and looked over at her. "How was your week?"

"I cleaned a few houses, hosted two dinners for *Englishers,* and did other chores."

"Oh, so you had a very slow week," he teased.

She laughed and he joined in.

Duane chuckled for longer than he should have as he struggled to find something else to say. It seemed like they only knew how to exchange pleasantries.

An awkward silence stretched between them, and Duane cleared his throat as Tricia sipped her iced tea.

Then Tricia faced him. "Wilmer isn't all that subtle, is he?"

A burst of laughter escaped Duane's lips, and Tricia joined in too.

Duane wiped his eyes, feeling as if the ice had been broken between them. "That's so true. At first I thought he wanted me to come for a friendly visit, but it's very obvious that he had a plan for us."

Tricia glanced behind her as if looking for spies. "Marlena told me you and I would make a *gut* couple."

Duane nodded slowly. "Aha. At least she was forthright with you. Wilmer hasn't come out and said it to me, but I did notice he was watching us when you and I spoke earlier."

"Marlena suggested we get to know each other better. Then she reminded me about how much time and money my family is costing the community, and she said that it would be best if I were married." She sighed. "As if I don't know what a burden I am." She shook her head.

Duane hated that Tricia would be made to feel that way. "No one has the right to pressure you or me to get married, Tricia."

"I agree."

She looked out toward her three children while they played on the swing set. "Tomorrow is Harley's birthday. He would have been forty-three."

Duane frowned. "I'm sorry. Are you planning to do anything special to remember him?"

"*Ya.*" Tricia sniffed. "I'm going to cook his favorite meal—steak and potatoes—and I thought we'd walk out to the cemetery to visit him after supper. The *kinner* are going to make him cards. I plan to talk to them about their favorite memories."

"That's sweet." Duane rested his elbow on the arm of the chair and his chin on his palm.

As Tricia talked on about her late husband, Duane found himself unsure of how to respond to Wilmer's pressure. He shouldn't have been surprised by it. After all, widows and widowers often remarried in their community, but the thought had never entered Duane's mind that he would be expected to marry Tricia. She was kind, attractive, hardworking, and easy to talk to, but he didn't feel a spark with her.

His heart did come alive when he thought of Crystal, however.

Later, Duane said good-bye to Tricia and then stepped into the kitchen, where Wilmer sat talking with his wife. "*Danki* for the visit. Have a *gut* week," Duane said before stepping outside.

"Duane! Wait!" Wilmer followed him. "I need to speak with you."

A black feeling filled his gut as he turned to face his bishop. "*Ya*, Wilmer?"

"I realized something earlier today when I saw you speaking with Tricia. It was as if the Lord himself put the revelation in my mind. You and Tricia belong together."

Duane held his hands up. "Now, hold on—"

"Let me finish," the older man interrupted. "Tricia needs a husband to take care of her and her *kinner*, and you need a *fraa* to help you at home. It's obvious you two get along. I noticed it the day you stopped by her *haus* for the estimate, and I saw it again today. It's apparent you like each other and are *freinden*, which is always a *gut* start for a marriage."

"I think you're jumping to conclusions."

"Just think about it. You would be doing a service for your community and family. Plus, you're both alone. Well, you're not alone yet, but your *sohns* are grown men now and will soon have families of their own. Do you really want to spend the rest of your life just running your business and coming home to an empty *haus* every night?"

Duane's mouth opened and then closed.

"You and Tricia together make *gut* sense." Wilmer patted Duane's arm. "Spend some time with Tricia, and then let me know when you want to get married. I'll give my blessing." Then he turned and marched back into his house, leaving Duane standing on the porch staring after him.

Duane's thoughts spun like a cyclone as he guided his horse home and pondered the bishop's instructions. While he understood that Tricia and her children needed help, he couldn't comprehend how the bishop expected Duane to solve her problems and relieve the community with a lifelong commitment.

Although he felt comfortable with Tricia and felt compassion toward her, she didn't warm his heart the way a spouse should. She was attractive and sweet, and he appreciated her sense of humor. Still, he couldn't imagine being married to her.

As he approached the road that led to his house, his thoughts turned back to Crystal—as they tended to do of late. He couldn't deny that he felt a spark for her . . . The kind of attraction he hadn't felt since—well, since Connie.

But Crystal wasn't Connie. She was just young enough to still want a family, and she deserved one. And Duane wasn't certain he could provide that. After all, Connie had wanted more children after Jayden, but it never happened. It could have possibly been Duane's fault that their family never grew beyond their three sons. He would never want to deny Crystal small children of her own.

He groaned.

As Duane guided the horse down the road to his house, he began to pray:

"God, please help me sort through these confusing feelings. Tricia is a lovely woman and I wish her and her *kinner* the best, but she doesn't warm my heart. I have feelings for Crystal, but it's obvious we don't belong together due to our age difference. Still, I can't get her off my mind. And I don't even know how *mei sohns* would react if I started dating or decided to get married. I need to be respectful of their hearts as well."

He took a deep breath. "Lord, I don't want to spend the rest of my life alone after *mei sohns* are gone, but I don't want to marry someone out of convenience. Please help me choose the right path for me. Help me do what's best for my family."

Duane guided the horse up his driveway and tried to focus on spending a relaxing evening alone with a new book, but he couldn't stop himself from wondering how Crystal had enjoyed her Sunday.

Thursday morning Crystal carried the large gift bag containing a package of diapers, a pack of baby wipes, and a package of pink onesies as she walked down the street and started the three-block journey toward Jeannie's farm.

It was a warm day, but the sky above her was clogged with gray clouds and the air smelled like rain. Still, she was happy to walk and wouldn't allow the threatening weather to dampen her happy mood. She couldn't wait to see her best friend and meet her new baby girl.

When she reached the road that led to Jeannie's farm, she picked up her pace. The colorful and cheerful flowers in Jeannie's garden greeted her as she strolled up the rock driveway toward the large, two-story, white house with its sweeping front porch. A line of buggies sat by the barn, indicating visitors.

Crystal climbed the porch steps and knocked on the storm door. A moment later, heavy footsteps sounded, and Wanda Stoltzfus, Jeannie's mother-in-law, appeared at the door.

"Hi, Wanda. I was hoping today would be a *gut* day to see Jeannie and meet her new *dochder*," Crystal said.

"Of course." Wanda's smile was wide as she opened the door. "Just wait until you see our little cherub. She's perfect, just like her *dat*."

A short and portly woman, Wanda had bright-blue eyes and dark hair, which she had passed on to her four sons. She also had a loud voice and was known for speaking her mind. In fact, when Crystal dated Owen, she found his mother to be intimidating and overbearing as she constantly gave Crystal unsolicited advice on how to care for her father and also how to be a good girlfriend to Owen.

Crystal nodded as she followed Wanda through the large family room and kitchen toward the downstairs bedroom. She fingered the handles of the pink bag while Wanda knocked on the door.

"Yes?" Jeannie called from the other side.

"You have a visitor, Jeannie," Wanda sang.

"Come in."

Wanda pushed the door open and then moved to the side. "I'll give you some privacy."

"*Danki*," Crystal told Wanda. She stepped into the spacious bedroom, where Jeannie sat on a rocking chair beside a bassinet.

Jeannie smiled as she held the baby wrapped in a blanket. "I'm so glad you're here."

Crystal rushed over to her and gasped as she peeked down at the little pink face. "She's just gorgeous."

"*Danki*. I think she has her *dat*'s blue eyes, but Wanda says it's too early to tell." Jeannie looked radiant, despite the dark circles under her pretty eyes.

Crystal set the large bag on the floor beside the rocker. "This is for you."

"*Danki* so much." Jeannie stood and then held the baby out to Crystal. "Would you like to hold Lila Grace?"

Crystal took the baby in her arms. "Oh! Lila Grace. What a perfectly lovely name!"

Jeannie pointed to the rocker. "Please sit." Then she perched herself on the edge of the large bed across from the bassinet.

Crystal sank down onto the chair and began to rock as she stared down at the baby's tiny face. "What do you think about motherhood so far?"

"It's tiring. Exhausting, really, but *mei mamm* and Wanda say we'll eventually get into a routine. Jared has been helping some, but he has to take care of the milkings too. It's not like he can take time off work, you know?" She laughed. "We'll figure it out eventually. Wanda has been cooking and cleaning. *Mei mamm* came over to help some too."

Crystal nodded as Jeannie talked on about how her family members were pitching in to handle the household chores, but she wasn't really listening. Instead, she was transfixed by the tiny baby in her arms and how this child meant so much to so many people.

Crystal suddenly felt an all-consuming ache that started deep in her heart and branched out toward every part of her.

And the pang was deeper and more powerful than she'd ever felt in her life—she knew to her very core that she craved a husband, a home, and a family. She desperately desired children of her very own.

But how could Crystal ever have those things if she had no prospects for a husband? She had no one who loved her or wanted to build a life with her. All she had were Kane's children, but they would never truly be hers.

Grief mixed with her yearning, and Crystal's eyes started to burn and water. She held her breath, hoping to keep the tears at bay. She couldn't allow her own selfishness and self-pity to ruin this special moment with her best friend.

After all, she was happy for Jeannie! She deserved all the joys of motherhood.

"Crystal?" Jeannie was at her side, rubbing her shoulder. "You okay?"

Crystal sniffed and smiled up at her. "*Ya*. I'm just so *froh* for you. You and Jared have waited so long, and the *gut* Lord answered your prayers with this perfect little bundle of joy."

Lila started to squirm and then cry, her little pink face turning bright red as she howled.

Crystal held her out to Jeannie. "Here you go. I think she wants her *mamm*."

"*Ya*, it's time for another feeding." Jeannie took the baby, and when Crystal stood, Jeannie sank back down onto the rocker. "*Danki* for the gift and for coming to visit us," she said over the baby's cries.

"I couldn't wait to visit you." Crystal touched Jeannie's arm. "You take care. And I'll see you soon."

Crystal closed the bedroom door behind her and walked to the kitchen, where she found Wanda standing at the counter washing dishes. As she walked over to say good-bye, she peered out the window toward the row of barns.

And she froze in place when she spotted Owen standing there.

# CHAPTER 16

CRYSTAL'S LUNGS SEIZED. HER EX-BOYFRIEND, THE MAN WHO had smashed her heart into a million pieces, who had abandoned her when she needed him most, stood out by one of the barns, talking and smiling with his brother Jared and their father, Hershel.

And to make matters worse, he had barely changed since leaving five years ago. He was still attractive with his dark hair, bright-blue eyes, and handsome smile that always had a way of lighting up a room and her heart.

But Crystal knew better this time. She wouldn't allow herself to be conned by his rugged good looks and his empty promises. She knew that even when Owen claimed he would always put her needs before his, he would choose himself and his desires every time.

"I guess you saw him."

"What?" Crystal spun toward Wanda's smug smile. "I'm sorry. What did you say?"

Wanda motioned toward the window. "Owen. He's back."

Crystal's stomach lurched. "When did he get back to town?"

"Yesterday, and he's back for *gut*." Wanda took a step toward her. "Are you dating anyone?"

Oh, how she wanted to lie and say yes! But lying was a sin. And even if Crystal lied and insisted she had a steady boyfriend, Jeannie would set the record straight.

"No, I'm not."

Wanda's blue eyes danced with delight. "Well, perhaps God sent him back here so that you two could finally get married. He's looking for work right now, but I'm sure he'll be back on his feet soon and ready to provide for you in no time."

"Oh, I . . . I think our time has passed." Crystal started for the door. "It was nice seeing you. I really have to get going. Lots of chores, you know!"

"Wait a minute, Crystal."

When she stopped moving, Crystal closed her eyes and silently counted to five. Then she fastened a bright smile on her face and turned back toward Wanda. "*Ya?*"

Wanda's face clouded with sympathy. "I know Owen hurt you. He left you when your *dat* was so *krank* . . ." She clutched her chest. "My heart still hurts for you, and I'm so very sorry *mei sohn* was so immature and selfish."

Crystal swallowed back a bitter response.

"But listen to me when I tell you that Owen has changed. He's learned from his mistakes, and he's ready to be the man you need and deserve."

"Did he actually say that?" Crystal challenged her.

Wanda nodded. "*Ya*, he did. He says he still cares for you. He asked about you last night. We were having supper, and he wanted to know if you were dating anyone. I told him that I didn't think so. I asked Jeannie this morning, and Jeannie said that you were still single, but I asked you to make sure. When I relayed that information to Owen, he was so *froh* to hear it. He said he couldn't wait to see you, and here you are!"

Crystal held her hands up. "Please, Wanda, I'm perfectly *froh* with my life. I'm not worried about getting married."

"Why not?" Wanda's large forehead wrinkled. "You're not getting any younger. If you want your own *kinner*, then you need to get started now. Your clock is ticking."

"I'm sorry, but I really don't have time for this. I need to get home to take care of my chores. Have a *gut* day." Before Wanda could say more, Crystal marched out of the kitchen and through the family room to the front door.

When she pushed it open, she stepped out onto the porch and walked right into Owen's hard chest. Her shoulders tightened, and her hands began to tremble as she looked up into his deep-blue eyes.

The scent of rain wafted over her as drops began to beat a steady cadence on the roof above them. She took a step back as the pain and heartache came rushing back. Memories of their happy times together—talking and laughing while he helped her hang out laundry, picnics by their favorite pond before her father became too ill to stay by himself, sitting together on her back porch while holding hands and watching the sunset . . . Oh, how in love she had been!

But he had abandoned her. As much as she'd tried, she could not erase the pain of the memory.

"Crystal, hi." He looked just as surprised as she felt. "It's so *gut* to see you. You look fantastic."

Why did he have to be so handsome? And why did she have to notice just how attractive he was? If only she could banish all her feelings for him from her heart! Her hands balled into tight fists, her fingernails biting into her palms. With her nostrils flaring, she pushed past him.

"Crystal."

She walked to the edge of the porch and looked out toward the rain beating on the green grass and flowers. "Perfect," she muttered.

"Crystal, wait." He touched her arm.

She whipped her arm out of his grasp and spun. "Please don't touch me."

Owen held his hands up, palms facing her. "I'm sorry. I'm . . I'm sorry for everything I did to hurt you." His posture sagged, and he looked exasperated. "Just let me give you a ride home. I'll go hitch up Jared's horse. I promise I won't talk."

"No, *danki*. I'll be fine," she said. Then she stepped out into the cool rain and started down the stairs.

"Crystal!" Owen called after her. "At least let me get you an umbrella."

Ignoring him, she barreled forward, the cool rain soaking through her prayer covering, gray dress, and black apron.

Frustration and humiliation whipped through her as tears welled up in her eyes. How could she allow Owen to still affect her heart this way after all this time? Crystal hugged her arms to her chest and stalked down the road. She only wished she'd grabbed her umbrella on her way out the door this morning!

If only Jeannie had warned her that Owen was not only back but at her house!

Crystal gritted her teeth and then blew out a frustrated sigh. Jeannie had more important things on her mind than her brother-in-law, but Crystal hadn't been prepared for that shock.

The rain intensified, and Crystal kept her head bent, trying her best to dodge puddles as she continued down the first block toward her brother's farm.

The nerve of Owen to tell her she looked good! To apologize! To offer her a ride home!

She looked up at the sky and let out a growl. Why couldn't he have stayed in Ohio and out of her life?

The *clip-clop* of horse hooves and whirl of buggy wheels sounded in the distance and then grew closer and closer as she hurried down the road.

Crystal groaned as embarrassment soaked through her like the unrelenting raindrops. She kept her neck bent, hoping that the person approaching her wouldn't recognize her.

When the horse and buggy were upon her, Crystal squeezed her eyes shut for a moment. *Please ignore me! Please keep going!*

"Crystal?"

She stopped and faced the buggy, and her stomach plummeted when she found Duane staring at her, confusion and possibly concern clouding his handsome face. Both happiness and shame overcame her.

*Of course* she would run into Duane when she looked like a drowned rat! Could this day get any worse?

"Need a ride?" he asked.

"No, *danki*. I don't want to get your buggy wet." She pointed toward the corner. "It's only two blocks to *mei haus*."

He sighed, looking exasperated. "Crystal, please just get in."

Hurrying around the back of the buggy, she climbed into the passenger side. Then she hugged her arms to her middle.

Duane reached behind him and retrieved a quilt from the back of the buggy. "Here."

*"Danki,"* she whispered, her voice barely audible over the rain

pounding on the roof of the buggy. She wrapped herself in the blanket and sucked in a breath, hoping to keep her raging emotions at bay. She ran her fingers over the gray, blue, and green log cabin pattern quilt. "This is so *schee*. Did Connie make it for you?"

"*Ya*. It was a Christmas gift a few years before she passed away. She told me to keep it in my buggy in case I ever get cold, and I've done that ever since. Of course, I do wash it occasionally." He chuckled.

She hugged the quilt against her body and breathed in its scent. It smelled like him—soap mixed with fresh earth and musk.

Closing her eyes, she tried to imagine Duane's beautiful wife handing him the quilt and wishing him a merry Christmas. The scene sent all her sadness and grief bubbling up inside of her, and she choked back a sob. She sniffed and her lip trembled as her body felt heavy and hollowed out.

*Hold it together! Don't cry in front of Duane!*

When she realized that the horse and buggy hadn't moved, she looked over at him and found him watching her with compassion in his deep-brown eyes.

"Do you want to talk about it?" His tone was warm and consoling.

She shook her head. "No, *danki*."

He hesitated for a moment and then turned toward the road ahead.

When his hands lifted the reins, she felt something break apart inside of her, and she needed a friend to listen. Reaching over, she took hold of his arm, and he stilled as he faced her.

"Wait," she said. "I do want to talk about it. In fact, I desperately need a *freind* right now if you'll listen."

Duane angled his body toward her. "Of course I'll listen."

The sympathy in his eyes was almost too much to bear, and she looked down at her lap while hugging his quilt closer to her.

"This morning I went to visit my best *freind*. Her name is Jeannie, and she just had her first *boppli*. A girl." She sniffed and picked up a loose thread on the quilt. "I'm really *froh* for her. She and her husband have prayed for a child for a while now. And her baby's name is Lila Grace, and she's *schee* and perfect."

She paused and tried to swallow against the ball of grief clogging her throat. "And while I was holding Lila, it hit me harder than usual that I'll be thirty-four in a little over a month, and I have no prospects for a husband. That means I'll never have a family of my own. I'll never have my own *kinner*."

She kept her head down as she continued. "I know that sounds like I'm jealous, and jealousy is a sin. But it's not that. I'm truly *froh* for Jeannie. She will be a *wunderbaar mamm*. I'm grateful the Lord saw fit to bless her and Jared with a child, and I pray that they have more."

She took a deep breath. "But while I held sweet Lila in my arms, I couldn't help but wonder if life has truly passed me by. *Mei freinden* from youth group are married, and now they all have at least one *boppli*. All of them, except for me. I'm the only single one left." Her voice was gruff. "I'm grateful and blessed *mei bruder* took me in after *mei dat* died. I'm *froh* I can be such an integral part of *mei bruderskinners'* lives."

Keeping her eyes focused on the quilt's intricate stitching, Crystal took a shaky breath as the truth grabbed her by the throat. "But as much as I tell everyone I'm grateful for what I have, I do want what *mei freinden* have. I want a husband, a home of my own, and my own *kinner*. Yet for some reason God doesn't want those things for me, and it hurts. I'm going to be all alone in my old age, and that truth has nearly broken me in two." She sniffed as tears trickled down her hot cheeks.

She felt the seat shift beside her.

"I don't believe life has passed you by." Duane's voice was close to her ear, sending a flutter deep in her veins. "The Lord hasn't forsaken you either. And to be honest, I don't understand why one of the young men in your community hasn't already asked for your hand in marriage. You're sweet, funny, kind, thoughtful, hardworking, and *schee*. You're young, and you can still have *kinner*. Don't give up on yourself so easily. God will never give up on you and what he has planned for your life."

She looked up at him, and he was so close to her that his leg brushed against hers, sending goose bumps chasing one another up her arms.

"That's so kind of you to say, but that's only part of why I'm upset right now." She sucked in a breath and squeezed her eyes shut as they stung with fresh tears. "To make everything worse, I walked out of Jeannie's bedroom and into the kitchen, and when I looked outside, I saw my ex-boyfriend was there. His name is Owen, and Jeannie's husband is one of his older *bruders*. We dated for three years, and we talked about marriage. He left me five years ago to go to Ohio to start a business with his cousin." She opened her eyes and swiped the back of her hand down her cheeks.

Duane blinked and something unreadable flashed across this face. "He left you to start a business in Ohio?"

She nodded. "*Mei dat* was on dialysis back then and so very *krank*. I needed Owen's help, but he said that if I loved him, I'd move to Ohio with him and bring *mei dat*. Of course, I chose to stay. Owen hadn't even asked to marry me. *Mei dat* was in no shape to travel, and he was comfortable with his doctors and the dialysis center here. Six months after Owen left me, *mei dat* came down with pneumonia and died."

"I'm so sorry, Crystal." The warmth in his voice gave her the courage to go on.

"Owen left me when I needed him most. Jeannie told me that his business failed and that's why he came back." Crystal's grief transformed into frustration. "His *mamm* was in the kitchen when I saw him, and she started lecturing me about how the Lord brought Owen back so he and I can try again. She said that my clock is ticking, and I need to give Owen another chance so I can have a family. But how could I ever trust him again?

"If he had truly loved me, he would have stayed in Gordonville and helped me with *mei dat*. He never would have given me an ultimatum as a marriage proposal. Instead, he would have put us first, not his dream to run a business with his cousin. Still, his *mamm* says I should give him another chance. She says he'll get his life together and then try to make things right with me."

She shook her head. "Jeannie has said things that like too. She always talks about how we'd be *schweschdere* if I married him. I'd rather be alone than married to a selfish man. Why does everyone think we belong together when it didn't work out the first time? Why does everyone have opinions about my life?"

Crystal groaned and covered her face with her hands. She'd said too much. Surely Duane regretted stopping and picking her up.

"I understand how you feel."

She sat up and faced him, shocked by his words. "You do?"

Duane nodded as he rested his arm on the back of the buggy seat. "My bishop is pressuring me to marry a widow in my congregation."

"Really?"

"Yes. He says it makes sense for us to get married since we're both alone." He looked down at the back of the seat and picked at a seam. "The congregation members are helping run her farm, and community funds are paying her bills. After her husband passed away, she lost some of her cows in a fire. Then her cows stopped producing as much milk, and the county raised the property value of her land. She's doing what she can to make money while the men in the congregation take care of her dairy farm, but she has a big tax bill coming and is running out of time. The community fund can only cover so much. The bishop thinks I need to take over the responsibility of taking care of her and her *kinner*."

Crystal gaped, her mind reeling at the thought of him marrying someone new. "How . . . how do you feel about it?"

"It makes sense, I suppose." Duane peered over at her and shrugged. "Her *kinner* need a *dat*, and I'll be alone once *mei sohns* get married and start their own families."

"Do you care about her?"

"She's nice. We get along well."

Envy stole her breath for a moment. "Do you love her?" She braced herself for his answer.

"No." He sighed. "And that's what I've been wrestling with. I don't see myself ever dating her or marrying her. I remember hearing stories about couples who were *freinden* when they married, and that friendship transformed into love. I keep wondering if I married Tricia, would I eventually fall in love with her, or would I wind up resenting her?"

She nodded, relief easing her twisting stomach. "Does she want to marry you?"

He rubbed his beard and looked down at the seat once again.

"We haven't really talked about it. We know that the bishop wants us to get together, but we both agree no one can tell us to marry."

"So, you're seeing her?"

"No, but the bishop would like me to. We're just *freinden*." Duane opened his mouth to say something else and then shook his head and turned his attention toward the windshield. "I'm sorry you've had such a hard day. I . . . I should get you home."

"No. Wait." Crystal shifted in the seat as curiosity gripped her. "Were you going to say something else?"

Duane snorted, looking sheepish. "If I tell you, then you're going to know all of my secrets."

"You already know all of mine now, so we'd be even." She chuckled, feeling completely at ease with him.

When his mouth hitched up in a smile, she felt happiness open up in her like a flower. How did this man have such a strong command over her emotions?

"Fine. The truth is that spending the rest of my life alone is one of my biggest fears," he began. "I wonder if I should marry Tricia if only for that reason. Still, I ponder if being alone is better than marrying someone I could never love. But in addition to all of that, I don't know how *mei sohns* would react if they found out that the bishop wants me to get married. I need to take their feelings into account. This would affect them as well, and their *mamm* hasn't been gone all that long."

He shook his head. "So, there you have it. These are the issues that keep me awake at night. While marrying Tricia makes *gut* sense, I still wrestle with if it's the best decision for my family and me." He held his hands up. "Now you know everything about me."

She studied him as his words soaked through her, and her

heart stuttered in her chest. She knew at that moment that she was falling for Duane, and it thrilled and terrified her at the same time.

Duane smiled. "I take back everything I just told you because you're looking at me like I'm *narrisch*."

"No, it's not that. I was just thinking that I'm so grateful for your friendship."

"And I am grateful for yours." He paused, his handsome eyes seeming to search her own. Then he cleared his throat and pointed toward the windshield. "Look at that. The rain stopped, and the sun came out."

Crystal peered out the window at the sun and the blue sky peeking past the clouds. "Wow."

"I should get you home. I'm sure you want to change into dry clothes."

They made small talk about the weather as he guided the horse to Kane's house and halted the horse in the driveway.

Disappointment overtook her as she turned toward him. "*Danki* for the ride and the conversation. I obviously needed both."

"You're always welcome. I'm just grateful I had my horse and buggy today. We're working across the street. I needed to run an errand, and my driver had to take his *mamm* to the doctor today and won't be back until this evening."

She untangled herself from the quilt and folded it on her lap. "I'll wash this for you."

"That's not necessary. I'll take care of it." He tossed it into the back of the buggy and then held his hand out to her. "Would it be all right if I checked on you soon?"

"I'd like that." When she shook his hand, a spark ignited in her soul and sizzled out to every part of her body.

She pushed the door open and climbed out. "Have a *gut* day."

"You too."

Crystal hurried up the back porch steps and into the kitchen, where she found Leona sitting on a chair beside Hope as she dropped cookie dough onto a pan.

Hope took her in and gasped. "You're soaked, *Aenti*!"

"I was wondering where you were," Leona said. "Hope wanted to make *kichlin*, and I told her that I would have to sit by her since I need to stay off my feet."

Crystal gave them a wave and continued toward the stairs. "I promise I'll be right down to help. I need to get cleaned up."

As she jogged up toward her room, Crystal wondered if Duane cared for her—and she prayed her fragile heart could handle the truth of his feelings.

# CHAPTER 17

Duane watched Crystal disappear into the house, and then he studied the empty porch as he tried to unravel the emotional conversation they'd shared.

He had been stunned by how Crystal had opened up to him, sharing personal details of her feelings and her past failed relationship. He'd also been surprised to hear she was convinced she would grow old alone when she was still young enough to fall in love and have a family.

Despite all of that, Duane was most shocked by himself. He had bared his own soul to Crystal. How easy it was to be honest with her! Talking to her felt natural—as if they'd known each other years instead of weeks. And when he touched her hand, he felt his heart come alive for the first time since Connie died. Crystal was not only his friend, but she had become important to him.

Duane could no longer tell himself he wasn't falling for Crystal. When he had least expected it, he had met a special woman who seemed to understand him, but now he had no idea what to do about it.

He scowled as he led the horse back down the driveway

and across the street to the Beilers' farm. After all this time, he finally met a woman he wanted to spend time with, but she was fourteen years younger than he was! And she wanted a family. Duane wasn't sure he had the stamina to start over with another child—or children for that matter—or if he could even have more if he chose.

Still, Duane couldn't deny that he cared for Crystal. He felt a strong connection to her that strengthened each time he saw her, and today the connection went as deep as his heart. Confusion overwhelmed him as he considered his quandary—the bishop wanted him to marry a widow to help her and the community, but his heart craved a younger woman who desperately wanted to start a family.

Which was the right choice?

*Lord, help me sort through this!*

Duane was still contemplating his conundrum after he had taken care of his horse and walked toward that day's jobsite.

"*Dat?*"

Duane turned and found Jayden studying him, his face full of concern. "*Ya?*"

"You okay?"

Duane smiled. "I think I'm going to be just fine."

Jayden nodded, but he looked unconvinced. "Let me know if you want to talk about it."

Duane gave Jayden's shoulder a gentle squeeze. "*Danki, sohn.* Now, how's it going with this roof?"

"Fine. Tyler is in charge as usual and keeping us on track."

"*Gut.*" As Duane turned his attention toward the job, thoughts of Crystal floated at the back of his mind—and he wondered how he was going to handle the tricky situation before him.

"You never told me how it went at Jeannie's today," Leona said while she scrubbed the dinner dishes later that evening. Although Crystal had warned her to sit down and take it easy, Leona had insisted she felt well enough to help with the dishes instead of putting her feet up and watching everyone else work.

Alisha stood beside her, drying and stowing the dishes while Hope sat in the family room with the twins, who were playing in their play yard.

Crystal stopped wiping down the table and looked over at Leona. "Jeannie looked fantastic, and the *boppli* is precious."

"Did you hold her?" Alisha asked.

Crystal nodded. "I did."

"What did they name her?"

"Lila Grace," she said.

"Oh, what a *schee* name." Alisha set a handful of utensils in the drawer.

Crystal kept working as her mind replayed her conversation with Duane. When would she see him again? She hoped he would stop by to see her since he was working across the street.

"Kane told me he ran into Hershel Stoltzfus at the hardware store yesterday, and Hershel said Owen is back."

Leona's words yanked Crystal from her thoughts and back to the present.

Crystal craned her neck over her shoulder as she took in her sister-in-law's expectant expression. "Yesterday, you say? I sure wish Kane had looped me in on that . . ."

"So it's true?" Leona spun to face her and leaned back against the counter.

Crystal turned back toward the table and tried to ignore her indignation. If her brother had warned her, then perhaps she could have been more prepared for her encounter with him. "*Ya*, it is true."

"You saw him?"

Crystal nodded. "I did."

"And . . . ?"

Crystal shook the dishrag out into the trash can and then set the rag on the counter. "And nothing. We had a brief conversation and then I walked home." She opened the door to the utility room and grabbed the dustpan and broom before walking back into the kitchen, where Leona stood waiting for her, hands on hips.

"Wait a minute." Leona wagged a finger at her. "That can't be the full story. What did he say to you?"

Crystal shrugged. "Nothing much. He told me he that I looked good, he was glad to see me, and he was sorry for everything."

"And then he let you walk home in the rain?" Leona looked aghast.

"Excuse me." Crystal moved past Leona. "He offered me a ride, but I told him no thank you. Then I walked home."

"Why would you choose to walk home in the rain?" Leona followed her.

Crystal sighed. "Because I didn't want to be stuck in a buggy with him. We said everything we needed to say five years ago. That's it. It's over."

"But he's back now. Perhaps the Lord sent him back so that you can make amends and try again."

"You sound like Jeannie and Wanda," Crystal muttered as she began to sweep the kitchen.

"They could be right," Leona said. "Everything happens for a reason. Don't get me wrong, though. I'm not saying I want you to get back together with him after the way he treated you."

Alisha set a pot in the cabinet and then faced them. "Who are you talking about?"

"No one, *mei liewe*," Leona said. "Please start washing the glasses for me while I talk to your *aenti*."

"*Ya, Mamm*," Alisha said, sounding disappointed.

Leona moved in front of Crystal. "Did he say he wanted to get back together?"

Crystal leaned on the broom. "Like I told Wanda, Owen and I missed our chance. End of story."

Leona seemed satisfied with that. She moved to the counter and started drying the glasses that Alisha had washed.

"Wait a minute." Crystal held her hand up. "I'm confused. You're not going to tell me that Owen is my last chance at happiness before my clock stops ticking, and my time to be a *mamm* is up?"

Leona looked over at her and shook her head. "No, I'm not. Kane was concerned that you would go back to Owen after the way he had hurt you. Owen wasn't there when you needed him, and that's the most important part of a relationship in my opinion. If he's not reliable now, what kind of *dat* would he be?"

Stunned, Crystal could only nod.

"We completely support you if you decide to not get involved with him, but I still don't understand why you chose to walk home in the rain." Leona pivoted back to the dishes.

Crystal returned to sweeping as thoughts of Duane churned in her mind. Considering the ages of his sons, would he even *want* more *kinner* if he married again? He most likely only wanted to concentrate on his business. Crystal craved her own family, and she wasn't sure she could marry a man who didn't want children.

As she swept the dirt and crumbs into a little pile, she searched her mind for something nice she could do for Duane to thank him for their talk and the ride home in his dry buggy. When an idea formed in her mind, her eyes widened, and a smile lifted the corners of her lips.

*"Gude mariye!"*

Duane turned into the Beilers' driveway just as Crystal and Hope walked toward him. His heart warmed as he took in her beautiful smile. She carried a tray with Styrofoam cups on it while Hope held a small box.

He rushed over to meet her. "Let me help you." He took the tray from her. "What do you have here?"

"We have cinnamon rolls!" Hope lifted her chin. "Me and *aenti* made them this morning."

Duane bent down to her level. "That is *wunderbaar. Danki* so much."

"Did you say cinnamon rolls?" Tyler called from the roof.

Korey walked to the edge of the roof. "Yum!"

Then they both headed for the ladder with Jayden close behind them.

"We brought *kaffi* too." Crystal pointed to the cups.

"It's perfect, but you didn't have to do it," he told her.

Korey walked over, rubbing his flat abdomen. "Where are those cinnamon rolls?"

"Here!" Hope jumped up and down.

Duane's sons laughed as they approached her. He handed

Korey the tray with the coffees. "Why don't you take these over to that picnic table?"

Korey gave him a strange expression and nodded. "Okay." Then he turned to Hope. "Walk with me. I've missed you."

"I've missed you too," Hope said, holding his free hand as they walked together toward the picnic table, where she sat down with the three young men and opened the box of rolls for them.

Crystal clucked her tongue and looked over to where Hope and Duane's sons began digging into the rolls. "Your *sohns* are so nice to her."

"She's adorable." Duane studied her green eyes. "How are you feeling today?"

"Much better. I wanted to apologize for being so emotional yesterday. I'm embarrassed for crying in front of you. That's why I brought the rolls and the *kaffi*. It's an apology and a thank you."

"You need to stop apologizing. It was my pleasure. I'm grateful I came along at the right time to help you, and I'm honored you trusted me."

"I do trust you." Her expression was serious.

"I trust you too." Something unspoken seemed to pass between them, and he felt a surge of courage. "I'd like to come by and visit you sometime. How would you feel about that?" He held his breath, awaiting her response.

Crystal blinked. "I would enjoy that very much."

"Great. We're going to finish this job up tomorrow, and I'll be able to get off work early. We'll only work a half day to do the second small barn. Would tomorrow evening work for you?"

Her smile was wide. "Perfect. You can come for supper."

"Great." Excitement bubbled up in him like a warm spring.

They made small talk about his job and the weather until she announced she had to get home to start on chores.

Duane headed over to the picnic table and sat down next to Tyler after Crystal and Hope walked back toward their house.

"I feel like I'm missing something here," Korey quipped from across the table. "What's going on between you and Crystal?"

Tyler pointed his cup of coffee at Duane. "I was thinking the same thing."

"You're not missing anything. We're just *freinden*." Duane picked a cinnamon bun from the box and took a bite. The sweet bun melted in his mouth as his taste buds danced with delight.

Korey's snort was derisive. "I'm not blind, *Dat*. I see how she looks at you."

"And how does she look at me?" Duane asked.

"Like she has a crush," Tyler finished. "Isn't she like twenty years younger than you?"

Duane glared at him. "Fourteen years, not twenty."

"You really care about her, don't you?" Korey's expression filled with concern or possibly worry.

"I told you. We're *freinden*. She's sweet and easy to talk to." Duane picked up his cup of coffee and took a sip. "That's all it is—friendship." *But I want so much more!*

"Let's get back to work. We need to finish this project tomorrow," Tyler said.

Korey gave Tyler a look before they both stood and dropped their empty coffee cups in the trash can and then started up the ladder to the roof.

Duane took another sip of coffee and waited for Jayden to say something, but instead, his youngest son remained silent while eating a cinnamon bun.

Finally, Duane gave his quiet son a palms-up. "Go ahead, Jayden. Tell me how you feel."

Jayden cleared his throat. "I can tell you like her."

"That's true."

"From what I've noticed, she makes you *froh*."

Duane studied his son. Jayden seemed to be just as intuitive as his mother had been. "That's also true."

"If she makes you *froh*, then I think it's great."

"Wait a minute." Duane held his hand up like a traffic cop. "You'd be okay with me dating Crystal?"

Jayden looked down at his cup and then up at Duane. "*Mamm* actually discussed the idea of your dating and remarrying with *mei bruders* and me before she died."

"What?" Duane leaned forward as his son's words rocked him to his core.

"She said that there would come a day when you'd fall in love again and remarry, and she asked us to support you because she didn't want you to be alone for the rest of your life."

Duane's eyes stung as he recalled a similar conversation he and Connie had shared when she'd encouraged him to find love again. He'd told her he'd never find anyone to love as much as he'd loved her, and she'd told him to try—no, *begged* him to try. "I had no idea she discussed that with you." His voice came out in a rasp.

"She did." Jayden wiped his eyes and sniffed. "I've prayed and talked to God about it a lot to prepare myself for this day. And I realized *Mamm* was right. You're entitled to happiness."

Speechless, Duane swallowed.

"Someday we're going to move out and start our own families, and when we're gone, you're going to be alone in the *haus*. It's selfish if all we're worried about is how much we miss *Mamm* when you miss her too."

"Wow. You're just like her."

Jayden tilted his head. "Who?"

"Your *mamm*. She was thoughtful and insightful like you."

"Thanks."

Duane nodded. "You're welcome. If something happens with Crystal, I might need your help convincing your *bruders* to support me too."

"We might all need to rely on prayer for that," Jayden said.

Duane laughed. "I think you're right."

# CHAPTER 18

DUANE SMILED THE FOLLOWING AFTERNOON WHEN HIS DRIV-
er's pickup truck pulled into the Beiler family's driveway. "I'm
going to head home for the day, so you three can finish up the job.
Drew will come back for you and the supplies."

"What?" Tyler stood up from the other side of the barn roof,
his face filling with confusion. "Why are you leaving us?"

"You said you wanted more responsibility. Now you have it.
You can finish up and talk to the customer. I have plans." Duane
headed toward the ladder.

"*Dat*, wait," Tyler called after him.

Duane spun to face Tyler's frown.

"You have plans?" Tyler challenged him. "How can you leave
early when we have this job to finish? You've always said that finishing our jobs is the most important thing we do. We've talked about
growing our little business, and we all have to pitch in to make that
happen. I showed you my business plan the other night, and part of
it includes sticking to the project schedule, and that means all of us."

"We're almost done here, and I trust you three to finish up.
I'm not abandoning you with something you can't handle." Duane
gestured around the roof.

Korey's brow furrowed as he studied Duane. "Where are you going?"

"I said I have plans, so I need to go home to get cleaned up."

"Tell us what's so important that you need to leave a jobsite before the work is complete," Tyler demanded.

Korey's eyes narrowed. "Wait a minute. Do you have a date?"

"*Ya*, I do." Duane smiled.

Korey frowned. "With whom?"

"I'm going to see Crystal." Duane looked over toward her house. "And I need to be back in time for supper, so I have to go now." He turned back toward his two older sons, who looked flummoxed. He hesitated, worry threading through him. "Are you three okay with the idea of me going to see her?"

Tyler just stared at him while Korey's jaw flexed.

"Come on, now. Tell me how you feel. I'm ready to listen. I realize this affects all of us."

"We can finish up here," Tyler said, his words soft.

Korey folded his arms over his chest, his expression impassive.

When Duane met Jayden's gaze, his youngest son gave him a nod. "Okay then. I'll see you all later. I have faith that you all can handle this." Then he started down the ladder as his stomach flip-flopped.

Later that afternoon, Crystal fluttered around the kitchen while the twins cried in the next room.

Crystal glanced at the clock on the wall above the sink and gasped. It was almost five. She was running out of time! Panic seized her, and she thought her heart might beat out of her chest.

As if reading Crystal's thoughts, Alisha appeared at her side. "What can I do to help, *Aenti*?"

"Well, I have to get the garlic bread ready for the oven, and I need to check on the lasagnas." She looked down at her apron, which was covered in tomato sauce. "I still have to get cleaned up. He should be here around five."

Leona sat in the family room balancing a sniveling Evie on her lap. She had taken to caring for the twins while keeping her feet up as the doctor had instructed.

Crystal opened the freezer and pulled out the boxes of garlic bread. "Please get the baking sheets out of the cabinet, Alisha."

"I'm on it!" Her niece sprang into action, retrieving the pans.

Crystal set the boxes of bread on the counter. "Put the bread on the pan and read the instructions."

"Okay."

Then Crystal turned toward the table. "Oh, and we need to set the table." Then she sucked in a breath. "*Ach* no! I forgot the salad!"

"*Aenti*, I got it." Alisha rubbed her arm. "Go get ready. I'll take care of the bread, the table, and the salad."

"Once I get Evie settled, I'll help," Leona said, speaking over Evie's whines.

"*Danki*." Crystal hurried upstairs, where she stripped off her soiled dress and apron and pulled on her favorite emerald-green dress along with a fresh back apron. Then she washed her face and checked her hair and prayer covering.

When she stepped out of the bathroom, she was greeted by the delicious aroma of dinner floating up the stairs, and she smiled. She could always count on Alisha to save the day.

The sound of men's voices rumbled from below, and her heart rate picked up speed. Duane was early! She smoothed her hands down her apron and squared her shoulders before starting down the stairs.

When she entered the kitchen, she found Alisha carrying two large bowls of salad to the table, which had already been set. Hope followed her with a bottle of homemade dressing. The twins sat in their highchairs while Jevon and Nate stood at the sink washing their hands. Leona gathered four baskets from the cabinet and then opened the oven, which overpowered the kitchen with the delectable scents of supper.

Crystal's gaze moved to the doorway, and her legs felt as weak as uncooked noodles as she found Duane holding a handful of beautiful wildflowers while standing with Kane. Duane looked more handsome than usual in his gray shirt—or maybe she had begun seeing him in a new light after their emotional conversation on Thursday.

When Duane's eyes met hers, a warm smile turned up his lips as he walked over to her and held out the bouquet of flowers. "These are for you."

"*Danki.*" She took the flowers and breathed in their sweet scent. "They're lovely."

"So are you," he told her softly, and her pulse skittered.

"Crystal," Leona called from the oven. "I think the lasagnas are done. Would you please check them?"

"Excuse me," Crystal told Duane. Then she motioned toward the table. "Please have a seat."

Crystal hurried to the oven and peeked in on the two pans, which were bubbling. "They look *gut.*"

"The bread is ready too," Leona said. "I'll handle the food while you take care of your flowers." She gave Crystal a curious expression when she said the word *flowers*, but Crystal ignored her and searched for a vase.

While Leona and Alisha took care of the lasagnas and bread, Crystal focused on her gorgeous flowers. She filled a vase with water, set the flowers in it, and breathed in their scent once again as happiness twirled in her chest. She couldn't recall a time that Owen had brought her flowers during their relationship.

*Stop! Don't compare Duane to Owen!*

Crystal put the vase on the counter and then turned toward the table, where Leona and Alisha had set the bread and the lasagna. "I think that's everything."

"It looks and smells amazing," Duane commented as he sat to Kane's right.

Crystal moved to her usual seat, but Alisha touched her arm, stopping her.

"I'll sit with the *zwillingbopplin* and feed them," Alisha said. "You take my seat." She pointed to the empty chair next to Duane. "I like when I can sit next to *mei freinden* at school. So, I thought you might want to sit with your *freind* tonight."

Crystal's heart trilled with love for her sweet niece. *"Danki."*

*"Gern gschehne."* Alisha sank down between her baby sisters.

Crystal hurried around the table and sat between Duane and Jevon while Leona took her seat at the other end of the table.

After a silent prayer, the sound of utensils scraping plates, along with the murmur of conversations, filled the large kitchen.

Crystal picked up the basket of bread, took a piece, and then handed it to Duane. "Here you go."

*"Danki,"* he said, his leg brushing hers and sending a tingle through her. He took a piece of bread and then passed the basket to Kane.

"So, Duane," Kane began, his expression still stoic, "I saw you and your *sohns* were working for the Beilers' farm this week."

Duane scooped a large slice of lasagna onto his plate. "*Ya,* that's right, and we thank you for the recommendation. It was a great job. We took care of his *haus* and three barns." He leaned so close to Crystal that his arm brushed hers, sending her senses spinning. "May I serve you a piece?"

"*Ya.* Please." She nodded, hoping to keep her expression serene despite his closeness.

Her gaze flicked to Kane, and his lips pressed downward. If only she could figure out why her brother seemed so perturbed tonight. She wondered if he and Leona had a disagreement earlier, but she couldn't recall overhearing any cross words. Also, Leona hadn't acted as if she were upset this afternoon.

"I'm glad it worked out. Where are you working next?" Kane asked.

Duane began cutting up his piece of lasagna. "We have a job in Paradise that starts on Monday and then two in Ronks." He forked a piece of lasagna into his mouth, and after swallowing, he leaned over toward Crystal again. "Your lasagna is superb."

"I'm thrilled you're enjoying it." She glanced down toward the end of the other side of the table, where Alisha cut up some lasagna and handed it to the twins, who were each happily gnawing on pieces of garlic bread.

When Crystal turned toward Leona at the end of the table, she found her sister-in-law watching her with a somber expression. Perhaps her brother and sister-in-law had engaged in a disagreement earlier, and Crystal had been so engrossed in preparing supper that she'd missed it.

Duane and Kane continued to talk business during supper and dessert when Crystal and Alisha served lemon meringue pie and coffee.

After dessert, Kane directed Duane out to the porch, where they sat and talked. Crystal and Alisha cleaned up the kitchen, and Leona tended to the children, taking the twins and Hope to the downstairs bathroom for their baths.

"Let's clean this up quickly, okay?" Crystal told Alisha. She didn't want to risk a repeat of his last meal and miss a chance to have a decent conversation with Duane before he left. "We'll clear the table and then I'll start washing."

Alisha pointed toward the table. "*Ya*. Then I'll wipe the table and then dry the dishes."

"*Danki*." Crystal and Alisha worked together, and soon the dishes and serving platters were cleaned and stored, the table wiped, and the floor swept.

Crystal smiled at her niece when their work was complete. "*Danki* so much for always being such a great helper. Would you please see if your *mamm* needs you?"

While Alisha trotted toward the downstairs bathroom, Crystal took off her apron, which was splattered with dishwater, and hung it on the back of a kitchen chair before stepping out onto the porch, where Duane and Kane sat beside each other in rocking chairs.

Duane looked up at her.

"Would you like to go for a walk?" she asked.

Duane pushed himself up from the chair. "*Ya*, I would."

Kane shot her a pointed look, but she ignored him and started down the porch steps with Duane in tow.

"We can walk around the pasture," she suggested. "I'll show you my favorite spot."

Duane's expression was warm. "I'd love that."

They walked toward the fence, which showed its age and was

in desperate need of a good painting, with the paint chipped off the slats and broken and missing boards in other areas.

"I'm so glad you could come tonight," she said.

"Me too."

She pointed to a bench overlooking the pond on her brother's property. "This is my special spot. Would you like to sit?"

"After you, Crystal."

She sat down on the bench, and he lowered himself down beside her.

The late May sky was bright blue and dotted with white, fluffy clouds, and the air smelled like honeysuckle. The water shimmered in the light of the sun, and tiny bubbles appeared, evidence that the fish swam just below the surface. Crystal breathed in the glorious evening and smiled as contentment settled over her.

Duane leaned back on the bench and crossed his arms over his wide chest. "I can see why this is your favorite spot."

"I used to sit here a lot when I first moved in. I would work on needlepoint projects and pray while taking in God's beauty. I'd think about my parents and talk to them and God."

He tilted his head as he looked over at her. "You like to needlepoint?"

"I used to before Hope and the *zwillingbopplin* were born. Back then, I was able to find some time to work on projects. I even could sneak in some time here and there after Hope was born, but once the *zwillingbopplin* came, it became more difficult. Now I'm grateful when I get to work in the garden."

He studied her and she was almost certain she found pity in his eyes. She shifted her weight on the bench, itchy under his stare.

"You should make time for the things you love, Crystal."

"That's easier said than done." She crossed her feet at her ankles. "What about you? What do you do for fun?"

"Well, I love to read."

"Oh *ya*? What kind of books?"

"Mysteries mostly. I try to get to the library every couple of weeks and stock up on some new novels. I like to try authors I've never read. Other times, I tinker in my shop. I like to build toy trains out of pine and then donate them to the children's hospital during their toy drive at Christmastime. They're very amateurish, but I enjoy doing it."

"When did you start making trains?"

He shrugged and looked down. "I built a train for Tyler when he was little, and he loved it. It's just a little engine pulling two cars. Not very fancy. I also created one for Korey, and he enjoyed it too. Connie thought it was so wonderful that she encouraged me to make them as sort of a ministry. So, I've been donating them to different Christmas toy drives since the *buwe* were little." When he looked up at her, he gave a sheepish smile. "Honestly, the trains are very plain. I'm a much better roofer than carpenter, thank goodness."

She smiled. "I have a feeling you're very humble."

He looked out over the pond, and a comfortable silence filled the air around them.

"I love my flowers. *Danki* so much," she said.

"*Gern gschehne.* I wanted to bring something since you've spoiled *mei sohns* and me with your *appeditlich* snacks, but I couldn't decide what. So, I thought maybe you'd like some flowers. I just hoped that you liked wildflowers."

"They're perfect."

Duane rested his right ankle on his left knee. "Your *bruder-skinner* are a hoot. I enjoy your loud suppers."

"You do?" Crystal laughed. "I forget what it was like before the *zwillingbopplin* were born. The *haus* would be too quiet without them." She turned to face him on the bench. "Tell me more about your *sohns*. Were they rambunctious as *buwe*?"

He chuckled, and she relished the sound. "Oh yes—especially Tyler and Korey. They would constantly get into mischief."

"Like what?"

"Oh my." He shook his head. "One time, they were playing softball in one of our fields, and Korey hit the ball so hard that it shattered our *Englisher* neighbor's window."

"No! What happened?"

"Well, I found out when the neighbor came over and told me. Korey and Tyler were too afraid to tell me."

"You must have been so upset."

"You could say that." He patted his leg as he nodded. "Another time they went out sledding by pulling a sled behind Tyler's buggy. A police officer pulled them over and told them to stop before they got hit by a car."

"They were doing that on a main road?"

"Of course they were," he deadpanned.

"Oh no!"

"*Ya*, they were a handful. They're much better behaved now, and Jayden never got into the trouble that they did. He's always been a very compliant, thoughtful, and obedient young man. The older two were the ones that gave me ulcers when they were younger and out together with *freinden*."

"They sound like two peas in a pod. They must be very close."

He grimaced. "Sometimes."

"What do you mean?"

Duane picked at a loose piece of wood on the bench. "They

usually get along. I'm sure they would always have each other's backs when needed, but some days they bicker about everything. It really irritates Jayden too. They get under his skin when they argue about trivial things."

"Huh." Crystal nodded. "That's interesting. I never would have guessed that."

"Well, I'm glad you haven't witnessed it. Connie used to say it was because they were close in age and felt as if they were in competition. I do my best to never favor one *sohn* over the others, so I don't really understand why they feel that they're in competition. I hope they work through it. I never had siblings, and sometimes I remind them how blessed they are that they have each other."

"I understand. I'm grateful for *mei bruder*. It meant so much to have him when I lost my parents. I'm sorry you didn't have anyone."

He gave her a sad smile. "It's okay. I was always blessed with *gut freinden*."

Silence overcame them again as the sun began to set, and the pond reflected the beautiful gold-and-crimson beams of light that bathed the sky above them.

Duane's smile slipped a fraction of an inch, piquing her curiosity.

"Penny for your thoughts," she said softly.

He looked over at her, and when his lips thinned, she sucked in a breath.

"I need to be honest with you about something," he said.

# CHAPTER 19

CRYSTAL'S HANDS TREMBLED AS SHE TOOK IN DUANE'S SOMBER expression. She waited on what felt like pins and needles for him to finish his thought.

He swallowed and laughed, then cracked his knuckles. What was he so nervous to say?

"I'm too old for this," he finally said.

"Too old for what?"

"To be so *naerfich* while talking to a *schee maedel.*"

He thought she was pretty! Her heart swelled as hope crept back into her chest.

"I'm too old to play games too, so I'm going to lay it all out on the line." He took her hands in his. "Crystal, I care about you."

"I care about you too." Her voice was soft, and she relished the feeling of his skin against hers, sending a heat rushing through her body.

"So, the age difference doesn't bother you?"

She shook her head. "If it doesn't bother you, then it doesn't bother me."

"Oh, thank goodness." His bright smile returned. "I would like to date you."

197

She gasped as happy tears filled her eyes. "I would like that very much."

"*Gut.*" Then his smile faltered. "Problem is, I can tell your *bruder* doesn't approve of me. Have I done something to offend him?"

She shrugged. "I doubt that. He's been in a foul mood this evening, but I couldn't tell why."

"It's pretty obvious that it's because of me. He's just being an overprotective *bruder*, and I don't blame him."

"I'll talk to him." She bit her lower lip as she recalled their conversation in the buggy. "What about you and Tricia?"

His brow furrowed. "What do you mean?"

"Are you still considering her?"

"She's not the woman I want to see. You are."

"*Gut.*" She felt herself relax, but she still had one more concern. "And your *sohns* are okay with the idea of you dating?"

"They'll get used to it."

"That sounds like they aren't supportive."

His lips pressed into a thin line. "I haven't spoken to Tyler and Korey about it much yet, but Jayden is supportive—of you."

She sat up straight as anxiety nipped at her. "Are you sure? I don't want to be the reason why your *sohns* are upset with you."

"*Mei sohns* are going to have lives of their own soon. I feel the Lord led me to you, and I intend to enjoy the blessings I have." He traced a fingertip down her cheek, sending a quiver of heat through her. "I'm so grateful I met you. I was certain I'd never feel a connection to another *maedel* after I lost Connie. You brought my heart back to life."

She smiled. "I'm so grateful to hear you say that."

"You have no idea how special you are. You're sweet, beautiful, thoughtful, and hardworking. And I admire your dedication to your family. I'm honored to have the chance to get to know you better." He leaned down and brushed his lips over her cheek, sending her stomach into a wild swirl.

Then he stood and held his hand out to her. "We should probably get back to the *haus* soon."

Holding hands, they started back toward the house together. As they approached the back porch, Crystal spotted a horse and buggy in the driveway.

"Is that yours?" she asked.

"No." Duane pointed toward the barn. "Nate and I put my horse in the barn. My buggy is over there."

"I wonder who's visiting this late in the evening."

They continued walking, and soon Crystal's eyes focused on a man standing on the porch with his back to her while talking to Kane. The man was a few inches shorter than Kane and had dark hair under his straw hat.

When the man turned around and his face came into clear view, the air rushed from Crystal's lungs. Panicking, she released Duane's hand.

"No," she muttered.

Concern seemed to be etched on Duane's face. *"Was iss letz?"*

"That's my ex-boyfriend."

Duane looked at Owen and then at her once again. "That's Owen?"

"*Ya*. I have no idea why he's here."

Duane held his hand back out to her. "Let's go find out."

When she threaded her fingers with his, she felt her courage swell. Together they walked to the porch, where Owen divided a look between her and Duane, his face filled with confusion or perhaps amusement.

Duane held his free hand out to her ex-boyfriend. "Hi, I'm Duane Bontrager." Although his tone was pleasant, Crystal saw his eyes narrow for a fraction of a second.

Owen shook his hand. "Owen Stoltzfus. Nice to meet you."

"You too." Duane looked past him toward Kane. "*Danki* for a nice evening."

Kane gave him a curt nod. "*Gut nacht.*"

Then Duane turned toward Crystal. "Would you please walk me to my buggy?"

"Of course." Crystal reached up onto the porch and grabbed a small flashlight from the railing and stuck it in her pocket.

She and Duane walked in silence to the barn, the flashlight guiding their way. Crystal stood by as Duane hitched up his horse, her temper rising as she pondered why Owen had come to her house.

She kept glancing toward the porch where Owen and Kane continued to talk. It didn't make sense that Owen would come to visit Kane. Something seemed off about the scene. What was she missing?

She kicked a rock with the toe of her shoe, hoping to release some of her irritation.

"Are you going to be okay?" Duane asked after his horse and buggy were readied for his journey home.

"I think so." She sighed. "I'm sorry the evening didn't end on the right note."

He smiled and touched her shoulder. "I had a fantastic time." He took her hand in his. "I can't wait to see you again."

"How about I bring a meal to your *haus* next time?"

"That sounds perfect."

"Since tomorrow is an off-Sunday, we're going to church in Leona's *schweschder*'s district. How about I call you, and we'll arrange a time for next week?"

"I'd love that." He gave her hand a gentle squeeze and then climbed into the buggy. "Have a *gut* night, Crystal. I look forward to hearing from you."

She waved as his horse and buggy moved down the rock driveway, past the house, and toward the road, his taillights blinking until they disappeared into the night.

For a moment, Crystal felt as if she were floating on a cloud. Had she really just become Duane's girlfriend? She was so happy her heart might burst!

She crashed back to earth, however, as soon as she turned back toward the porch. Owen was still there, talking to her brother.

Crystal spoke to neither Kane nor Owen as she hurried through the back door and mudroom to the kitchen, where Leona sat at the table flipping through a catalog. The house was so quiet that she assumed the children were already in bed.

"Why is he here?" Crystal asked.

Leona looked up at her, and her brow puckered. "Who?"

"Owen." Crystal pointed toward the porch. "Why is he talking to Kane?"

"I have no idea. But you owe *me* an explanation."

Crystal crossed her arms in front of her. "About what?"

Leona pointed to the seat across form her. "Sit. Tell me the truth about Duane."

Crystal dropped into a chair, resting her elbow on the table and her chin on her palm. "We like each other, and I invited him for supper so that we could spend more time together. And . . . he asked me if I'd like to officially start dating him."

"He's your boyfriend?" Leona scrunched her nose as if smelling something foul.

Crystal sat up straight. "Why do you say it like that?"

"He's nearly fifty, Crystal. He probably just needs a *fraa* to take care of his *haus* while he runs his business."

Crystal opened and closed her mouth as she studied her sister-in-law. "That's not true. We care about each other and have a lot in common. He's lost his *fraa*, and I lost my parents. He's handsome and easy to talk to."

Just then the back door opened and shut with a loud bang, and Kane appeared in the doorway.

Crystal jumped up from her chair and wagged a finger at her brother. "Why was he here?"

"Calm down." Kane held his hands up. "Owen is just looking for work. He called me earlier and asked me if I needed help."

She snorted. "And are you planning to hire him?"

"You've seen what a state of disrepair this farm is in, and I haven't had time to take care of it myself. Owen says he'll fix the fence, the barn doors, and the chicken coop. Then he'll paint the barns, the *daadihaus*, and the *haus*. He's also going to pitch in with the cows. I've needed the help for a long time, and he needs the work. We help each other in this community. It's just a job. That's it. Just avoid him, and you'll be fine."

Crystal folded her arms over her middle. "That's really something else, Kane. You're telling me to be an adult, but you didn't even have the decency to ask me how I'd feel about my ex-boyfriend coming to work here. Did it even occur to you that this might be uncomfortable for me?"

"I'm sorry, but I thought you could handle it."

"I'm a part of this family. Don't my feelings matter?"

"*Ya*, of course they do." Kane sighed. "You're right. I should have asked you first. I'm sorry."

"And another thing," Crystal said. "Why didn't you tell me Owen was already in town before I went to visit Jeannie?"

Kane shook his head. "It wasn't deliberate. I just didn't think of it."

"Seeing him every day will not be pleasant for me, Kane. I wish you'd thought of that."

Kane's lips puckered. "I'm sorry, and you're right, but I've already hired him. Let's see how it goes. If it's too painful, then I'll let him go. Is that fair?"

Crystal stared at him, her lips pursed. Then she turned and started for the stairs. "*Gut nacht*," she muttered.

"Hold on," Kane called after her.

She stilled and slammed her eyes shut. "What?"

"Please come back here."

She spun to face him.

"I assume since you were holding Duane's hand when you walked back from the pond that you're dating him." Kane's expression remained impassive.

Crystal nodded. "*Ya*, that's true."

"I'm not *froh* about it."

"I didn't ask for your permission, and I don't have to. I'm a grown woman."

Kane's lips worked for a moment. "I'll say it again, Crystal. I think he's too old for you."

"I think that's my decision to make."

Leona's eyebrows shot up toward her hairline as she divided a look between Crystal and Kane.

Her brother was silent for a moment, but she could almost

hear the wheels turning in his brain. "Why wouldn't you want a man closer to your age?"

"We don't choose who we love," Crystal said. "God guides us toward that person."

Leona shook her head. "He already has *kinner*, Crystal. He probably won't want more."

"Are you both done? I'd like to shower and go to bed. We have church in the morning." Crystal's body shook with her frustration.

Kane nodded, seemingly resigned, and Crystal padded upstairs. She'd hoped to wash her irritation down the shower drain, but she continued to fume over her brother's behavior while she stared up through the darkness toward the ceiling. Why were Kane and Leona so resistant? None of this made any sense.

Then she closed her eyes and smiled as memories of how Duane had touched and kissed her cheek filled her mind.

She rolled to her side and opened her heart to God:

*Lord, thank you for bringing Duane into my life. Please help our families accept our relationship and help us grow closer through our love of you.*

Then she let happier thoughts lull her to sleep. She felt her body relax just as one of the twins started to sob.

Sighing, Crystal sat up, flipped on her lantern, and carried it to the twins' room. Another long, sleepless night awaited her.

Duane grinned, feeling like a smitten teenager as he walked from the barn toward his house later that evening. He looked up at the stars twinkling in the sky, certain that they were rejoicing with him.

He couldn't stop his mind from replaying how it had felt to hold her hand, touch her face, and kiss her cheek. His pulse trotted as he recalled the feel of her warm, soft skin.

The storm door creaked in protest as he wrenched it open. He stepped into the mudroom and kicked off his boots before setting them under the bench. Then he hung his straw hat on a peg by the back door beside his sons' hats and set his flashlight on the bench.

A murmur of voices floated in from the kitchen, and when he walked through the doorway, he found his three sons sitting at the kitchen table. The room was illuminated by a lantern on the table and another sitting on the counter. His three sons looked up at him, and while Jayden's expression was blank, Tyler frowned and Korey scowled.

"Am I late or something?" Duane joked.

Tyler rubbed his clean-shaven chin. "How'd it go?"

"Did you ask her?" Jayden inquired.

Duane leaned back against the counter, facing them. "It went well, and *ya*, I asked her." His heart felt light as he smiled. Then his smile faded. This wasn't only about his happiness. He had to think of how his sons would feel about this too.

"Asked her what?" Korey divided a suspicious look between Duane and Jayden.

Tyler's eyes narrowed for a moment and then recovered. "You asked her out?"

Duane nodded.

Korey stood. "Are you kidding me? You're *dating* again?" His voice echoed around the kitchen.

"Hold on now." Duane took a step toward him, holding his hands up. "Calm down."

"Don't tell me to calm down." Korey's words were measured,

his eyes narrowed to slits. "I thought you two were just *freinden*, but now you're dating? Aren't you moving a little fast, *Dat*?"

"No one is getting married," said Duane. "Crystal and I are just getting to know each other, and we'll see how it goes."

Korey walked over to him and lifted his chin in defiance. "And what if we don't like this new development in your life?"

"Let's talk about it then," Duane said. "Why are you upset?"

Korey's nostrils flared and his lips worked, but no words escaped his mouth.

"Tell me how you're feeling, Korey," Duane encouraged him.

Korey turned toward Tyler, who looked down at the tabletop as Jayden folded his hands on the table, his expression open.

Duane held his breath, but his sons remained silent. "I'm listening, so just talk to me. We're a family, and we'll work through this together."

"If I have to explain why I'm upset that you're dating, then it's not worth it to even discuss it. It should be obvious to you, *Dat*." Korey shook his head.

"Why are you so angry, Korey?" Duane worked to keep his words even, despite the frustration with his older sons' silence. "You had to know that someday I would start dating again. Jayden told me that your *mamm* asked you three to accept when I decided to move on and get married."

"Don't try to make me feel guilty." Korey raised a shaky finger at Duane. "You won't even talk about her, so don't throw that back in my face!"

"What do you mean?"

"I talk about *Mamm* all the time. I bring her up, but you just look away or remain silent. You're trying to forget her!" His voice croaked as his dark eyes sparkled with tears.

Duane held his hands up, hoping to calm his middle son. "That's not true."

"*Ya*, it is. You act as if *Mamm* never existed."

"No, I don't." Duane pursed his lips as his son's words stung him like a swarm of wasps. As much as he had hoped to work through this tonight, it seemed that Korey was too upset. He would try again another day. "Go get some rest. I think you need to calm down and cool off. *Gut nacht.*"

Korey and Jayden pulled their flashlights from their pockets before heading to their bedrooms, but Tyler lingered by the table.

"What is it, Tyler?" Duane asked, hopeful that at least one of his sons might want to talk.

"Don't you think now is a bad time for you to start dating?"

"What do you mean?"

"We're trying to grow our business, *Dat*," Tyler said. "You need to focus on that and not on a girlfriend."

Duane shook his head. "I don't think my dating will interfere with the business. You can trust me to make sure we're on track with our work and have enough to sustain us." He studied his son's hard expression. "Is there anything else you want to discuss?"

"No," Tyler muttered before heading toward the stairs.

Duane took a deep breath, rested his hands on the edge of the counter, and dipped his head as his thoughts tumbled through his mind.

"Lord, I don't know how to do this. Dating with three grown *sohns* is uncharted territory for me . . . Help me find the path forward because I certainly do not know the way."

Standing up straight, Duane flipped off one lantern, grabbed the other, and padded toward his room, hoping he'd find a way to turn off his jumbled thoughts and find some rest.

# CHAPTER 20

CRYSTAL HUNG A PAIR OF HER NEPHEW'S TROUSERS ON THE clothesline Monday morning. While laundry was a tedious task, she enjoyed the solace of the late-May morning with the warm sun on her face and the happy sounds of the birds singing in nearby trees.

The colorful array of shirts, aprons, dresses, and trousers flapped in the gentle breeze as a dog barked in the distance. She retrieved two more pairs of trousers from the basket and pulled clothespins from her apron just as the *clip-clop* of hooves and the whir of buggy wheels sounded in the distance.

As she pushed the clothesline out toward the tree where it was attached, a horse and buggy moved up the rock driveway toward the house. Her heart did a funny little flip as the horse halted, and she waited for the driver to emerge from the buggy.

She hoped for a moment Duane was stopping by for a surprise visit. But Duane had said he had a job in Ronks today, so the odds of him being in Gordonville were slim to none.

The door opened, and Crystal rolled her eyes at the sight.

"*Gude mariye,*" Owen called to her.

Ignoring him, she returned to her task, grabbing one of her nephew's shirts and securing it on the line with two clothespins.

She and Kane had avoided the subjects of both Owen and Duane yesterday, but she was still hurt by his decision to hire her ex-boyfriend. She couldn't imagine having to see him every day when her feelings for him were so muddled.

Out of the corner of her eye, she spotted Owen walking toward her. She kept working, hoping he'd take the hint and head out toward the barn so she could avoid looking at his handsome face and into his bright-blue eyes that reminded her of her hopes for a future with him.

"Crystal," he said. "Could we please talk?"

She craned her neck over her shoulder and peered out toward the steps, where he stood watching her, his expression hesitant. "I can't stop you from talking, but I have chores to do."

She glanced down at the basket, grateful she was almost done. She grabbed two more shirts and turned back to the line while his heavy footsteps climbed the stairs.

"I'm sorry for hurting you. I was self-centered and terrible to you. I never should have given you an ultimatum. Instead, I should have stayed here and helped you care for your *dat*." He paused. "And I'm sorry about your *dat*. I should have come back for the funeral, but I was too focused on my own needs to realize how much you needed me."

With her lips contorted and her eyes narrowed, she pivoted toward him. "Who coached you to say those things to me?"

He winced as if she'd struck him. "What's that supposed to mean?"

She took a step toward him, her body vibrating with her frustration. "There's no way you could have figured out on your own how much you messed up. So, who was it? Was it Jeannie?" She began counting the names off on her fingers. "Your *mamm*? Your *dat*? Or one of your three older *bruders*?"

"No one told me to say it." His voice and his eyes seemed to be full of humiliation, confusing her.

She turned back to the laundry basket, her hands shaking as she picked up one of the twins' dresses.

"Will you please forgive me?"

"I forgave you a long time ago." She hung the dress on the line and picked up four more, working as quickly as her hands would allow her.

"Oh, praise God." The relief in his voice was palpable. "So, maybe we can start over."

She hung the dress on the clothesline and then faced him. "What do you mean by that?"

When he stepped toward her, she took a step back. "Letting you go was the biggest regret of my life." He placed a hand over his heart. "I still love you, Crystal."

"You love me?" she squeaked. "That's rich! Is that why you disappeared for five years?" She held her hand up, the palm facing him. "You ran your business into the ground, and I know that's the real reason you're back."

He huffed out a breath. "Let me explain. I didn't run the business into the ground. My cousin did. We were building garages, and it was going well. I actually believed we had a future. Then Mervin started booking jobs and not showing up. I was on my own running a small crew. Soon I realized I didn't have enough money to pay my crew and myself. It turned out that Merv was misusing the money. He was spending it on alcohol and gambling, and he wouldn't stop. We lost everything."

"And now you're back with nothing to show for it."

His shoulders sagged. "It took losing everything to realize that I left my heart here."

She shook her head. "So, if your cousin hadn't run your business into the ground, then you wouldn't have realized you made a mistake when you left me?"

"That's not what I mean, Crystal." He looked pained. "My words aren't coming out right."

"So what do you mean then?" Her hands trembled.

He took a deep breath. "I know I messed up, and if I could fix the past, I would. I can't do that, but I can work toward a better future." He reached for her hands, and she took a step back. "I'm sorry for hurting you and for disrespecting your *dat*. I'm sorry for not being here when you needed me. And I promise right now that I will work the rest of my life to show you how much you mean to me."

Speechless, she could hardly breathe.

"I know you're angry with me, and you have every right to be. But I'm asking you to just take a moment and recall all the *gut* times we had. Don't you remember the fun we had with our *freinden*—hiking, fishing, ice skating, and just laughing together?"

She licked her lips as memories tumbled through her mind.

"We can get that back again if you give me a chance to prove to you that I've grown up and I'm ready to be the man you deserve."

She shook her head. "Owen, I'm not that naïve *maedel* you remember. I've learned a lot during the past five years, and one thing I've learned is to not pin my hopes and dreams on you." She pointed to the laundry basket. "Now, if you'll excuse me, I have chores to finish."

When Crystal picked up the last two small dresses, she expected to hear his footfalls stomping down the stairs, but instead, she only heard the sound of the birds singing and muffled voices coming from inside the house.

While trying to stop her joyful memories with him from taunting her, she hung the last two dresses on the line, pushed it out, picked up the empty basket, and balanced it on her hip before facing her ex-boyfriend once again.

"What else do you want me to say, Owen?" she kept her words measured.

"I just . . . I wish you'd give me another chance. Let me prove to you that I'll treat you right this time."

"No." She shook her head, and when she tried to move past him, he stepped to the side, blocking her.

"Please, just . . ." He motioned around the farm. "Is raising someone else's kids truly going to satisfy you? If you give me a chance, maybe I can make you *froh* and give you the family you deserve. I'm saving money, and I'll find us a *haus*. We can get married and fill it with *kinner* and happiness."

She drew in a ragged breath. "Why did you want to work for *mei bruder*? Is it just so you could try to get me back? If so, then you're wasting your time." She nodded toward the house. "Now please excuse me."

He cast his eyes down, looking defeated, then took one step to the right.

Crystal moved past him and made a beeline toward the back door. She reached for the knob on the storm door and wrenched it open.

"Tell me you're not dating that man," Owen quipped.

Frozen in place, Crystal closed her eyes.

*Lord, give me strength.*

Then she peeked over her shoulder and met his smug expression. "Duane is a *gut* man."

Owen scoffed and then jogged down the steps toward the barn.

Crystal continued into the house, where she disappeared into the utility room and dropped the basket on the floor with a clatter before looking up at the ceiling and letting out a groan. She massaged her temples where a headache brewed. Then she tried to get ahold of herself.

She couldn't allow Owen to hurt her again, no matter what he said to her. She was strong! She couldn't let anyone see how much his words irritated yet also tempted her. When he spoke of their past, her heart had clung to those precious memories, longing for the comfort of them. But that was a long time ago. Even if he truly cared for her and wanted to make amends, she was wiser now. Maybe he had changed, but so had she.

After silently counting to ten, Crystal stepped out into the kitchen, just as Leona rushed in, rubbing her distended belly while working to catch her breath.

"I thought I heard something fall. I hurried down from the *zwillingbopplin*'s room." Leona studied her wide-eyed. "Are you okay?"

"*Ya.* Sorry." Crystal crossed to the window and stared out toward the barn, expecting to see Kane and Owen but finding the area empty.

"*Was iss letz?*"

Crystal faced her. "Owen is here."

"Just take Kane's advice and ignore him." Leona shook her head and opened the refrigerator, pulling out the pitcher of water.

"Well, it's a bit difficult to ignore someone who won't stop talking to you."

"You'll need to work on it then. This will make you stronger." Leona poured two glasses of water and then put the pitcher back in the refrigerator.

Crystal suppressed an eye roll.

Leona motioned toward the glasses. "Have a drink."

*"Danki."* While she took a sip of the cool water, Crystal rested her eyes on the beautiful vase of flowers that Duane had brought her on Saturday. The vibrant, colorful wildflowers looked as if they were smiling at her and reminding her of all the wonderful blessings she had in her life that Owen could never steal from her—especially Duane's affection.

A cozy feeling that reminded her of being wrapped in Duane's quilt overcame her as she imagined seeing him again. It couldn't happen soon enough!

Smiling, Crystal pivoted to face the calendar hanging on the wall. "I'm going to take supper over to Duane's *haus* this week. Which day would work the best for you to handle supper without me?"

"I-I suppose Thursday," Leona said, looking dumbfounded.

"Thursday it is. I'll leave Duane a message, and if it's okay, I'll go to the market tomorrow and buy all of the supplies, so I won't take away from our groceries here. I'll use the money from my savings account." Crystal opened her favorite cookbook and began flipping through it. "Now, what should I make?"

"You really care for him, don't you?"

Crystal laughed as she met her sister-in-law's stunned gaze. "I already told you that."

Leona's expression became worried as she rubbed her large belly.

Later that evening, Duane dialed the voicemail and began writing down messages. There was one message for Korey and three from customers asking for estimates.

When the final message started, Duane poised his pen, ready to write down the pertinent information.

"Hi, this message is for Duane," a sweet feminine voice said. "This is Crystal."

With a grin, Duane sat up taller as happiness seeped through him. She'd been on his mind all day, and a message from her was just what he'd needed.

"Saturday night we talked about getting together for supper at your *haus* this week," she continued. "I was wondering if Thursday would be okay. If so, then please leave me a message. Also, let me know what time is best. I look forward to hearing from you. Have a *gut nacht*."

Duane replayed the message, enjoying the sound of her voice. Then he dialed her number, and after several rings, Kane's voice filled the receiver. "You have reached the Glick family. Please leave us a message. Thank you."

"Hi," Duane said. "I'm calling for Crystal. It's Duane. *Danki* for your message. It made my day. Thursday is perfect for supper. How does six o'clock sound? I look forward to seeing you. Take care. *Gut nacht*."

He hung up the phone and couldn't wipe the smile off his face as he hurried back into the kitchen, where Korey was setting the table.

Jayden stood at the stove, stirring pasta while the meatballs and tomato sauce he'd prepared last night warmed up in the pot beside him. "Dinner will be ready in a few minutes."

"*Danki*." Duane crossed the kitchen and washed his hands at the sink. "Where's Tyler?"

Korey put the utensils at the last place setting. "He'll be down soon."

Duane handed Korey his message. "This is for you."

"Oh?" Korey stared down at the piece of paper. "Michelle called?"

Tyler entered the kitchen rubbing his hands together. "Those meatballs smell divine. When are we eating?"

"As soon as the pasta is done," Jayden said from the stove.

Tyler rubbed his flat abdomen. "I feel like I haven't eaten in a week."

"Why don't you fill our glasses instead of whining?" Korey suggested as he folded a napkin under a fork.

Tyler seemed to ignore his brother's snide tone as he took the water pitcher from the refrigerator and did what he was told.

Duane was impressed. Maybe they would have a pleasant meal tonight without his two oldest sons' bickering.

After Jayden dumped the spaghetti into the colander in the sink, Duane helped him bring the meatballs and tomato sauce, salad, a jar of dressing, and the pasta to the table.

After the silent prayer, they began filling their plates with the delicious food.

"So, tell us, Kore." Tyler beamed as he scooped a pile of pasta onto his plate. "What did Michelle say in her message?"

Korey spooned meatballs and sauce onto his pasta. "Not much. She just said hi and asked me to call her."

"That's a great start." Jayden placed some salad onto his plate and then passed the bowl to Duane.

Korey pointed toward the counter. "Who were the other messages from?"

"New customers," Duane said. "I need to call them back and set up times for estimates."

"Fantastic," Tyler said. "We're staying busy these days. I told you that those ads would work. My business plan is already a success."

They spent the remainder of supper talking about the business, and once their plates were clean, Duane cleared his throat. "I wanted to let you know we're going to have company for supper on Thursday."

"Who's coming?" Jayden asked.

"Crystal is going to bring us a meal. Isn't that nice?" Duane held his breath as his three sons looked over at him.

"What is she going to make?" Jayden asked.

Tyler set his fork down on his plate, pressing his lips together.

"I'll most likely have plans," Korey said with a glower. "I'm going to call Michelle back and see if I can go to her *haus* for supper on Thursday."

Jayden pointed at Korey. "You need to grow up."

Pushing his chair back, Korey stood. "I'm going to go take care of the animals." After setting his plate and glass on the counter, he walked toward the back door.

"I'll go help him." Tyler set his dishes on the counter and then followed him.

"Wait," Duane said, and his two older sons stopped and faced him.

While Korey glowered, Tyler's lips formed a flat line.

Duane held his hands up. "Instead of storming off, why won't we talk about this?"

"What's there to say if you've already made up your mind?" Korey spat the words at him before spinning and marching out the door with his older brother in tow.

The door slammed behind them, and Duane pinched the bridge of his nose.

"Just give them time," Jayden said.

Duane shook his head. "I just hope Thursday isn't a disaster."

"It won't be," Jayden said. "I'll make sure of it."

Duane smiled, grateful for his youngest son.

# CHAPTER 21

*"Aenti!"* Alisha hurried into the kitchen late Thursday afternoon. "I can't get the *zwillingbopplin* to stop crying. I need your help."

The sound of the twins screaming in the family room filled the kitchen. Just then, the oven timer buzzed, announcing that Crystal's pork roast was ready.

Crystal grabbed two pot holders, opened the oven, and pulled out the roast. "I'm sorry, Alisha, but I can't help you. I have to get this food ready to take to Duane's *haus*. Where's your *mamm*?"

"She went to her room to lie down. Her stomach hurts."

Anxiety pressed down on Crystal's shoulders. Nothing had gone right today. Leona had awoken with a bad headache and spent most of the day resting on the sofa, while Crystal had made breakfast, took care of the twins, cooked lunch, cleaned, and then prepared two suppers—one to take to Duane's house and one for her family. While Crystal understood that Leona had to follow the doctor's directives for her health and her unborn babies' safety, she was also overwhelmed with all of her chores.

Now she had thirty minutes to finish preparing both suppers and get ready before Kane's driver arrived to take her to Duane's house. Since Leona had taken to her bed, it seemed Crystal couldn't leave.

Disappointment grabbed her by the throat. She had looked forward to this since Monday, and now everything was falling apart. She pressed her lips together as reality hit her in the face. She needed to call and cancel with Duane now.

But first—she had to tend to her crying nieces.

"Can you stir the stew and the mixed veggies, Alisha?" Crystal said.

"Yes, since you're the only one who can calm Evie." Alisha pointed to the doorway.

Crystal hurried into the family room, where the twins stood up in the play yard, their little faces red as ripe tomatoes while they screamed.

"*Ach, mei liewes,*" Crystal cooed. "Don't cry." She lifted Evie into her arms and balanced her on her hip while reaching down and rubbing Morgan's back.

Morgan soothed herself by sucking her thumb while Evie buried her face in Crystal's neck and sobbed. Morgan sat down in the play yard and picked up a board book.

When Crystal felt a tug at her skirt, she turned to where Hope stood staring up at her. "*Ya?*"

"*Aenti,* my tummy hurts," Hope whined, hugging her arms to her middle.

Crystal sighed. Her dream of seeing Duane tonight had now fully dissolved. "Let's walk to the bathroom."

Holding her hand out to Hope, she led her to the bathroom and told her to sit. Then she balanced Evie on her hip and waited outside the door.

"Hope," Crystal said through the door. "I'm going to check on supper. Call me when you're done."

"Okay." Hope's voice trembled.

Crystal hurried into the kitchen, where Alisha set dishes and utensils out on the table. "What can I do to help?"

Alisha opened her mouth to respond just as Kane walked into the kitchen from the mudroom.

"Trevor is going to be in here in fifteen minutes to pick you up to take you to Duane's. Aren't you getting ready to leave?" Kane asked Crystal.

Crystal shook her head. "I don't think I can go."

"Why?"

"Leona isn't feeling well. She went to lie down, which she needed to do." Crystal looked down at Evie, who rested her head on Crystal's shoulder. "Evie was upset, and Hope is in the bathroom with a stomachache."

Kane hesitated. "What do you need to do before you can leave?"

"I have to pack up the food and get changed."

"Go. I'll take Evie and check on Hope." Kane held his arms out to Evie. "Alisha can start packing up your food."

Stunned, Crystal stared at her brother. "Are you sure?"

Kane's reddish-brown eyebrows lifted as he pointed toward the doorway. "Yes, go on!"

Crystal handed Evie to him and then rushed upstairs and changed into a rose-colored dress and fresh black apron. She then checked her hair and prayer covering before hurrying back down the stairs. She found Kane bouncing Evie in his arms while he stood outside the bathroom.

"Is Hope okay?" she asked.

Kane kissed Evie's strawberry-blond head. "She'll be fine."

"I can still cancel," Crystal offered.

Kane shook his head. "I got this."

"What if I dropped the food off and then had Trevor bring me back?"

Her brother pressed his lips together. "I promise you I will take *gut* care of the *kinner* while you're gone."

"I know you will." Crystal hurried into the kitchen.

Alisha pointed to a tote bag sitting on a kitchen chair. "I packed up the pork roast, mashed potatoes, and vegetables before stacking them in the bag. Don't forget your lemon cake. It's on the counter."

"You're a lifesaver." She hugged her niece. "Now, you're all set to serve the stew with the biscuits I made earlier?"

"I'm all set, *Aenti*."

*"Danki."* When the sound of a car engine rumbled outside the house, Crystal picked up the tote bag and grabbed the cake saver. "My ride is here. See you later."

"Have fun and tell Duane we said hi," Alisha called as Crystal rushed to the door.

After a short ride, Trevor Davis's van steered into the driveway of a two-story, brick home with a small front porch. A barn sat behind it, along with a long, cinder block building.

"Thank you so much for the ride," Crystal said as she pushed open the back door. "I'll call you when I'm ready to come home."

"No problem. Have a nice time."

Crystal hefted the large tote bag onto her shoulder, balanced the cake in her arms, and then climbed out of the back of the van, shut the door, and walked up the brick path to the porch. She lifted her hand to knock just as the door opened, and Duane walked out onto the porch.

"Crystal, hi!" He held his hands out. "Let me help you."

She handed him the heavy tote bag. *"Danki."*

"How are things at the farm?" He held the door open and motioned for her to walk inside.

"It's been a challenging day. I almost didn't come."

"Why?"

She stepped into a large family room with a sofa, two wing chairs, and a recliner, along with a coffee table, two end tables, and two propane lamps.

"Leona didn't feel well. Her doctor is concerned about her blood pressure, so she has to take it easy—especially when she gets headaches. The goal is to get her *zwillingbopplin* as close to their due date as possible. So she had to rest, and I had no help with the *kinner*. I had to do my chores, cook, and prepare a meal to bring here as well as supper for my family. I thought I wasn't going to make it since Alisha can only do so much to help me." She shook her head while gripping the cake saver. "Then Kane came in and surprised me by offering to help."

Duane's smile was wide. "I'm so glad he did. I've been looking forward to this since you called."

Duane touched her cheek, and she enjoyed the feel of his skin on hers.

"I'm so grateful that you took the time to cook for me and came to see me. I think you deserve time away from your family." Then he grinned. "And I'll admit it—I'm selfish. I don't want you to go home." He beckoned her toward the doorway. "Let's enjoy this fantastic meal together. It smells heavenly."

"I hope you and your *sohns* like pork roast."

"We love it," Duane said.

They stepped into the kitchen, where Jayden set plates and utensils out on the table.

"Hi, Crystal," Jayden said as he arranged the fourth place setting.

"Hello, Jayden." She set the cake on the counter and then turned toward Duane. "The table is only set for four?"

Duane put the bag on the counter beside the cake. "Korey has plans tonight."

"Oh." Her smile wobbled. "We'll miss him."

Jayden gathered four drinking glasses from a nearby cabinet. "He's eating at Michelle's *haus*."

"Oh." Crystal rubbed her hands together. "Is she his girlfriend?"

Jayden arranged the glasses on the table. "Not yet, but I have a feeling he'll ask her soon."

"That's exciting." Crystal looked around the kitchen. "Your home is lovely. Have you lived here long?"

"*Danki*. Connie and I moved in just after we were married." Duane began pulling the containers out of the bag.

Crystal leaned over. "Please, let me help you." Then she clucked her tongue. "Oh, no, I forgot the salad. What a stressful day!"

"We have some salad left over from last night. I'll get it out." Jayden opened the refrigerator and began rooting around.

Duane opened a cabinet and pulled out a serving platter and a few bowls. "How about we put your amazing meal out on serving dishes?"

While Crystal and Duane worked on serving the meal, Jayden gathered up a salad and dressing.

Duane stood by the table once the food was ready. "Now we just need your *bruder*."

"He said he was just going to change after taking care of the animals. Do you want me to check on him?" Jayden asked.

A peculiar look came over Duane's face, and an unspoken conversation seemed to pass between father and son. "No, I'll handle it." He turned toward Crystal. "Excuse me. I'll be right back."

"Take your time," Crystal said.

Duane disappeared around the corner and then heavy footfalls sounded in a stairway.

Crystal smoothed her hands down her apron and smiled at Jayden. "How's work?"

"*Gut.*" He gestured toward an empty chair. "Why don't we sit?"

She sat down across from Jayden. "So, the job in Ronks is going well?"

"It is." Jayden talked about their current project, roofing a strip mall, while muffled voices sounded from upstairs.

A few moments later, heavy footsteps echoed in a stairwell once again and then Duane entered the kitchen.

Tyler sauntered in behind him, his expression grim as he met Crystal's gaze. "Hello. *Danki* for supper."

"*Gern gschehne.* I was *froh* to bring it." She smiled, but when he looked away, she felt a pit in her stomach as the truth hit her—Tyler didn't approve of her visit.

"All right." Duane clapped his hands. "Let's enjoy this fantastic meal that Crystal prepared for us." He sat down at the end of the table to her left while Tyler took a seat beside Jayden.

After a silent prayer, they began filling their plates with the food she had prepared.

As they ate, Crystal tried to peek across the table to discern if the boys were enjoying the meal. Jayden smiled, seemingly contented, while Tyler mostly stared down at his plate.

Her heart felt heavy. Although Duane had admitted that his sons wouldn't accept their relationship, she had still hoped to win their favor. How could they move forward as a family if Duane's sons didn't approve of her? How could Crystal cope as a step-mother without her stepsons' love and respect?

Crystal cleared her throat. "So, Jayden was telling me that you're busy roofing a large strip mall in Ronks. That must be a big project for you all."

"*Ya*, that's true." Duane lifted his glass of water. "We'll have it finished up tomorrow."

"*Wunderbaar.*"

Jayden pointed his fork at his plate. "This is *appeditlich.*"

"*Danki.*" Crystal sipped her water and looked over at Tyler, who continued to stare at his plate. When she glanced at Duane, he frowned, shaking his head. She gave him a reassuring expression.

"How's Hope doing?" Jayden asked.

Crystal cut up her roast. "She was feeling a little under the weather when I left, but I'm sure she'll be all right."

"Oh no." Jayden's expression flickered with alarm. "What was wrong?"

"She just had an upset tummy. Nothing unusual for little ones."

Jayden smiled. "She's a character. I imagine she's never met a stranger."

"That's true," Crystal said.

They spent the remainder of the meal discussing Crystal's nieces and nephews as well as their upcoming jobs. Jayden and Duane participated in the discussion while Tyler kept his focus on his food.

After drinking coffee and eating lemon cake for dessert, Crystal, Duane, and Jayden started cleaning up the table.

Tyler carried his dishes to the counter and then turned to Crystal. "*Danki* for bringing supper and dessert. It was *appeditlich.*"

She smiled at him. "*Gern gschehne,* Tyler. I'm glad you joined us."

"Excuse me," he said, giving his father a look. Then he walked straight out of the kitchen and up the stairs.

Duane sighed and shook his head as he picked up the platter of leftover pork roast and carried it to the counter.

Crystal's posture sagged and she once again regretted bringing supper to Duane's family tonight. Though Tyler hadn't been rude toward her, she could feel the rift between Duane and his son. It broke her heart to think she was responsible for it. Did this mean she and Duane could never have a future? That they could never be a family?

Jayden flipped the water on in the sink and then faced his father. "Why don't you and Crystal visit on the porch while I clean up the kitchen?"

Duane looked relieved. "*Danki,* Jayden." Then he took Crystal's hand. "Let's refill our *kaffi* cups and go outside."

# CHAPTER 22

"It's such a lovely night." Duane gazed out toward his neighbor's large pasture as the sun began to set, painting the sky in vivid streaks of red, orange, and yellow. The gorgeous colors seemed a fitting backdrop for another evening spent with his beautiful girlfriend at his side.

He breathed in the warm, clean air, enjoying the scent of new earth and animals. He relished the late-May weather, which seemed to hold the promise of summer.

He turned toward Crystal beside him and found her cradling her mug of decaffeinated coffee in her hands, her eyes fixed on the sunset. A crestfallen look had overtaken her pretty face ever since Tyler had retreated to his room.

Duane bit back his disappointment with his two older sons. Although he had spoken to them individually and asked them to give his relationship with Crystal a chance, when he'd asked Tyler to join them for supper, Tyler said he'd eat with them but could not yet muster enthusiasm about the situation. And to Duane's complete embarrassment, his oldest son had kept his word.

His two oldest sons still refused to talk to him about their feelings when he tried to coax them into a conversation about his relationship with Crystal. His heart broke as he considered how upset his sons were, but he couldn't help them work through this if they refused to talk to him.

Although Duane had been grateful for Jayden's support, he still couldn't shake his frustration with Tyler and Korey. They were supposed to set the example for Jayden, but Jayden had been the one on whom he could count—the one acting mature beyond his nineteen years.

Now as he sat on the back porch next to his lovely girlfriend, Duane felt his spirit deflate. Would he lose her over this? He couldn't let that happen, and instead, he had to face the issue head-on, no matter how humiliating it was.

Taking a deep breath, he searched for the words to express how he felt. Finally, he decided on complete honesty. "I'm sorry about Tyler's behavior."

Crystal turned toward him. "Tyler was respectful tonight."

"I know, but he wasn't exactly warm. When I went upstairs earlier, I asked him to join us and be hospitable. He's old enough to know that he should have been friendly and participated in the conversation." He sucked in a breath, awaiting her response.

She set her mug on the small table beside her and then rested her hand on his, the sensation of her warm skin sending his senses spinning. "You don't need to apologize for him."

"I feel like I do." He turned his hand over and threaded his fingers with hers. "They're *mei kinner* and a reflection of me."

"They're also adults with minds of their own."

He sighed. "You're right."

"Is Korey really at Michelle's *haus*?"

"*Ya.*" He looked out toward the pasture and breathed in the clean air.

She angled her body toward him, her expression clouding with something that looked like worry. "I don't mean to sound prideful, but am I the reason why he made plans with Michelle?"

Duane felt his lips press down. He didn't want to lie to Crystal, but he also didn't want to hurt her with the truth.

She shook her head. "I don't want to disrupt your family, Duane. Maybe coming here was a bad idea."

"No, don't say that." He gave her hand a gentle squeeze, and worry seized him. "I'm not going to give up on *mei sohns*. I've been trying to get Tyler and Korey to talk to me, and I'll keep trying. I believe in my heart that the Lord led me to you, and that's why I'm not going to give up on us either. If God blesses this relationship, then it will work out."

When her pink lips turned up in a smile, he felt his body relax. She faced the pasture again and rested her head on his shoulder.

The simple gesture sent joy buzzing through him. He pushed the swing into motion with the toe of his shoe as the cicadas began their nightly chorus, singing the day into the night.

Duane continued to hold Crystal's hand and enjoy the closeness of her. Lightning bugs danced through the air as if celebrating them, and the propane light in the kitchen poured out through the open windows behind them, casting a happy yellow glow on the porch floor.

"I didn't tell you about Owen," she suddenly said.

Duane felt his happy mood dissolve as he recalled his brief encounter with her ex-boyfriend. "What about him?"

She sat up and faced him, releasing her hold on his hand as he halted the swing. "Remember how he stopped by the farm Saturday?"

*How could I forget?* He nodded.

"Kane hired him to work at the farm. He's going to do all of the maintenance *mei bruder* hasn't had time to do." She frowned. "He's been looking for work, so Kane hired him without asking me how I felt about it."

Duane studied her as envy doused him. "How do you feel about it?"

"Upset, of course." She shook her head. "I told Kane too. I said he should have asked me and considered my feelings." She pointed to her chest.

"You're an integral part of that family."

"*Danki.*" She turned toward the pasture again. "That's not the worst of it, though."

Duane's eyes widened. "What do you mean?"

"Owen started working there Monday, and he cornered me on the porch while I was hanging out laundry."

He felt his brow wrinkle. "What do you mean by cornered you?"

As Crystal described the conversation, Duane was certain his jealousy might swallow him whole. "And how did you respond to him?"

She snorted. "I told him I forgave him a long time ago, but I'm not interested in trying again. I asked him who helped him prepare his apology, and he had the nerve to look offended and shocked."

He nodded, but worry still taunted him. "Has Owen left you alone since Monday?"

"*Ya,* he has. I think he got the message."

Silence fell between them once again, and he pushed the swing back into motion. He rested his arm on the back of the swing behind her shoulders and tried to calm his sparking irritation toward Owen.

"Have you told Tricia about us?"

Her question slammed him back to the present.

"No, I haven't seen her, but I plan to tell her and the bishop."

She nodded slowly, looking concerned. "Won't the bishop be upset?"

"I suppose so, but I want to be with you."

"I want to be with you too." She rested her head on his shoulder once again. "Duane, I have a question for you."

He looked down at the top of her prayer covering. "Okay."

"If you were to get married again, would you consider having more *kinner*?"

He hesitated, and she peeked up at him. He took in the hope in her beautiful green eyes, and he couldn't bring himself to admit that he might not be able to. "*Ya*, I would."

"*Gut*."

He smiled as more lightning bugs lit up the sky like tiny, glittery confetti. Pure contentment slid through him.

"This is the perfect evening," she whispered.

He looked down at her. "I was just thinking the same thing." He felt the overwhelming urge to kiss her but knew it was too soon.

"Tell me about your parents," he said.

"Well, *mei dat* looked just like Kane," she began.

Duane enjoyed the sound of her voice as she shared stories of her childhood. Soon the entire pasture was cloaked in darkness, a signal that their evening was coming to an end.

She looked up at him. "I guess it's time to say good night," she said as if reading his mind.

"*Ya*, the evening flew by too quickly."

"It did, but we have to get up early tomorrow for work."

The *clip-clop* of horse hooves and whir of buggy wheels drew

Duane's attention to the driveway just as a horse and buggy arrived.

"That'll be Korey," he said.

The horse stopped in front of the barn, and then Korey climbed out of the buggy. After unhitching his horse by the light of a lantern, he led it into the barn and then stowed the buggy.

When Korey exited the barn and started toward the house, Duane sent up a silent prayer that Korey would be friendly and respectful to Crystal.

Korey's pace seemed to slow as he approached the porch.

"How was your evening?" Duane asked.

His middle son climbed the porch steps. *"Gut."*

"Hi, Korey," Crystal said with a pleasant smile.

Korey nodded, continuing into the house.

"I'm sorry," Duane whispered once Korey was gone. "I'll talk to him again."

Crystal smiled, but her expression seemed to have lost the sparkle he'd seen earlier. "We'll get through this. I'll pray about it too."

"May I take you home, Crystal?"

Crystal's eyes seemed to warm at the idea. "I'd like that."

They returned to the kitchen, where Crystal insisted Duane keep the leftovers. While she gathered up her tote bag and purse, Duane grabbed a lantern and then led her out to the barn.

Crystal called her driver to let him know she had a ride while Duane hitched up the horse and buggy.

"Duane," she said as she walked over to his buggy. "Would you please show me one of those trains you make?"

He smiled. "Sure. I'll go get one." He hurried over to his workshop, the beam of his flashlight guiding his way. The aroma of pine overwhelmed him as he fetched one of the finished trains sitting on his shelf before bringing it over to her. "Here you go."

Crystal gasped as she turned the wooden locomotive and its two train cars, attached with little metal rings, over in her hands. "Duane, this is fantastic! The *kinner* who receive them must love them."

"*Danki*." He felt his cheeks heat.

She held the train out to him. "Who taught you how to work with wood?"

"*Mei dat* dabbled in it. We worked together in his shop when I was a *bu*."

"He would be proud."

His heart swelled at the compliment. He gently pushed the train back toward her. "Give it to your *bruderskinner*. Tell them it's from me."

"That's so kind, and I know they will love it."

They climbed into the buggy, and soon they were on their way, heading down Beechdale Road. The sounds of the horse's hooves and the hum of the buggy wheels filled the space between them.

Duane glanced over at Crystal beside him and a crush of memories took him by surprise. It had been so long since he'd had a woman in his buggy that he felt transported back in time to his younger years when Connie sat beside him, smiling and sharing stories.

"Tell me about the book you're reading," she said.

"Oh," Duane said, surprised. "Let's see. It's a murder mystery."

"Really?"

"*Ya*, but it's a cozy mystery." He spent the remainder of the ride to her house talking about his book and some of his other favorites.

When they arrived at Kane's farm, Duane halted the horse by the back porch and then turned toward her. His lantern highlighted her beautiful face with a warm yellow glow.

"I had a really nice time tonight," she suddenly said, her voice filling the buggy.

Duane looked over at her through the darkness. "I did too. Let's do this again soon."

He leaned over and caressed her cheek with his hand, using the most featherlight touch. When he leaned in closer, she sucked in a breath. The air around them felt charged, as if they struck a match, it would explode.

He brushed his lips over her cheek, and she released a quiet sigh as a warm glow rushed through his body.

"*Danki* again for the amazing meal," he whispered. "Have a *gut* night."

"You too." Crystal climbed out of the buggy carrying the train along with the bag with her food containers, and he waited until she was in the house before he guided the horse to the road.

Duane spent the ride home daydreaming about Crystal and imagining future dates with her. He found himself stuck on her question about having a family. While he hoped for a future with her, he wasn't certain he could deliver on the promise of children. Still, he couldn't bring himself to break her heart. He wanted to see what God had in store for them first.

When he arrived home, he took care of his horse and buggy and then headed into the house, where he found Korey sitting at the kitchen table, sulking. Seeing his son's sour expression brought him crashing back to earth.

Duane crossed his arms over his chest and prepared himself for a heart-to-heart with his middle son. "Are you ready to talk?"

"What would *Mamm* say?" Korey seethed. "Don't you think it would hurt her to see you with Crystal?"

Duane took a deep and cleansing breath. "Korey, I know that you're hurting, but I hope you will hear me. No one will replace your *mamm*. I'm not trying to hurt you or your *bruders*, and I'm not trying to replace my old life. Your *mamm* was my everything. We fell in love and we built a life together."

He gestured at him. "We loved our family, and nothing will change what we had. But, at the same time, she's gone. I'm finally at a place where I'm ready to start thinking about the future. I didn't plan to meet Crystal or expect to have feelings for her. You'll learn that you can't plan when you'll fall in love. God puts that person in your life when he sees fit. I happened to find Crystal, and I want to see where God leads us. I'm only asking you to give her a chance. Tell me how you're feeling, and we'll work through this. You and your *bruders* are important to me, and I don't want to hurt you."

"Wait a minute. You're in *love* with her?" Korey sat up straight. "Are you going to marry her?"

"Hold on now." Duane held his hands up. "I don't know if I love her. I like her a lot, and I want to get to know her. You, Tyler, and Jayden will be the first to know when and if I'm ready to get married again."

"This is ridiculous. You say that you'll always remember *Mamm*, but here you are ready to replace her as your *fraa*. It hasn't even been two years since she's been gone. You never talk about her, so it seems like you've already moved on. How could you do this?" Korey's voice broke and he wiped at his eyes.

Something inside of Duane broke apart, sending grief rushing in. "I'll never forget your *mamm* or what we had together. She's in my thoughts all the time, and I miss her every day. I may not talk about her, but I will always grieve her. Everyone grieves differently, Korey." His voice trembled. "I'll always miss your *mamm*. No one will ever replace what she and I had."

Korey's eyes flashed as he stood. "You say that, but this is wrong. Are you going to replace us with new *kinner* too?" His voice was as sharp and cold as glass.

Duane scrubbed his hands over his face as Korey stalked away and up the stairs.

His steps felt bogged down with the weight of his situation as he picked up his lantern and walked to the downstairs bathroom. He couldn't stop his confusion over the entire situation.

He felt like a boat adrift on the ocean as joy, frustration, and grief pummeled him like waves crashing on the shoreline. He'd never expected to become a widower in his midforties, left alone to parent three sons. He missed Connie with every fiber of his being. And he'd never expected to find the possibility of love with someone younger so soon after Connie had passed away. And now he struggled to make their relationship work while wading through his sons' hurt and bewilderment.

How would he find his way through all of this?

He climbed into the shower, hoping the warm water would wash his worries down the drain, but the water did little to alleviate his sore muscles or burdens. After dressing, he climbed into bed and stared up toward the ceiling.

Duane rolled over onto his side as Korey's criticisms echoed through his mind. If only he could turn off his son's words! Did he belong with Crystal, or was Korey right? Was it too soon for him to date and possibly even plan a future with a new wife?

"Lord," he began, "I don't know how to navigate these strange waters. I feel like I might go crazy with all these confusing feelings. I'm still trying to accept that I'm a widower, and I miss Connie so much that my heart hurts. I never expected to care for Crystal, but when I'm with her, everything feels right with the world. In my heart, I feel as if she might be my future, but I never want to do anything that will hurt my children. Please grant me the right words to explain to my sons that I'm not trying to hurt them. If it's your will, help Crystal and me find our way."

Memories of Connie hit him hard and fast, taking away his breath. He recalled their dating days when he took her on picnics to a nearby lake and when they visited their favorite pizzeria. He recalled holding her hand and laughing until they couldn't breathe.

The sound of her voice and her laugh echoed through his mind. Oh, how he missed her! How he longed to touch her face and kiss her lips once more.

Then he did something he hadn't done in a long time, he began speaking to his late wife. "Connie, I miss you. I still love you and I always will. You're forever with me in my heart."

He paused, licking his dry lips. "I hope you can understand what I see in Crystal. She's sweet, funny, and kind. I admire her gentle spirit and her love for her family. I want to get to know her and I'm not sure where it might lead. I just want you to know that no one will ever replace you. I'll always love you. Forever."

Then he closed his eyes and hoped to sleep.

# CHAPTER 23

CRYSTAL TOOK A BITE OF BREAD SMEARED WITH PEANUT BUT-ter spread while she sat in the Byler family's barn beside Lorraine and across from Jeannie and Jolene after the church service on Sunday.

"I'm surprised you came to church today," Crystal told Jeannie. "How have you been feeling?"

"I'm okay." Jeannie cupped her hand to her mouth to cover a yawn. "Jared said I should stay home today, but I wanted to get out of the *haus*. Wanda offered to keep Lila so I could come and see *mei freinden*."

Jolene clucked her tongue. "That's so sweet of her."

Crystal took another bite of her sandwich to stop herself from frowning as she recalled her conversation with Jeannie's mother-in-law just last week. As far as she was concerned, there was nothing sweet about Wanda.

"Is Lila eating well?" Lorraine asked before popping a pretzel into her mouth.

Jeannie nodded. "*Ya*, we had a slow start, but she's doing well now."

Crystal sipped her coffee while her three friends discussed

their experiences with both bottle feeding and breastfeeding. She was used to feeling left out of these sorts of conversations, but today it didn't bother her quite as much.

Instead of feeling like an outsider, she lost herself in thoughts of Duane. Memories of how they'd held hands in the swing with her head resting on his shoulder and thoughts of the chaste kiss he'd given her in the buggy had kept her heart quivering since she'd seen him Thursday evening. She couldn't wait to see him again.

"Crystal?"

"*Ya?*" She looked over to where Jeannie watched her.

"I heard something interesting about you from Wanda."

Crystal's stomach dipped, but she worked to keep a serene expression on her face. "Oh *ya*? I doubt it was all that interesting."

Jolene leaned in. "Do tell."

Lorraine dropped a couple of pieces of lunch meat on her bread.

"Wanda heard you're dating someone," Jeannie said.

Lorraine and Jolene gasped in unison and then both began firing off questions.

"Do we know him?" Jolene asked. "Is he a member of our church district?"

Lorraine tapped the table. "What does he look like? Is it serious? Are you going to finally get married?"

Crystal held her hand up. "Slow down now. You have to give me a chance to answer you." Then she leveled her gaze with her best friend. "I'm assuming Wanda heard this from Owen, right?"

Jeannie nodded. "*Ya.* I heard Owen is working with Kane now."

"Wait a minute!" Jolene's voice was so loud that the women at the next table turned and stared. "Sorry," she said, her cheeks turning red. "Owen is working for Kane? *And* you have a new boyfriend?"

Lorraine turned toward Crystal, her mouth shaped like an O. "Are you back with Owen?"

"No, no, no." Crystal shook her head. "I'm not dating Owen."

"Well, who is he?" Jolene asked.

Crystal sat up straight and lifted her chin. "His name is Duane Bontrager. He's a roofer who lives in Bird-in-Hand."

Jeannie pressed her lips together. "Owen said he met him."

Crystal wanted to roll her eyes. Leave it to Owen to start a rumor about her. "And he's a *wunderbaar* man and *dat*. He's a widower."

Lorraine's nose scrunched. "He has *kinner*?"

"He has three *sohns*," Crystal said and then sipped more coffee.

"And?" Jolene asked. "How old are they?"

Crystal shifted on the bench. "They're nineteen, twenty-three, and twenty-four."

"What do they think of you?" Lorraine asked.

"They're nice young men," Crystal said before picking up a pretzel and tossing it into her mouth. She ate another pretzel as her appetite dissolved. She looked over at Lorraine, who seemed to watch her with confusion. Why couldn't her friends just be happy for her? She wished their lunch would end so she could return home and escape this scrutiny.

"What do you and Duane possibly have in common?" Jolene finally asked.

Crystal tried to calm her frayed nerves. "We've both experienced loss. He's a kind man, and I care about him. He makes me *froh*."

"But don't you want a family?" Jeannie asked. "I know he

makes you *froh*, but I'm worried that happiness will end if he tells you he doesn't want more *kinner*."

Crystal shook her head. "We just started dating. I'm not worried about having a family with him yet."

"What about Owen?" Lorraine asked. "Would you ever want to work things out with him?"

Jolene nodded. "*Ya*, you two were such a cute couple and so in love. You're both older now, and I'm sure he's learned his lesson."

"He really cares for you, and he's truly sorry," Jeannie said. "I know he hurt you badly, but you might want to consider giving him a second chance."

"Owen and I are over, and there's nothing else to say about that." Crystal dropped the pretzel she'd been holding.

"Do you love Duane?" Jolene asked.

Crystal hesitated. "We're just getting to know each other at this point." She pushed herself up from the bench. She'd had enough of their criticism. It was time to go home. "I need to get going. Have a *gut* week."

She climbed off the bench and hurried out of the barn toward the line of buggies waiting for the families to ride home in them.

Crystal hugged her arms to her chest as she walked over to Kane's buggy and crawled in. Then she closed her eyes and opened her heart in prayer.

"God, why are my *mei freinden* rejecting Duane when they've never met him? Can't they just trust my judgment? When I'm with him, everything seems so right. Is Duane the one for me if he makes me *froh*? If Duane is the one you've chosen for me, then please help me stand up to *mei freinden* and family who are against him. Guide me, Lord. I'm lost."

Duane sat with Ed and Ray at lunch after their Sunday service that afternoon. His heart lifted as he thought of Crystal and wondered if she was enjoying her lunch after church as well.

"What are you smiling about?" Ed asked as he lifted his piece of bread smothered with peanut butter spread.

Duane cleared his throat. "Well, I'm seeing someone."

"You are?" Ray gasped.

"That's great!" Ed leaned in. "Is it Tricia Mast?"

Duane felt his brow pinch. "No, it's not Tricia."

Ed and Ray shared a look.

"What's going on?" Duane asked.

"You know *mei fraa* goes to quilting bees with Wilmer's *fraa* and other ladies in the congregation," Ray began, and Duane nodded. "Apparently Marlena said that Wilmer invited you to visit after church at his *haus* and told you to consider dating and marrying Tricia. Marlena also said she spoke to Tricia about marrying you."

Duane's stomach twisted. "So, Wilmer's *fraa* is telling all of the women in our church district that I'm going to date and marry Tricia Mast?"

"That's right." Ed nodded.

Duane groaned.

"So, who *are* you dating?" Ray asked.

"Her name is Crystal Glick. She's from Gordonville." He explained how they met and became easy friends. "She's thirty-three and lives with her *bruder* and his family."

"She's thirty-three and single?" Ed asked.

"*Ya,* and she's *schee,* funny, sweet, and lovely. I care about her very much."

Ray seemed to study him. "But you seem to get along with Tricia. Why won't you consider dating her?"

"Why would I want to date Tricia when I care for Crystal?"

"Because it would be the right thing to do. You'd be helping to relieve the community's burden by helping her and her *kinner*," Ray explained.

"Exactly," Ed said. "I've seen you and Tricia talk at church, and it's obvious you like each other. I saw you laughing together, and a shared sense of humor always helps with a marriage. Besides, Crystal is young enough that she'll want more *kinner*. Do you want to have a newborn when Tyler is almost twenty-five already?"

Duane felt his shoulders tighten. "I'm not going to marry someone just because it's *gut* for the community. I want to marry for love."

"You should really spend more time with Tricia," Ed said. "Give her a chance before you just fall head-first into a relationship with someone younger."

"Ed's right."

Duane rested his elbows on the table as his best friends' words settled over him. As much as he wanted to reject their comments, doubt still nipped at him. Did he belong with Tricia because it made good sense, or did he belong with Crystal because his heart desired her?

*Lord, help me find the way to your plans for me!*

Duane climbed the front steps of Tricia's house Wednesday after work. He lifted his hand and knocked. Then he brushed his hands down his shirt and trousers. He had hurried home from work, showered, pulled on fresh clothes, and then rushed out to visit her.

The door opened, and Kathleen, Tricia's eleven-year-old daughter, looked up at him.

"Hi, Kathleen. Is your *mamm* available?"

The girl nodded. "Just a moment." She hurried into the house.

Duane walked over to the edge of the porch. He had hoped to visit with her after church, but then he'd been invited to spend the afternoon with his old friend Quill and his family.

Despite Ed's and Ray's warnings about his relationship with Crystal, he had decided that he couldn't allow another week to go by without being honest with Tricia. Although they hadn't made plans to date, he wanted to stop the rumor mill before it got out of control. And to do that, he had to make her aware of what the community members were saying about Tricia and him.

The door opened, and he spun to face Tricia.

"Duane, hi. What a surprise."

"I hope I haven't caught you at a bad time."

"Not at all. I was just making supper. Would you like to stay and eat with us?"

"Oh, no *danki*. I was just hoping to have a moment to speak with you."

She nodded, but confusion seemed to flash over her face. Then she pointed toward the glider. "Why don't we sit?"

"Perfect."

They walked over to the glider, where he waited for her to sit before he lowered himself down beside her.

Tricia gave him a tentative smile. "What did you want to discuss?"

"I wanted to tell you about a rumor I heard at church on Sunday." He turned toward her.

"Oh." Her pretty face flickered with concern.

"I ate lunch with Ray Lambert and Ed Allgyer, and they told me that Marlena has been telling her quilting circle members that you and I are dating and planning to marry."

"*Ach* no." She rolled her eyes.

"I thought you'd want to know so we could set them straight. People should know that it's not true."

"Right." She nodded slowly and then studied him.

"Is there something else?" he asked.

"Duane, I've known you a long time. You're a *gut* man, and a superb *dat*." She took a deep breath. "I know that this is forward and not the norm, but I need to ask you. Would you consider making the rumor true?"

He gave her a hesitant smile. "I like you, Tricia. I admit that I feel comfortable with you, but I need to be honest. I've met someone, and I started seeing her last week. I wanted you to know. I plan to tell the bishop too."

"Oh." Tricia blushed. "You met someone?"

"*Ya.* It was completely unexpected."

"Who is she?" she asked.

"She lives in Gordonville, and I met her on a job."

Tricia smiled, but he was almost certain he spotted disappointment in her lovely gray eyes. "*Gut* for you. You deserve happiness. I appreciate all you've done for me and my *kinner*." She stood. "*Danki* for coming by."

"Let me know if you ever need any more help."

"And let me know if you need any sewing done."

He laughed. "Have a *gut* night."

Duane watched Tricia disappear into the house and then jogged down the steps toward his waiting horse and buggy. After climbing into his buggy, he stared out the windshield as confusion over Tricia's suggestion settled into his mind. It seemed that everyone in his community believed he and Tricia belonged together, but his heart longed for Crystal. Was his heart wrong and the community right?

He rubbed his temple. He needed some relief. He needed a friendly ear to listen to him and calm him.

He needed Crystal. He craved the chance to look into her eyes and feel the overwhelming happiness that she always brought to his soul. He needed to touch her hand and know that she was the right choice for him.

Duane led the horse out toward the road and started toward her house, hoping she would be available to talk with him.

When Duane reached Kane's farm, he halted his horse by the back porch, and as he climbed the steps, he recalled when he had first met her. He smiled as he contemplated how much she had come to mean to him since that day.

He reached the door, and he heard a child screaming on the other side. He grimaced, assuming it was most likely Evie. He knocked, waited a few moments, and then knocked again.

Soon the door creaked open, and the screaming become louder as Alisha stood in front of him.

"Hi, Alisha," Duane spoke over the cries coming from inside the house. "Is everything okay?"

Alisha looked behind her and then at him, her expression seeming worried. "Evie is upset."

"I'm sorry. Is your *aenti* busy?"

"She's trying to calm Evie down, but I'll go get her. *Mamm* doesn't feel well and went to bed." Alisha ushered him in and then disappeared as Duane stepped into the mudroom. He moved to the doorway leading to the kitchen, which he found empty.

A few moments later, Crystal walked into the kitchen, her expression forlorn and dark shadows under her eyes. The screaming continued from the next room.

"Duane. Hi. I wasn't expecting you."

"I was hoping we could talk."

Crystal frowned. "Is it an emergency?"

"No, it's not."

"This really isn't a *gut* time. Leona went to bed because she doesn't feel well. She was having some labor cramps earlier, and when she called the doctor, she instructed her to try to keep her feet up as much as possible. Kane is out getting supplies and hasn't returned yet. I can't get Evie to stop screaming. I've tried everything. Can we talk another day?"

"Of course we can."

Alisha appeared in the doorway, balancing a screaming Evie on her little hip. *"Aenti!"* she yelled over her sister's cries. "Would you please help me?"

Crystal's entire body seemed to wilt as she looked at her niece. *"Ya."* Then she looked at Duane. "I'm sorry, Duane."

"Don't worry. I'll see you soon." As she trudged into the family room, Duane stood in the doorway and wondered if Crystal's life would ever get easier.

Crystal rocked Evie while looking out the twins' bedroom window later that evening. Exhaustion weighed her down like a heavy blanket as the toddler sniveled into her neck.

Today had been a long, tiresome day. While Leona rested in bed, Crystal had struggled to manage all her chores, coupled with caring for the twins, Hope, and Jevon. She'd been so consumed with the children that she'd forgotten to set the timer, and her cheesy chicken casserole had burned to a crisp. She had to toss it into the trash and instead serve simple sandwiches for supper.

Later, Evie was inconsolable. And although Alisha had done her best to care for her, Crystal had to step in, leaving the kitchen cleanup to Alisha. And, in the middle of the chaos, Kane had to run out after supper for the diapers he had forgotten earlier, leaving Crystal to handle it all.

Yes, the day had been a disaster, but then Duane had appeared. Oh, how she'd been relieved to see her boyfriend's handsome face, but he had arrived at the wrong moment. If only she could have frozen time and found out what he'd wanted. Guilt and chagrin dug into the already strained muscles in her back.

Footsteps sounded in the hallway outside of the twins' room before the door creaked open, and Leona appeared in the doorway, a flashlight glowing in her hand.

Crystal looked up at her. "How are you feeling?"

"The cramps have stopped." Leona nodded at Evie. "I heard her crying. I guess she's finally asleep?"

Crystal sighed. *"Ya."*

They were silent for a moment. Leona walked over and touched Evie's hair. The toddler sighed and snuggled against Crystal's neck.

Leona rested her hands on her protruding belly. Her due date was fast approaching. Soon there would be eight children, and Crystal wondered how they would cope. While Crystal was excited to meet her new nieces or nephews, tonight the thought of another child made her even more fatigued. She squeezed her eyes closed as the guilt of the thought threatened to drown her.

*Help me, Lord. Grant me patience with* mei bruderskinner.

Leona gingerly lowered herself into the rocking chair beside Crystal and pushed it into motion while rubbing her belly. "Alisha told me Duane stopped by earlier. What did he want?"

"I don't know." Crystal frowned. "I didn't have a chance to talk to him."

"I feel terrible that I wasn't any help today. This pregnancy has been much more difficult than the others. I'm sorry that you have to carry the burden."

"It's not your fault. We need to get you to July, and it's important that you rest." Crystal looked down at her sleeping niece as questions tumbled through her mind. She hoped she would have a chance to talk to Duane again. She prayed he would understand why she couldn't talk to him.

*Please forgive me, Duane.*

Crystal looked over at Leona, and suddenly Duane's words from when she'd brought him the meal floated through her mind:

*I think you deserve time away from your family.*

Perhaps Duane was right, and she had earned a much-needed break from running her brother's household and caring for all of his children alone.

"I don't know what Duane wanted, but when you're feeling better, I plan to find out." Crystal would choose a night when Leona was feeling well and spend time with him. Then she'd find out why he'd stopped by and what he'd wanted to tell her.

# CHAPTER 24

CRYSTAL PICKED UP HER PORTABLE CAKE CARRIER, THEN climbed out of Kane's buggy Sunday afternoon. "*Danki* for the ride. I expect Duane will bring me home."

Although the air was warm, the early June sun was blocked by gray clouds, and the scent of rain floated over her.

"See you later." Kane looked toward the porch and waved. "Hi, Duane."

Duane sauntered toward the buggy and greeted them both.

Crystal's heart flopped around like a fish as Duane closed the distance between them.

He held out his hands. "Let me carry that for you."

"*Danki*," she said as he took the cake saver. "I brought a special dessert since you insisted upon cooking for me today."

"*Danki*," he said.

Kane wished them a good evening and then guided his horse toward the road.

Once her brother's buggy was gone, Crystal looked up at Duane. "I'm glad today was convenient for me to come see you. I wanted to apologize in person for not being able to talk to you Wednesday."

He touched her hand. "I understood. You were preoccupied."

"It was a terrible day, but I didn't mean to take it out on you."

"You didn't take anything out on me." He tilted his head. "But I'm glad Leona is feeling better and you were able to take time for yourself today. I can tell you don't get much of a chance to recharge your batteries."

"That's true." She smiled. "What did you want to tell me when you stopped by?"

He looked sheepish. "It wasn't that big of a deal. I just wanted to tell you I found out at church that a rumor is going around that I'm planning to marry Tricia Mast."

Crystal's eyes widened. "Oh really?"

"*Ya*, two of *mei gut freinden* told me during lunch after church. So, I went to see Tricia to tell her about the rumor."

"How did she take the news?"

"She was surprised to hear it." He hesitated.

"Is there something else?" Crystal's stomach dipped.

"She asked me if I wanted to date her."

Crystal gasped. "What did you tell her?"

"I explained that I'm already seeing you."

"Oh," Crystal said, relieved. "I was surprised you wanted to cook for me. What did you make?"

"It's a Mexican lasagna casserole I put together yesterday."

"*Danki* for preparing it."

"*Gern gschehne. Mei sohns* will be *froh*. They love Mexican food." He lifted the bag up onto his shoulder.

Crystal lifted an eyebrow. "Your *sohns* are all here today?"

"Yup." He beckoned her toward the house. "I told them all to be friendly. They wanted to go to youth group, but I made them stay to at least see you. They can catch up with their *freinden* after lunch."

She felt her smile flatten. "Are you sure that was a *gut* idea?"

"It will be fine. Let's go inside."

Crystal walked with Duane into the house. They found the three young men in the kitchen, and the table was set for five. Tyler and Korey sat at the table while Jayden stood by the counter.

*"Wie geht's?"* she said, her voice seeming a little too loud and cheerful.

Tyler nodded. "Hello."

Korey's lips twisted as he looked down at the tabletop.

"Lunch smells divine," Crystal said.

Duane opened the oven and pulled the casserole out. "I hope you like it."

"We're so glad you're here." Jayden joined his father by the counter. "Let me help serve the meal." He carried the casserole dish to the table, and Korey shot him a dirty look.

Crystal's stomach knotted, and a shaky feeling swept through her. Perhaps this had been another bad idea. She turned toward Duane, who gave her an encouraging expression before he gathered up a knife and a spatula.

"Let's enjoy this *appeditlich* lunch," Duane announced, his words seeming to hold a warning for his older sons.

Crystal took a seat beside him and across from Jayden. After a silent prayer, Duane cut the first piece of casserole and then scooped it onto Crystal's plate. Then he cut a piece for himself and pushed the dish over to Jayden.

She took a bite and swallowed, her taste buds dancing with delight. "This casserole is wonderful, Duane. *Danki* for making it."

"I'm so glad you like it," he said. "I found the recipe in one of the cookbooks you gave me."

"I'll have to look for it." She glanced around the table. "How did your projects go this week?" Crystal asked, hoping to get Duane's sons to talk to her.

"They went well," Duane began. "We finished up that strip mall and then had a couple of farm jobs."

Duane talked on about their work while Jayden smiled and his older brothers ate their food, eyes focused downward.

When the work discussion petered out, Crystal searched her mind for a subject that might engage his sons. "Where is the youth gathering today?"

"It's over in Paradise," Jayden told her. "We're meeting up with a couple of other youth groups."

"And we're missing out," Korey snapped, his brown eyes seeming to spark.

Duane pinned him with a sharp look. "Korey . . ."

"What, *Dat*?" Korey's eyes were hard and angry, and Duane's mouth tightened at the edges.

"We'll get there in plenty of time," Jayden said, as he gave Crystal an apologetic look.

Crystal pushed back her chair. "Why don't I serve dessert, so you all can get on your way?"

"Let me help you," Duane said, pushing back his chair and standing.

While Duane gathered up the lunch plates, Jayden picked up the casserole dish and carried it to the counter. Duane retrieved five dessert plates from the cabinet along with a knife and a cake server, and Jayden passed out dessert forks.

Crystal set the cheesecake in the center of the table. "I hope you like chocolate cookie cheesecake."

"It looks amazing," Duane said. "Will you cut it for us? I'm terrible at slicing cakes."

Crystal cut and served the pieces before sitting down.

"It's fantastic," Jayden said.

To her surprise, Tyler looked over at her after eating a bite. "It really is great. *Danki*, Crystal."

Her heart warmed. "I'm thrilled you like it."

Silence filled the kitchen while they ate.

"*Mei mamm* used to make chocolate cheesecake," Korey suddenly said.

"Oh?" Crystal asked.

Korey's face was stormy, a brooding scowl wrinkling his forehead. "Hers was much richer."

Duane dropped his fork on his empty plate with a clatter, and Crystal jumped with a start. "Korey, that's enough!" his voice boomed.

Jayden peered over at Korey. "Stop being disrespectful."

"Disrespectful?" Korey demanded. "This whole situation is disrespectful to *Mamm*! You're erasing her memory!"

A chasm of dread opened in Crystal's chest. She stood and started stacking their dishes, her body vibrating with nervousness. Korey would never accept her, and if she were honest with herself, she wasn't sure how to handle becoming a stepmother to a young man who might never treat her with kindness and respect. Perhaps the idea of having a happy future with Duane was preposterous!

She carried the dishes to the sink and gazed out the window, where rain had started to fall, beating a light and steady cadence on the roof above them.

"Korey, stop now before you say something you might regret." Duane's voice was laced with a warning.

Just then a knock sounded on the back door.

"I'll get it," Korey said, shoving his chair back and ambling toward the back door.

Crystal didn't know what to say or do, so she turned on the faucet and added dish detergent to the sink.

"I'll do that." Duane's voice was behind her. "I'm sorry," he whispered in her ear.

She plastered a smile on her lips as she looked up at his face, which was full of contrition. "It's not your fault. I expected this."

He shook his head. "I raised him better than this," he whispered.

Jayden brought the rest of the cheesecake to the counter and also gave Crystal an apologetic expression. "We don't all feel that way."

"Michelle brought strawberry cheesecake for the youth gathering," Korey announced as a young woman with light-brown hair and bright-blue eyes followed him into the kitchen, carrying a cake saver. "I wonder if it will taste like *mei mamm*'s."

"Hi," the young woman said, smiling. "I'm Michelle." She crossed the kitchen and set her cake saver on the counter.

Crystal held her hand out to her. "I'm Crystal." She pointed to the cake saver. "You brought cheesecake too?"

"*Ya.*" Michelle glanced at the half-eaten cake on the counter. "Oh my! Is that chocolate cookie cheesecake?"

"It is."

"I've never tried to make it. Maybe I can get the recipe from you sometime?"

"*Ya,* I'll give it to Korey."

Jayden sidled up to the sink. "I'll take care of the dishes."

"Korey," Duane said, his words measured. "Come into the *schtupp* with me. I'd like to speak with you in private for a moment."

Korey and Duane disappeared into the family room. Tyler stood, grabbed a dishcloth, and wiped down the table. Behind him, Jayden started washing the dishes.

"Do you live close by?" Michelle asked.

Crystal tried to ignore the tension knotting in her stomach as she shook her head. "I live over in Gordonville. How about you?"

Muffled voices floated into the kitchen from the nearby room. Although she couldn't hear their words, it was obvious from their tones that Duane and Korey were embroiled in a heated conversation.

"I don't live far," Michelle said. "I walked here."

"In the rain?"

Michelle lifted a shoulder in a half shrug. "*Ya.* I had my umbrella." She looked past Crystal. "Oh, look. It stopped already. It was just a quick spring shower. I can't believe summer is almost here. I love this time of year, don't you?"

"I do. I love working in my garden."

"I do too!" Michelle's smile widened. "My younger *schweschder* and I spent hours working in ours yesterday."

Crystal continued to make small talk with Michelle, and soon Duane and Korey returned, both looking irked.

"Let's go to the youth gathering, Michelle," Korey announced.

Michelle spun to face him in the doorway, her smile wobbling. "Oh, okay." She picked up her cheesecake. Then she turned to Crystal. "It was very nice meeting you. I hope to see you again soon."

Crystal smiled. "Me too. Enjoy the youth gathering."

Michelle said good-bye to Duane and then followed Korey out the back door.

When Duane met Crystal's gaze, he shook his head. She forced a smile, hoping to calm him.

Then Crystal turned to Jayden, who scrubbed the utensils. "Why don't I finish up so you can leave?"

Jayden lifted an eyebrow. "You sure?"

"Of course." She faced Tyler, who had started drying the dishes. "You too. Go have fun with your *freinden*."

Tyler's expression seemed hesitant. "Okay. *Danki* for dessert."

"*Gern gschehne*." She smiled as some of the weight lifted from her shoulders. Maybe—just maybe—she'd made some headway with Tyler today.

After his sons left, Duane rubbed his forehead and leaned against the doorway leading to the family room. "I don't even know what to say about Korey."

Crystal walked over to him and cupped her hand to his cheek. "There's nothing to say. Let's clean up the kitchen and then sit on the porch."

"Leave the dishes for later. I'd rather just sit with you." He threaded his fingers with hers.

Duane steered her outside, and she breathed in the smell of soil after the rain. Still holding his hand, she sat down beside him on the swing just as a bee buzzed past, most likely on its way to find a flower.

"You were right," he began, giving her hand a gentle squeeze. "Making them stay home was a disaster."

She smiled over at him. "The good news is that I feel like I made some headway with Tyler. He was nice to me today, and hopefully Korey will come around too. Just have faith and keep praying." She held on to those words, despite her worry and doubt.

"I will." He looked out toward his neighbor's pasture. "Let's talk about something else."

"That's a *gut* idea. Tell me about the book you were reading. Did you finish it? Was the chef the murderer?"

His handsome face lit up with excitement. "I did finish it, but it wasn't the chef. It was the mechanic."

"No!" she exclaimed. "Tell me everything."

They spent the rest of the afternoon discussing books before moving on to stories of their childhood. Later, they recalled holiday memories while eating leftover casserole for supper and slices of her cheesecake along with cups of decaffeinated coffee for dessert.

Crystal felt a deep connection with him as she talked about her parents and he shared stories of his.

Her heart felt heavy later that evening when she sat beside him in his buggy and he steered his horse toward her house.

"You okay?" he asked, giving her a sideways glance.

She settled back on the seat. "*Ya.* I was just thinking that today went by too quickly."

"Me too. I had a great day with you."

"I don't want our time together to end."

"Well, that just means we need to plan another day together soon."

After halting the horse in Kane's driveway, Duane leaned over to her, and she held her breath as his lips brushed her cheek, sending a shiver of pleasure trilling along her spine. For a moment, she was light-headed.

"Have a *gut* week," he said.

"You too." Her voice sounded breathy.

She climbed out of the buggy and waved as Duane moved down the driveway, the buggy's taillights flashing.

Crystal's heart sang as she ambled toward the porch, happiness enveloping her. When she reached the steps, she stopped as she took in the scene in front of her. Kane sat on a rocking chair, smiling and talking to Owen.

She stilled, confusion replacing her joy.

"You're finally home," Kane quipped, lifting his mug. "How was your day?"

"*Gut*." Crystal climbed the steps.

Owen lifted his mug as if toasting her. "It's *gut* to see you."

Crystal blinked at him and then hurried past him to the kitchen. She was grateful the house was quiet when she rushed toward the stairs.

Once in her room, she tried to push away her thoughts and confusion toward Owen. She'd had a wonderful afternoon with Duane, and she felt her heart warming more and more toward him each time she saw him. Was this what true love felt like? The idea sent joy flittering through her.

But still doubt weighed heavily on her shoulders. Could she and Duane have a future if Korey refused to accept her? And did she truly want to be his stepmother if he would pepper her with insults and cruel comments, constantly comparing her to Connie?

She sank down onto the corner of her bed and opened her heart in prayer:

"Lord," she whispered, "I feel myself falling in love with Duane, but I'm not sure if we belong together. I don't want to be the one who causes a rift between him and his *sohn*, and I don't want to push my way into a family. Perhaps I don't have what it takes to be a stepmother."

She took a shaky breath. "Please guide my heart toward the path you've chosen for me and find a way for Duane and me to be together if it's your will."

Hugging her arms to her waist, she tried to imagine a future with Duane where his sons accepted her.

Duane's happy mood dissolved when he found his three sons standing by the barn when he arrived home. He gripped the reins with such force that it hurt his hands. He halted the horse by the barn and then climbed out of the buggy.

"Let me help you." Jayden appeared beside him and began unhitching the horse.

Duane muttered a thank-you before turning toward Tyler and Korey. "You really embarrassed me today," he began, his voice already shaking. "And before you ask me what *Mamm* would think, I'd like to ask you how your *mamm* would have felt if she'd seen how rude you were today. She raised you both better."

Tyler hugged his arms to his chest and hung his head while Korey took a step toward Duane.

"I'll never accept her, *Dat,* so stop trying to force me to." Korey's face contorted as he wagged a finger at him.

Duane's fury sparked. "I never said I was going to force you to accept her. I just want you to treat her with decency and respect, and you can't seem to figure out how to do that."

Korey took a step toward him, storm clouds gathering across his face. "She has to *earn* my respect."

"Korey, just listen to me," Duane began before pausing to take a deep breath. "I know you're angry with me and not Crystal. You're allowed to be angry with me, but I'd prefer you take it out on me and not her." He pointed to his chest. "I've begged you to talk to me and tell me how you feel so we can work through this together. Now I'm going to ask you again. What can I do to make this better, Korey? You're *mei sohn*. I love you and I can't stand the thought of losing you."

His middle son's eyes narrowed as he took a step toward Duane. "You want to know how I feel? Fine! I'll tell you. I can't believe you're dating already, *Dat*. You let *Mamm* go so quickly. You act like she was never here." His voice was brittle.

Duane scrubbed his hand down his face. "Korey, that's not true. You wear your grief on your sleeve, but I don't." He touched his shirt. "I carry my grief with me here all the time. I miss your mother every minute of every day."

"So then how can you date Crystal and behave like you were never with *Mamm*?"

"You have to face the fact that I hope to marry again someday, and your *mamm* warned you and your *bruders* of that."

Korey's eyes narrowed. "*Mamm* didn't mean for you to remarry right away."

"I'm not getting married," Duane said. "We're just getting to know each other."

Jayden jumped between them and held his hands up. "That's enough." He turned toward Korey. "After *Mamm* died, *Dat* told us that all we had was each other, and we have to hold on to each other tightly. You need to remember that. *Mamm* would want us to stay close, no matter what."

"You're a traitor, Jayden." Korey sneered and then stalked toward the house, his flashlight bouncing along the path.

Duane stared after him, unmoored. He had no idea how to set things right with Korey.

"I'm sorry for letting you down, *Dat*." Tyler's voice was almost a murmur.

Duane swiveled toward his oldest son.

"You're right. You and *Mamm* raised me better, and I shouldn't have embarrassed you." Tyler swallowed. "I hope you can forgive me."

"Of course I do, *sohn*," Duane said.

Tyler rubbed the back of his neck. "I'll treat her with respect, but just don't ask me to be excited about the idea of having a stepmother. I need some time to adjust to the idea."

"I understand, and no one is getting married yet."

When Tyler gave him a hesitant smile, Duane felt some of his anger uncoil around his heart.

But deep down a thread of worry gripped him that he would lose Korey forever. As his sons walked toward the house, he felt grief and loneliness creep up on him. A vision of his late wife's beautiful face filled his mind, and he looked up toward the stars sparkling in the sky above him.

"Connie," he whispered, his voice husky. "I feel like I'm failing you. I told you I'd do my best with our sons, and I'd try to fulfill the roles of mother and father. I never expected to meet someone this soon after you passed away, and in a way, I'm sorry. I'm sorry if it's disrespectful for me to care for someone and imagine a future with her, but my heart is drawn to her. It's killing me to think that this relationship is hurting our sons, and it's clear Tyler and Korey are struggling. The truth is, I don't know what to do. I'm lost, adrift in these confusing emotions." He sniffed as his eyes stung.

"Korey is convinced I'm replacing you and acting as if you were never here, but that's not true. You're with me always. You're in my heart, my mind, and my bones. You're part of me. I can't stand the pain in Korey's eyes. My fear is that I'm going to lose him forever. I don't want to lose Korey, but I also don't want to lose

Crystal. I'm begging God for guidance, but I feel more befuddled every day. Forgive me, Connie. I miss you. I always will and I'll always love you."

With his heart clogging his throat, Duane trudged toward the house. "Please relieve my confusion, Lord. My heart seems to believe I belong with Crystal, but Korey and Tyler act as if I should remain alone. What is the right answer? Please calm my heart and show me the answer."

The questions followed him up the steps, through the mudroom and kitchen, to his bedroom.

# CHAPTER 25

Duane walked into the kitchen Thursday evening and dropped the mail onto the counter. He flipped through the stack of advertisements and bills and tried to chase away his frustration as Korey rooted through a nearby cabinet for a pot.

For the past four days, Korey had been in a foul mood, only giving brief responses to Duane's questions when he struggled to encourage his son to talk to him. He'd noticed both of Korey's brothers take him aside on different occasions to talk to him at the worksite, but his middle's son's attitude hadn't improved.

Instead of starting another argument with Korey, Duane had turned to prayer. He'd found himself praying constantly during the day, begging God to heal his rocky relationship with his middle son and to help him through his confusion over his feelings toward Crystal. Thoughts of Crystal and memories of Connie had haunted him during the day and filled his dreams at night.

Jayden entered the kitchen and walked over to the stove. "What are you making?"

"Hot dogs," Korey muttered.

Jayden walked over to the breadbox and flipped it open. "I'll set the table and grab the buns."

"Thanks." Korey's response was barely audible.

Duane shook his head as Jayden once again reminded him of his late wife. He could recall so many times when he and Connie had argued, and he said things to her that he had later regretted. Yet, instead of holding a grudge, Connie had immediately forgiven him and then acted as if they'd never traded barbs.

And, just like Connie, Jayden had set out to help Korey prepare supper even though Korey had called him a "traitor" only a few days earlier. Jayden truly had his mother's forgiving and patient heart.

Tyler stepped into the kitchen and pointed toward the back door. "There's a horse and buggy coming up the driveway. Is anyone expecting company?"

"I'm not," Duane said.

Jayden shook his head while setting the table. "I'm not either."

Korey kept his head bent while dropping the hot dogs into the pot and then covering them with water.

Tyler headed toward the back door just as a knock sounded. "I'll see who it is."

Duane opened the refrigerator, found the mustard and relish, and carried them to the table.

"*Dat.*" Tyler stood in the doorway, his expression grim. "It's the bishop. He wants to talk to you."

Duane's stomach twisted as he set the condiments on the table. *Oh no, not Wilmer.*

He felt his sons' eyes on him as he walked toward the mudroom. He stepped out onto the porch, where the bishop stood, scowling.

"Wilmer, hi. What brings you out here tonight?" Duane shook the older man's hand.

The bishop's mouth puckered as he scrutinized Duane with dark, beady eyes. "I heard a rumor and wanted to find out if it was true."

"What's the rumor?" Duane crossed his arms over his chest.

"Belinda Allgyer told *mei fraa* that you're seeing a *maedel* from another church district. Is that true?"

So Ed had told his wife that Duane was dating Crystal, and the word had now spread through the church district. "*Ya*, it's true that I'm seeing someone."

"But I had told you to consider dating Tricia."

"You did, but I met someone else."

Wilmer's forehead crinkled. "I don't understand. You and Tricia make a *gut* match, and your marriage would be *gut* for the community. You two make sense."

"Getting married is a lifelong commitment, and I wasn't ready to make that kind of commitment to her."

"Who's this *maedel* you're seeing?"

"She lives in Gordonville."

"Is she a widow?"

"No."

"How did you meet her?"

Duane pressed his lips together. For some reason, he felt protective of Crystal and their relationship, and he wasn't ready to share details about her life.

But if he didn't give Wilmer the information he craved, then he wouldn't leave. And Duane was ready to eat his supper and relax after a long day working on a roof in the June heat and humidity.

So, he took a deep breath and pressed on. "We had a job on her *bruder*'s farm."

"She lives with her *bruder*?"

"*Ya*," Duane said.

"And she's never been married?"

"No, she hasn't."

Wilmer rubbed his long, gray beard. "What's her name?"

"Crystal Glick."

The bishop hesitated, and Duane held his breath, hoping the bishop would give up and leave.

Instead, Wilmer's eyes narrowed. "I believe the Lord is leading me to instruct you to marry Tricia Mast."

Duane took a ragged breath in an effort to calm his erupting temper. "I disagree. I believe the Lord led me to Crystal."

"You *belong* with Tricia. You both have lost your spouses, and it's the best solution for our community. Break up with Crystal and ask Tricia to marry you."

Duane shook his head. "No. If I get married again, it will be for love, not simply because it's *gut* for the community."

"You and Tricia will learn to love each other in time," the bishop said.

"Wilmer, you're entitled to your opinion, but we're talking about my future," Duane said, pointing to his chest. "Have a *gut nacht*."

"I believe you're making a mistake," the bishop said.

"Actually, Wilmer, I don't believe I am. Now, I'm going to have supper with *mei sohns*. I'm sure Marlena is expecting you too. *Gut nacht*." Duane shook the bishop's hand and then stepped inside the house, where Tyler met him in the mudroom. He studied his son. "Did you hear the whole conversation?"

"I did."

"And?"

Tyler frowned. "Why didn't you tell me that the bishop was pressuring you to marry Tricia Mast?"

"I didn't want to upset you or your *bruders*."

Tyler touched his clean-shaven chin, and Duane could almost hear his eldest son's thoughts working through his mind.

"What is it, Tyler?" When Tyler hesitated, Duane said, "You can be honest with me."

"To tell you the truth, *Dat*, I'm having a tough time imagining you remarried, but if I had to choose a *fraa* for you, I would say that Tricia is a better match."

Duane flinched as if Tyler's words had struck him. "What do you mean?"

"It just seems like Tricia is the logical choice. I mean, you've both lost your spouse, you're both parents, and it's obvious that you get along. Plus, she needs help, and she's a member of our church district. She seems like a suitable match. It's just my opinion, though." Tyler shrugged as if his words hadn't rocked Duane to his very soul. "Let's go eat. I'm starved."

As his oldest son walked away, Tyler's words burrowed under Duane's skin.

Could Tyler and the bishop be right that Duane belonged with Tricia and not Crystal?

Duane scrubbed his hands down his face as doubt settled heavily over his heart.

Excitement buzzed through Crystal as she stepped into the kitchen on Friday evening, two weeks later. It was her birthday and time for her party. She couldn't wait! The kitchen smelled heavenly with the lingering fragrance of the carrot cake that Hope and Alisha had helped Leona bake earlier in the afternoon.

"I think everything is ready for your party," Leona said as she stood by the oven.

"*Danki* for planning this for me. I really appreciate it."

"Well, we appreciate you and wanted to do something nice for you. I just hope your *kuche* turned out well."

"I'm sure it will be perfect."

Just then, Alisha, Jevon, Nate, and Hope walked into the kitchen. "Happy birthday, *Aenti*!" they sang in unison.

Alisha held something behind her back.

"We love you," Nate said.

Jevon nodded. "*Ya*, we do."

Hope hugged Crystal at her waist. "I love you, *Aenti*."

"Aw." Crystal's eyes stung with tears. "I love you all very much too."

Alisha held out a large manila envelope. "We made you something."

"Oh wow." Crystal took the envelope.

"Open it!" Jevon called. "Open it!"

Inside, Crystal found a colorful drawing. She laid it on the table and carefully examined the nine stick figures, a house, and barns. At the top, the words "Happy Birthday, Auntie" were written in multicolored letters.

"We drew our family," Alisha explained, and then she pointed out the different people. "That's *Mamm* and *Dat*. And then that's you, me, Jevon, Hope, Nate, and the *zwillingbopplin*."

Nate pointed to colorful flowers. "Here's your garden, and those are the barns."

"And the cows and the barn cats," Jevon chimed in.

"And I drew *mamm's bopplin* that are coming soon," Hope announced.

"This is so precious." Crystal sniffed as tears trailed down her cheek.

Hope tugged at Crystal's dress. "Why are you crying? Don't you like it?"

"I love it, and I love all of you. That's why I'm crying. These are *froh* tears." She kissed each of their heads. *"Danki."*

Leona peeked over her shoulder. "Oh, that is just perfect. You all did a great job."

Just then a knock sounded on the back door, and Crystal hurried through the mudroom. "I'll get it."

Outside, she found Jeannie and Jared standing on the porch while Jared hefted a baby seat that held a sleeping Lila.

"Happy birthday!" Jeannie held up a gift bag.

*"Danki!"* Crystal smiled. "Hi. Come in." She and Jeannie had shared a few pleasant conversations during the past couple of weeks, and Crystal had forgiven her friends for their critical questions about Duane. She was grateful her friends had stopped sharing their opinions over her relationship with him, and conversations with them had been much more relaxing.

Jeannie took the baby seat and shouldered the diaper bag. "Is Owen still here?"

Crystal nodded. "He's in the barn."

Jared jammed his thumb toward the barn. "I'm going to find him." Then he jogged down the porch steps and started across the field.

"It's so *gut* to see you." Jeannie gave her a side hug.

"You too." Crystal clucked her tongue as she looked down at Lila. "She's gotten so big."

"I know!"

Just then two horses and buggies made their way up the driveway, and Crystal's heart flipped. Perhaps Duane was here!

When the horses halted by the barn, Jolene climbed out of one buggy while Lorraine climbed out of the other. Their husbands also exited their buggies and joined Kane, Owen, and Jared by the barn.

Crystal forced her lips to turn up in a smile. While she appreciated her friends for coming to celebrate her birthday, she wanted to see her boyfriend the most. She'd missed him since their last visit.

Lorraine and Jolene hurried up to the house, their children trailing behind them. While their children began playing on the swing set, Lorraine and Jolene came up the porch steps.

Jolene pulled Crystal in for a hug. "Happy birthday!"

"*Danki*," Crystal said before hugging Lorraine.

They each handed her a gift bag.

"Let me get Alisha to come out here with the *kinner*, and we can talk in the kitchen." Crystal directed the older children outside and then invited her friends in to sit in the kitchen.

She served bowls of chips, pretzels, nuts, and a vegetable tray while they sat and talked.

Leona put the twins in their highchairs, handing them each a bowl of Cheerios before she sat down.

Soon the kitchen was buzzing with activity as the children ran in and out, grabbing handfuls of chips before returning to the swing set. Crystal kept checking the clock, wondering and worrying about Duane and his whereabouts.

Nearly an hour later, she peeked out the window and spotted a horse and buggy.

Crystal popped up from her chair. "Excuse me."

With her pulse racing, she hurried outside. The late-June air was warm and smelled like summer as the sun began to set. The cicadas began their familiar chorus while lightning bugs floated about.

She rushed down the porch steps just as Duane climbed out of his buggy. She bit back the urge to launch herself into his arms.

Oh, how she'd missed him! The past weeks had been torture.

"Happy birthday," he said, handing her a bouquet of red roses.

She took the flowers and breathed in their sweet scent. "*Danki.* What a lovely gift!"

His smile faded. "I'm so sorry I'm late. We were finishing up a big job over in Leola, and we ran into some trouble. Then I had to go home and get changed."

She took his hand in hers. "Don't worry. I'm just so grateful you're here now." She gave his hand a tug. "Come and meet *mei freinden.*"

"Okay." He tied his horse to the fence and then picked up a bag from inside the buggy before permitting her to steer him up the porch steps and into the house.

"Hi, Duane!" Alisha called while pushing Hope on a swing as they walked past the swing set.

"Hi!" Hope hollered as her brothers echoed the greeting.

"*Danki* for the train," Nate said. "I love it."

"*Gern gschehne.*" Duane nodded.

Crystal towed Duane through the mudroom and into the kitchen. "Everyone," she announced, and conversations stopped, "this is Duane." Then she pointed to her friends. "Duane, this is Jeannie, Jolene, and Lorraine."

He smiled and waved. "Hello."

"Hi," Lorraine said.

Jolene nodded. "Nice to meet you."

"Hi, Duane." Jeannie smiled. "We've heard a lot about you."

Crystal pointed to the table. "Please help yourself to some snacks. I'm going to take care of these gorgeous flowers and get the cake out."

While Duane sat down beside Leona, Crystal moved over to the counter and found a vase.

"Let me help you." Jeannie appeared at her side and took the roses from her. "How are things with Duane?" she whispered.

"*Gut*. Why?" Crystal filled the vase with water and then stuck the flowers in.

"I was just wondering."

Crystal looked over her shoulder, relieved to see Duane laughing at something Leona had said while she rubbed her large belly. Then she turned to Jeannie. "Duane and I are *froh*."

Jeannie leaned in close. "I'm glad to hear that."

Leona sidled up to Crystal. "Why don't I get out the *kuche* I baked earlier?"

"Perfect." Crystal rubbed her hands together. She couldn't wait to celebrate another year of life with her friends and family.

# CHAPTER 26

"Happy birthday to you," Duane sang with the rest of Crystal's friends and family. "Happy birthday, dear Crystal. Happy birthday to you!"

Crystal laughed and then blew out the candles on her carrot cake. She looked as if she were glowing tonight dressed in a green dress that he had decided was his favorite. Her cheeks were pink, and her green eyes sparkled in the light of the lanterns set around the large kitchen.

Duane scanned the crowd in the kitchen while Crystal cut her cake, and Leona and Alisha handed out pieces. Kane carried over a carafe of coffee and began filling and distributing mugs.

It had not escaped Duane's notice that he was the oldest man in the room. If he and Crystal remained together, he would most likely always be the oldest member of the group. At least, he'd be the oldest if they were with her friends and family. He wondered if that would eventually bother Crystal. When he had asked her to be his girlfriend, she said she wasn't concerned about their age difference. Still, that might not always be the case as their years together wore on.

Duane swallowed back his worry. Perhaps he was

overanalyzing the situation. Maybe he would blend in with her friends, and the age difference wouldn't bother her at all.

Leona held out a piece of cake. "Would you like a plate, Duane?"

"*Ya. Danki.*" He breathed in the delicious scent of carrot cake with cream cheese frosting. "Did you bake this?"

She nodded. "*Ya*, Hope, Alisha, and I did. It's Crystal's favorite."

"It smells fantastic," Duane said.

"I hope you enjoy it."

"*Mamm*, could I have one, please?" Jevon asked, tugging on the skirt of her dress.

She bent and touched his nose. "Of course."

Duane moved over to the counter and leaned against it. He forked a piece of cake and enjoyed the sweet, delightful flavor as he took in the scene.

Conversations had broken out in the kitchen while the party guests enjoyed the cake. To his left, he spotted Alisha and Hope leading the other children into the family room to eat while Leona had returned to the table and sat between the twins' highchairs.

Kane stood in the corner talking to three men, who were the husbands of Crystal's friends.

Duane continued to enjoy his cake while conversations swirled around him. When he spotted Crystal holding Jeannie's newborn, he sucked in a breath. He felt a lead brick form in his gut as Crystal peered down at the baby in her arms, her expression full of longing.

Duane scooped more cake into his mouth, feeling older by the minute. He wasn't sure he was truly ready to start over with a newborn, but if they were married, he would try for her sake.

But what if he couldn't give her a child? Would she resent him for the rest of her life? He didn't want to ruin her future in that way. Crystal was a lovely, special young woman, and he didn't want to destroy her prospect of a happy life as a mother of her own children.

But still doubt crept into Duane's mind and settled.

He set his plate down in the sink. He considered starting to wash the dishes for her, but then he stopped himself. What would the other men think if they spotted him washing the dishes? Surely they would find him strange.

"Duane."

He turned and found Kane beckoning him. *"Ya?"*

"Come sit on the porch with us," Kane said as Owen frowned at him.

Duane followed the men outside and sat on a rocker while they began discussing their farm work. He moved the chair back and forth and contributed to the conversation when he could think of something interesting to say.

After enduring what felt like another hour on the porch listening to Kane and the other men talk about farming, the party guests began to leave.

Duane leaned on the porch railing as he watched Crystal say good-bye to Jolene and Lorraine before they loaded their families into their buggies and started toward the road.

Crystal said good-bye to Jeannie and Jared next, hugging Jeannie and kissing the baby before they secured her in the buggy and headed out on their way.

When Owen walked out toward the barn, Crystal brushed past him and climbed up the porch stairs. Duane tried not to grin at how she'd disregarded Owen as she made her way to him.

"We can finally talk," she said as she walked over to him. "*Danki* for coming tonight."

"I never would have missed your birthday."

"I'm sorry I couldn't spend more time with you." She motioned toward the glider. "Would you like to sit?"

They sat together, and then he held up the bag that he'd carried in earlier. "Would you please open this now?"

"Oh. *Danki*. You shouldn't have. The flowers were more than enough."

"Please. Open it."

She peeked into the bag and pulled out a needlepoint set. "Oh my goodness."

"I hope it's a *gut* set. I really didn't know what to get, and I didn't have anyone to ask." He pointed to the picture. "It's flowers in a vase. I thought it might include your favorite things—needlepoint and flowers."

Crystal ran her fingers over it. "This is lovely."

"Now you need to make me a promise." He placed his hand on hers.

Her eyes seemed to search his. "What's the promise?"

"Promise me that you'll make some time to go to your special spot and work on this or something else of your choosing. You deserve time to yourself."

She smiled. "You're so thoughtful. I'm so grateful God brought us together." Then she leaned over and kissed his cheek.

The feel of her lips on his cheek made every cell in his body come alive, a feeling he hadn't experienced since he'd been with Connie.

"I'm so glad you're here," she whispered, threading her fingers with his. "I had wanted to introduce you to *mei freinden*." Her green eyes sparkled. "I hope you enjoyed meeting everyone."

"I did."

"Isn't Jeannie's *boppli* adorable?"

Duane nodded as the memory of her excitement while holding the baby filled his mind. His stomach tightened. "She is."

"Sometimes I wonder about us and our future."

His throat dried.

"I mean, if we got married and had *kinner*, I wonder how many the Lord would see fit for us to have."

"Crystal," he began, lowering his voice in hopes that their conversation wouldn't be overhead. "I need to be honest with you about something."

Her brow puckered. "What is it?"

"I just don't know about *kinner*." He huffed a deep breath as embarrassment crept up his neck.

She angled her body toward him. "What do you mean, Duane?"

"Connie wanted more *kinner*, but we never had any after Jayden. I don't know if that was my fault." He looked down at his lap. "If it was my fault, then I would feel terrible if I prevented you from having the family you've always dreamed of."

"Duane." She rested her hand on his arm, and his eyes darted to hers. "You don't know that for sure."

"But it's a possibility, and I don't want to lie to you."

She nodded, and he hoped it wasn't doubt that he found in her eyes. "Does that mean you wouldn't want to try with me?"

"No, no," he said. "I just don't want you to pin your dreams on me and then be disappointed."

She nodded, looking thoughtful, then cupped her hand to her mouth to cover a yawn. "Excuse me."

Duane gave her hand a squeeze, taking that as a cue that it was time to go. "It's getting late. I should probably get going."

"*Danki* again for everything."

"I hope you had a *wunderbaar* evening and a *gut* birthday."

"I did." She stood and wrapped her arms around his middle, pulling him into a warm embrace.

He breathed in her scent—coffee mixed with carrot cake and the flowery aroma of her shampoo. He wanted time to freeze so that he could hold her forever.

When she pulled away, she smiled up at him. "I look forward to seeing you again."

"*Gut nacht,*" he told her.

Duane strolled out to his waiting horse and buggy and then climbed in. As he guided his horse toward the road, he pondered the evening.

And one question pummeled his heart over and over—could it even be possible for him and Crystal to have a long-lasting relationship that would sustain her for a lifetime?

Later Crystal walked into the kitchen and filled a glass with water. After Duane had left, she had headed into the kitchen and helped Leona and Alisha finish cleaning up, even though they told her that it was her birthday and she should relax. She couldn't imagine not helping when there was work to be done. Then she had read a story to the twins and tucked them into bed.

As she drank the water, she contemplated her evening. She smiled as she recalled her time spent with Duane. She was grateful that they had enjoyed a few minutes together, and she'd snuck in one kiss. Her blood rushed through her veins at the memory.

But then her heart sank a little as she considered what he had said about having children. Would she be satisfied if they were married and he couldn't have more children? Would being his wife and a stepmother be enough to sustain a happy life with him, especially while facing daily animosity from Korey?

She washed the glass and then set it in the drainboard. When she turned, she found Owen standing by the table. Startled, she gasped. "I didn't expect to see you here."

"Sorry. I didn't mean to scare you." He smiled and held out a package. "I have something for you."

Her stomach soured. "You really don't need to give me a gift."

"I insist." He closed the distance between them and held out the package. "Please take it. I just wanted to remind you that I'm sorry. I wake up with regret every day and go to bed with the same feeling because I always think of you and what we had. You were my best friend, and I stupidly sacrificed everything because I believed my cousin's business was going to be profitable. I never should have chosen the promise of money over a future with you. If you give me a chance, I will put you first. I promise you from the bottom of my heart." He touched his chest.

She shook her head. "Owen, you need to give this up. We're over, and I'm not interested in taking you back. Please take your gift and leave."

He set the gift on the counter beside her and then leveled his gaze with her. "Crystal, just listen to me. I know you're upset with me, and I don't blame you. I treated you and your *dat* badly, and I'm sorry. I'll never stop apologizing until you see just how sorry I am."

She took a step back from him, putting necessary distance between them. "Owen, please go."

"Let me just say what I came to say." He held his hands up. "I can tell that Duane is a *gut* man. I will give him that, but I loved you first. We have a shared history, and you're still important to me. If you give me a chance, I'll make a life for us. We'll have a family. I know that's what you want. I saw the look in your eyes when you held Lila."

She studied his face, and she saw honesty, remorse, and hope there. Memories welled up inside of her—long walks they'd taken around his father's pasture, late-night talks with stolen kisses, Sunday afternoons spent visiting with his family.

Her chest swelled as she recalled how much she loved him and how she'd wanted to marry him, settle down, and have a family with him.

She shook her head, hoping to dislodge the feelings she still harbored for him. She felt as if his bright-blue eyes were pulling her in, beckoning her to a familiar place. Why did he have to be so handsome?

"It's too late, Owen." Her voice sounded rough.

"It doesn't have to be," he continued. "I believe in us. I believe that God led me back here to you." He pointed a finger between them. "I'm willing to try again if you are."

"Owen, I've told you no. Now, I need you to leave."

"Fine." He started across the kitchen, and when he stopped by the doorway, she held her breath.

"I'm not going to give up on you," he said.

"Well, then you are wasting your time," she said, hugging her arms to her chest as if to shield her heart from the man before her.

Owen headed out the door, and once he was gone, Crystal released the breath she'd been holding.

She opened the package Owen had left and stared down at

a box of her favorite cookies, fudge-striped, and shook her head. "Well, the *kinner* will enjoy these."

After setting the box of cookies on the counter, she gathered up the picture her nieces and nephews had drawn and the needle-point kit from Duane and carried them up to her room where she set them on her dresser before she changed into her nightgown.

When she crawled into bed, she closed her eyes and prepared herself for another night of restless sleep.

# CHAPTER 27

On Thursday, one week later, Crystal thought she heard a loud knocking and then the sound of someone saying her name. Half asleep, she rolled over and snuggled deeper into her pillow.

"Wake up, Crystal! Come quick. Leona is in labor!"

Crystal sat up and gulped in air. Was that Kane calling for her? Her room was shrouded in darkness, and the green digital numbers on her clock read 4:05.

She grabbed her flashlight from her nightstand, flipped it on, stumbled out of bed, and pulled her door open.

"Crystal," Kane said, his hazel eyes wild, and his face contorted with worry. "Please get dressed. She says the contractions are starting, but they're far apart. I'm going to call for a ride soon. I need you to be ready when the *kinner* wake up."

"I'll be right down."

"*Danki.*" Kane rushed down the hallway and descended the stairs.

Crystal hurried around her room, grabbing a gray dress, black apron, and her prayer covering. Soon she was dressed and down the stairs. She heard noises coming from Kane and Leona's room but stayed away out of respect for their privacy. She busied herself by mixing up cinnamon rolls and then popping them into the oven.

Crystal enjoyed the heavenly aroma of the rolls when she took them out of the oven. She expected Kane to come out and share that it was time to call for a ride, but he remained in the bedroom.

Worry started to creep into Crystal's mind when more time passed, and Kane still hadn't emerged from the room. She set the cinnamon buns on a tray and then glanced at the clock. It was almost six thirty, and the children would wake up soon.

"Crystal," Kane rushed out into the kitchen. "Leona says something isn't right. I was going to call for a ride, but I think I need to get the paramedics in case she needs medical attention before we get to the hospital."

Crystal's eyes widened as fear grabbed her by the throat. "Oh no!"

"Please take care of the *kinner*," he called over his shoulder as he hurried out the door.

"Of course!" Crystal paced the kitchen and opened her heart to God:

*Please, Lord, protect Leona and her babies. Please let the babies come into the world safely. Hold them in your arms, Lord. Please!*

Kane returned a few minutes later. "They're on their way. I left a message for Owen and asked him to run the farm for me. Now I need to pack a bag for Leona."

"Do you need help?" Crystal called after him.

"No, *danki*."

Crystal felt useless as she stood in the kitchen while Kane led the three young paramedics through the front door and to his bedroom. Several moments later, they exited the bedroom and took Leona out the front door on a stretcher.

Crystal walked outside with Kane and touched his hand. "Don't worry about anything here. Just call me later and let me know how it's going. I'm praying for you all."

"*Danki*, Crystal." Kane jogged toward the ambulance as the paramedics loaded his wife into the back.

While Crystal watched the ambulance drive away with her brother and sister-in-law inside, she prayed once more:

*Lord, protect Leona and her babies. Bring the babies into the world safely.*

She walked back into the house and heard one of the twins cry out. She forced herself to smile. She had to be strong for the children.

Later that afternoon, Crystal hurried out toward the barn to check the messages. The early July sun was hot on her neck as she walked through the lush, green grass dotted with bright-yellow dandelions.

She'd spent the morning silently praying while taking care of the children. Worry had followed her around like her shadow as she wondered how Leona and the twins were doing. Had she arrived at the hospital in time to have the babies in the delivery room with her doctor's help? Were the babies healthy? And was Leona okay?

And what if Leona wasn't? If she needed to be hospitalized or if something happened to her, Crystal's nieces and nephews would depend on her more than ever.

The thought was too much for the moment. Turning to prayer,

she said, "Please God, protect Leona and her precious babies. Bring them home safely to our family."

When the children asked about their parents, Crystal told them that their mother had gone to the hospital to have their baby brothers or sisters and promised their parents would be home soon. She was careful to keep any worry out of her voice, and all the children had accepted her explanation.

Once she'd gotten Nate and Alisha off to school, Hope and Jevon had kept the twins happy in their play yard while she cleaned up the kitchen and put together a casserole for supper. After feeding Jevon, Hope, and the twins lunch, she had put the twins and Hope in for their afternoon naps and then hurried outside to check the messages to see if Kane had left any news. She couldn't wait to hear how Leona and the babies were doing. Oh, how she prayed they were doing well!

Crystal looked over toward the pasture fence and spotted Owen hammering in new slats. While she hated to admit it to herself, the farm had improved since Owen had started working there. The fresh coat of red paint and new doors made the barns look almost new. Now the fence was shaping up as well.

She rushed into the barn and found a message from Kane. She prayed once again as he started to speak.

"Crystal, it's Kane. We had a rough start, but everything is okay," he said, and she could hear the exhaustion in his voice. "Leona had a healthy boy and girl. They were born by cesarean section. I'm going to stay the rest of the day. I'll come home tonight and go back tomorrow. I should be able to bring her and the *bopplin* home in a few days. They both weigh close to five pounds, so they shouldn't have to stay in the hospital too long. *Danki* for being there for the *kinner*. Tell them we love them, and we'll be home soon. Oh, and Leona wants to name the boy Kane Junior and the girl Josie. After what she's been through, I told her that it's definitely her choice. Good-bye."

Crystal breathed a sigh of relief, and her thoughts immediately went to Duane. Oh, how she missed him! They hadn't seen each other since her birthday last week, and now she wouldn't see him for a least a week or so since Leona was recovering.

She dialed his number and then smiled when his voice came through the line. "Thank you for calling Bontrager and Sons Roofing. Please leave a message, and we'll call you back."

She cleared her throat while she waited for the beep. "Hi, Duane. This is Crystal. I have news. Leona had her *bopplin* today—a boy and a girl. It was a tough delivery, but she should be able to bring them home in a few days."

She paused. "I just wanted to let you know what's going on because I won't be able to see you for a while. I'm going to have to care for the *kinner* alone while she's in the hospital, and then Leona is going to need me to take care of the *kinner* and help with the newborns while she heals from the delivery. It might be a couple of weeks before we can get together. I'll miss you. Take care."

She hung up the phone and started out of the barn. When she stepped out into the bright sunlight, she spotted Owen waving at her from the fence. He jogged over, and she frowned, her stomach tightening at the thought of having to talk to him once again.

"Have you heard any news?"

She nodded. "She had a boy and a girl."

"That's fantastic! Are they okay?"

"*Ya*, but she had a tough time. I've been so worried since the paramedics came to get her. She'll be in the hospital for a few days. Kane said he'll be home tonight and then go back tomorrow."

Crystal sniffed as happiness and relief for her brother and sister-in-law overtook her.

"Crystal." Owen's voice was full of empathy. "Are you okay?" He reached for her and then pulled his hand back.

"*Ya*, I am. I'm just feeling a little overwhelmed."

"Do you need anything?"

"No, *danki*."

"I miss you. I miss us." Regret seemed to flicker over his face as his gorgeous blue eyes studied her.

Crystal's heart clutched as she backed away from him. Why couldn't she leave behind her old feelings? What was wrong with her? "I need to go check on the *kinner*, Owen."

She spun and then hurried into the house. When she reached the mudroom, she looked up at the ceiling. "Lord, keep Leona and the babies safe and give me strength."

Duane walked into the barn later that evening. His back and neck ached from another day of hard work in the hot July sun. He picked up the phone, and after writing down two messages for his sons and three from prospective customers, he was grateful to hear Crystal's voice.

He settled down on the chair by the phone and listened as she shared the news of her new niece and nephew. He felt a pang of longing when she said she wouldn't be able to see him for a while.

When her message was over, he dialed her number and waited for the voicemail to pick up. After the beep, he started to speak.

"Hi. This is Duane calling for Crystal. I'm sorry to hear Leona had a tough delivery. Praise God she and the *bopplin* are fine. I understand you and the family need a few days to adjust. I will stop by to see how you are soon. Give my regards to Kane and Leona. I miss you too, Crystal."

Duane hung up the phone and then headed back toward the house. Of course, Leona would need some time to recover, but surely he could stop by to see Crystal sooner than a couple of weeks.

He'd wait a few days and then he would go see her. Maybe seeing him would brighten her day. He couldn't wait.

Tuesday evening Alisha stepped into the bathroom where Crystal had the twins in the tub. "*Aenti*. Duane is here to see you."

Crystal looked down at her apron, which was splattered with breakfast and lunch. She'd been up nearly all night helping Leona with the newborns, and now she was giving the toddler twins a bath after they had decided to rub their SpaghettiOs into their hair during lunch. Embarrassment whipped over her. How could she spend time with Duane when she felt and looked like such a mess?

"I'll take over," Alisha offered.

"*Danki*, but where are Jevon and Hope?" Crystal asked as she stood.

Alisha pointed toward the doorway. "They're coloring at the kitchen table and talking to Duane. He brought a box of donuts."

"Okay." Crystal stepped out into the hallway just as Leona called her name from the bedroom.

"Crystal!" Leona bellowed. "Would you please bring me more

diapers, wipes, and burp cloths? Also, would you please make more formula?"

Pressing her lips together, Crystal sucked in a breath. "*Ya.* Just give me a minute, please."

As she walked toward the kitchen, Crystal felt as if her legs and arms were made of lead. She was so exhausted that her eyes burned. She tried to smile as she stepped into the kitchen, but it felt more like a grimace. If only she'd had the time to change before Duane arrived.

Her heart lifted when she saw Duane sitting at the table talking to Jevon and Hope, who beamed at him while they ate glazed donuts.

When his gaze tangled with hers, he stood and walked over to her.

"Hey." He held his hands up in defense. "I know you told me to stay away, but I brought donuts." He pointed to the large box in the center of the table.

"That's really sweet, but I wish I'd known you were coming."

"Why?" His handsome face clouded with a frown.

She glanced down at her messy apron and embarrassment crept up her neck, heating her face. "I'm a wreck. I was up nearly all night helping with the newborns. I got a total of two hours of sleep. Today has been horrendous. I have Evie and Morgan in the bathtub because they decided to wear their SpaghettiOs instead of eat them."

"I'm so sorry, but you still look beautiful to me. Plus, I remember those tough times when *mei buwe* were young. Connie and I had plenty of those days."

She cupped her hand to her mouth to stifle a yawn. While she appreciated the sweet compliment and his empathy, she still longed for a chance to clean herself up. "How about I call you when things are a little less chaotic? Then we can enjoy each other's company on the porch without any interruptions." Saying the words nearly broke her heart, but she didn't have the emotional or physical energy to be good company for him today.

He hesitated and then a warm smile lifted his lips. "Sure. If that's what you want."

"I promise I'll call you Friday. I'm hoping to get some sleep by then. We'll make plans. Maybe you can stop by to visit on Saturday or Sunday, okay?"

"Call me when you're ready. I'll look forward to seeing you."

"I will too. *Danki* for the donuts."

Duane said good-bye to Jevon and Hope and then headed out the door.

Despondency weighed heavily on Crystal's chest as she made the formula and gathered up the other supplies Leona needed.

When she carried everything into Leona's bedroom, she found her rocking her newborns in a chair, one in each arm. The sweet smell of baby lotion and diaper cream filled her senses. She set the diapers, wipes, and burp cloths on the dresser before handing the bottle to Leona.

"*Danki*," Leona said before she began to feed Josie.

As Leona gazed down at the baby's tiny face, Crystal felt an overwhelming ache grab her heart and squeeze it. Would she ever have that? Would it be possible with Duane? After all, he admitted that he and Connie wanted more children but couldn't have them. Would she be satisfied with a future if they never had children of their own? Or would that ache become a gaping hole in their marriage?

And how would she maneuver the choppy waters of becoming

a stepmother to three full-grown sons, one of whom clearly didn't want her in his life, let alone the home where he'd grown up? Would Korey's belligerence toward her fester and tear down the foundation of her relationship with Duane?

It all seemed too complicated and painful when what she truly craved was a loving family of her own. She wanted one more than ever.

Her grief ran deep, mixing with her sadness and exhaustion. The room was suddenly closing in on her. She had to get out of there.

Crystal pushed those thoughts away and headed for the door. "I need to check on Evie and Morgan. Call me if you need me."

Thunder rumbled in the distance as Duane hammered another shingle onto the hardware store roof Saturday afternoon. The scent of rain had become stronger throughout the day as more and more dark clouds clogged the sky.

"*Dat*, I think we need to call it a day." Tyler's voice held the hint of a warning. "We're really taking a chance up here. You heard about the *bu* who was struck by lightning in the pasture last week in Paradise, right? It didn't even look like rain when he was hit. The Lord is telling us to finish this up on Monday."

Duane sighed. "You're right, but that means we're starting out next week behind schedule."

"Not necessarily," Tyler said. "Kore and I can finish this job up on Monday, and you and Jay can start the teardown at the other job on Monday. It'll work out. I'm sure of it. I'm a *gut* project manager."

Jayden nodded. "Sounds good to me."

Korey just shrugged as he picked up supplies.

Duane's middle son still was giving him the cold shoulder, and the silence between them was eating away at his heart. Oh, how he missed his son! To make matters worse, he hadn't heard from Crystal since he'd stopped by and delivered donuts on Tuesday. She had promised to call and make plans to see him over the weekend and then didn't. Perhaps something had happened. What if one of the children or Leona had taken ill? He was worried about her. But if something had happened, wouldn't she have called?

Duane longed for closeness, and he and Crystal had barely begun seeing each other—but already he wondered if they were moving away from one another. After all, she was busy with her new niece and nephew.

Bishop Wilmer had left a message yesterday saying that he wanted to talk to Duane about Tricia since her farm's tax bill was coming due in a month. And although Duane hadn't called Wilmer back, the message had sent more doubt twisting up Duane's insides. Was God trying to speak to him? He recalled how the bishop, Duane's friends, and even Tyler had told Duane that they all believed he should give Tricia a chance. Maybe they were right, and Crystal's silence had only confirmed that.

Perhaps his relationship with Crystal was too complicated to stand the test of time. He would only know for sure by going to see her.

"Okay, let's call it." Duane started picking up supplies as another peal of thunder gently shook the roof. The four of them descended the ladder, and Duane pulled out his cell phone to call his driver just as the rain started.

Duane sent Tyler in to tell the storeowner they would finish up the job on Monday, and then Duane helped Jayden and Korey pack up their supplies while they waited for their ride.

Once they were ready, Duane stood under the store's awning and stared out toward the pouring rain as lightning lit up the horizon.

"You okay, *Dat*?" Jayden asked.

Duane huffed a breath. "Not really. I'm worried about Crystal." *And our relationship.*

"What do you mean?" Jayden asked as Tyler joined them.

"Bryan said it's fine if we finish up Monday," Tyler interrupted. "He was surprised we stayed on the roof that long since it's been thundering for a while."

Duane nodded. "Thanks."

"*Dat*, what's going on between you and Crystal? You seem upset." Jayden looked concerned.

He explained how she had promised to call soon to make plans, but her family's situation had monopolized her time. "I haven't heard from her all week. I'm worried about her and her family. It's not like her to not call at all. I'm going to have Drew drop me off on the way home and then pick me up after he takes you all home."

"Okay, *Dat*," Tyler said.

Jayden gave a solemn nod. "I hope everything is okay."

"I do too," Duane agreed as worry threaded through him.

# CHAPTER 28

CRYSTAL STOOD IN THE MIDDLE OF THE KITCHEN AND HEAVED out a heavy sigh. She felt as if her world was crumbling as exhaustion made her arms and legs feel heavy. Thunder rumbled outside the house and the scent of rain wafted in through the open windows.

She glanced down at her apron, which was splattered with formula along with ingredients from the casserole she'd thrown together earlier. She was a mess for sure!

It had been a horrendous week as Crystal had pushed herself through each day, helping with the newborns, taking care of the older children, cooking, cleaning, and washing clothes on barely a few hours of sleep each night. She wasn't sure how much longer she could sustain this chaos, but she would do what she had to for her family.

Leaning back against the counter, she covered her face with her hands as her eyes filled with frustrated tears.

*Lord, give me strength. Help me be a better sister and aunt.*

When she heard the back door open and close, Crystal sniffed and cleared her throat, hoping to make herself presentable before her brother stepped into the kitchen.

"You okay, Crystal?"

Her gaze snapped to Owen's. He stood before her in the middle of the kitchen, his handsome face clouded with worry.

Her mouth opened, and instead of saying she was fine, her truth came out in a rush. "No, I'm not. I'm a wreck. I feel more overwhelmed than I've ever felt, and I-I-I can't keep up." Her voice broke as a sob bubbled up and spilled out of her throat without warning.

"Hey, it's okay." Owen closed the distance between them. "Just tell me what's going on."

She picked up a napkin from the counter and wiped her eyes and nose. "I haven't slept since the newborns came home, and I'm doing my best to take care of the *haus* and the *kinner*, but I'm just so tired, Owen. I feel like I'm losing my mind."

"It will get better. Jared told me that he and Jeannie are still trying to get Lila on a schedule. It just takes some time, and I would imagine that it's even more challenging with *zwillingbopplin*." He touched her shoulder.

She nodded and sniffed, feeling silly for being so emotional, especially in front of him. "I know."

Something unreadable flickered in his eyes. "You're so strong, Crystal. In fact, you're the most courageous person I know. You'll get through this."

"I don't feel very strong right now," she whispered as her lip trembled, and more weary tears spilled down her hot cheeks.

She closed her eyes and tried in vain to stop the tears. When Owen's strong arms pulled her in for a hug, she stilled and then relaxed against him for a moment, remembering the old, familiar comfort of his embrace.

Then guilt gripped her. She took a step back from him out of his embrace, wiping her eyes.

When she glanced behind Owen, she spotted Duane standing in the doorway to the mudroom, his mouth agape and color rising up his neck. Her stomach dropped.

"Duane?" She reached for him.

Shaking his head, he looked dejected before he spun and headed through the door, his footsteps heavy.

Crystal rushed after him, her heartbeat pounding in her ears. "Duane! Wait!" She stepped out onto the porch just as thunder crashed in the distance and rain pounded on the roof above them. "Duane, please stop! Talk to me! That wasn't what you thought it was. That wasn't . . ."

He stopped at the edge of the porch and faced her. "Then what was it?"

"Today was a really bad day. Actually, it's just been a tough week. Owen just happened to walk in while I was having a breakdown, and I let him hug me." Her shoulders sagged with her defeat. "That's it."

"Do you care about him?" A thread of hurt vibrated in his voice.

She shook her head. "No, not in that way, and I'm sorry if I hurt you."

Duane took a step toward her. "I've missed you, and I came here to check on you. I've been worried about you and your family."

"I've missed you too, and I'm sorry I haven't called. I meant to, but I'm burning the candle at both ends. I haven't slept since the newborns came home. I'm running myself ragged trying to keep this household running."

He nodded and glanced around as if putting puzzle pieces together in his mind.

"What are you thinking, Duane?"

"I'm feeling at a loss right now." He touched his beard as sadness filled his gorgeous, dark eyes. "It seems like everything is against us."

"What are you saying?" Worry filtered through her.

"We're both working through things in our lives." He gestured toward the house. "You're going through a hard time with your family, and I'm still dealing with Korey and his silence and anger. Maybe we should take a break."

She opened her mouth and closed it. Then she rubbed her temple, where a headache brewed. "I'm sorry, but I can't even think straight. I got three hours of sleep last night, and my head is pounding. But this doesn't sound like a good solution right now. Can we talk about this another time?"

"No, I think we need to talk about this now."

Confusion doused her as the rain pounded harder above her and lightning electrified the sky above. "What do you mean, Duane?"

"It's obvious that you belong with someone like Owen who can give you what you want." The pain in his eyes nearly broke her in two. "If you stayed with me, there's a huge chance that I might not be able to give you your greatest desire, and that's *kinner.*"

"You don't mean that." Her voice sounded thick and reedy.

"Actually, I do. I saw how you and Owen were together, and as much as it destroys me to say this, I would rather see you *froh* with him than have you pin all of your hopes on me and then I let you down." He took a step back toward the edge of the porch. "Maybe the bishop is right, and Tricia is more suited for me."

She blanched. "How can you say that?"

"I'm just stating the truth as I see it." He held his hands up. "You want a future with a man who can give you *kinner,* and I'm not sure I can. You said yourself that everyone thinks Owen came back so that the Lord could give you another chance. Maybe everyone is right about Owen. Plus, Korey is upset that I'm dating you, and the rift between us is taking a toll on me."

His words were like a knife to her heart. She breathed in a shaky breath as her eyes filled with tears. "I'm sorry. I had worried that the problems between you and Korey would morph into something even more painful. I wish I hadn't been the cause of that."

He took a step toward her, and his expression became so intense that her heart thudded against her rib cage. "It's not your fault. It was bound to happen. I care deeply for you, but I don't think I'm the best match for you. As much as I hate to admit, I can tell that you and Owen still care for each other. The Lord may be leading you to him instead of me, and I'm prideful to think that I can be enough for you, even as much as I care for you."

She stared up at him as his words soaked through her. "So you think we should break up?"

"Unfortunately, yes." His voice caught, and he cleared his throat roughly. "I think Owen might be the best choice for you, and Tricia is the practical one for me."

She tried to swallow, but her throat felt like it was full of sand. "So, that's it then. It's . . . over?" The words nearly crushed her.

His Adam's apple bobbed, and she was almost certain she spotted unshed tears sparkling in his brown eyes. "*Ya*, I guess so."

"I'm sorry." The statement punched her in the chest, and she felt as if she couldn't breathe, her insides knotted up.

"I'm sorry too," he croaked.

Then she wrenched open the back door and walked into the kitchen, where Kane and Leona sat across from each other at the table, each of them holding one of the newborns while Owen leaned on the counter.

"Are you okay?" Leona asked, concern clouding her face.

"It's over between Duane and me." When her words broke, she rushed up to her room, closed the door behind her, and began to cry.

Duane headed into the house as his driver steered his truck down the driveway toward the road. Above him, the rain continued to pound on the roof, and his heart shattered more and more with each step he took.

After kicking off his muddy boots and hanging his damp straw hat on a peg in the mudroom, he stalked into the kitchen, where he found his three sons sitting at the table, eating sandwiches along with macaroni and cheese.

"We tried to wait for you," Jayden said. Then his expression clouded, and he stood. "*Dat*, are you all right?"

"What happened?" Tyler asked.

Duane's body vibrated with a mixture of grief and humiliation as his eyes moved from Tyler's concerned expression to Korey's widening eyes. "Crystal and I broke up." His voice sounded gravelly.

Then Duane forced his legs to carry him toward his bedroom, where his bitterness melted away, leaving anguish.

"*Dat?*" Jayden rushed after him.

Ignoring him, Duane sank down on the corner of his bed, which creaked under his weight, and dropped his head into his hands. He'd finally allowed someone into his heart after losing Connie, and now he regretted it.

A dull ache overcame him.

*"Dat?"* Jayden's voice sounded close to his ear, and then the mattress shifted beside him. "Please talk to me."

When Duane felt a hand on his shoulder, he sat up straight and turned to Jayden, who looked stricken with worry. "We realized it could never work out," he said.

"I'm sorry."

Frowning, Tyler stepped inside the room. "The last thing I wanted was to see you this *bedauerlich*. I'm sorry, *Dat.*"

*"Danki."* Duane cleared his throat. "I think you were right, and I need to give my relationship with Tricia a chance." The words were painful to admit.

"What are you talking about?" Jayden asked.

"The bishop suggested I date and eventually marry Tricia, and I think she's a better match for me. We have more in common, and it will help the community."

"But is that what you want?" Jayden asked softly.

Duane swallowed against his dry throat.

"Don't rush into anything, *Dat*," Tyler cautioned him. "No matter what, you have us."

"That's right," Jayden said.

*"Danki,"* Duane whispered, grateful for the sons God had given him. The Lord had walked with him through the death of his beloved wife. Surely God would not forsake him now.

*Be with me, Lord. I need you now as much as ever.*

Crystal rolled over and stared out through the darkness toward her bedroom wall later that evening. Anguish wrapped around her chest and squeezed, sucking the air from her lungs as tears streamed down her cheeks.

She had somehow managed to push herself out of bed and propel herself down the stairs to finish preparing supper and clean up the kitchen. Although her nieces and nephews had asked her more than once if she was okay, Leona and Kane had barely spoken to her, only giving her sympathetic expressions and offering to help with the chores.

After Crystal had gotten the children cleaned up and ready for bed, she had hidden in the upstairs bathroom, where she'd taken a long, hot shower and cried until she was certain she'd run out of tears, while Duane's words about how they didn't belong together ran through her mind.

Crystal sniffed as she rolled onto her back.

"Lord," she whispered. "Please help me. Please take away my pain. I think I'm in love with Duane and I think he may love me too. But I'm so confused. If he truly loved me, then why would he say we belong with other people? Why would he insist that we can't make it work? I agree we had unresolved issues, but I believed somehow we could work them out through prayer and faith."

Her voice shook as her tears began to flow once again. "Now I have a hole in my heart. I've lost the love of my life. After thirty-four years, I believed I found a man who truly loved me, and I've lost him. Help me heal, Lord. Please."

She covered her face with her hands as her sobs echoed throughout her room. She couldn't breathe due to the grief packed around her heart.

When a soft knock sounded, she rolled over and pulled her sheet over her head. Then her bedroom door creaked open.

"*Aenti?*" a soft voice called.

Crystal held her breath, trying in vain to stop her tears.

"*Aenti,* we're sorry you're so *bedauerlich.*"

Sniffing, Crystal swiped her hands across her face.

The door creaked closed and then soft footsteps padded across the room. After a moment, the bed shifted on either side of her and she felt two little bodies snuggle up beside her.

"*Ich liebe dich,*" Hope whispered as she held Crystal's hand.

"That's right," Alisha said from the other side of her. "We love you, and we won't leave you alone tonight."

Crystal sniffed. "*Danki.*"

Then she closed her eyes, grateful for her nieces with their little hearts of gold.

"Are you sure you want to stay home from church today?" Kane studied Crystal while they sat around the breakfast table the following morning.

Crystal looked down at her bowl of oatmeal sprinkled with cinnamon. "*Ya.* I'll take care of Kane Junior and Josie so that Leona can see her *freinden.*" She peered down to the end of the table where Leona sat watching her.

Leona seemed to share a look with Kane. "Okay. *Danki.*"

"May I stay home with *Aenti?*" Alisha asked.

"No, Alisha," Kane said. "You need to go to church."

"*Ya, Dat.*" Alisha gave Crystal a sympathetic look.

Hope shifted in her seat. "*Aenti* was *bedauerlich* last night. Me and Alisha heard her crying, so we went into her room to check on her. We slept with her to try to make her *froh* again."

"Yes, and I am the luckiest *aenti* in the world." Crystal's heart turned over in her chest as she looked at her precious nieces across the table. When she turned toward her brother, Crystal spotted another concerned look pass between him and his wife, and she cleared her throat. She was tired of being the subject of their unspoken worry and pity. "We need to finish up so you can get on your way to church."

After their plates were clean, Kane brought the bassinet into the kitchen so that Crystal could keep an eye on the newborns while she washed the dishes and wiped down the table. She had just finished up when the family filed back into the kitchen, Leona and Kane each holding one of the toddler twins.

Leona gave Crystal a hesitant expression. "I'm *froh* to stay home if you want to go to church. I can care for the newborns."

"*Danki*, but I need some time alone to think and pray." Crystal looked down at the two sleeping infants in their bassinet. "We'll be fine."

"If you say so." Leona walked over to the bassinet and peered down at her son and daughter. "We'll be back soon, Junior and Josie." Then she touched Crystal's arm. "The Lord will heal your broken heart."

Crystal nodded as a lump began to swell in her throat.

"We need to go, Leona," Kane said. Then he looked at Crystal. "*Danki* for caring for Junior and Josie."

Crystal waved as the children and their parents made their way out the back door.

When the babies started to cry, she carried them into Kane

and Leona's bedroom and changed their diapers while she sang "Jesus Loves Me" to them.

Then she warmed up bottles in the kitchen and moved into the family room as she rocked them and took turns feeding them, silently praying for God to heal her splintered heart.

Her mind replayed her relationship with Duane as more sadness gripped her, stealing her breath. She recalled all the times Duane had gone out of his way to talk to her nieces and nephews, and her heart constricted.

He was such a good man, a good father, a good friend.

Crystal shoved the painful memories away and lifted Kane Junior to her shoulder to burp him. She rubbed his back and sniffed. It was going to be a long day.

*Please, God. Give me strength. I fear I might crumble into a million pieces and never recover.*

Duane stepped out of the Dienner family's barn Sunday afternoon after church. As he took in another gorgeous mid-July day with the singing birds, cheerful chirping squirrels, and crystal-blue, cloudless sky, the beauty all seemed to mock his grim mood.

He had somehow made it through the long service with the ministers' holy words of the Lord's promises while trying to hold back the grief that had haunted him all night long, stealing his slumber.

During the service he had lost himself in memories of his too brief relationship with Crystal. Her beautiful face, her smile, and her laughter echoed down the corridors of his memory.

Still, he had held fast to his belief that perhaps he and Tricia belonged together, and now he planned to do something about it. If only he could stop the bleak feeling that had curled in his chest ever since he'd broken up with Crystal.

When he spotted the bishop talking with the minister and deacon, he quickened his steps. "Bishop. May I speak with you?"

Wilmer excused himself from his conversation and stepped over to Duane. *"Wie geht's?"*

"I received your message regarding my relationship with Tricia, and I wanted to tell you that I'm considering what you said."

"Is that so?" The older man's bushy eyebrows lifted and then his beady eyes narrowed. "What about Crystal?"

"We broke up." Duane cleared his throat and then nodded over to where Tricia stood with her children and a few other women. "I'm going to speak with Tricia now and see if we can talk this afternoon." His stomach twisted. Why was his body so averse to this conversation?

The bishop patted Duane's arm. "I'm so glad to hear it. Just let the deacon and me know when you're ready to set a wedding date. The sooner, the better since that tax bill deadline is getting closer and closer."

Duane nodded and then ambled over to Tricia.

She met his gaze and her gray eyes sparkled as she walked over to meet him. "Duane. *Gut* to see you."

"I was wondering if we could visit this afternoon," he said. "Could I possibly follow you to your *haus*?"

"Of course. I have some *kichlin* the girls and I baked. We can sit on the porch and enjoy this *schee* July day."

"Perfect."

Tricia set a tray with two glasses of lemonade and a plate of peanut butter cookies on the small table between the rocking chairs on her porch nearly forty-five minutes later. "Here you go."

"*Danki*." Duane lifted a glass of lemonade and looked out to where her three daughters played on the wooden swing set nearby.

As he sipped the lemonade, the muscles in his shoulders tightened, and questions about how he would make a life with Tricia and her daughters in his house assaulted his mind.

First and foremost—where would her daughters sleep? His three sons currently enjoyed having their own rooms, which left no extra bedrooms. He could add on to his home, but would two of his sons agree to share a room until that additional room was built? He doubted Korey would agree to any upheaval, but perhaps he would accept Tricia more willingly than Crystal, as Tyler had.

*Crystal.*

He felt his mouth turn down in a frown. Oh, how he missed her. She had carved out a piece of his heart.

"Duane?"

He turned toward Tricia, who was staring at him. "*Ya?*"

"You seem to be lost in thought. You okay?"

"Of course." He forced his lips into a smile.

"Then . . . do you have something to tell me?"

Duane set the glass down on the small table and rubbed his sweaty hands on his trousers. "I've been thinking about your offer to make the rumor about us true, and I believe that the bishop might be right. I think you and I should see if we belong together. It makes *gut* sense for us to marry so that I can help out your family and the community." He hesitated, wishing his hands and his voice would stop trembling. "So I came here to see if you'd still like to consider dating me, and then, when the time is right, marrying me."

Tricia blinked and then shook her head. "I thought you were dating a woman from Gordonville."

"We broke up." How he hated saying the words out loud! He picked up a cookie, but his appetite had disappeared.

Sympathy seemed to fill her pretty face. "What happened?"

"It just didn't work out." Duane shrugged as if the breakup hadn't crushed his soul. "Crystal and I both agreed that we should move on."

Tricia looked out toward her children and then back at him. "Are you sure dating me for the sake of the community is what you really want?"

"It makes *gut* sense. Even Tyler told me that being with you is the practical choice. We have a lot in common, and we get along. It's obvious to everyone that we like each other."

She was silent as she picked up her glass and took a long drink.

"What do you think, Tricia?"

She set her glass down, and a serious expression overtook her pretty face. "Do you love Crystal?"

Duane hesitated.

"Please be honest with me, Duane. Do you love her?"

"Yes, I do."

"So, if you love her, then why do you want to date and then possibly marry me?"

"It just won't work out between us. *Mei sohn* Korey is having a hard time with the idea of Crystal, and it's caused a rift between us. I can't stand the idea of losing *mei sohn*."

"What makes you think Korey will accept me?"

"Tyler doesn't see you as a threat to his mother's memory, so I have a feeling Korey will feel the same way. But it's not just that. Crystal wants *kinner*, and I'm not sure that's possible for me anymore." Duane gestured toward her children. "You and I have had our *kinner*, so expanding our families won't be a priority to us. Crystal deserves someone younger who can give her the family she craves."

"But does she love you?"

Duane looked out toward the row of Tricia's barns as his heart sank. "I think so."

"Did she want to break up?"

"No."

Tricia fell silent, and when he turned toward her, she reached over and touched his hand. "Duane, I appreciate that you want to help me and do what's right for the community, but I realized something when you turned down my offer to date me."

"What's that?"

"I don't want a marriage of convenience any more than you do." She heaved a deep sigh. "You and I have both learned how precious true love is. When God leads us to it, we shouldn't give up on it. Instead, we need to hold on to it tightly and guard it with everything we have."

"What are you saying?"

"I'm saying that I would hate for you to marry me and then resent me for the rest of your life because you regret giving up on Crystal." She gave a melancholy smile. "If you love Crystal, then you shouldn't let her go. You should try to find a way to make it work."

His pulse sped up at the thought of working it out with Crystal, but that was an impossible dream. "But what about you?"

"I keep hoping that the Lord will find a way for my family and me. And maybe the Lord will bless me with love again as well."

"I hope he does," he said.

"I do too." She smiled. "I'm grateful for your friendship, Duane."

"I'm grateful for yours as well."

Later, after hitching up his horse, Duane started on his short journey from Tricia's farm toward home. His thoughts ran rampant as the lush, green patchwork of farmland dotted with cows and horses rushed by his window.

Tricia's words about how he should fight to make it work with Crystal echoed through his mind, but it seemed impossible to work it out with her. It seemed so obvious that Owen was the right choice for her, and that truth cut him to the bone. If only there was a way for Crystal and him to be together.

All he knew for certain right now was that he needed divine guidance. "Lord," he whispered as his horse continued toward his home. "I'm lonely, broken, and confused. Please help me carry on, as you've done so graciously for me in the past."

As he steered the horse onto Beechdale Road, he felt a flash of sadness and waited for the Lord's healing hand. Until then, he would keep his eyes on Jesus and pray.

# CHAPTER 29

THURSDAY EVENING CRYSTAL SET THE PLATTER OF PORK CHOPS
on the table between the large bowl of rice and the two smaller
bowls of green beans Alisha had delivered.

"Oh, we forgot the applesauce," Alisha said, hurrying to the
refrigerator.

Crystal nodded. *"Danki, mei liewe."*

She was so grateful for her sweet niece. Alisha had not only
helped with the chores before and after school every day this week,
but she had also frequently checked on Crystal, asking her how
she was feeling, while the rest of the family seemed to go about
their business without even noticing that Crystal's heart fractured
a little more every day that passed without seeing Duane.

Leona stepped into the kitchen and lifted the twins into their
highchairs while Hope took her seat at the table.

When Kane appeared in the doorway with Owen close behind
him, Crystal sighed. She'd done her best to avoid Owen all week
after their awkward encounter, but now he stood in the kitchen
watching her with a sympathetic expression. She had resigned herself to the possibility that they might someday become friends, but
she still couldn't see herself as his girlfriend, despite what Duane

had said. She swallowed back the hurt the memory of his words brought.

"Let's set another place," Kane announced as he walked to the sink and began scrubbing his hands.

Crystal opened the jar of applesauce and carried it to the table.

While Nate retrieved a folding chair from the utility room, Alisha set a place for Owen across from Crystal. It was going to be an awkward meal with her ex-boyfriend across from her, watching her eat.

After the table was set and Kane and Owen had finished washing their hands, they all sat down and bowed their heads in silent prayer.

Crystal was grateful Kane and Owen filled their meal with conversations about the farm. Whenever she felt Owen's eyes focus on her, Crystal busied herself with cutting up more pork for the toddler twins and checking to make sure Hope and Jevon had enough to eat.

After supper, Crystal brought out the pan of brownies she and Hope had baked earlier while Alisha retrieved the vanilla ice cream. She sat down and began cutting up and distributing the brownies while Kane scooped the ice cream.

"*Aenti*," Hope began, "remember that time when Duane stopped by, and we gave him brownies, and I told him to warm them up and have them with ice cream?"

Crystal tried to swallow as she felt the faces around the long table focus on her. Duane had been so sweet to her nieces and nephews, and they had cared for him in return.

"Do you think he warmed them up and had ice cream with them?" Hope asked.

Crystal tried to clear her throat as she dropped a brownie onto

Jevon's plate. "I don't know, *mei liewe*. Maybe he did." The gravel in her throat came out in the rasp of her words.

"I'm sure he did because he likes ice cream," Hope continued. "Remember that other time he took us out for ice cream? That was so fun, wasn't it?"

Crystal nodded. "*Ya*. It was." Her eyes stung with the memory.

"I miss Duane and his *sohns*. Why haven't they come by to see us?"

"Eat your dessert, Hope," Kane instructed.

Crystal set a brownie on Owen's plate, and her eyes defied her and locked on his face. He gave her a hesitant smile, and she tore her gaze away.

Hope looked worried. "Are you okay, *Aenti*? You look kind of *krank*."

"Eat, Hope," Leona instructed.

Crystal served herself a brownie and dropped a dollop of ice cream on top of it, but her appetite had started evaporating the moment Owen had walked into the kitchen. She pushed the ice cream around on her plate and considered how it resembled her heart, melting into a shapeless blob that no longer had a use.

She was grateful when their plates were empty and she could focus on keeping her hands busy by cleaning up the dishes.

"Crystal," Owen said as she stood with her back to him at the sink. "Would you please take a walk with me?"

"Not now, Owen. I need to clean up these dishes." She kept her back to him and flipped on the hot water.

"I'll handle them." Leona appeared at her side. "Go talk to him. It'll help you feel better."

"Help me feel better?" Her laugh was humorless. "I don't think so. Besides, you need to feed Junior and Josie."

"I'll feed the *kinner* with Alisha's help," Kane volunteered.

Then her eyes found Owen, who watched her with an unreadable expression. Agreeing to speak to Owen was her best option, but she wouldn't allow him back into her heart no matter how much his promises of a future tempted her.

"Okay." She looked at Owen. "But we can't be gone long because I need to finish my chores."

Owen had the nerve to look relieved. *"Danki."*

Crystal followed him out to the porch and stopped when he continued down the stairs.

He stopped at the bottom of the steps and faced her, wrinkling his brow. "Are we going to walk?"

"I'd rather not." She folded her arms over her middle. She wouldn't walk with Owen to her special spot. That was where her beloved relationship with Duane had begun, and even though Duane had broken her heart, she wouldn't permit Owen to tarnish that place. "We can stand right here."

Owen huffed out a breath as he walked up the porch steps. "Fine." He hesitated and raked his hand through his dark hair.

She held her breath, awaiting whatever was weighing on his heart.

"I love you, Crystal." His voice sounded rough around the edges. "I never stopped loving you. I know I've messed up again and again, and I will make things right if only you will let me try."

She shook her head and took a step back. "Owen, I'm sorry, but it's too late for us." She started back toward the door.

"Wait, Crystal. Let me finish. Please."

Something in his voice caused her to stop and face him once again.

Owen rubbed the back of his neck and then cleared his throat, his expression humble. "Could you find it in your heart to not only forgive me but also marry me?"

She froze. Surely, she had imagined that he had just proposed to her!

"Before you say no," he began, edging toward her, "I promise I will show up for you. I was young, selfish, and foolish when I left you here . . . I was wrong to expect you to uproot your *dat* when he was so ill. I'm older now, I know what's important, and I care for you and your whole family. Right now, I'm still saving money, but we can live with my parents until I can afford to rent a place. I promise it won't take long. We'll build a life together based on love and respect, and we can have all of the *kinner* you want."

She pressed her hand to her chest as memories of their shared happiness filled her mind.

Owen had been her best friend, her confidant, the love of her life. They had made plans and shared dreams of a future together. She had loved him with her whole heart. He'd been the first man to make her feel beautiful and worthy of love. He'd been the first man she'd wanted to call her husband.

But he was also the first man to break her heart.

Then her mind flashed forward to the hug they'd shared the night Duane had broken up with her. As much as she hated to admit it, Owen had comforted her. Did that mean that they still had a chance to build a happy life together—one that God would bless?

Then visions of a baby, her own baby, filled her mind. Oh, how she wanted a family of her own, along with her own home and her own life! She could almost hear her baby crying and see herself sitting on a rocking chair in a nursery while she sang to her child.

Perhaps Owen was the key to that dream, and maybe the Lord

had been trying to tell her that Owen was her future all along. Maybe the Lord *had* sent Owen back to Gordonville so that they could try again. If so, then her friends had been right, and she'd just been blinded by resentment.

Suddenly, she saw a vision of not only the baby in her future but of her husband—the man whom she would love and cherish for the rest of her life, and the man who would love, cherish, and take care of her and her child.

She squeezed her eyes tighter, and that vision became more concrete—and at first she was certain her husband was Owen.

But then the vision came into clear focus. Not Owen, but Duane stood beside her, smiling at her while they peered into a bassinet, and her chest constricted with such force that she gasped, her eyes opening wide.

No, she didn't want that future with Owen. She wanted it with Duane—another man who had let her down.

"Crystal?" Owen reached for her arm, his expression hopeful. "Is that a yes?"

She looked at him as her chest heaved with a mixture of grief and disappointment. "No. I'm sorry, Owen. While I forgive you, I could never be more than your *freind*."

"Why can't you just give me another chance?"

"You're not the right man for me, Owen. Instead of focusing on me, try to find another *maedel* who will cherish you the way a *fraa* should cherish her husband. I'm just not that *maedel*. But *danki* for trying to work things out with me. I can see the sincerity in your eyes, and I'm grateful to see how you've grown up. But I can't, Owen. I'm sorry."

As she walked into the house, she hoped to finally put the past behind her.

Crystal walked over to where Leona stood in the Yoder family's large kitchen after helping the women clean up after lunch on Sunday, a week and a half later. "I'm going to head home. Would you like me to take Evie and Morgan with me?"

"Why are you going home now? Don't you want stay and visit the Yoders with us?" Leona asked softly.

"No, *danki*." Crystal pointed toward the doorway. "It's a *schee* day. I'll push the *zwillingbopplin* home in their stroller, change them, put them in for a nap, and then rest."

Leona studied her. "I'm worried about you. You've been spending too much time alone."

"I appreciate your concern, but I'm fine. Just tired." Crystal pointed to where the twins sat in their highchairs, eating buttered pieces of bread. "I'm *froh* to take them with me."

"*Danki*. We'll see you soon."

After saying good-bye to the Yoder family, Crystal quickly wiped the twins' faces with a cloth, located their double stroller, loaded them into it, and started toward the road. She breathed in the humid air and pointed out colorful butterflies that crossed their path during their short journey home.

Once inside the house, Crystal took the twins upstairs to their room, changed their diapers, and set them in their cribs for a nap.

Then she went into her room, changed out of her church clothes and into a work dress, and sat on her bed. She stared out the window toward the large, beautiful oak tree that seemed to be her only companion as her heart sank.

She flopped back on her bed and tried to nap, but sleep

wouldn't come. Instead, she closed her eyes and pretended to sleep while thoughts of Duane assaulted her mind.

When she heard her family arrive home, Crystal tiptoed over to the twins' room and put her ear against the door, listening for any sign that they were awake. She started down the stairs and then stopped, realizing she had forgotten her shoes.

Crystal stepped into her room, slipped on her shoes, and then looked over at her dresser. Her eyes found the gift bag Duane had given her on her birthday on a corner of the bookshelf next to her dresser. She had forgotten that she had set it there the week after the party. Her heart stuttered as she picked it up and opened it. When she examined the needlepoint kit, his words rolled through her mind.

*Promise me that you'll make some time to go to your special spot and work on this or something else of your choosing. You deserve time to yourself.*

"Oh, Duane," she whispered. "I miss you. Why couldn't we work things out?"

Crystal picked up the bag and strode down to the family room, where Leona rocked the babies, and Alisha, Jevon, Nate, and Hope sat on the floor looking at books. She nodded at them and kept moving.

"Where are you going?" Leona called after her.

Crystal kept moving forward. "I'm going for a walk. The *zwillingbopplin* are sleeping."

In the kitchen, Kane gave her a confused look as he craned his neck over his shoulder while warming up two bottles.

Crystal waved at him and strolled out the back door, down the porch steps, and around the pasture until she came to her favorite spot.

She lowered herself onto the bench and squinted out toward the pond as the bright afternoon sunlight caressed her face and sparkled on the water, reminding her of how the stars had shimmered in the sky the night she sat on the back porch with Duane.

She sat in silence for a little while, then pulled the needlepoint kit from the bag and studied it while Duane's words tossed around in her mind. When the overwhelming urge to pray filled her, she squeezed her eyes shut.

"Lord," she whispered, her voice barely audible over the chorus of happy frogs nearby. "I miss Duane. I love him, and I can feel in my heart that I always will. He is the one who fills my nighttime dreams, my daydreams, and my every prayer."

She turned the needlepoint kit over in her hands. "Although I love him, perhaps we don't belong together. He believes he's more suited for Tricia while I belong with Owen. Deep in my heart, I know Owen is not the right man for me, even though he promised to fix what went wrong between us. I also believe Duane loves me because of the pain I saw in his eyes when we broke up. Still, how can Duane and I overcome the obstacles between us? Am I capable of being a stepmother to a young man who might resent me? Do I have the capacity to love Korey even if he can't accept or respect me? I don't know if I'm that strong, God. I need your guidance, Lord. Is it possible for Duane and me to work through these issues and forge ahead toward a happy life together? Are you able to help me find true love with Duane despite these complicated issues?"

Crystal pondered that thought, and once again the vision of Duane by her side while they looked down at their baby in a bassinet filled her mind.

Then the vision transformed, and she saw herself sitting on the porch with Duane, laughing and talking while they watched the sunset. She imagined eating meals with him, riding in his buggy, and sitting in a barn during church while peering over at him sitting in the married men's section. She could see herself experiencing everyday life with him.

And then suddenly it hit her like a ton of hay crashing down from the loft in Kane's barn: She *wanted* to start her life as soon as possible with Duane—if he would still have her. Her dream had morphed from having a family to having him in her life, weathering whatever storm came their way. They would make it together, as long as they relied on God and each other.

But then another thought hit her: Perhaps Duane didn't fully understand how important he was to her. Though she didn't regret caring for her nieces and nephews, the work had come between them and their time together. She would now have to talk to Kane and Leona about scaling back the time she spent caring for the children so that she could show Duane how important he and their future were to her.

"*Danki*, God, for sending me the answer," she whispered as she stood and started toward the house. "But now I need your help. Please help me lovingly tell Kane and Leona that I need space to build my own life without hurting them or the *kinner*. And also please lead Duane back to me and don't let it be too late for us to try again."

When she reached the house, she found her brother and sister-in-law in the family room. While Leona rocked Junior in a chair, Kane read a book and sat in his armchair.

"Where are the *kinner*?" Crystal asked.

"In their rooms resting," Kane said. "Why?"

Crystal sank down onto the edge of the sofa and looked down at the gift bag.

"Are you all right, Crystal?" Leona lifted Junior up onto her shoulder and began rubbing his back.

A surge of courage and clarity overtook Crystal as she looked up at them. "I'm actually better than I've been in a long time." She paused to gather her thoughts while they watched her. "You know I love *mei bruderskinner*, and I would do anything for them."

Kane nodded slowly. "*Ya*, of course we do."

"I need to say something, but I don't want to hurt either of you."

Leona blinked, her eyes widening. "What is it?"

"Please just give me the benefit of the doubt while I explain how I feel." Crystal took a deep breath. "I love you and the kids, but I am so exhausted. Sometimes I feel like you take advantage of me. And I fear that over the years I've missed out on a lot because I took care of *mei dat* and now all of you. I don't regret doing those things, but this is not sustainable. *Danki* for keeping a roof over my head, but I think I have a chance to be *froh* with Duane and I don't want to miss that chance. That means I need to scale back what I do around here so that I can show Duane how important our relationship and the possibility of a future with him is to me."

"You're leaving?" Leona gasped, leaning forward in the chair. "What will we do?"

"No, no." Crystal leaned over and patted Leona's hand. "I don't mean I want to leave right away. I would never abandon you or the *kinner*. But I do hope I have a chance to build a life with Duane—if he'll agree to give our relationship another chance—and that would mean moving out."

Kane and Leona stared at each other, and Leona's face was etched with panic.

"We understand," Kane said. "Perhaps we've been taking advantage of you for too long."

"You could hire someone to help," Crystal said as an idea filled her mind. "You could even have someone move into the *daadihaus* to help you in exchange for a place to live. That might work."

Leona nodded and some of her worry seemed to subside. "Okay."

"Can I stay with you for a little while longer while I figure out what to do next?"

"Of course," Kane said. "And we'll miss you."

"I'll miss you all too." Crystal sniffed as she imagined leaving her precious nieces and nephews. "But I want to always be close to my *bruderskinner.*"

Kane frowned as regret flickered over his face. "We've been selfish, thoughtless, and blind for too long. I'm truly sorry."

Crystal shook her head. "No, you're just overwhelmed parents doing the best that you can."

"I hope you can mend things with Duane," Leona said. "Please forgive me for not realizing the toll we were taking on you."

"Of course I forgive you." Crystal's voice became soft, her eyes burning with threatening tears. But until she and Duane worked out their differences about their relationship, it might be too late.

And the thought sat cold and hard over her heart.

# CHAPTER 30

DUANE STRODE OVER TO HIS HORSE AND BUGGY FRIDAY AFTER-
noon and climbed in beside Jayden. Since they had been working
close to home all week, they had saved money by taking the horse
and buggy to give an estimate instead of paying for an additional ride.

"Did we get the job?" Jayden asked.

"*Ya*, we did." Duane examined his notepad and then his calendar. "We're three weeks out for work now, so it will be late August
before we work here."

"That's *gut* news."

Duane looked out toward the road just as a young Amish
couple walked past, holding hands and smiling, and his chest
tightened as he once again thought of Crystal.

Although his grief and remorse had clung to him like a second
skin since they broke up, he suddenly felt something inside of him
shift, and Tricia's wise words filled his mind:

*You and I have both learned how precious true love is. When God
leads us to it, we shouldn't give up on it. Instead, we need to hold on to
it tightly and guard it with everything we have.*

He swallowed, and his heart opened to the idea of not only

trying again with Crystal, but also marrying her, making a home with her, spending the rest of his life with her, and possibly even having children with her—if the Lord saw fit to make him a father once again.

*Lord, I hear you loud and clear. Crystal is my future. She is the one you've chosen for me. Help me tell my children that I want to build a life with Crystal, but I need their blessing. Guide me to the words that will make them, especially Korey, understand how much they mean to me and how Crystal will never replace their mother. Help my children realize that they are the most precious people in my life but that I feel led to be with Crystal and include her in my life as a way to expand our family, not to replace them or Connie. I can only do this through your love and guidance.*

"*Dat?* Are we going back to the worksite, or are you going to stare off into space for the remainder of the afternoon?"

Duane looked at Jayden, and for the first time since he and Crystal had parted ways, he smiled. "We're going to leave."

Duane flicked the reins and guided the horse toward the road.

"So, Jayden," he began as they headed to the job. "How would you feel if I got back together with Crystal?"

"*Dat,* you've been so *bedauerlich* these past few weeks, and it's been difficult to witness. I'd be grateful. Go get her."

Duane gave him a sideways glance. "What if I were to propose to her?"

Jayden studied him. "If it made you *froh,* then I'd adjust."

"But what about your *bruders*? I can't stand the distance between Korey and me, and I don't know how to fix it. I don't want to hurt him, Tyler, or you, but I can't stop myself from believing that the Lord has led me to her."

"Just tell Korey what you said to me. He'll eventually work through it and realize that you're not replacing *Mamm*. Instead, you're just following your heart toward a *froh* life."

"*Danki*," Duane said.

Now he just had to make a plan to tell his two other sons and then find the right words to express to Crystal how much she meant to him.

*Lead me, Lord.*

Duane glanced around the table during supper that night. The aroma of steak, baked potatoes, and corn filled the kitchen.

He had come home early and made the special meal in preparation for telling his sons what he had planned to do. While he knew trying to bribe his older sons with steak was outlandish, he was desperate for their blessing and hopeful that Korey might finally understand the depth of Duane's love for him and also his love for Crystal.

"So what's going on, *Dat*?" Tyler suddenly asked.

Duane lifted his water glass. "What do you mean?"

"We rarely have steak." Tyler gestured at the delicious meal. "Did you close a big deal that I don't know about?"

Duane took a long drink of water and then set his glass down. "No, Tyler. You've been working beside me while we plan our schedule. I haven't kept any deals from you."

"So what is it?" Tyler asked again.

When Duane met Jayden's gaze, his youngest son gave him an encouraging nod.

"Wait a minute." Tyler pointed between Duane and Jayden. "You and Jay have secrets. That's not fair."

Korey looked up from his plate. "What secrets?"

Duane wiped his mouth and beard with a napkin and gathered his thoughts. "I've made a decision today, and I wanted to discuss it with you all."

Korey and Tyler shared a worried look.

"If Crystal will have me, I want to try again with her."

"I should have known," Korey snarled like a furious dog as he pushed his chair back and started to stand.

"Korey, please hear me out. I know you're angry, but I'm really trying here. Let's talk about this like adults."

Frowning, Korey sank back into his seat, folded his arms over his chest, and stared down at his lap.

"As I was saying," Duane continued, frustration churning in his gut. "I plan to go see Crystal and try to fix things between us. I want to know how you feel about it. Let's get everything out in the open."

All three of his sons stared at him for a moment, and then Jayden shifted in his seat.

"I support you, but I ask that you keep us in mind before you make any big decisions about the future," Jayden said.

Tyler nodded. "I agree with Jay. If you're thinking long-term, then please let us know ahead of time. It will be an adjustment for us if she becomes our stepmom."

"I promise not to keep any secrets from you," Duane said. "We're a family, and you three are my priority. Your emotional well-being is important to me."

Korey glowered. "I don't want her as my stepmom. I don't support the idea of you getting remarried so soon after losing *Mamm*."

"I understand that you're hurting, Korey, but we all are," Duane said, working to keep his voice gentle.

"You don't show it," Korey snapped.

"We all grieve differently, and you need to respect that," Duane explained. "Tyler has thrown himself into work." He gestured at Tyler. "That's how he copes."

Tyler blinked at him, as if shocked at this revelation.

Duane pointed at his youngest son. "Jayden is the one who works to keep the peace. He wants us to remember we're a family. And I keep it inside. I break down when I'm alone." He touched his chest. "But you need to share your grief with all of us."

Korey's eye widened, and he started to open his mouth in protest.

"Wait, Korey," Duane cut him off. "I'm not saying you're wrong, but you need to respect that we're not all alike. None of us are wrong, but you can't keep telling me that the way I grieve is wrong. It's just different from how you grieve. I miss your *mamm* more than you'll ever know."

"Replacing *Mamm* with a new girlfriend isn't grieving, *Dat*. It's moving on, and I'm not ready to move on. I miss her every day. I look for her in the married women's section at church. I expect to see her in her garden weeding and planting flowers. I can't imagine seeing another woman in her place yet," Korey snipped.

Duane huffed out a breath. "I understand, and I miss her too."

"This is pointless." Korey shook his head and looked down again.

"No, it's not, Korey. I'm trying to tell you that I'm still your *dat*," Duane said. "I didn't plan to meet Crystal so soon, but God put her in our lives. And if Crystal will have me, I want to try again. I don't need your permission, but I am telling you out of respect, which is in turn what I expect from each of you. I expect you to respect my relationship and Crystal. And I want you to remember that I'll always love the three of you. Nothing will ever change that, and no one will ever replace you in my life."

He looked around the table, taking in his sons' expressions. While Korey continued to study his lap, Tyler watched him with worry etched on his face, and Jayden continued to look hesitant.

"I prayed about it, and I believe God led me to Crystal for a reason," Duane continued. "I think she's my future. I will always love your *mamm*, and no one will replace her. But I believe God is granting me a second chance at happiness and answering my prayers. I need to guard this chance with my life. I'm choosing to love again, and I want love back in my life. It's important to me."

He took a deep breath as he looked around the table at his sons. "Someday you three will move out and start your own lives, and I don't want to spend the rest of mine alone. I don't know if Crystal will even consider giving me another chance, but I am going to ask her. I hope you all will understand, and I hope you will learn to care for Crystal too, which is why I'm telling you now."

Tyler pressed his lips together.

"I don't need your blessing, but I sure would like to have it," Duane said, hopeful.

Jayden nodded. "It will take some getting used to, but I'll support you, *Dat*."

Duane turned to Tyler. "Ty?"

"Like Jay said, it will take time, but I'll support you too." Tyler rubbed at his shoulder as if a knot had formed there. "I don't want you to be lonely in your later years."

"All I can ask is that you try." Duane turned to Korey.

When Korey met his gaze, his face was contorted into a deep

glower. "May I be excused?" His voice was low and vibrating with bitterness.

"*Ya*," Duane said, disappointment whipping over him.

Korey stood and dropped his plate and utensils in the sink before stomping up to his room.

Duane rubbed his eyes with his fingers. He hoped he would choose the right words when he went to see Crystal and that she would believe in him more than Korey had.

The following morning, Crystal was certain she was dreaming when she looked out the storm door and found Duane standing on the back porch.

She pushed the door open and stepped outside, hoping it wasn't a dream. "Duane. Hi."

"*Gude mariye.*" He held his straw hat in his hand and began to spin it. "Do you have a few minutes to talk?"

"*Ya.* Would you like to sit?" She pointed to the glider.

He nodded and then they sat down together. Crystal folded her shaky hands in her lap and sat up straight as worry threaded through her.

Duane took a deep breath. "I wanted to say I'm sorry for giving up on you and on us. I was wrong when I told you that I didn't think we were meant to be together. I was completely wrong when I said that Tricia was the woman I was supposed to be with, and I regret telling you to go after Owen." He swallowed, and his eyes seemed to sparkle.

"I've realized that love is precious, and when we find it, we need to hold on to it, no matter the cost. Letting go of you so easily was a mistake that I regret deeply. My most fervent prayers are that you love me, and you'll give me another chance because the truth is that I love you and I want to be with you."

His handsome face seemed to plead with her, and she blinked as his words floated through her mind.

"I do love you," she whispered, her eyes filling with tears. "I've missed you so much."

"I've missed you too." He cupped his hand to her cheek, and she leaned into the touch. She felt the apology in his hand, and it left her breathless.

"You're my best *freind* and my confidante," he said. "I know your family depends on you heavily, but I hope that there's a way we can be together because I want to plan a future with you. I just hope that I'm not too late and that you haven't already made a promise to Owen."

Crystal shook her head. "You're not too late. I never wanted Owen, and I'm so sorry you saw me hug him. I was just overwhelmed that night." She sucked in a deep breath. "My family has depended on me for years, but I've realized that it was my fault for not drawing boundaries with them and allowing myself the time to build my own life. I've told them that I want to have my own life and my own family, and I want those things with you, if you'll give me a chance to show you how important you and our relationship are to me."

"Of course I'll give you a chance. In fact, I've been praying for a chance to show you how much you mean to me."

"*Danki.* Now they just have to find someone to help Leona."

"I thought of an idea for help on the way over here."

"What is it?" she searched his eyes.

"What if Tricia Mast and her three *dochdern* moved into the *daadihaus*? She could help with the *kinner*, and Kane could give her a place to live."

"That's a great idea! I'll mention it to Kane."

"Perfect."

She swallowed against her dry throat. "What about Korey?"

"I've talked to *mei sohns* and asked them to try to accept you."

"What did they say?"

"Tyler and Jayden are supportive. Korey needs more time, but he will adjust. We have to be patient with him. We need to just keep praying and encouraging him to talk about his feelings." He hesitated. "When I realized that I was falling for you, I thought I could date you without any repercussions from *mei sohns* because I believed they were growing up and wouldn't need me anymore. I've learned now that even though my sons are older, they still need me. They just need me in a different way. I'm learning my new role as a parent as I go along."

She smiled. "I'm willing to also take my time to learn my role in their lives. I'll do my best to treat their feelings with respect since this is a difficult transition for them."

"We'll figure it out as we go along." He took her hands in his. "But I need to know how you feel about possibly not being able to have *kinner* with me. If that is the case, will you resent me the rest of our life together?"

She gave his hands a gentle squeeze. "Duane, I'll love you, and even if we can't have *kinner* of our own, we can be *froh* together."

"I'm so relieved to hear you say that. I love you, Crystal," he whispered, sending a trill along her spine. "I believe you're the future God has chosen for me. Your love is the foundation of my heart. Would you please give me a chance to build a future with you?"

His words were a sweet melody to her ears.

"*Ya*, I will. And I love you too," she said.

He leaned down and brushed his lips over hers, and she melted against him, losing track of everything.

Duane smiled, and happiness radiated in his chest as he sat at his kitchen table and ate supper on Saturday evening one month later.

His sons, Crystal, and Michelle surrounded him, and everyone listened as Tyler shared a story about one of their recent roofing jobs at an *Englisher*'s house and the silly questions the owner's son asked them about the Amish culture.

When Duane looked at the other end of the table, Crystal's gorgeous green eyes locked on his, taking his breath away.

The past month had been full of joy and promise as he and Crystal had fallen into a comfortable routine. Kane and Leona had invited Tricia Mast and her family to move to the farm, and Tricia had accepted. Now Tricia helped out with the children and had a place to live while her farm went up for sale. Tricia thanked Duane for thinking of her, and she was relieved to no longer have to work several part-time jobs and also rely on members of the community to care for her farm. Tricia's help with the children had enabled Crystal and Duane to spend a few evenings together every week.

Tonight Crystal had brought supper over for Duane, his sons, and Michelle. Although Korey remained quiet when Crystal was around, he was no longer disrespectful. Tyler was friendlier and seemed to be adjusting to Duane's relationship with her.

Throughout the past month, one thing had become

clear—Duane wanted to spend the rest of his life by Crystal's side, and tonight he was going to officially ask her to marry him. He just hoped and prayed she would say yes.

Duane had told his sons last night that he planned to propose to her after supper tonight, and while Korey remained silent, Tyler and Jayden had given their blessing. He hoped one day Korey would accept Crystal, but until then, he would just continue to pray for him and also for his relationship with his son.

When supper was over, Michelle carried a coffee cake to the table while Crystal started the percolator. Jayden gathered up mugs, sugar, and creamer, and Crystal picked up cake plates.

Soon they were all gathered around the table together and enjoying their dessert. Duane scanned the table and smiled while his sons and Michelle discussed their friends at youth group.

"Duane," Crystal called to him from the other end of the table. "Why are you smiling like that?"

He lifted his mug toward her in a toast. "I was just thinking about how *froh* I am."

"I feel the same way."

"Let's take our *kaffi* out on the porch," he told her. "Jayden and Tyler said they'd do the dishes."

Crystal nodded. "Okay."

Duane's pulse galloped.

*Please, Lord, let her say yes!*

Crystal sat beside Duane on the porch swing. The late August

evening air was heavy and humid as the cicadas and birds serenaded them.

She peered over at Duane and longed to read his mind.
He'd been acting strangely all evening. He seemed to be lost in
thought—as if he were trying to figure out an intricate puzzle.

He pushed the swing into motion and stared out toward his
neighbor's farm.

"I can't believe that September will be here next week."

"*Ya*, the summer flew by."

He nodded, his eyes still trained on the pasture.

Crystal stopped the swing and turned toward him. "Are
you okay?"

When he hesitated, worry filled her.

He took a deep breath and then faced her. "This past month
has been one of the best of my life. I've realized that I want it to
last forever, and that's why I can't wait any longer. I want our life
together to start now. I would be honored if you would be *mei fraa*.
Will you marry me so that we can build a life together?"

"Yes! Yes!" She sniffed as her eyes stung and joy curled
through her.

He leaned over and kissed her, sending heat humming through
her veins. He deepened the kiss, and the contact made her feel as if
all the cells in her body were lit on fire.

"I can't wait to be your husband," he said, his voice husky.
"Let's get married right away."

# EPILOGUE

CRYSTAL THREADED HER FINGERS WITH DUANE'S AS THEY stepped out onto his porch on a Thursday evening three weeks later. Her heart sang as she smiled up at his handsome face. As of this afternoon, Duane was now her husband!

Earlier in the week, Crystal had packed up her room before Duane, Kane, and Jayden helped her move most of her boxes last night. She brought the last of her things with her this morning when Kane dropped her off for the ceremony.

Although her nieces and nephews had been weepy when she told them she was moving out (and Crystal had shed a few tears of her own in private too), Crystal promised to visit them often, and she intended to keep that promise. Her nieces and nephews would always be an important part of her life.

The events of today had passed by at lightning speed. Crystal and Duane had been married by both of their bishops in Duane's family room. Since it was his second marriage, it had been a small, private ceremony with only Duane's sons, Leona, and Kane in attendance, while Tricia and her daughters cared for Leona and Kane's children.

Both Jayden and Tyler had quietly congratulated her and

Duane after the ceremony, but Korey had stood off near the kitchen doorway, glowering and wiping his eyes. Crystal would continue to pray that Korey would soften his heart toward her someday soon.

Later that afternoon, Tricia had brought her daughters and Crystal's nieces and nephews over to enjoy lunch and cake to celebrate. Crystal had been both surprised and delighted that Jeannie, Lorraine, Jolene, and their families had stopped to congratulate them and also share desserts they had made.

And now the house was quiet since her family and friends had gone home, and his sons—now her stepsons—had retreated to their rooms for the evening.

Crystal leaned against Duane as they stood on the porch and looked out toward the pasture. The sun began to set, sending gorgeous bands of red, yellow, and orange across the sky while lightning bugs danced around as if celebrating their nuptials.

She turned toward him and snapped her fingers. "I almost forgot. I have a gift for you."

She hurried into the house and to the kitchen, where she had left the shopping bag before they prepared for the wedding. She carried the bag out and handed it to him. "I hope you like it."

She held her breath as he pulled the pillow out of the bag and grinned.

"I love it!" He ran his fingers over the needlepoint picture of the colorful flowers in the vase that he had given her for her birthday. "You added our names and the wedding date at the bottom. It's perfect. We have to put it on our bed every day."

She smiled as her heart tripped over itself. "That's exactly what I thought."

"Now I need to give you my gift."

He took her hand and guided her down the porch steps and toward the fence that separated his property from his neighbor's farm. He stopped and pointed to a wooden bench that overlooked the patchwork of lush, rolling, green fields behind them. The bench sat alone as if patiently waiting for someone to enjoy it.

"You left your special spot behind, so I wanted to give you a new one." He made a sweeping gesture toward the bench. "Please try it out."

Crystal sat down on the bench and looked out toward the fields, taking in their beauty as frogs serenaded her. She smiled up at him as warmth flooded her. "It's perfect."

Duane sat down beside her. "So, you'll come out here and work on more needlepoint projects?"

"Oh, I don't know," she teased him. "Now I have four grown men to care for. Between the cooking, cleaning, laundry, and sewing, I don't think I'll ever have the time to—"

When he brushed his lips across hers, interrupting her, the contact sent her stomach fluttering with the wings of a thousand butterflies. She closed her eyes, wrapped her arms around his neck, and leaned into the kiss, savoring the taste of his mouth against hers. This was how true love was supposed to feel.

Duane broke the kiss and rested his forehead against hers. "Promise me you'll make time to enjoy your special spot."

"I promise," she whispered, still breathless from the kiss. "*Ich liebe dich*, Duane."

"*Ich liebe dich*, Crystal. I'm so glad God gave me a second chance at love. I promise I will cherish you forever."

As Duane pulled her close for a hug, Crystal felt overwhelming gratitude—and silently thanked God for allowing her to love him. She couldn't wait to see what God had in store for their future as husband and wife.

# ACKNOWLEDGMENTS

As always, I'm thankful for my loving family, including my mother, Lola Goebelbecker; my husband, Joe; and my sons, Zac and Matt. I'm blessed to have such an awesome and amazing family that puts up with me when I'm stressed out on a book deadline.

Thank you to my mother and my dear friend Maggie Halpin, who graciously read the draft of this book to check for typos. I'm also grateful to my special Amish friend, who patiently answers my endless stream of questions.

Thank you to my wonderful church family at Morning Star Lutheran in Matthews, North Carolina, for your encouragement, prayers, love, and friendship. You all mean so much to my family and me.

Thank you to Zac Weikal and the fabulous members of my Bookworm Bunch! I'm so grateful for your friendship and your excitement about my books. You all are amazing!

To my agent, Natasha Kern—I can't thank you enough for your guidance, advice, and friendship. You are a tremendous blessing in my life.

Thank you to my amazing editor, Jocelyn Bailey, for your

friendship and guidance. I appreciate how you push me to dig deeper with each book and improve my writing. I've learned so much from you, and I look forward to our future projects together.

Special thanks to editor Becky Philpott for polishing the story and connecting the dots. I'm so grateful that we are working together again!

I'm grateful to each and every person at HarperCollins Christian Publishing who helped make this book a reality.

To my readers—thank you for choosing my novels. My books are a blessing in my life for many reasons, including the special friendships I've formed with my readers. Thank you for your email messages, Facebook notes, and letters.

Thank you most of all to God—for giving me the inspiration and the words to glorify you. I'm grateful and humbled you've chosen this path for me.

# DISCUSSION QUESTIONS

1. Crystal has a special spot on Kane's farm where she likes to needlepoint. Do you have a special hobby and a place where you like to enjoy it?

2. When Crystal and Duane begin dating, many of their family and friends express that their age difference would complicate the relationship. What are your feelings about this?

3. Kane hires Owen to work for him without asking Crystal her feelings about the offer. What do you think of Kane's actions?

4. The bishop feels Duane should marry Tricia Mast, a widow who is struggling to run her farm and raise her three children. He feels that Duane should consider marrying her for the good of the community. What do you think of the bishop's point of view?

5. Duane's sons grapple with the idea of his dating Crystal. Can you relate to their point of view? Do you think their feelings are valid?

6. Leona relies on Crystal to care for her children, and she

often expects Crystal to carry the load of caregiver as well as doing a majority of the household chores. Do you believe that Leona is taking advantage of Crystal? If so, do you think her actions are deliberate? Why or why not?

7. Throughout the story, Owen pursues Crystal, insisting he has changed and will put her first in his life. Why do you think we are drawn to familiar people and patterns? Do you agree with her decision not to date him again? Why or why not?

8. Crystal realizes throughout the story that she made caring for her family her first priority instead of building her own life. Although she adores her nieces and nephews, she decides by the end of the book that she must prioritize a future with Duane. What do you think caused her to make this decision?

9. Both Duane and Crystal have suffered great losses. Duane lost his wife, and Crystal lost her parents. Think of a time when you felt lost and alone. Where did you find your strength? What Bible verses helped?

10. Duane recognizes that he and his sons grieve differently. Have you ever felt that your grief was different from someone else's? If so, did you feel judged for your way of grieving? Have you judged others if their way of grieving seemed different from yours?

# ABOUT THE AUTHOR

Dan Davis Photography

AMY CLIPSTON IS THE AWARD-WINNING AND bestselling author of the Kauffman Amish Bakery, Hearts of Lancaster Grand Hotel, Amish Heirloom, Amish Homestead, and Amish Marketplace series. Her novels have hit multiple bestseller lists including CBD, CBA, and ECPA. Amy holds a degree in communication from Virginia Wesleyan University and works full-time for the City of Charlotte, NC. Amy lives in North Carolina with her husband, two sons, and six spoiled rotten cats.

Visit her online at AmyClipston.com
Facebook: @AmyClipstonBooks
Twitter: @AmyClipston
Instagram: @amy_clipston
Bookbub: @AmyClipston